SWELL
FOOP

PIERS ANTHONY

SWELL

FOOP

A TOM DOHERTY ASSOCIATES BOOK

NEW YORK

SWELL FOOP

Copyright © 2001 by Piers Anthony Jacob

This book is printed on acid-free paper.

A Tor Book
Published by Tom Doherty Associates, LLC
175 Fifth Avenue
New York, NY 10010

www.tor.com

Tor® is a registered trademark of Tom Doherty Associates, LLC.

Library of Congress Cataloging-in-Publication Data

Anthony Jacob, Piers.
    Swell foop / Piers Anthony Jacob.—1st ed.
        p.   cm.
    "A Tom Doherty Associates Book."
    ISBN 0-312-86906-1
    1. Xanth (Imaginary Place)—Fiction. I. Title.

 PS3551.N73 S86 2001
 813'.54—dc21   2001041444

First Edition: October 2001

Printed in the United States of America

0 9 8 7 6 5 4 3 2 1

Contents

SWELL
FOOP

1
QUESTION

C ynthia crested a hill and spied the Good Magician's castle. She paused, surveying it, her pulse accelerating with maidenly excitement. She was here; could she handle the three Challenges? She knew they would be possible but not easy.

Suddenly her Question seemed foolishly inadequate. She really didn't need to bother Magician Humfrey with it; there was one sure way to get the answer on her own. The trouble was, that way was dangerous. If she proved to be unlucky, she could regret it for the rest of her life. So she could not afford to gamble; she had to know before she married Che Centaur.

She spread her fair white wings and leaped into the air. She had been trotting, perhaps to give herself more time to think, but now she would fly in before she had a chance to change her timid mind again. After all, centaurs weren't supposed to be femalishly irresolute. They were supposed to be intelligent and decisive. She had been a centaur only half her life, or one-third of it, or five-sixths of it, depending on how she chose to see it at the moment. She was still learning.

The castle looked deceptively placid. The tower windows were open, the moat was calm, and the drawbridge was down. Just as if anyone could walk right in. Well, there was one way to make proof of that.

Cynthia Centaur glided to a four-hoof landing, folded her wings, and trotted up to the drawbridge. Sure enough, it lifted just before she got there. Unsurprised, she walked down the bank to the water. As her fore-hoof touched it, colored fins appeared. Loan sharks. She backed off; she did not want to let them take an arm or a leg. There would be no swimming today.

She spread her wings and leaped. The feathers found no purchase; she landed back on the ground. She nodded, having confirmed another limit. She could not walk, swim, or fly across the moat. It was a Challenge.

So what was the way? There had to be something likely but difficult, and she would have to figure out how to make it work. That was the way of it. The Good Magician did not like to be bothered with frivolous Questions, so he made it awkward for querents to get in to ask them. Then they had to pay a year's service, or the equivalent, for the Answers. Even so, there seemed to be a fairly constant stream of them. Many of them worked off their Services by becoming parts of Challenges for later comers. So it amounted to a cottage industry.

None of which helped her to cross the moat. What had Magician Humfrey cooked up for her? For the Challenges tended to relate to the abilities of the ones whose progress they barred. It would require centaur savvy to get through.

She walked around the moat, seeking some hint. All was quiet. Until she was halfway: 180° in precise centaur terminology. There she saw a rope supported by a system of pulleys on either side of the moat. One end was attached to a small boat at the outer bank, and another end was in the hands of a lovely human woman.

"Ahoy there, centaur!" the woman cried. "Do you mean to anger?"

"Why, no," Cynthia said, surprised. "Am I somehow giving offense?"

"Frustrate, interfere, balk, thwart, oppose—"

"Cross?"

"Whatever," the woman replied crossly. "Do you intend to navigate this moat?"

"Why, hello, Demoness Metria!" Cynthia said. "Are you operating this Challenge?"

"Yes, I'm stuck here until I help someone get across. If you want to come in, get in the boat and I'll haul you over."

"But I weigh a lot more than you do," Cynthia protested. "It would be difficult for you to pull me."

"That's why I have the pulley. It gives me the magic of buy."

"Of what?"

"Shop, browse, patronize, bargain, purchase—"

Cynthia fixed on the last word. "Leverage?"

"Whatever. Get in the stupid boat. I'll use the crastination to haul you across."

Crastination? Cynthia hesitated to inquire. It was probably the name for the fancy pulley. She wasn't sure about this, but nothing better offered, so she set four feet in the boat and hunkered down so as not to tip it over. This was hardly her most comfortable mode of passage, but of course the Challenges were not designed to be comfortable.

Metria pulled on her rope. It swung her halfway across the moat. Cynthia's boat hardly budged.

"↑↓→↖!!" the demoness swore up, down, and sideways. The water beneath her bubbled and clouded as if abruptly heated.

"I think I'm still too heavy for you," Cynthia said.

"You're *not* too heavy! I'm just too amateurish. I can't get it right."

Obviously true. Cynthia watched as Metria swung back to her side of the moat and landed on the bank. "Maybe if you pulled it more slowly, to get more leverage?"

The demoness pulled more slowly—and was hauled across the moat even faster. "⤳⤵⤴⤶!!" The green grass around her wilted and turned brown.

"I am not sure this is working," Cynthia said delicately. "Perhaps if I looked for some other way to get across—"

The demoness vanished from the outer moat bank in a puff of vile smoke and reappeared at the inner bank, rope still in hand. "Absotively posilutely not! I am supposed to haul your donkey rear across this fetid pool of snot, and I shall do it if it vetoes us all." Now steam rose from the water, and chips flaked from the castle wall behind her. What little vegetation remained in the area gave up the ghost; little plant-shaped spirits were floating into the sky.

Cynthia's maidenly ears were hurting. She had never before seen a demon quite this enraged, and wasn't sure she would survive with her health if it got any worse. She decided not to argue. "Of course, Metria," she said soothingly. "It will surely work out."

"It had *better* moil out," the demoness gritted wrathfully, "or I might become annoyed." Thin plumes of smoke jetted from her ears, and veins stood out in stark red relief on the crackling surfaces of her eyeballs.

This was still beneath the level of annoyance? Three of Cynthia's knees felt weak, and the fourth was none too strong. She had to pacify Metria before she exploded, destroying the whole castle. Obviously the present approach wasn't working. The demoness did not seem to know how to operate the pulley correctly, but surely would not be amenable to suggestions by an outsider. How could this be handled posilutely— oops, positively?

Maybe if she reverted to basics. "Metria, I'm sure there's some mistake, and something is interfering with your effort. Maybe if we explore this from the start, we can find out what's happening."

"Maybe," the demoness snorted. A little smoke ring spun clear of her nose, expanding as it floated across the moat. The fin of a blue shark sliced through it—and the fin blistered before it hastily submerged.

So far so good. "Now, I am somewhat inexperienced about demonly matters, and perhaps my vocabulary is deficient. You mentioned a crastination, which I assumed to be the pulley. Possibly I am in error." It galled her to say this, because true centaurs were seldom in error, and their vocabularies were never deficient.

Metria laughed. Waves of heat rippled outward from her; the rage was dissipating. "Maybe I misspoke. I am trying to use the pulley to keep me here while I pull you across. I am trying to crastinate, so I can stay here long enough to find out what is so infernally important about your quest."

"But there's nothing important about me or my quest," Cynthia said. "I just want to find out whether my offspring will breed true. You see, I'm not a natural centaur; Magician Trent transformed me from human eighty years ago. So my children might turn out human, instead of winged centaur. I can't face the threat of such a horror, so I must find out before the fact."

"That's right; I remember now," Metria said. "You tried to fool the Magician, and he was diseased."

"He was what?"

"Instead of being at ease, he was—"

"Oh. Not eased. Perturbed."

"Whatever," the demoness agreed crossly. "So he punished you."

"Yes. But now I like being a winged monster, and I love Che Centaur, and I want to be sure that when I marry him I'll be able to do my part. But however important that may be to me personally, I recognize that in the larger scheme of the cosmos, it is inconsequential. So it must be some other quest that is the one you want."

"No, you are the only querent scheduled for today, so it has to be you. Humfrey's in such a dither he didn't even notice how I'm subbing for Demon Tension in the Challenge. I'm the most curious of demonesses, and I've just got to know what's so awful it can make even the Good Magician get all up in a heaval. So I have to get you into the castle, not me out of it. Until my oddity is sated."

"Your what is sated?"

"Eccentric, irregularity, peculiarity, abnormality, quirk—"

"Curiosity?"

"Whatever! So I gather you don't even know what's so important about your Question."

"Well, it's important to *me*. But I think not to many others. Does it seem important to you?"

"No. Who cares whether your baby is a stinkweed? So it must be something else. I've just got to know."

Cynthia was beginning to be just the merest suggestion of concerned. The Good Magician was dithered about her Question? It was true that if the Answer turned out to be negative, she would have to seriously consider not marrying Che, which would break both their hearts, but since when did Humfrey care about centaur hearts? She hardly rated any such concern. "I fear you will be disappointed. But I'll be happy to share my Answer with you, at such time as I obtain it. Then you can rest undisgruntled."

"Rest how?"

"Calm, placid, peaceful, quiet, serene, tranquil—"

"That's six."

"I beg your pardon?"

"I usually give only five explications."

"Five whats?"

"Analogues, meanings, expressions, translations, identities—"

"Synonyms?"

"Whatever. You gave six. That damages the cadence. *I* should have filled in the sixth."

"I apologize." Actually Cynthia remembered her giving six on more than one prior occasion, but she didn't care to argue the case. "I meant merely to say that you can rest easy, once you know what I learn from the Good Magician."

"Well, why didn't you say so?" the demoness demanded crossly.

"I fear I got distracted. Now about this crastination: I remain unclear as to its precise application. How will crastination help you?"

"By delaying my departure, so I can overhear Humfrey's verdict. I'm trying to stall."

Cynthia nodded. "Perhaps the word you want is 'procrastination.' "

"Yes! That's it. I couldn't quite get it. 'Amateur crastination' was as close as I could come."

"And when an amateur does a job a professional should do, it can go wrong," Cynthia said.

"It can get downright bungled. I want to stand here and pull you across, using the—" She hesitated.

"Leverage."

"Of the pulley. Instead it's been reversing, leaving you slow while I zoom across the moat."

"Try it again, this time thinking pro instead of amateur."

Metria pulled on the rope. This time she remained in place, and Cynthia's boat slid smoothly across the moat. She had figured it out.

"Remember—you promised," the demoness said. "And souled folk keep their promises."

"I will tell you what I learn," Cynthia agreed. "Though I suspect it will disappoint you. Nothing about me or my concerns is important to Magicians or demons."

"We'll wash."

"We'll what?"

"Brine, water, pool, bay, ocean—"

"Sea?"

"Whatever." The demoness looked cross as she faded out.

"We'll see," Cynthia agreed with half a smile. There was something

almost amusing about the demoness's problem with words. Was the
Good Magician really unaware of Metria's presence? The Challenge
seemed remarkably apt for this particular individual.

She stepped out of the boat and surveyed the castle. There was a
door in the wall. She tried the handle, and it turned, and the door opened.

Beyond was a spacious chamber filled with harpies. They were dancing, strutting in messy patterns. Feathers were flying, the walls were
filthy, and the smell was appalling. No wonder: there was bird poop all
over the floor, getting stirred up by the claws of the dancers. Cynthia
stepped back, wrinkling her nose. Centaurs were natural about natural
functions, but their manure was inoffensive and good for flowers. Harpy
dung, in contrast, was truly nasty. It required special facilities for detox-
ification. To have it spread about a sealed chamber—that was dangerous.

But this seemed to be the only way into the castle. The first Challenge
had been a test of her understanding; she had found the key word and
thus gotten through. This second Challenge seemed to be a test of her
fortitude; how could she pass through this muck and stench without
fainting?

The answer was that she couldn't. Cynthia had been cleanly all of
her life, whether in human or centaur form. She had regularly washed
or replaced her human clothes, then had to get used to going bare as a
centaur. She had finally reached the point where she could trot past a
group of human boys, knowing that their eyes were riveted to her bounc-
ing breasts, and not be unduly embarrassed. After all, clothing fetishism
was a human trait, not a centaur trait, and centaurs were not responsible
for human hang-ups. Boys weren't supposed to see the sexual parts of
girls, so naturally they lived to sneak peeks, and the upper foresection
of a centaur was similar to that of a human person. So human boys did
stare at centaur fillies, and thought they were getting away with something, but if there was embarrassment, it should be on the part of the
boys. But going bare did not mean going dirty. The idea of going among
these dirty birds repelled her.

Surely the Challenge could not be merely a matter of getting through
filth. There must be a way to avoid it. But how? The ceiling of the
chamber was not high; that was why the harpies were footing instead of
flying. Cynthia could not fly through it, assuming her wings were working now. She had to walk. Her very hooves curled inward at the thought.

So how could she pass through this noisome chamber without tracking putrid gook? How could she breathe? The stuff would surely get on her wings, even when tightly folded, making them reek. The very notion was nauseating. She wanted no part of this foul ball.

Foul ball. Could this be a pun? Puns were the bane of Xanthly existence. They were everywhere, like poisonous toadstools, and of course even the toads did not muck about in their stools. Puns were the lowest form of humor in much the way buns were the lowest form of bread, and even buns had naughty connotations to make boys snicker. Puns brought worse reactions than snickering. So it was conceivable that an obscene dance might be called a foul ball. But puns were also the main avenue for changing things.

Suppose she thought of another meaning for ball? She concentrated— and in a moment the dancers rolled into one feculent mass, a huge sphere that squeezed the limits of the chamber. But there was no way to pass it; the ball blocked the way. So that was evidently not the answer. She relaxed her focus, and the ball dissolved back into dancing harpies, who seemed not to have noticed their brief transformation.

Then a dim bulb flashed just over her head. The other word—foul. That could also be fowl. This could be a fowl ball. Harpies resembled fowl, which were barnyard birds—chickens, ducks, turkeys, pheasants, and the like. But by a further extension, all winged monsters could be said to have an affinity, because of their wings. Even winged centaurs.

She concentrated, and the harpies became winged centaurs engaged in mannerly dancing, their hooves keeping the cadence. The stench became odor, and the odor became smell, and the smell became healthy centaur musk. Now the chamber was bearable.

She moved on in and joined the dance. It was the Centaur Stomp, and she loved it. In a moment a centaur stallion came to join her. The Stomp did not require partners, but there could be couples if they wanted to be. "May I join you?" he inquired politely. "I am Center Centaur."

"Join me to what?" she inquired in return, with a smile as she matched his hoofbeats.

He laughed. "I knew you were clever and nice," he said.

"Oh? How?"

"It is my talent. Insight. I can see inside a person and know what is wrong."

"Being clever and nice is what's wrong with me?"

"Yes, because these are nasty challenges that make you feel uncomfortable. You could handle them better if you had a trifle more meanness of spirit."

It was her turn to laugh. "That is a flattering liability."

"True. I regret that you are emotionally committed to another stallion. I will let you go now."

"Thank you." He was evidently not a challenge in himself, just a bit player who perhaps was not allowed to help her, but felt no need to be unpleasant. She appreciated that.

Then she got a sudden headache. That was weird; she hadn't had one of those in a long time. Was it part of the Challenge?

A filly caught her eye. "Oh, I'm sorry," she said. "It's my talent: causing random headaches within a set radius. I can't control it, but fortunately it is intermittent. Let me get clear of you, and you will be all right."

"Thank you," Cynthia said weakly as the filly stomped away. Sure enough, her headache eased. She appreciated the filly's consideration. It was interesting how the thoughtless messy harpies had been replaced by thoughtful centaurs with obvious character; they weren't mere illusion. The Good Magician set up his Challenges in style.

She stomped steadily across the hall, until she reached the far door. Then she exited, and closed the door on the dancers. Let them have their fun; she was through the second hurdle. She had figured out the pun and morphed it to her own design.

She was in a short hall. In alcoves to either side were young human men. She recognized them by their forms, though she could as readily have done so by their action: both were looking fixedly at her breasts. They were young men, all right. She could simply trot between them and be through.

Or could she? This was likely to be the third Challenge, which meant that there would be something to challenge her progress. She had better discover its nature, rather than suffer it by surprise. Sometimes the worst threats were the least obvious ones.

First she tried the direct approach. "Hello, men. Shall we exchange introductions?"

"If you want to," the one on the right replied, not removing his eyes from her torso. Young men did tend to stare, but these ones were becoming downright obvious.

There was a pause, and she realized that it would be up to her to initiate the exchange. "I am Cynthia Centaur, coming to ask a Question of the Good Magician."

"We are the human twins Metros and Chronos," he replied. "We are here to serve as your third Challenge." His eyeballs seemed to be expanding.

Cynthia had schooled herself to be a true centaur, and to ignore incidental human crudities. But there were limits. The way these men were staring disrupted her aplomb. "May I inquire as to the nature of this Challenge?"

"You may." Both of them licked their lips. They were actually slavering.

There was another pause. They were answering, but not volunteering. "What is the nature of this Challenge?"

"You must pass by us." They were breathing hard. This was becoming embarrassingly obvious. Had they never before seen a maidenly chest?

But she maintained her dignity, with an effort. "Is there some reason this is not as simple as it seems?"

"That depends on how simple it seems to you." Never once had they looked away. The man on the left was locked on her left side, the one on the right on her right.

Cynthia sighed inwardly. These characters were bound to make it other than simple. But how? "Will you tell me your talents?" Then, before they could complete the routine of agreement and silence, she continued: "Please do so."

Metros nodded. "My talent is to make any object I touch larger or smaller, by four-fold." His right hand twitched, as if eager to make something on her right side four times as large.

"And mine is to make it older or younger, by a similar margin," Chronos said. His left hand twitched, as if ready to make something on her left side a quarter its present age.

Cynthia managed not to wince. "And if I try to walk past you, you will make me larger or smaller, or younger or older—four-fold?"

"Yes. You may choose which, by taking our right hands, which make larger or older, or our left hands, which make smaller or younger. Or one of each, so as to become larger and younger, or smaller and older."

"Four-fold," Cynthia said soberly. She had already gathered which hand did which; it was elementary logic. "So I will become a monstrous centaur, too big to squeeze through this passage, or a little one, readily balked. Or I will become sixty-four years old, or four years old—too old or young to accomplish those things I wish to."

"Precisely. You may be able to avoid one of us, but not both of us. If you do not touch us, we will touch you. So you must choose, or be chosen. Or retreat."

This did seem to be a sufficient Challenge. So competent that there needed to be no surprise element. So deadly that she could not afford to choose any of the alternatives. So certain that she could not avoid it. She *had* to figure it out, and nullify it.

But how? She was sure the twins were not bluffing. Illusion could be spectacular, but the Good Magician had no need to use it. He could afford the real thing, as the harpy/centaur ball had demonstrated. She really would be rendered older or younger, larger or smaller, depending on how she chose to be touched. Yet how could she avoid it? There seemed to be no way.

But there *had* to be a way. That was the nature of each Challenge. If only she could figure it out. She was supposed to have a fine centaur mind. She should be able to use it now. If she was a real centaur, instead of an imitation one. Unfortunately she wasn't sure she *was* genuine. That was why she was here, after all.

This reminded her of the problem of age. She had been delivered as a human baby in the year 1005, and been transformed to winged centaur in 1021. So technically she had been in this form for eighty of her ninety-six years. That was how she made it as five-sixths of her life. But when transformed she had fled to the Brain Coral's pool, and remained there seventy-two years, until 1093, when she was released, and traveled with Gloha Goblin-Harpy and Magician Trent, and joined Che Centaur. So her conscious life was twenty-four years. Then she had been rejuvenated by eight years, so was now physically sixteen. So if she were touched by Chronos, would she become three hundred eighty-four or twenty-four? Or ninety-six or six? Or sixty-four or four? Which of her ages would the magic talent fix on to multiply or divide?

She couldn't risk it. None of them were good for her. She wanted to stay sixteen, parallel to Che, so they could marry as approximate equals. That was why she had been rejuvenated: to match him. She didn't want to throw that away. As for changing her size—she had changed it when transformed, and that was quite enough. So she could not tolerate any more change of either size or age.

In addition, the very thought of having these freaks touch her body revolted her. She knew exactly where they would grab. Even if their talents didn't change her size, she would get dirtily pawed. The dirt was all in their minds, not hers, but it nevertheless bothered her considerably. She had not, it seemed, yet abolished all of her original human conditioning.

So should she just give up, and go home, and hope it was all right? That did not appeal, either. There just had to be a solution! If only she could cancel out the twins, make them touch each other—

Surely they did touch each other, and themselves, often. How did they eat, wash, dress? Were they constantly changing size and age? She doubted it. Each might be immune to his own touch, but what about his brother? They must have a way to nullify brotherly touches. That was the way she needed.

Suppose they touched with both hands at once? Would they multiply or divide? Or would the hands cancel each other's effects?

A bulb flashed. They had to cancel. It was the only logical way. And therein was her answer. She should take *both* hands, simultaneously.

But there were two of them. She might nullify one, but what about the other? She didn't have four hands.

Another bulb flashed. She didn't need them. The twins' hands defined their talents, but the victims weren't restricted to hands, as far as she knew. Otherwise the victims could simply tuck their hands under their armpits and be immune. It had to be the touch anywhere on their bodies that counted. Not that there was any doubt where she would be touched.

Well, it was time to prove she was more centaur than human. She would use their fixations to nullify them. She would touch *them,* her way. "I'm coming through!" Cynthia cried. She galloped toward the twins.

Each of them reached forward to touch her. She reached to the right to catch both of Metros's hands in hers. Her size did not change. She hauled him in to her bosom. She was taller than he; his face got flattened against her right breast while his feet dragged on the floor. He was helpless.

But that was only half the job. She half unfurled her left wing and swept it out to enclose Chronos. It was awkward, but she angled her body to make it possible. She brought him in against her left breast, holding him down with the wing so that both his hands were under him, locked against her equine chest. She held him there, and clasped his twin brother as closely as she turned around. Then she shoved Metros quickly away, and reached across with her hands to do the same with Chronos. The twin brothers tumbled together as she backed hastily away from them. Both had silly vacant smiles on their faces, as if they had been stunned by something heavenly. That irritated her, on a background level; she had intended to nullify them, not to give them a treat. But it couldn't be helped.

She saw one of them become huge, then small. The other grew old, then young. Indeed, they had not been bluffing. They would have to sort themselves out. Meanwhile she was backing through the far door. She had gotten past them.

Not without some token injury, however. She discovered that there were scratches on her breasts and sides where the obnoxious men had scraped by. Her torso was stinging, and blood was starting to ooze.

She shut the door, and turned around again. Her pulse was racing; she wasn't used to physical violence, even in a good cause. But she had overcome the third challenge. She felt like taking a shower to get her front side clean. But it had done its job, paralyzing their minds while nullifying their hands. She had proved she was more centaur than human.

"Welcome, Cynthia." It was Wira, the Good Magician's daughter-in-law. She appeared to be about twenty-seven, but, like Cynthia, could be reckoned as different ages. She was blind, and very nice.

"I'm so glad to see you, Wira," Cynthia said. "I was afraid I wouldn't make it through those challenges."

"Maybe it would have been better if you hadn't."

Cynthia stared at her. "What do you mean?"

"Oh, I shouldn't have said that," the woman said quickly. "I'm sure everything's in good order." But there was a certain insincerity in her tone. That was quite unlike her.

"Now, Wira," Cynthia said in her most reasonable manner. "We have been friends for some time, because we have things in common. Remember, we were both sixteen when we went to sleep."

"Yes, we have been, and we were," the woman agreed evasively.

Cynthia didn't like taking advantage of guilt, but she was getting really nervous about what was going on with Magician Humfrey. "You woke in Ten-ninety, and were youthened twenty-two years to match Hugo, so you could marry him. I woke in Ten-ninety-three, and was youthened eight years to match Che. He introduced me to you, when we visited the castle."

"Yes, when I was nineteen physically, forty-one chronologically. You were eight physically and eighty-eight chronologically, so you were both half my age and twice my age. Wasn't that odd!"

"So we had to be friends," Cynthia said. "We pretended to be big and little sisters in spirit. Now you're twenty-seven and I'm sixteen, physically, and we've never deceived each other." She paused meaningfully.

Tears squeezed from Wira's blind eyes. "Oh, Cynthia, I'm not deceiving you! I just *can't* talk about the Good Magician's business."

This was really serious. "Did I do something wrong?"

"Oh, no. Not at all. You—you just came at a bad time, I think. Humfrey's in an awful mood. I think he set the Challenges not to stop you, so much as to make you change your mind."

"The ferociously angry demoness!" Cynthia said. "The loathsome dance. The boys gawking at my torso."

"Yes. But it didn't work. You prevailed."

"It came close to working," Cynthia muttered. "I must confess that last Challenge really bothered me. I hate being viewed as a naked object. It isn't centaury. But I just didn't want to admit defeat."

"I'm glad you won through. But I hope you don't regret it. Something weird is going on."

"So Metria thinks. I promised to tell her what it is."

"Well, I fear you will soon find out. I've never seen Humfrey so out of sorts."

"Seen?"

"I may be blind, but I speak the same language you do. There's not even a Designated Wife on duty today; none of them will go near him when he's like this." Then Wira looked at her. "Are you hurt?"

"Just some scratches. How did you know?"

"There is a slight tightness to your voice, as if you are in discomfort. Let me summon Robert."

"Robert?"

"He uses music to heal wounds." She elevated her voice. "Robert!"

"Please, I'm not wounded, just scratched."

But Robert was already appearing. He was an ordinary human man with some kind of instrument. He touched its strings. Music flowed—and the stinging abated.

Cynthia looked down at herself. The scratches had healed!

Robert, seeing that his job was done, nodded and departed. "Thank you!" Cynthia called after him. He had healed her with his music, and not even stared.

Cynthia returned to business. "So the Good Magician's been grumpy before. How did his wives handle it then?"

Wira pondered. "I suspect they stayed clear of him, as they are doing now."

"No one has mentioned long-ago episodes? There must be some hint."

"Well, the Maiden Taiwan did mention something once. But that wasn't really the same."

"Tell me anyway. Maybe it will help."

"Well, it seems that over a century ago Humfrey discovered the Fountain of Youth. He offered the water to King Ebnez. The king declined, and made him promise not to give any of the youth elixir to any person not of his own family, and not to tell anyone where it was. So Ebnez died, and Humfrey became king after him. He honored the restriction, but the Maiden Taiwan, who was his wife of the time, said that the restriction really chafed him, because he saw worthy people aging and dying when they didn't have to. He would be really grumpy for days on end when he thought about it. But finally Ebnez came to him as a ghost, and told him that he seemed to have good judgment so far, so he was releasing Humfrey from that restriction. Thereafter Humfrey felt free to use the elixir for other beneficent purposes, and did so, and was significantly less grumpy."

"You're right: That's not quite the same. I have no information that might free him from such a problem."

"Yes. I don't know what to advise you to do."

This sounded really bad. Cynthia's nervous tinge expanded into an apprehensive twinge. But her curiosity grew apace. "Well, let's discover what it is."

"I suppose we had better." Wira led the way up the winding stairway to the Good Magician's dingy little study. There was barely room for her equine body.

Humfrey looked up as Cynthia came to the doorway. "Go away," he grumped.

Not sufficiently daunted, she spoke formally. "Good Magician, I have come to ask a Question."

He grimaced. "I prefer not to Answer it. Please depart."

This was an astonishing response. Humfrey's entire business as the Magician of Information was Answering Questions. The required year of service enabled him to keep a fine castle, always well stocked, with competent help at all times. Why should he balk now? "Good Magician, if I have unwittingly given offense, I apologize and proffer whatever amends are feasible. But I do want my Answer, and stand ready to perform whatever Service is required."

"She did successfully navigate the Challenges," Wira said. "And she's my friend. She is deserving."

The Magician's fossilized countenance softened, as it tended to do when Wira addressed him. If there was any person in Xanth he could be said to like, it was her. "My dear, it is not that easy."

"My Question is straightforward," Cynthia said. "I am sure you will have no difficulty Answering it. It is—"

He stopped her with a suddenly lifted hand. "Desist, filly. I do not want to hear it."

"But—"

"I see I must explain. There is an indirect crisis facing Xanth which will require horrendously risky action. The Muse of History has decreed that I must select for this mission the first querent whose Question I Answer. Your Question is so simple, and the mission so difficult and dangerous, that there is a complete lack of proportion. In addition, you are a nice person, and Che Centaur's fiancée. I prefer not to disrupt your lives so pointlessly. Please do not ask your Question. It is better for me to wait for someone with a more difficult one."

This was indeed serious. But she had fought through the Challenges, and was not about to quit now. "You don't think I'm up to this mission," Cynthia said, nettled. "Because you know I'm not a real winged centaur, I'm only a transformed human girl." There was the crux of her insecurity.

"If the Muse of History selects you for this mission, then you must be up to it," he said. "You are fully your present species, in every particular but memory. But for such a simple Question, and with so much to risk, with your mating ceremony looming soon, it seems unfair. Now abandon this query and go your way untroubled."

"No! I want to know. I'll do the mission. Give me my Answer." She realized as she spoke that she hadn't even asked the Question yet. But obviously Humfrey knew what it was.

"I believe you could fathom it for yourself. Depart, and enjoy your future with a fine centaur."

Cynthia took a determined breath, but Wira touched her elbow before she could translate it into a sentence. "He has really Answered you," she whispered. "He's trying to let you go without a Service."

Indeed, he had. He had said she was fully centaur in everything but the memory of her human origin. Breeding was not memory. But she was unwilling to accept her Answer free. "No. I will do the Service. I insist on having my Question Answered."

"The answer is yes!" he snapped. "Now begone!"

"But I haven't yet asked."

"So you need do no Service. Scram!"

"You must go," Wira whispered urgently.

She stood unmoved. "Yet it seems that you have indeed Answered. You tell me that my issue will breed true to my present nature."

"Yes! All transformees breed true. Half the present winged centaurs are transformees. You know that. So there is no need to come here."

Cynthia realized with a start that she *had* known that. A number of her friends were transformees, and some had already mated and bred true. She had been concerned about nothing. Still, she felt obliged to honor the forms. She had come for an Answer, and she had gotten it. "What is my Service?"

Humfrey sighed. "You will not relent?"

"I am a centaur. You have confirmed that." Centaurs were known for their stubbornness.

"Then so it must be," he said, resigned. "The Demon E(A/R)th has disappeared, and must be rescued before his magic of Gravity fades, destroying Earth and taking Xanth with it. My Book of Answers has nothing on this subject; it is beyond the scope of mere magic. You must handle this matter yourself." He put his head down on the musty tome before him.

Cynthia heard Wira's horrified intake of breath. This really was a horrendous mission, perhaps impossible. But she had to do it. She had no idea how to proceed.

$\overline{2}$

CASTLE ZOMBIE

S im was thoroughly tired of geometry. It was true that he had to learn all the knowledge of the realm, but mathematics in all its forms was just plain dull. He would much rather be out learning how to tame dragons or spook foolish nymphs.

"So then what is the formula for determining the hypotenuse?" Che Centaur asked.

"The what?" Sim squawked. He was unable to speak human fashion, but Che understood his peeps and squawks perfectly, so it made no difference. Che was his tutor, and a good one.

"I'm not sure your avian mind is completely on this lesson," Che said, frowning.

"I'm bored!"

Roxanne Roc, snoozing nearby, opened an eye. She was Sim's governess, and she did have authority over him. But she preferred to leave his schooling to the tutor. Only if Che glanced her way would she intercede. Then Sim would have to get back to work on math, no matter how boring it was. He had caught on early, being a very bright bird, that one defiant twitch of a feather in Roxanne's direction would cause her to summon the Simurgh, who would quickly make him wish he had never been hatched. When it came to discipline, his best chances for tolerance lay first with Che, then with Roxanne.

Che paused, considering. He was a good teacher, as all centaurs were, but he was young, just sixteen. That meant that he had not quite yet joined the Adult Conspiracy, though it hardly applied to winged monsters, and had some sympathy for a six-year-old bird. "Let's take a break," he said. "We can fly around and see if we can find anything interesting."

"Let's look for the origin of puns!" Sim squawked.

Roxanne winced. She knew this was a waste of time. But she also respected Che's judgment, so gave him considerable leeway in tutoring. He favored the carrot over the stick, and while Sim had not yet figured out who would even want a carrot, let alone a stick, it seemed that Roxanne was satisfied that it worked. But neither choice was certain at the moment; math was more likely.

To Sim's surprise, Che agreed. That meant that Che was bored too. No one knew the origin of puns, so it was probably an endless search.

They spread their wings and took off. The centaur flicked himself with his tail to become light enough to remain aloft. Che was larger, because of his centaur mass, but Sim was destined to be huge, the size of a roc, when grown. He was not a roc, of course; he was the chick of the Simurgh, the oldest and wisest bird in the universe. She had seen the universe expire and be re-created three times. Sim might be on duty for the next change of universes. But first he had to learn all there was to know. There was a lot of that, and much of it was dull, unfortunately.

They flew across the Land of Xanth. It was beautiful in its crazy fashion, with fields and forests, rivers and lakes, hills and mountains, and of course the great Gap Chasm across the center. But there was no sign of the origin of puns.

"Do you think the puns will ever run out?" Sim squawked.

"If they do, Xanth will dissolve into chaos," Che said with just a hint of a muted smile. "It is mostly made of puns."

"Maybe some bloated ogre has magic indigestion, and constantly emits them."

"Perhaps," Che agreed, this time with five-eighths of a smile. He allowed Sim some juvenile humor, since he was a young bird.

Then Sim's sharp eyes spied a flying figure in the distance. "Cynthia Centaur!" he squawked. "She has returned!"

That preempted Che's attention. "My betrothed."

Soon Cynthia joined them. Her bare bosom was heaving with more than the routine effort of flight. Sim knew that had there been any human men nearby, they would have stared. He had not yet figured out why hard breathing attracted their attention, but would surely do so in time. "I have horrendous news! I must rescue a Demon, and I have no idea how to proceed."

"You used a capital *D*," Sim squawked. There was more difference between a Demon and a demon than between a centaur and a microbe.

"The Demon Xanth is in trouble?" Che asked, dismayed.

"No. The Demon Earth."

Both Che and Sim almost fell out of the sky. "Surely we miscomprehend," Che said as he righted himself. "We have no dealing with that particular Demon."

"It's my Service for the Good Magician," she said. Then, evidently reminded of something, she clasped Che's foresection in air and kissed him while the two hovered in the sky. "I have my Answer. I will breed true."

Centaurs spoke of breeding rather than of stork deliveries. This related to their alternate system of reproduction. Birds of course were more sensible, using eggs as the delivery mechanism. How it was that a bird brought live babies to other creatures was another thing Sim had not yet discovered.

"That is good to know," Che said. "But I don't understand what—"

"She must rescue the Demon Earth," Sim squawked helpfully. "And she doesn't know how."

"That much I had gathered," Che said somewhat wryly. "But why should you be selected for so momentous a task?"

"The Muse of History said Magician Humfrey had to assign whoever got an Answer this day, and I was the one. As for the Demon Earth— it seems he originates the force of gravity, which the Land of Earth really needs, and which also has some relevance to the Land of Xanth. So I need to rescue the Demon before this force fades, in much the way magic would fade were the Demon Xanth incapacitated. I just wish I had some notion how to do it."

Che nodded. "It is true. We do have some use for gravity, despite the way we winged centaurs require magic to abate it so we can fly. Losing it would be a serious matter, and not just because it holds obnoxious land creatures down. But having any effect on a Demon, let alone rescuing one, is prodigiously beyond the capacities of any creature of Xanth. We are as dust motes compared to them."

"Mother should know," Sim squawked. "She knows everything."

"Suddenly I perceive a certain logic to the selection," Che said. "Cynthia is my affianced, and I tutor Sim, whose mother knows everything. Thus Cynthia has a certain access to essential information."

"I'll go ask her," Sim squawked eagerly. This sounded far more interesting than basic math.

"I think we should all go ask her," Che said. "Roxanne can take us more rapidly."

That was true. The three of them were about to fly back when the roc's huge form lifted into the air, and joined them in a single wingbeat. She had powers of flight beyond those of any ordinary roc. Actually, she had more; she could command the cooperation of any of the leading figures of Xanth, when necessary to safeguard Sim. But she had never needed to invoke such authority. "You spoke my name?" she squawked.

"We need to go to the Simurgh," Che said. "Something has come up." He had some authority in his own right, because every winged monster was sworn to protect him. That was one reason why Roxanne had been able to be low-key. He was also destined to change the history of Xanth, but no one knew whether this related to his tutoring of Sim or some other thing. Sim hoped it was the latter, because tutoring was so, well, mundanish.

Without further squawk the roc hovered in air and extended her monstrous claws. They formed an enclosure into which the three of them flew. They settled, and Roxanne accelerated.

Xanth passed below in a blur of mixed magic color. Then they were over a complicated range of mountains whose colors were pure: blue, red, green, pink, yellow, white, and black. "The mountains of Qaf," Sim squawked happily, recognizing them. "Each a different color of beryl. The green is emerald, which is fairly common, but the red is bixbite, which is rare, and of course black beryl is not encountered elsewhere. No one other than Mother or Roxanne or me can fly here." That was literal; all other winged creatures found themselves magically grounded. Not even small *d* demons could conjure themselves here without special permission.

Roxanne hovered over a white peak and opened her talons. They slid out to land on a level platform. Roxanne glided across to a blue peak and settled.

The Simurgh approached. Her wingbeats were like waves of mist, and as she landed on a red peak her feathers showed like light and shadow, with a crest of fire on her head. Sim knew himself to be the most beautiful bird in Xanth, scintillating with twice the colors of the rainbow, but the sheer splendor of his mother awed him. WHAT IS IT, SON? Her voice was in their minds, a dauntingly powerful thought.

"Cynthia must rescue the Demon Earth," Sim squawked. "She needs to know how."

THIS REQUIRES DIALOGUE. Then the scene changed. Sim found himself and the others in a lush garden with vegetables and fruits of many colors. There was yellow corn, white turnip, blue berries, black berries, red strawberries complete with straws for drinking, green melons, and pink lemonade. But it was not a meal; it was a display. Sim himself was a handsome navy bean. "Squawk?" he inquired.

"The Simurgh has rendered us into an illusion scene for more comfortable dialogue," another navy bean said in Che's voice.

"A lovely display of garden produce," a cute chick pea said in Cynthia's voice.

"But I'm a real chick," Sim squawked. "Why am I not a chick pea?"

"The term has a colloquial as well as a literal meaning," Che-bean explained. "It refers to a pretty girl. Navy beans are symbolic of virile seafaring men."

Oh. Suddenly he was satisfied to be a bean.

"Now let's hear more about your mission," a brightly shining sunflower said, turning her light on the chick pea.

"Magician Humfrey requires me to rescue the Demon Earth," Cynthia said. "He says this matter is not in his Book of Answers, so I am on my own. I desperately need advice."

"This is true," the Simurgh said. "Only another Demon could incapacitate a Demon. Since all other Demons are therefore under suspicion, the matter must be handled by mortals. This is a considerable Challenge."

That seemed to be a more than considerable understatement to Sim. The power of any Demon was virtually absolute in his realm. All of the magic that made the Land of Xanth what it was stemmed from the incidental leakage from the surface of the body of the Demon Xanth. Similarly all of the natural forces of the Land of Earth derived from leakage from the Demon Earth's body. They might as well be ants trying to govern invisible giants.

"Is it even theoretically possible for a mortal centaur to accomplish such a mission?" Che asked.

"Yes. But it is neither easy nor direct."

"There is a way?" Cynthia asked, eagerly surprised.

"Yes. You must acquire the use of the Swell Foop."

There was a brief silence. "I don't believe I am familiar with the term," Che said, embarrassed for his ignorance.

"Unsurprising. It is an unclassfied device that was lost several centuries ago."

"Lost!" Cynthia exclaimed. "Then how—"

"You must find and recover it. To do this you must first obtain the Six Rings of Xanth, for they are the only artifacts capable of handling the Swell Foop. That will be a considerable challenge of its own."

"But if this wonderful Foop is lost, how can anyone use it?" Cynthia asked. "What use would it be to get the Rings, if there is nothing for them to handle?"

"The Rings will also enable you to locate the Foop. When they are stacked and aligned, a person who sights through them will be able to see the Foop—if the stack is pointing the right way, and if it is the person destined to use it."

"How will we know who that person is?"

"It will be one of the holders of the Rings. Perhaps the one who is first able to spy the Foop. I am not sure."

There was a startled pause. None of them had ever imagined the Simurgh not knowing something.

"Let me summarize, if I may," Che said. He had a very organized mind.

The sunflower seemed to smile. "You may."

"Cynthia needs the Swell Foop to rescue the Demon Earth. She needs the Six Rings of Xanth to find the Foop. If I infer the implications correctly, the Rings are not easy to obtain, and each must have a separate holder. This will necessitate a party of at least six."

"Correct."

Sim cut to the essence. "Where are the Rings?"

"Because they are so powerful as to be dangerous in the wrong hands," the sunflower said, "they are well hidden. No living person knows the location of any of them."

A silence hovered above the group, then slowly settled on it. But Sim had a faint notion how his mother thought. "You did not exclude nonliving persons, such as the demons."

"No demon knows, either."

Sim was chagrined. He thought he had made a smart observation, for he was supposed to be a very bright bird.

"Maybe a ghost," Cynthia said.

"No ghost."

Then a tulip bulb flashed over Che's head. "Zombies!"

The sunflower nodded. "Only living persons may use the Rings. Only the zombies know where the Rings are hidden. This is a precaution to make it unlikely that their power will be abused."

Sim nodded. Living folk did not like to associate with zombies, so seldom got close to them or asked favors of them.

"But what do the Rings do, aside from locating the Swell Foop?" Cynthia asked.

"They control the six known Regions of Xanth. Any one has absolute power over its Region; the six together would have power over all Xanth rivaling that of the Demon Xanth. It is felt that such power should not be invoked casually."

"And the massed power of the Rings is required to handle the Foop," Sim squawked. "That must be an extremely potent device."

"It is no ordinary foop," the Simurgh agreed. "It is an almost perfect one. That makes a difference."

The other navy bean nodded. "Surely so."

"Then I think we must go to see the zombies," the chick pea said with imperfect enthusiasm.

"This is recommended," the sunflower agreed. "And I think this is a suitable mission for Sim to support."

"Saving a world?" Che asked.

"It is best for him to begin small."

A world was small, to the Simurgh, who knew the entire universe. If Sim could not save a world, he would hardly be fit to tackle the universe. Still, this seemed like a formidable enterprise. He firmed his beak; he would make his best effort.

Then the illusion faded, and they were back on the mountaintop.

Roxanne spread her wings and lifted into the air. She came to hover just above them, her talons descending. There was no downdraft; she could prevent it from happening when she chose, as part of the enhanced powers of flight she had been granted for her task of caring for Sim. She was a good nanny, and he felt closer to her on a personal basis than to the Simurgh. She had time for him. Which was of course the point: Roxanne did not have to run the universe.

They got into the enclosure, and the roc flew rapidly away from the beryl mountains of Qaf. In just a few wingbeats she was gliding down toward Castle Zombie. It was a decrepit structure, overgrown by sickly moss, with a moat filled with rotting goo. Sim was not particularly partial to this site, but he kept his beak shut, knowing that this visit was necessary.

Roxanne set them down on a high slimy ledge, then went to seek a more pleasant resting spot for herself. This was not selfish on her part; it was uncertain that the tottering castle could sustain her weight. She would return the moment Sim squawked. In fact, she would bash down a wall to reach him, if she had to. But she would not have to; the fact was that no one in the Land of Xanth would offer Sim any trouble. That did not make him feel great; it was just the way things were.

A rickety door squeaked open and a zombie emerged. "Whash?" it asked. A bit of its lip fell off as it spoke.

"We have come to see the proprietors," Che said.

"Thish whay." It turned and led the way into the castle.

Inside was a platform, with a zombie maid in attendance. "Take theze creaturez to Zombie Mashter," the zombie man said. Then, to the group: "Donth ashk her to tawk."

"She can't talk?" Cynthia asked.

"Muzzn't."

"Mustn't talk?" Che asked. But the guard had already gone back outside.

The maid nodded and turned toward the far exit.

Cynthia got a look on her face. Sim tried to caution her, but she brushed aside his squawk. "Let's introduce ourselves," she said to the maid. "I am Cynthia Centaur. You are?"

"Anna Gram," the maid said.

"That's interesting. I know a game with that name."

The zombie maid resumed progress toward the door, not responding. "I think she's not supposed to talk," Sim squawked.

"Nonsense," Cynthia said. "She spoke her name perfectly well. I do not accept the notion of servants being forbidden to speak. They are people too." She returned to address Anna. "This is your station? Where you work? This platform?"

"Sklatform," Anna agreed, slurring slightly in the zombie manner.

Then Cynthia turned about and walked stiff-legged back out the entrance.

Che and Sim stared after her. "She looked angry," Che said. "What brought that on?"

Anna bowed her head. "Zorry," she said.

"Oh, I'm sure it's not your fault," Che said. "Though I've never known her to be temperamental. This is quite unlike her."

Then a light flashed over Sim's beak. "Anagrams!" he squawked. "Her talent!"

Anna nodded abjectly.

"I don't understand," Che said, seeming quite displeased. He was supposed to be the one who always understood.

"Anagrams," Sim squawked. "Rearranging the letters of words or sentences to form other words. Her talent is to make that literal, only her zombie pronunciation messes it up. She tried to say 'platform' but slurred it. 'Sklatform.' That became 'stalk from.' She spoke to Cynthia, so it affected her."

"You're right!" Che agreed. "That's why she's not supposed to talk. There's no telling what will happen. Apparently her name is immune, and when she speaks briefly enough, there's no anagram to be made. Cynthia forced the issue, and paid a consequence."

"Zorry," Anna repeated.

"Not your fault," Che said. "We won't require you to talk anymore. I'll get Cynthia, and you can lead us silently downstairs."

In a moment Cynthia was back, and Che explained. "Sim figured it out."

"Bright bird," she agreed tightly.

They followed Anna down several sagging flights of steps. Sim was afraid that the stairs could not support the weight of the two centaurs, but they turned out to be stronger than they looked. Indeed, the castle was stronger than it looked, Sim remembered from lessons. Its seeming oldness was largely magical, and had been from the day it was constructed.

They were met on the ground floor by a comely old woman. "Why, hello, Che and Cynthia," she said warmly. "And Sim, the most beautiful bird in Xanth. But whatever brings you here?"

"We are glad to see you, Millie," Che said. "We have need of the Six Rings of Xanth. We understand that only the zombies know where they are."

Millie the Ghost, as she was still called though her ghostly days were long gone, paused. "This must be something Jonathan knows about."

"We hope so," Cynthia said.

"Let me fetch him. Come into my parlor." She brought them into the section of the castle that she maintained zombie-free. It was completely clean, and there was no smell of rot. It was a relief.

While she was away, they consulted. "Do you think he will know?" Cynthia asked. "If we never heard of the Rings or the Foop, maybe he hasn't, either."

"He must have," Che said, but he did not seem completely certain.

"The Good Magician would not have given Cynthia this mission if it wasn't possible to accomplish," Sim squawked.

"But he didn't want to give it to me."

Then Millie returned with the Zombie Master. "You are looking for the Rings of Xanth?" he asked. "Why?"

"The Good Magician says the Demon Earth needs to be rescued, and the Simurgh says we need the Swell Foop, and to find it we need the Six Rings, and only the zombies know where they are."

"This is true. Even I do not know, but there are zombies who do." He glanced at Sim. "This is an extremely ambitious project. Your mother supports this?"

"Yes," Sim squawked. "She wants me to start small. To practice for the big one later."

"Like saving the universe," the Zombie Master agreed. "This is a mere world or two."

"Yes."

"Nevertheless, I think you will need some help."

"Why?"

"Because this group consists of only three people. You will need six to handle the Rings."

"Six?" Cynthia asked. She had evidently forgotten their prior dialogue on this subject. That was because she had not been a centaur all her life.

"Each Ring requires the full attention of one person to use it. They must be used together to handle the Swell Foop. Therefore there must be six people to complete the mission."

"But I thought I was supposed to rescue the Demon Earth myself, once we get the Rings," Cynthia said, dismayed. "It's nice of Che and Sim to help me, but I couldn't ask anyone else to get involved. The Good Magician said it's dangerous."

"Fortunately I am not restrained by any such consideration," the Zombie Master said. "As it happens, Millie and I are about to retire, and Castle Zombie will be occupied by a new couple. They need to gain experience, and this should be excellent practice." He went to the door and called. "Justin! Breanna! This one's for you."

"Justin and Breanna!" Cynthia exclaimed. "Of course! She just turned eighteen, so they can marry."

"That may have to wait," the Zombie Master said. "The Demon Earth's magic is gravity, and Xanth needs that almost as much as Earth does."

"They might float away during the ceremony," Sim squawked, laughing.

"So might the rest of us," Che said, not finding it as funny.

Another person appeared at the door. Justin Tree was no longer a tree, but a completely ordinary man, so that it was not possible to notice such details as the color of his hair or eyes or the size of his nose. He looked about twenty-one, but had a courtly aspect. "A salutation to each of you," he said. "I believe we met at Jenny's wedding."

"I don't remember that," Cynthia said.

"I was with Breanna at the time."

"But she attended alone."

Che interceded. "He was *with* her—in her mind."

"Oh." Cynthia managed to blush. It was another remnant liability dating from her time as a human being. It was embarrassing, but Che claimed to like this aspect of her personality. So did Sim; it was amusing.

Breanna of the Black Wave appeared. She had lustrous waist-length black hair, glowing green eyes, and the rest of her was duskily appealing in the human manner. "What's this about delaying our wedding?" she demanded with moderately masked outrage. "It's taken me three years to nail Justin down, and now he's going to get a reprieve?"

That was of course a pose. Everyone knew that the last thing Justin wanted was a reprieve from Breanna.

"These folk must try to save the Demon Earth," the Zombie Master explained. "They need your help, and since it involves liaison zombies, it seems you two are elected."

"The Demon Earth! Why the bleep should we try to help *him*? He tried to trap the Demon Xanth in Mundania and ruin Xanth. He's no friend of ours."

"You underestimate the gravity of the situation," the Zombie Master said.

Cynthia tried to stifle a titter, and Sim clamped his beak shut to avoid a hilarious squawk.

"What's so funny?" Breanna demanded with barely subdued annoyance. She had been a pretty girl at innocent fifteen; now in her more mature irritation she was darkly beautiful.

"I believe he refers to the magic of the Demon Earth," Justin said. "This relates to gravity, which is vital to Earth, and convenient in Xanth."

"Without gravity, your skirt would fly up," Sim squawked, losing the battle of amusement. Human maidens were inordinately sensitive about such details. "Something might show." Why human women insisted on wearing skirts, or, for that matter, panties, was another minor mystery Sim had not yet fathomed.

She fired a dusky glare at him. "I knew that, Birdbrain!"

Che looked as if he were biting his human tongue, and even Millie averted her fair old face. They knew that Sim was not only the most beautiful but also the smartest bird in Xanth, after his mother. Breanna knew it too, but she was a respecter of little that wasn't black, as a matter of principle. It was a privilege to be mildly insulted by her.

"It seems that the Demon Earth has been abducted or imprisoned or somehow confined, and with him the force of gravity is hostage," the Zombie Master said. "He may not be our favorite Demon, but if it falls on us to restore him to his normal place, self-interest behooves us to do this. Cynthia Centaur has been assigned by the Good Magician to accomplish this mission."

"And I need a whole lot of help," Cynthia said.

"But Justin and I are about to get *married*," Breanna said. "At long lengthy last. He has escaped this fate too long already. Find someone else to help." She caught Justin's hand and squeezed it. He showed signs of melting.

It was clear that if his fiancée told him to jump through a flaming hoop or to chew on a stink horn, Justin would make his best effort. Breanna was completely in charge of his situation, and she knew it. It would require a monstrously compelling reason to make her postpone the nuptial.

"Che and Sim are helping," the Zombie Master said. "But they must locate the Swell Foop, which can be done only by the use of the Six Rings of Xanth, which in turn are hidden. Only the zombies know their locations. Therefore a liaison to the zombies is required. Millie and I are a bit old for such activity."

"And you're retiring," Breanna said, a small black cloud forming over her head. "So *we* have to do it." A tiny jag of lightning speared out in his direction. It didn't reach him, but it didn't fall short by much.

"I did think it would be good experience," he agreed, unperturbed. Evidently he had come to know Breanna well in the past year or so. "And, knowing your generous nature—"

The cloud exploded, drenching her glossy tresses with a bucket of rain. "That's not fair! You're using false flattery." Fortunately the water was soon steaming away from her hot head.

"Flattery, yes. False, no. When did you ever let a friend down?"

"All *right*! We'll help find the stupid Rings." She turned on Justin. "But that will be only a brief respite. As soon as they have their Rings, you're sunk."

"I was sunk the day I met you," Justin murmured fondly.

"For sure." Breanna spun to face Sim. "Your mother's in on this, right? I never heard of these Rings, let alone this swelled poof, and I'll bet hardly anybody else has, either, but she knows everything."

"Yes," Sim squawked.

"So how does a zombie know about a ring? Which zombie is it?"

Sim shrugged his wings.

She rolled her eyes, making miniature cataracts form. Fortunately their wild water faded almost as fast as it flowed, and did not interfere with her vision. "So we have to figure out which zombie. I should have known. Well, let's get on it. I want to get this done today so we can schedule the wedding for tomorrow. Come on." She whirled and led the way out of the castle.

"That's some human woman," Che murmured as they set out after her.

"I believe my zombies will be well represented after my retirement," the Zombie Master agreed. "Justin is a fine and knowledgeable man with good judgment, but some fire is also good, and she has that in excellent measure."

Sim could only agree. But he wondered how Breanna would react when she discovered that she would have to wield one of the Rings, surely extending her participation and further delaying the wedding. They all might need lightning rods and raincoats.

They walked out the sagging front gate and across the warped drawbridge. Once they were beyond the moat, Breanna put two fingers into her mouth and made a piercing whistle. Soon zombies were shuffling in from all around. It was an impressive if macabre sight. Some zombies were relatively fresh, but others were in abysmal state. Sim knew that it depended not on the length of time they had been subject to this condition, but on their state of decomposition when they had been made zombies. A zombie never really changed form, though constantly sloughing off moldering bits of itself. That was part of their magic: to live their half-lives interminably, neither fully alive nor fully dead. Sim could not think of a worse situation for a person to find himself in. Surely full death would be better.

"I dread this," Cynthia murmured, mostly to herself.

Breanna heard her. "Why, wing-mare? Because you have to work with zombies?"

"Well—"

"Zombies are people too, you know. They serve Xanth loyally, and don't deserve to be stigmatized."

"Oh, I wouldn't think of—" Cynthia started somewhat lamely.

"And they aren't all rotten. Some are very fresh, so you wouldn't even know they're zombies if you weren't told. If you took the trouble to get to know them—"

"Cynthia apologizes for any inadvertent slur," Che said. "Her mind is distracted by the magnitude of the task ahead."

"I will try to get to know a zombie well," Cynthia said apologetically.

"Okay." Breanna let it go, this time. Sim made a mental note never to imply anything negative about a zombie, at least while in Breanna's vicinity.

Sim took a brief walk while waiting for the zombies to assemble. He didn't fly, because that would suggest that he was trying to get away from the company of zombies, and after the way Breanna lit into Cynthia about that, he knew better. So he walked and hopped along, exploring the region, for he was interested in everything and more.

He spied two human girls looking at a brownish pool. "Hello," he squawked.

They jumped. "Don't gobble us up!" one cried. "We don't mean any harm."

He realized that they had not understood him. That was what came of walking alone, instead of having Che near to translate for strangers. He stopped moving, doing his best to look innocuous.

"Oh, you're just a bird," one girl said, reassured. "A big chick." Sim nodded.

"A beautiful one," the other agreed. Sim tried to blush, but couldn't manage this human expression. His feathers got in the way.

"We'll introduce ourselves," the first girl said. "We're twins, twelve years old. I'm Mol, and this is Ly."

"I'm Sim," Sim squawked.

"We do springs," Mol said.

"But it's random," Ly added.

"Squawk?"

They laughed. "That confuses everyone, even us," Mol said. "It's like this: I can make springs, but there's no telling what kind they will be. I mean, they can be water, or green jelly, or castor oil." She made a face. No one liked the oil from the wheels on chairs.

"And I change those springs," Ly said. "But I'm random too. So I might change her jelly to happiness elixir, or purple grunge. I wish we could control it, but we can't."

"I just made this one," Mol said, looking at the pool.

"But we don't know what it is," Ly said. "We don't want to just leave it here if it's bad. But how do we tell?"

"You see, we can make springs, but we can't unmake them," Mol said.

"We have to leave them where they are," Ly said. "If they aren't too bad. We left one in the Ever-glades that's a mere."

"A what?" Sim squawked.

"It makes you feel insignificant," Mol explained.

"We didn't like leaving it," Ly said, "but at least it's out of the way."

Obviously they needed help. Sim poked his beak cautiously into the pool. And got kicked in the tail.

Startled, he looked at the girls, but they were not close enough to kick him. No one was. So he tested the pool again, this time watching his tail, and got kicked again—by nothing.

A bulb flashed. "Boot rear!" he squawked. It was a popular drink, though somewhat wild.

"Oh, thank you," Mol said. Evidently they were coming to understand him.

"I'll change it," Ly said. She focused, and the pool changed from brownish to greenish.

Sim dipped his beak again. This time nothing booted his tail. "Lima soda," he squawked.

The girls exchanged twin glances. "Let's leave it at that," Mol said.

"Yes, it won't hurt anyone," Ly agreed.

"We have to go now," Mol said.

"Thank you so much," Ly said.

Sim nodded and gave them a parting squawk. Then he returned to the zombie gathering.

At last the assembly was complete. There was an astonishing number of zombies of every type—human, animal, and crossbreed. Several were birds. Some did indeed look fully alive, with no rot showing.

"Now pay attention, friends," Breanna said loudly, showing no aversion to either the sight or the stench of the throng. "We need your help."

The zombies focused on her as well as they could. Some had rotten eyes, and most had rotten brains, so their attention was not universally great, but they tried. It was clear that they had come to know her and like her to the extent they were able. Sim wasn't sure exactly why she had decided on this odd profession, but she seemed to be good at it. When all were listening, Breanna nodded to Justin.

"We have a need to locate the Swell Foop," Justin said. "Its nature need not concern you. In order to locate it, we must have the Six Rings of Xanth. We understand that only you know where the Rings are."

The zombies looked around in confusion. They did not seem to know anything about this.

"Maybe Xeth knows," Breanna said. "Where is he?" Then she answered her own question. "Of course—he's in his palace. We'll go there."

Xeth was the king of the Zombies, Sim knew. Justin Tree and Breanna of the Black Wave were to take over Castle Zombie, to serve as the liaison between the zombies and the living folk, but they did not govern the zombies. Xeth and his wife Zyzzvya did. Their palace was a bit apart from the common run of zombies, so they had not heard the whistle.

The five of them trooped through the forest until they came to a well-kept structure shaped like a military barracks. The trees and shrubs in its vicinity were lined up in a square formation, the largest at one corner, the smallest at the opposite corner, and the ones between changing size evenly. Everything was in perfect military order.

Breanna approached the door and touched the brightly polished brass doorknob. "King Xeth," she called. "Queen Zyzzvya—may we speak with you?"

The door opened and an attractive human woman stood there. No, Sim realized after an instant as his sharp bird's eyes caught the detail. She was a zombie, a very fresh one, with no rot showing. She must have been zombied within hours after death. She was proof of Breanna's statement about the variability of the type. She wore a sword, and was evidently an amazon woman. "Why, hello, Breanna. What is your concern?"

"We need to find the Six Rings of Xanth, and only the zombies know where they are, but the folk around the castle don't seem to know. I thought you and Xeth might be able to help us."

"I can help you with one, if you truly have a need-to-know," Zyzzvya said.

A very-well-preserved male zombie wearing a crown appeared behind her. This was King Xeth. "And I can help you with another," he said. He glanced at his wife in surprise. "But I did not know you had a Ring."

"I did not know *you* did, dear," she replied.

"I have always known; my mother taught me when I was young. But you have not been a zombie very long."

"Just long enough to meet you, dear." She turned back to Breanna and the others. "But this is not good protocol; we must properly entertain our visitors."

"My wife has military discipline," Xeth told the group. "She was a warrior in life. She has some excellent zombied pickles, and sourbread with sour cream spread." He spoke with a barely noticeable lisp; his tongue evidently had a trace of rot.

"We have no need of entertainment," Sim squawked quickly. He regarded himself as reasonably tolerant, but somehow zombie food did not appeal. "We wish to locate the Rings as soon as possible." Then Breanna speared him with a dark glance. He had just violated his resolution! "But perhaps a beakful to eat would be good."

Zyzzyva brought out a plate of appetizers, and they all tried them. They turned out to be quite good.

"The location of each Ring is known to but a single zombie," Xeth said. "No one knows who that is. But I can find the zombies in a few hours. I will send out messengers to question every zombie, and to summon the Ringers here."

"A few hours!" Breanna exclaimed, evidently appalled by the delay. But in half a moment she caught herself. "Of course, and thank you, King Xeth. Meanwhile, will you and Zyzzvya be able to help us with the first two?"

"As soon as we complete the directives to the messengers," the king agreed. "We should be able to start tomorrow."

"Tomorrow!" But again she stifled herself; she had had enough experience with zombies to know they couldn't be rushed. "Of course. Thank you so much."

Xeth nodded graciously. "I will commence the summoning now."

The living group walked back to Castle Zombie. "Maybe we can get it done in the morning, and have the wedding in the afternoon," Breanna said. "You must all come, of course. Meanwhile, you must stay the night with us; Castle Zombie has excellent facilities, believe it or not."

"We are sure of it," Che agreed politely. And of course they were; Sim knew that Millie the Ghost took perfect care of the castle, and the human section was completely human. The zombies hardly needed shelter, and were satisfied to snooze in shallow graves when not active.

Still, Sim might have preferred some other practice mission, if he thought about it. He made sure not to think about it while in the black girl's presence, however.

3

RING OF FIRE

King Xeth was as good as his kingly word: In the morning the four other zombies were there, ready to guide their charges to the general vicinity of the Rings. Breanna saw the others pairing off with their zombies; they would split up to search out all the Rings simultaneously, saving time, so as to get this chore done in a couple of hours. That would leave the afternoon free for the wedding.

She also saw Roxanne Roc, still waiting patiently for Sim to finish his business here. She walked over to the huge bird. "We each have to go with a Zombie to find a Ring of Xanth," she said. "Sim too. I don't think you should try to help him in this; it's his training mission. Why don't you check with him, and then take a few hours off? I'm sure you deserve a rest."

Roxanne nodded. She sent a glance into the throng, neatly catching Sim's eye. Then she nodded again, turned gracefully around, spread her wings, and took off. She was a good governess, knowing when to let the line slacken.

"Let's do it," Breanna said to Xeth, satisfied.

The king nodded and set off down a path. Breanna paced him. "It's funny how things have changed in three years," she said. "The first time we met, I fled you; now I like you just fine."

"Yes," he agreed. Zombies were not much for conversation, even well-preserved ones like him. His brain was perfectly good, and he could speak with only the slightest slurring, but he had never developed the habit of dialogue.

"You found me lying in the Pavilion of Love, and kissed me awake, and wanted to marry me. But I didn't want anything to do with a zombie. Isn't that hilarious, considering that I'm about to become the Zombie Mistress?"

"Yes." He could also speak at some length, when it was expedient, with good organization of thoughts, but seldom found it necessary.

"And it was all my mistake," she continued. "I thought it was just a vacant bed for anyone to use. You were perfectly within your rights to assume that I was looking for a prince or king to marry. You couldn't understand why I didn't follow through."

"Yes."

"Fully living folk can be prejudiced in various ways, and I was prejudiced against zombies. Until I heard myself talking about them exactly the way I'd heard others in Mundania talk about blacks." She looked down at her brown arm. "That they're all right in their place, but I wouldn't want to marry one."

"Yes."

"Of course I still wouldn't marry a zombie, or any other kind of creature. Justin Tree is the only one I want to marry, and I made him change to young human man form for that. But meanwhile you did marry Zyzzyva, so you are happy."

"Yes."

"Any luck summoning the stork?" This query might be considered out of order among fully living folk, but zombies didn't mind direct questions; in fact, they preferred them, as being less confusing.

"Storks are slow to answer zombies."

"Well, keep trying, and you'll get there. I understand that the Demoness Metria summoned the stork more than seven hundred and fifty times before getting its attention."

"Yes."

A swirl of smoke formed. "Did I hear my cognomen?"

"Your what?"

"Appellation, designation, patronymic, personage, identification—"

"Name?"

"Whatever," the cloud agreed crossly.

"It was just an incidental reference. We were talking about storks."

"Bothersome birds." The cloud formed the semblance of a stork as it faded.

Breanna was relieved. The demoness was usually more mischief than she was worth.

They passed a boy looking at a stone. "Oh, are you a rock collector?" Breanna asked.

"No, I'm using my talent," the boy said. "I can see the future of any object. The trouble is, most objects never have more future than they have past. So I keep checking, hoping to find a really interesting one." He dropped the stone.

"That may be the case with things out in the wilderness," Breanna said. "But maybe the objects in castles would be more interesting, because so much more happens there."

"Gee, yes," the boy agreed. "I'll go find a castle. Maybe I'll find an object that will be used to kill somebody. Thanks."

"Welcome," Breanna said with a quirk of a smile as he departed. The boy had a good talent, when he learned to use it well.

They came upon an older woman of about Breanna's height but heavier, who looked confused. Breanna was impatient to get her business done, but didn't like to pass someone by who might need help. "Hello. Are you all right?"

"I don't know. I thought I was ill, then suddenly I was standing in this forest. I walked, but have not found my way out of it. In fact, I tried to follow this dog, but he seems to be lost too."

Now Breanna saw the dog. He was of a rusty color. "True, Rusty?" she inquired.

He wagged his tail.

Breanna got a glimmer. This was not far from the realm of madness, where some who had died appeared. "Are you from Mundania?"

"Mundania?"

"The real world. Sometimes people come here from there. Animals too."

"Yes. I am Vanna Jane Morrow Shelton. I live at—"

"I am sorry to tell you that you can't go back, Vanna. This is—this is a weird place. But you can find new friends here. If you will just follow this path behind us, you will come to Castle Zombie. It looks awful, but it's not. Ask to talk to Millie the Ghost."

"A ghost!"

"It's just a name. She's a nice person. She will help you to get comfortably settled. I know you will like it here."

"I don't want to impose—"

"Don't worry about it. I'd show you the way myself, but I'm on an urgent mission."

"Of course." The woman set off down the trail, looking more confident now that she had somewhere to go.

The dog hesitated. "You too, Rusty," Breanna said.

The dog ran after the woman.

But that reminded Breanna of their own objective. "Say, just where are we headed?"

"To the Demon Realm."

"The Demon Realm! Do you even know how to get there?"

"No."

"Then where are we walking to?"

"If we just keep trying, we'll get there."

Breanna was accustomed to zombies' ways, but still got caught on occasion. "I prefer to find a shortcut," she said. "Do you know one?"

"No."

"But the Ring is in the Demon Realm?" It was best to be quite sure.

"Yes."

"Which Ring is it?"

"The Ring of Fire."

"And what does it control?"

"All demonic creatures, including Com Pewter's kind."

"Oh, I thought it might relate to the Region of Fire."

"That too," he agreed.

"But it's not necessarily *in* the Region of Fire. Just somewhere among the demons."

"Yes."

"So maybe we should get demon help to locate it."

"Yes."

"Do you have a particular demon in mind?"

"Demon Professor Grossclout."

She nodded. "I know of him. He is said to terrorize demon students. So he's in charge of the Ring?"

"Yes."

"Okay, let's see if we can find Grossclout quickly. For that we'll need the help of a lesser demon." She pondered half a moment. "The only one I really know is the Demoness Metria, because she's always messing into human business. Usually we just want her to go away."

"Yes."

"But this time I guess we need her. So I'll see if I can summon her. This time on purpose." She stopped walking, looked around, then called out, "Demoness Metria! Are you there?"

There was a faint swirl in the air before her. "Maybe," it said.

"We need your help."

"Too bad," the swirl said. "Maybe you should just go ask a stork."

Maybe the demoness had a grudge about being dismissed before. "Usually we just want to be rid of you. Aren't you pleased that we want your presence for a change?"

"No, that's boring."

"But we need you!" Breanna said, frustrated.

"Maybe if you beg hard enough."

So that was it. The demoness liked to annoy, and so she did the opposite of what was wanted. "Then I guess we'll just have to ask some other demon to help us. Maybe—" Breanna cast about for a name, but couldn't think of any, because she didn't know many demons.

"Demon Molish," Xeth said.

"D. Molish?" the swirl demanded, outraged. "He's no good at anything express."

"At anything what?" Breanna asked.

"Incontestable, absolute, certain, categorical, explicit—"

"Positive?"

"Whatever," the swirl said crossly. "All he does is destroy. You don't want him."

"Demon Lete," Xeth suggested.

"D. Lete? He's a total subtraction!"

"A total what?" Breanna asked, beginning to appreciate what the zombie king was doing.

"Remove, obliterate, eradicate, damage, ruin—"

"Loss?"

"Whatever! All he does is take things away. You don't want him."

"Demon Flower," Xeth said.

"D. Flower? He's a rogue! All he does is—"

"Never mind," Breanna said. "I'm sure one of them will do. They all surely know the way."

The swirl became a shimmering female shape. "Know the way where?"

"To the Demon Grossclout. But that's none of your business."

"The hades it isn't!"

"The what?" Xeth asked.

"Never mind!" Breanna repeated. "We don't want the likes of her annoying the good professor."

"It's my *right* to annoy Grossclout!" Metria flared, light flashing from her solidifying body. "I've been doing it for centuries."

"Then you must have lost your touch by now. He's seen it all."

"He *hasn't* seen it all!" The dress on the female form shrank dangerously. "I held some in reserve."

"Will you please go away?" Breanna demanded. "We are looking for someone else to lead us to Professor Grossclout, and we can't do it as long as you're in the way."

"Then you're stuck, because I insist on doing it. So there."

"But someone else could do it faster and better!"

"The purgatory they can!"

"The what?" Xeth asked.

"Never mind! I'm sure another demon could have us standing there before Professor Grossclout before I could count to ten. One, two three, four—"

There was a sudden wrenching, and smoke surrounded them. Breanna did not let it distract her from counting. "Five, six, seven—"

The smoke cleared. "And what is the meaning of this intrusion?" a commanding voice demanded.

Breanna stared. They were standing in a classroom before the Demon Professor himself. The young demons seated behind them tittered. Metria was nowhere to be seen.

"Uh, we needed to find the Ring of Power, and—"

"The *what*?"

"It's a—a—" Breanna stammered, daunted by the sheer over-whelming presence of Grossclout.

"I know what it is. Is your head filled with mush? What business do you have with it?"

"We—we have to—"

"In my office."

The room changed about them, and they were standing in his office, before his massive ironwood desk. Grossclout sat behind it, his visage menacing.

"To find it, to fetch the dandy poop—"

"The Swell Foop! Who put you up to this inanity?"

"Well, the Simurgh, actually, because—"

"Out with it! What's the phenomenal emergency to justify such a pursuit?"

"The Demon Earth is missing, and we have to save him, because—"

"Because we need the gravity. Of course. But this is not a thing for mortals to tackle. How did you get involved?"

"Because only another Demon could have abducted a Demon, and that means—"

"Another Demon is suspect. Now it registers. So mortals have to do it, and the only way they can accomplish anything at all is to use the Swell Foop."

"Yes," Breanna agreed. "So first we have to get all the Rings of Xanth, because—"

"Because they are the only way to locate the lost Foop, let alone control it," Grossclout said impatiently. "Let us cease belaboring the obvious. Why are you disrupting my class?"

This time Xeth answered. "Because the Ring of Fire is in your domain. You are the only one who knows where it is."

"I have no idea where it is."

"What?" Breanna asked, almost dumbfounded.

"No one knows precisely where any Ring of Xanth is."

"But then how can we—?"

"You will have to look for it. I will give you passes to search the premises so that the juvenile demons will neither hinder nor molest you. But only you can locate it."

"But I just came with King Xeth because—"

"You have been designated by blind fate. Concentrate your mind and you will get a notion of its direction."

Breanna had her doubt, but it was hard to deny Grossclout's overwhelming force of personality, so she tried. To her surprise, she did get a sense of a circular presence, as if there were a dim beacon whose light shone through walls and vegetation. "That way, maybe," she said, pointing toward a wall.

"I shall not have my study disturbed or my classes disrupted," Grossclout intoned dangerously. "You must use existing channels, rather than breaking through walls."

"Oh, sure," she agreed, realizing that he had a point. "I'll go around."

"Do so."

Breanna and Xeth exited by the study door, and found themselves back in the classroom. The class had evidently dissolved into mischief the moment the terrifying gaze of the Professor was absent. The male demons were trying to shape themselves into baskets that formed into a huge ball. The female demons were forming puffs of smoke that were drifting toward the basket cases, trying to get their attention. Breanna and Xeth walked cautiously around the edge, so as not to get caught by either a basket or a smoke ball.

Grossclout reappeared at his classroom desk. "Are your heads filled completely with mush?" he demanded horrendously. "You ignorant louts cease playing basketball immediately; this is not a sports arena. You scheming gamines stop sending smoke signals; this is not a boudoir."

The students quickly reverted to what appeared to be their normal state of muted terror, and the Professor resumed his lecture. "Now we come to the simplest and most basic technique of magic, that even a cranium three-quarters filled with mush should be able to grasp. Unfortunately that means a minority of you will grasp it. This is the magic of illusion, which requires the least effort for the greatest apparent result. It can actually be quite deadly when properly wielded, as when a deep pit in the ground is covered over by the illusion of a path. Mortal folk can find that quite uncomfortable. Even unwary demons can suffer if deceived. Can you provide an example, D. Ceive?" He focused his glare on a demoness who was burnishing her fingernails.

She glanced up, crossing her legs so that her well-fleshed thighs showed almost—but not quite—to her panty line. "Sure," Ceive said. "If a girl thinks there's something useful to be learned in this class, and wastes time attending it."

There was a murmur of admiration at this audacity. No one else dared respond to the Professor like that. Breanna, having made her way to the door, paused to see what would happen.

"That answer is incorrect," Grossclout said.

"You have a better one?" Ceive asked, adjusting her décolletage so that her very full breasts showed almost—but not quite—half their heaving globes.

"Indeed. When a demoness who has been banned from classes because of failing the course fourteen times in succession attempts to masquerade as a student, and discovers that the class she has crashed is an illusion."

"Really!" Ceive laughed, her flesh jiggling juicily.

Then the rest of the class dissolved into a single mass of warty flesh. Ceive was left sitting on the tip of the tongue of a horrendous monster. Huge teeth appeared as it slammed its jaws together. The demoness barely had time to puff into smoke before getting chomped.

The monster formed into a suction pump, and sucked the smoke into itself. "Eeeek!" the smoke screamed as it disappeared into the tank. Then the tank popped into the path of a giant steamroller and was instantly flattened.

The Professor extended a hand on an endlessly lengthening arm and picked up the paper-thin form. "Why, I do believe it is Metria," he said. "She seems to have lost weight."

"Metria!" Breanna exclaimed. "That's where she went!"

The Professor glanced her way. "This miscreant is with you?"

"I guess she is," Breanna said. "We needed her help to find you."

"Then perhaps you had better take charge of her." The Professor rolled the paper into a tight ball and tossed it across the re-forming classroom.

"Uh, thank you," Breanna said, catching the ball. "We'll try to keep her out of further mischief." Then she stepped out of the classroom.

"I had wondered where she went," Xeth said.

"For sure." She looked at the ball. "Do you think she'll recover? I was sorry to see her squished like that, after she helped us."

The ball dissolved into smoke. "Oh, I've been squished before," the voice of the demoness said. "That's when my personality got fractured into three identities."

"I didn't know that," Breanna said. "What happened?"

The smoke shaped into human female form, fully clothed. "In my youth I got stepped on by a Sphinx. It squished me into three aspects: Metria, with the problem of lexicon—"

"Of what?" Xeth asked.

"Vocabulary," Breanna said quickly.

"Whatever," the demoness agreed crossly. "And Mentia, who's a little crazy." She changed form, becoming cross-eyed with her pupils spinning around inside. "And cute little Woe Betide." She became a sweet, nice, adorable, innocent child. "Professional Grossmouth always puts me through the wringer when he catches me in class."

"I heard that!" the Professor's voice bellowed from the room beyond.

"Oh, go toast your ancient old eyeballs on this!" Metria said, re-forming in a short-to-the-nth-degree skirt. She faced away from the classroom, bent forward, and flipped up the skirt to expose huge polka-dot bloomers.

"I saw that!" the voice trumpeted.

Breanna realized that Metria and the Professor had an ongoing relationship that just possibly barely might include half a modicum of mutual respect. She liked to show him her wares and he liked to condemn her. Apparently no harm had been done to either, this time around.

"Let's go find that Ring," Breanna said. She started off down the hall.

"Isn't Xeth coming?" Metria inquired as she floated along beside.

Breanna realized that King Xeth wasn't with them. She turned and looked back. He was standing where he had been.

Then she added it up. "Your bloomers! They freaked him out!"

"Sorry about that," the demoness said, not too contritely.

Breanna went back and waved a hand before Xeth's face. "Xeth! Come out of it."

He blinked and looked at her. "Did something happen?"

"Metria freaked you out with her bloomers."

"Oh? I don't remember."

"If I had realized that zombies can be freaked out that way, I would have had a much easier time escaping you and your minions, way back when."

"Most zombies wouldn't freak. Their eyes are not good enough to see anything clearly."

"And most fully living men lose their freak the moment the sight ends," Breanna said. "So I guess you're in between."

"I suppose," he agreed. "I wonder if that explains those jumps in time when I'm at home with Zyzzyva."

"She's freaking you out when she wants to be left alone!" Breanna exclaimed. "The canny wench!"

"But I would rather not be freaked out. It is confusing."

"Well, you're married. I understand married men don't freak out much, at least not from seeing their wives' panties. They're too familiar."

"That's true," Metria said. "I can't freak out my husband anymore unless I assume the form of an unfamiliar woman. It's frustrating."

"Unfamiliar?" Xeth asked.

"Once I pretended to be a Mundane Chinese princess with the talent of making animals sing. That put him away for hours. Another time I emulated a woman who could form living things into useful shapes, such as making a tree into a chair."

"Ogres do that," Breanna said.

"Without twisting it into a pretzel, I mean. In the guise of doing that, I bent forward a bit too far, and he freaked right out." Metria frowned. "And he has the gall to claim he doesn't peek at other women!"

"Say, maybe if you just remember that, it won't happen," Breanna told Xeth. "Don't let Zyzzyva fool you into seeming unfamiliar."

"I will."

"And if you fake being freaked out, you can fool *her,*" Metria said. "Then you'll see whatever she's doing when she thinks you aren't watching."

"I will."

"Aren't we sort of betraying the female conspiracy?" Breanna asked her.

"Yes. Isn't it fun?"

"Yeah!" They giggled together.

Breanna focused on the faint glow in her mind. "This way," she said, opening a door. She peered in.

Then Xeth was waving a hand before her face. "Breanna! Come out of it!"

"Come out of what?" she asked. "I was just going into this room."

"You freaked out."

She laughed. "Silly! Women don't freak!"

"Then what is the demoness doing?"

Now Breanna saw that Metria was hovering quite still, like a weightless statue, staring into the room. She was, indeed, freaked out.

"What's in there?" Breanna asked.

"Male demons in underpants."

"Wow! You mean male pants freak out females?"

"Evidently these ones do."

"Demon pants!" she said, catching on. "They must have special potency. I never heard of a woman being freaked out by a living man's underwear."

Xeth put his hand in front of Metria's face, interrupting the view. She resumed motion. "Well, let's get on with it," she said, peering ahead—and freaked out again.

"We'd better try another route," Breanna decided.

Xeth covered Metria's gaze again, and this time continued to block her view until they got the door closed. "But we have to get moving," she protested.

"Not that way," Breanna said. "You freaked out."

"Oh—you mean they have those male hot pants on display again?"

"For sure."

"They're not supposed to do it *back*."

"Turnabout's not fair play?" Breanna asked.

"Of course not. Whatever gave you that idea?"

Breanna decided not to argue the case. "Well, I just want to find the Ring of Fire. I need to find an alternate route." She opened the next door.

There was an immediate chorus of screams, and a tangle of assorted limbs. "That's a demoness dorm," Metria explained.

"Why should they care?"

"They scream every time the door opens, just in case it's necessary."

"But demons can assume any form they want to, can't they?"

"Of course. They're just having fun, same as the boys. Soon one dorm or the other will stage a freakout raid."

"Well, I'm getting tired of demon fun. I just want to find that Ring."

"Then maybe you need an M-path."

"A what?"

"It's a path that feels what you need, and takes you there."

"But I already know where I'm going."

"But you don't know how to get there without getting into trouble."

Breanna nodded. "Right. So how do I get an M-path?"

"I just happen to have one here." The demoness reached into her own bosom, rummaged around elbow deep, and came up with a small length of tape. She presented this to Breanna.

"This is it? I can't walk on this."

"Just hold it in front of you and follow the glowing M."

"Oh." Breanna tried it, turning around while holding the tape. Sure enough, the M brightened in one direction. She went that way. Soon they came to a hall intersection, and the M brightened to the right. She followed it, and soon it brightened to the right again. When the path intersected a hall they had already been through, Breanna halted. "This thing's going in circles!"

"No it isn't," Metria said. "It's always right."

"But what if I need to go left?"

"It makes three right turns."

"Oh," Breanna said again. It did turn out that the M-path led across the hall and through a new one. It had made a looping left turn.

They continued until they came to a washroom. There the path ended.

Breanna looked around it. "I can't find any continuation from here," she said, frustrated.

"It must be here, then," Metria said. "Hidden."

They looked all around the small chamber, but found no ring. There was a pitcher of water, and a basin, a washcloth, and a towel, and that was all.

"It must have been here, and then been lost," Xeth suggested.

"But my sense of it indicated it was here!"

"It could have been here for centuries, leaving its trace, and been taken yesterday," Metria said. "We don't know how current your perception is."

Breanna wasn't sure she understood that, but certainly the Ring was not to be found. "So what do we do now?"

"We can ask Professor Grossclout," Xeth said.

"No!" Breanna and Metria said together.

"But who else might know?"

"Well, there's Ersup," Metria said. "She looks in her purse to find something personal about whoever she concentrates on."

"Would that help me find the Ring of Fire?"

"It should, if it's personal."

Breanna was dubious, but game. "Okay. Where's Ersup?"

"I don't know. I haven't seen her in months."

Breanna did her best not to explode. "You're a big help!"

"Thank you."

Breanna pondered. "Xeth, you say this Ring controls Com Pewter too?"

"Yes, he is demonic."

"He knows a lot, and I get along with him okay. I'll ask him."

"Those infernal machines are not to be trusted," Metria said.

"Neither are demons," Breanna retorted.

"How can you say that? I am a ghost."

"You're a what?"

"Apparition, specter, spook, phantasm, ghastly—"

"Aghast!" Breanna exclaimed, making the devious connection.

"Whatever," the demoness agreed crossly. "We demons can be trusted to be perfectly demonly."

"Which is to say, devious."

"True. So why trust a demon machine?"

"Because I set him up with his girlfriend, Com Passion. She'd be annoyed if he played me false."

Metria nodded. "Helm has no fury like that of a female annoyed."

That seemed close enough, considering. "So can you take us to Pewter—and if so, will you?"

"Of course I can, and will." She fuzzed into smoke. The smoke enclosed them, then dissipated.

There was Com Pewter's screen before them. **TO WHAT DO I OWE THE DUBIOUS PLEASURE OF THIS VISIT BY GIRL, ZOMBIE, AND DEMON-ESS?** the screen printed.

"We have a problem," Breanna said. "I need to find the Ring of Fire to save Xanth from a loss of gravity."

BUT XANTH HAS NO GRAVITY, ONLY HUMOR.

"Gravity as in staying on the ground. The Demon Earth's lost, and his gravity is fading. The Ring of Fire is supposed to be in a demon washroom, but I can't find it. Can you help me?"

NO

Breanna was used to this. "Can you direct me to any person, creature, thing, or idea that can, and if so—?"

Another machine appeared beside Pewter. ♥♥*Why, hello, dear mortal girl* ♥♥ the new screen scripted.

"Hello, Com Passion!" Breanna replied.

You must meet our offspring

A third machine appeared, smaller than the other two.

"You have a baby!" Breanna exclaimed, delighted. "What's his name?"

Its screen lighted. **♣ com ponent ♣**

"Hello, Ponent," Breanna said. "Welcome to the club." The small screen brightened and turned pink. The little machine was a bit shy as yet.

Breanna turned back to Passion. "I need to find the Ring of Fire, and it's not where it is supposed to be. Can you help me?"

No Passion scripted with evident regret.

Her spirits sinking, Breanna tried once more. "Ponent, maybe you can help me. Where do you think I should look for the Ring of Fire?"

♣ will you take a cookie? ♣

"A cookie?" Breanna asked, surprised.

♥*He insists on giving out cookies* ♥ Passion scripted fondly.

"Young folk do like cookies," Xeth reminded Breanna.

"For sure! But I thought they liked getting them, not giving them."

MACHINES DON'T EAT THINGS Pewter printed.

♥*Once you accept his cookie, he will always know you.* ♥

"Oh. Okay, Ponent, give me your cookie."

An oblong image of a cookie appeared on the little screen. Breanna reached down, and it jumped onto her hand. It was decorated like a printed circuit board, with a pastry foundation, colored sugar wires, and raisin resistors. She took a byte, and it was delicious. "Thank you. Now what is your input on the Ring of Fire?"

The little screen flickered as the machine pondered. Then it steadied.

♣ i dont have big data banks yet so i have to figure things

out a little at a time. i think if you cant find it where its supposed to be and it isnt where it isnt supposed to be it must be hidden where its supposed to be so you cant find it so you should look again maybe harder. ♣

Breanna considered. "Does that makes sense?" she asked the others.

DOUBTFUL

𝒫𝒪𝒮𝒮𝒥𝑩𝓛𝒴

"Ludicrous!" Metria snapped.

"Yes," Xeth said.

"Well, it makes sense to me," Breanna decided. "I'm going to go look again."

"I'll take you back," Metria said. "I love to see mortals make fools of themselves in vain quests."

"Thank you, Ponent," Breanna said. "I'll go look harder."

Then the demoness smoked up a cloud and transported them back to the demon's bathroom.

It was unchanged. The towel and cloth still hung by the wall, and the pitcher and basin remained on the counter. No Ring.

"Why do demons have a washroom?" Xeth asked.

Metria laughed. "It's a joke! Demons don't need to wash. We just fuzz into smoke and leave the dirt behind."

"So this is for mortal visitors?" Breanna asked.

"We hardly ever have visitors. So it's just a wasted chamber."

"Yet my sense tells me the Ring of Fire is here. Why should it be in a useless room?" Then she paused, a dim bulb blinking over her head. "So it won't be disturbed! No one ever comes here. It *must* be here!"

"Except that it obviously isn't," Metria said dourly.

"Said how?" Xeth asked.

"Dreary, dismal, forbidding, morose, dolorous—"

"It was the correct word the first time!" Breanna snapped.

They both looked abashed. "Sorry about that," the demoness said.

Breanna focused on the room. "We have to look harder. It must be here, only we can't see it."

"Sometimes the obvious is confusing as hades," Metria said. "That's the way it is in Grossclout's class. I remember when he demanded that we figure out why new human adults don't have magic talents, and washed me out when I missed it. I didn't realize it was a trick question."

Breanna was distracted for a moment, despite her better judgment. "But Mundanes *don't* have talents in Xanth. I'm the only exception I know of, and I made a special deal. It's because you have to be delivered into magic, not into science."

"You'd have flunked out too."

"But everyone knows—"

"The Demon Professor says everyone has mush for brains."

"But none of the Black Wave had talents when we came to Xanth. I didn't. Only the children who were delivered here later. So I *know* from personal experience that—"

"The interpretation of personal experience is mush, he says. This time he proved it."

"Proved it? How?"

"By bringing in a Mundane mortal man with a magic talent as Exhibit A. His talent was metallergy."

"You mean metallurgy?" Breanna asked, trying to cut short the multiple alternatives sequence. "Working with metals?"

"No. Met-allergy. His metalwork made folk sneeze."

"And he had immigrated from Mundania? The talent had grown after he lived here? I find that hard to believe."

"Me too," Xeth said.

"It turns out that magic infuses new Mundane folk too slowly to show until time has passed. So they think they have no talents, and stop looking for them. Children respond much more rapidly, so their talents show sooner. The professor says that anyone who has lived in Xanth for more than five years has a talent, if he only knew it."

"I'll be bleeped!" Breanna exclaimed. "I never thought of that!"

"Typical mush-filled skull."

"I guess so. But how come the word hasn't gotten out?"

"It's just one of those obscure facts Grossclout uses to flunk unwary students. Nobody's interested."

"Maybe no demons are. But I'll bet most mortals would be. I'll have to tell them to look, after this mission is done." Then Breanna brought herself back to business. "So maybe this is another mush case. I just have to see that Ring. By clearing the mush out of my thick skull."

"You got it, mushmind." The demoness formed momentarily into a big steaming bowl of cornmeal mush.

"Okay, I'm trying to look with a new perspective. To see whatever I missed before." Breanna crossed and uncrossed her eyes, looking around.

"But we can see everything," Xeth protested. "The pitcher, the basin, the dirt-ring where the basin sat—everything."

Breanna's jaw dropped half a notch. "The dirt-ring! That's a Ring."

"But not the one we want," Metria said.

"I wonder." Breanna approached the counter. She put her finger to the ring of dirt—and felt something hot. She closed her hand on it, and lifted—and the entire Ring came up. It was hot because little flames were dancing around it, though they did not actually burn her hand. As it moved it shrank until it was the size of a finger ring. "Got it!"

"It was masquerading as dirt!" Metria said, amazed.

"It was there all the time," Xeth agreed. "My mind was mush."

"Mine too," Metria agreed.

"And it was Com Ponent who put us on to it," Breanna agreed. "All it took was a little elementary reasoning." She put the Ring on her little finger, where it fit perfectly. The flames continued to flicker without burning her flesh. There was no doubt about the identity of the Ring of Fire.

"It fooled me," Metria said. "I thought it would look—"

"The way it does now," Xeth agreed. "So did I."

"For sure," Breanna agreed, well satisfied. "We were all mushbrains. But you really helped, with your story of that class lesson. That got just enough mush out." She looked around, invigorated. "Now I want to go home to Castle Zombie and get married."

4
RING OF EARTH

C he Centaur looked at the gathering of zombies. Which one should he choose as a guide? Breanna was already departing with King Xeth.

"I'll take you," Zyzzyva Zombie said. "Mine is the Ring of Earth."

"I thought I might look for the Ring of Air, since I can fly."

"No, that's for Sim. Anyway, they don't have to match up that way."

That made sense. "Very well. Where is it?"

"The Good Magician has it."

"Humfrey? But then he could have given it to Cynthia when he gave her the Service."

"No. He does not know where he has it, and he did not realize it would be necessary." She spoke with no detectable impediment, and there was no rot visible on her; she was an extremely fresh zombie. She was also a warrior woman, carrying a short sword, and she looked very fit generally.

"Very well. I will take you there."

She got on his back, and she was lithe and light, no problem to carry. Of course it was no problem to carry anyone who could stay mounted, since he flicked them light anyway. He did so, first flicking her, then flicking himself, so that they were light enough to fly. Then he spread his wings and took off.

"Oh, it's nice up here!" she exclaimed, exactly like a tourist. "I seldom have the chance to fly. That is why I wanted to go with you or Cynthia: to have that chance."

"This is a serious mission," Che reminded her. "Not an entertainment jaunt."

"I know it. Nevertheless, I can appreciate the wonder of flight better than most zombies, being better preserved, and probably am less onerous for you to carry."

She had a point. Che prided himself on being open-minded, but contact with far-gone zombies did not especially appeal. Now he appreciated the Land of Xanth anew as it spread out below them, seeing it through her eyes, as it were.

Indeed, it was beautiful, with green and yellow forests interspersed by blue and silver lakes and brown and red fields—and here and there an old gray mountain poked its head up, surrounded by its child mountains who did not yet reach its height. They would surely get there in time; mountains were slow to achieve maturity. Overhead the sun floated serenely on, radiating rays of contentment. It was a nice day.

"What is that?" Zyzzyva inquired.

Che looked. There was a small cloud to the side, moving swiftly to intercept their flight path. "A mischievous juvenile cloud, I think."

"That's interesting. I have a much clearer view of it from up here." Zyzzyva twisted around to get a better view. Her body was fit and firm; she was a warrior lass, and he could feel it as she moved. He wondered whether she had been killed in battle; if so, she must have given a good account of herself. "Are those pigtails?"

Che looked again. Sure enough, there were two vapor streamlets trailing behind, with misty bows at their ends. "It's a girl cloud."

The cloud got before them and began to huff and puff into a gray glob. There was an internal rumble, and lightning flashed. "She's trying to block us off," Zyzzyva said indignantly.

"Now I think I recognize her attitude," Che said. "A chip off the old cloud block."

"What block?"

"Fracto. He caught and married Happy Bottom, a storm from Mundania. They stay mostly in the Region of Air, but this one must have sneaked out of the nursery."

"Oh, yes—that encounter happened while I was still alive. The Land of Xanth almost got blown away."

"Fortunately Fracto decided to help."

A face formed on the cloud. It looked at them. Then the mouth opened, sucking in air.

"She is about to blow us away!" Zyzzyva said, alarmed.

"Fray!" Che called loudly. "Does your mother know where you are?"

The cloud choked on her breath, and her pigtails flounced. She scudded hastily away, leaving tiny balls of vapor behind.

"They're so cute when they're little," Zyzzyva said. "I hope I can get the stork's attention soon."

"Surely you will," Che said encouragingly.

They reached the Good Magician's Castle. Che was heading in for a landing on the roof, but unexpectedly lost elevation. He must have recovered too much weight, and was falling. He flicked his tail repeatedly to lighten his body, but it had no effect. Something was wrong.

"Hang on!" he cried. "Crash landing!"

Fortunately there was a large pillow bush growing beside the moat. He was able to steer for it, and landed with a dull whomp! Zyzzyva slid off his back, but seemed to be all right. Zombies were hard to hurt, even the well-preserved ones; it was part of their magic.

"I don't know what went wrong," he gasped. "Suddenly I lost my power of flight."

"No harm done," she said. "We can cross the bridge."

But as they approached the drawbridge, a group of five men appeared. They were bright colors, and were armed with assorted weapons. They arrayed themselves before the bridge in militaristic manner.

"That's a defensive platoon," Zyzzyva said. "We'll have to fight them."

"But I didn't come here to fight!" Che protested. "I just want to find the Ring of Earth."

"Maybe we can reason with them, then." She walked ahead, approaching the group. "We are here on important business. Please let us through to see the Good Magician."

"No," the orange man said, looking quickly around. He had large bright eyes.

"Who are you?" she asked, evidently nettled.

"I am Vita Man A. These are my companions, B, C, D, and E. Now go away, zombie."

Zyzzyva glanced back at Che. "I did ask them nicely," she said.

"Let me try." Che stepped forward. "It is urgent that we speak with Magician Humfrey. Please let us pass, or notify him that we are here."

"If you persist, we shall drive you off, crossbreed."

Che was getting a bit nettled himself. "But this can't wait. We have to find the—"

The orange man drew his sword and swung at Che. But Zyzzyva moved faster. Her own sword whistled as it moved. The orange man's head flew off his body.

Astonished, they both stared. "I thought he would dodge or block," Zyzzyva said.

"That annoys me," the Vita man said. He sheathed his sword, bent down to pick up his head, and set it back on his neck. Then he drew the sword again.

"He's a zombie!" Zyzzyva exclaimed. "He can't be killed."

"But he's not rotting."

"True. Xeth and I are the only zombies with no visible rot. So he must be a golem. An animated thing, not a real man. Curious to find organisms like that here."

"Do you know what?" Che asked. "I believe this is a Challenge! That's why I lost the power of flight."

"But we're not coming here as querents. We have legitimate business."

"There must be a mistake. But if we want to get in, it seems we must fathom the Challenges."

"I am not good at fathoming, since I died."

"Fortunately I haven't died. We simply have to figure out what is required."

"What is required is clearing these obnoxious men out of our way."

"There is surely a way without chopping them up, since that doesn't seem to hurt them."

"Very well. You fathom it, and if that doesn't work, I will chop them to small enough pieces so that we can cross before they get themselves back together."

"I don't think that's the proper way."

"What, are you a pacifist?"

Che hadn't thought about that. "I suppose I do try to find the most expedient solution to any problem. The Good Magician's Challenges generally do have some nonviolent way through, and I think it behooves us to find it."

"Well, it's your quest," she said doubtfully.

"If I can't find it, then we'll try your way."

"Fair enough."

Che considered. The five Vita men were five different colors. Did that mean anything?

"They look good enough to eat," Zyzzyva said. "Too bad I no longer have to eat."

"Eat!" Che said. "Vitamins!"

"Are you spelling that right?"

"Of course. That's the key. He said he was Vita Man A. We assumed he meant he was the first of five men denominated by letters of the alphabet. But it's a pun. These creatures really are supposed to be eaten."

"But zombies don't eat."

"This Challenge isn't for you, but for me. I have to eat them."

She remained dubious. "It will take you a long time."

"Probably one bite of each will do. Chop off a finger or toe, and I'll eat that."

"Coming up." She faced the orange man. "Prepare to be chopped, Vita men."

But Che was already reconsidering. "Maybe if I just identify them, it will do."

"Still trying for the peaceful way," she said, disgusted.

Che rifled through his excellent memory for obscure facts. He had been tutoring Sim for years, and so was very sharp on facts. The men were different colors, but also seemed to have different qualities. "Vita Man A, you are the one who sees well," he said.

The orange man nodded and stepped back.

Che addressed the gray man, who seemed to have very quick reactions. "Vita Man B, your nerves are excellent."

The gray man stepped back.

The green man seemed to have snow on his head and shoulders, as though freezing, but did not look at all uncomfortable. "Vita Man C, you can beat the common cold."

The next man was stoutly built and shining white, like a beam of sunshine. "Vita Man D, you have strong bones."

The last one was blood red. "Vita Man E, you have a strong heart."

Now they were all retreating across the bridge. Che nodded. "We cracked the riddle. They knew it. There was no point in continuing the Challenge."

"I think they are cowards."

She did have a militaristic mindset. "Maybe we'll have to fight in the next Challenge," he said.

They crossed the drawbridge, stepped onto the inner shore of the moat—and found themselves in darkness.

"Did night fall, or is my sight failing?" Zyzzyva inquired.

"It seems to be magical darkness. This must be the second Challenge."

"Well, it can't hurt me; I have no concern about darkness. Zombies thrive in it. But it may be a problem for you."

"Yes. I prefer light when I have something to accomplish." But he stepped forward, having no alternative.

"I can go first, if you want."

"I suspect that whatever is here will find me regardless." He banged into something solid, and stopped.

"Did it find you?"

"I found it. It seems to be a wall. The way must turn."

He turned to the left, but soon encountered another wall. He turned to the right, and found another wall. There seemed to be no open way forward. But behind was the moat; that was unlikely to be the route. Yet there had to be a way.

He felt the walls, but found no break. They extended high and low and to either side, blocking every avenue.

"Maybe you have to say a spell," Zyzzyva suggested.

"Open sez me," he said. But the walls remained solid.

He retreated, backing to the moat. Suddenly the castle returned to view, in full daylight. There was no sign of any tunnel, with or without walls. Could the darkness be illusion?

Still, the illusion of darkness was like the illusion of light: If it seemed to exist, it did exist. An illusory lamp worked as well as a real one. He could try to ignore the darkness, but that wouldn't banish the effect.

Zyzzyva appeared beside him. "Ah, there you are. That's one weird tunnel. I can't see into it from here, or out of it from there."

"It seems to be a structure of illusion. Made to conceal the wall. There must be some way around that wall, if I could only see it."

She laughed. "Too bad the wall's not illusion too."

Then they looked at each other with dawning surmise. Surmises were always best when dawning; they weren't much for evening. "Could it be?" he asked. "An illusion of touch?"

"Does that kind of illusion exist?"

"I don't see why not. It could be covered by darkness because otherwise we'd see that the wall isn't there, and be suspicious."

"Unless it's an invisible real wall."

"No need to cover that with darkness."

"One way to find out."

They forged back into the invisible darkness. Che put his hands forward to find the wall. When he did, he pushed against it—and his hands moved on through its seeming substance as if penetrating jelly. He forged on, feeling the pressure of the wall against his flanks and wings and finally his tail. Then he was beyond it, and in a moment emerged into light.

Zyzzyva reappeared just behind him. "That was interesting. I think you mortals have more fun than we zombies do."

"Also more frustration."

"I suppose so. We tend to take things more as they come, and relax under a nice blanket of dirt when nothing comes."

"We seem to be through the second Challenge. There should be one more."

She looked around. "We seem to be in an old workshop."

It was true. It was a roofless chamber filled with odds, evens, ends, middles, and whatnots. There were no doors, and the walls were too high to jump over.

"The Challenge must be to find our way out of here and into the castle."

"You still can't fly?"

Che spread his wings and flicked his side. He did not lighten. "Correct."

"It is interesting the way these Challenges are tailored to the querents," she remarked. "An ogre could bash his way out."

"I suspect an ogre would find his strength missing. He would have to use his mind."

"His what?"

Che had to smile. "True—ogres are justifiably proud of their stupidity. But he might make a face and scare a wall into collapsing."

"Yes, I understand that an ogress can curdle milk with half a glare."

"And crack a mirror just by thinking of looking into it. But this isn't solving this Challenge. I suppose you could reach the top of the wall by standing on my back and jumping, but I would be too heavy for you to pull up after you."

"Surely so. Still, it would not hurt for me to look. There might be a ladder on the other side that I could pass back to you."

Che looked down at his four hooves. "I don't think I could use a ladder."

"Maybe a long board for a ramp."

He nodded. "You seem to be thinking better than I am."

"Unlikely. Everybody knows zombies have rotten brains."

"What everyone knows is not necessarily true."

She glanced obliquely at him. "I gather you're not much for conventional prejudice."

"Not much," he agreed. But he had to admit to himself that he had made a reasonable effort of prejudice, before getting better acquainted with this zombie.

He went to stand beside a wall, and she got on his back, then carefully stood. "I can't quite reach the top."

"Maybe if I stand on a crate." But the crates were in poor repair, and he couldn't find any he could safely use.

"Maybe if you just lift me with your hands," she suggested.

"I can try."

"I'll delete some weight." She removed her small helmet, letting her hair hang loose, and her short sword.

He stood beside the wall again, and she stood before him. He put his hands on her waist just above her metallic skirt, and lifted. She came up, surprisingly light; she was a slender woman. In a moment her nice knees were before his face.

"Not quite high enough," she said. "My fingers can't quite catch the top."

"I can't lift you higher," he said. "In fact, I can't hold you here long. My arms aren't strong."

"Let me get on your shoulders." She lifted her right leg and put her metallic slipper on his left shoulder. Then she stepped up with the other foot. Now she was squatting over his head. "Don't let go; I'm unsteady. Just slide your hands down my legs and take another grip so I can stand."

He did so. Her legs were marvelously sleek and firm. He found her knees, and gripped just below them.

Then she straightened her legs. Her balance shifted. He glanced up, trying to judge which way she was leaning, so he could correct it—and caught a glimpse of her inner thighs and metallic panty. *I'm not human,* he thought determinedly. *I can't freak out.* That steadied him, and he in turn steadied her. He had thought that human men were foolish to freak out at the sight of female human underwear, but that peek under her skirt had given him a jolt. There was definitely magic there.

"Got it!" she said, and suddenly her knees slid out of his grasp as she hauled herself up. In two moments she was sitting on the top of the wall, dangling her feet. A light breeze ruffled her loose hair. She was looking increasingly feminine.

"Good enough," he said, gratified that they had succeeded to this extent. A silvery image remained in his mind, and he realized that it was the memory of that panty. The magic was still trying to get him, attacking his human aspect. "Anything you can fetch for me?"

Zyzzyva looked around. "Nice gardens all around, girt by similar walls. This seems to be one of those greenhouse puzzles, with hedges and paths and barriers every which way. We just happened to land in a closed section."

"By no coincidence, I think."

"I don't see anything I could fetch that could help you. Shall I come down?"

"No need. I'll just have to find my own way clear."

He reconsidered the yard. There were the battered crates, assorted wood boards, several partial rolls of canvas fabric, a short length of chain left over from something, a half full box of nails with a rusty hammer, and several huge feathers weighted down by stones. He smiled. Did someone think the feathers would fly away by themselves?

Then he re-reconsidered. Could those be roc flight feathers? If so, they could indeed fly; they were what enabled the big birds to do it.

He trotted to one of them, took hold of its quill, and rolled the stone off. Immediately the feather sailed up, eager to fly. It was indeed a flight feather. It was all he could do to hold it down. It took a lot of lift to launch a roc, so the magic was strong.

Now the rest of it fell into place. He could use the other junk to build a craft to anchor the feathers, a flying machine that would carry him out of here. That was the solution to this riddle.

He got to work. As it happened, the boards and bits and nails were the right size to make a crude boatlike vessel. Happened? That had been the point all along, just waiting for him to catch on. He felt stupid for not doing so before, and he did not like feeling stupid.

Soon he had a craft with a canvas rudder operated by the chain, a central basin large enough for a lying centaur, and oarlocks for six big feathers. He fitted the feathers one by one, weighting each down with its stone, until all six were securely in place.

Now at last he was ready to fly. But he paused. Once he removed the stones, those feathers would fly, carrying him up. But how would he land again? He would not be able to weight them down again once he was airborne.

"You have a problem?" Zyzzyva asked from above.

"Yes. I'm not sure how to land this flying machine, once I'm aloft."

"Why will you need to?"

This seemed like a stupid question, but he answered carefully. "Because a fall from the heights could be dangerous if not lethal."

"But once you're clear of the Challenge, won't your own power of flight return?"

Che's jaw actually dropped. She was of course correct. He would have no need to land the flying machine; he could land far more conveniently on his own. "Once again, your brains are functioning better than mine."

"Thank you. But I wonder: Assuming it flies away, never to return, what will happen to it?"

"I suppose it will crash somewhere. Does it matter?"

"Yes, it matters. That machine is like a zombie, having a kind of half-life. It should not be thrown away after it gives good service."

Che would never have thought of it that way, but he was coming to appreciate her zombie viewpoint. Zyzzyva herself was a fine and interesting person who was forever changing his conception of zombies. Naturally she had empathy for other neglected or disparaged creatures. He would have to do something about his flying machine.

"Suppose I name it, and give it a compatible destination? If it is capable of hearing and understanding, then it will know where to go on its own."

"I can enable it to do both," she said. "Toss up my sword."

He had no idea what she wanted with it, but she would need both sword and helmet when she went on. He picked up the helmet. "First this," he said, and tossed it.

She caught it neatly. "Thank you." She put it on, becoming more military. Had he been human, he might have been disappointed.

"And the sword." It was sheathed, so was safe to throw. He did so carefully, and she caught it as neatly. She buckled the sheath belt around her waist, then drew the sword. She put it to the side of her head and cut off her left ear.

"What are you doing?" Che cried, appalled.

"I am cutting off my left ear," she said. "Have no concern; I'll grow another, zombie style. Fasten this one to your machine, so it can hear you speak." She tossed the ear down to him.

He controlled his revulsion and caught it. There was no blood, just a little stickiness at the point of severance. He took it to the machine and set the sticky side against the prow. The ear adhered; indeed, in a moment it seemed as if it had grown there on its own.

"Now that is a zombie machine," Zyzzyva said. "It will hear you and respond to you."

This was weird! But he followed through, rather than embarrass Zyzzyva by openly doubting her. "Flying machine, I name you Rockie, because your animation is from roc feathers and your ear is female. You are a lady craft. Do you understand?"

There was no reaction. That hardly surprised him. "You have to tell her how to respond," Zyzzyva said. "She doesn't know anything yet."

Oh. "If you hear and understand, wiggle a flight feather."

Still nothing, as expected. Machines constructed of ends and odds did not come to life of their own accord. "You must tell it which one," Zyzzyva said. "It will not be very smart at first."

"The front right feather," he clarified.

The right front feather wiggled under its stone.

Che stared, but there was no doubt about it. It was now a living, or at least an animate, flying machine. Zyzzyva had been right all along.

So he continued. "I will use you to fly out of this yard. Then I will leave you, to go about my own business. Do you understand? Wiggle your left front feather if you do."

The left front feather wiggled.

"But I don't want you to feel out of sorts, because you are the only creature of your kind. So I will tell you who else to look for. There is a duck-footed boat named Para who normally plies his trade near the Isle of Women just west of the peninsula of Xanth. He's the only one of his kind too. You should get along. Simply fly over the coast until you see him. He should be glad to see you. If you understand, wiggle your right rear feather."

The right rear feather wiggled.

"One more thing," Che said, as an afterthought. Afterthoughts were almost as good as forethoughts. "Your ear is from a zombie, so if you ever have occasion to do a zombie a favor, please consider it. Zombies can be good folk when you get to know them."

Then he got into the craft and reached out to roll the rocks off the six flight feathers. They immediately vibrated, taking flight, carrying the craft and him with them. In nine-tenths of a moment he was up and out of the yard and flying over the walled garden.

"Wait for me!" Zyzzyva called.

But the flying machine wouldn't or couldn't wait; it was flying vigorously onward. So Che spread his wings and flicked himself, and felt himself getting lighter. He lifted out of the craft, hovered above it for the remaining tenth of a moment, then turned to face Zyzzyva. "You're going east, Rockie," he called. "You want to go west."

The craft turned and flew the other way. Meanwhile Che glided down to land on the top of the wall beside the zombie woman. He saw a lump on the left side of her head; the ear was already re-forming. "Thank you for your help," he said.

"Men need women's help," she said matter-of-factly. "That's why I married Xeth."

Che didn't argue. He lifted her onto his back, as there was not room on the wall for her to get to his side. "You have also educated me about zombies."

"Living folk need that."

He spied a woman waving in the center of the garden. He flew down to join her. "That's Wira, Humfrey's blind daughter-in-law," he murmured. "She's very nice."

"I have heard of her."

"Hello, Wira," he called as he landed. "I am here on business, and I brought Zyzzyva Zombie, King Xeth's wife and queen of the zombies."

"On business?" Wira asked. "We assumed you were a querent."

So that was it. "No, this is an urgent mission to save Xanth from destruction."

"In that case you had better see the Good Magician right away." She faced the zombie, who was dismounting. "Hello, Zyzzyva. We have not met before."

"We live apart," Zyzzyva agreed.

Wira stepped into her and embraced her. So much for prejudice; the blind woman had little way of knowing that this zombie was not rotten. "You seem remarkably fit."

"I am. I was killed in battle, and zombied within hours."

They followed Wira into the castle proper. There was room for Che's bulk; the Good Magician's castle always accommodated what it needed to. They made their way up the winding stairway to the Good Magician's dingy office. There was Magician Humfrey, poring over his Book of Answers.

"Che Centaur and Zyzzyva are here on business," Wira said, announcing them.

"I don't know where the Ring of Earth is," Humfrey said grumpily.

So he had known their business! "I understand you are in charge of it," Che said.

"True. But none of the Ring proprietors know where their Rings are. You will have to search for it."

"But doesn't your Book of Answers list everything?" Zyzzyva asked.

"No. The omission is deliberate. If the location were recorded, some nefarious entity might snoop and locate it."

Che considered. His zombie guide didn't know exactly where the Ring was, and neither did the Good Magician. But it had to be somewhere in this castle, because otherwise it would be out of Humfrey's control. "May we search for it?"

"Of course. We cleaned up the castle for you. The Designated Wife will help you." Humfrey turned back to his huge tome.

They went back down the stairs to the kitchen, where a cloud of smoke hovered over the stove. "Dara, this is Che Centaur," Wira said politely. "Also Zyzzyva Zombie. Che, this is Dara Demoness, the Good Magician's Designated Wife."

The smoke roiled, then formed into the figure of a lovely dusky woman. "A zombie! This could be interesting."

"Or it could be dull," Zyzzyva said, unimpressed.

"What are you up to?"

"We must locate the Ring of Earth," Che said. "We believe it is somewhere on the premises."

"The Ring of Earth! I haven't heard of that in centuries."

"It has not been used in centuries."

"That explains it. Why do you need it now? It controls all the land-bound creatures of Xanth. Are you preparing to invade Mundania?"

"We need it to fetch the Swell Foop."

She puffed into incoherence. "The Swell Foop! That thing is dangerous!"

"So we understand," Che agreed dryly.

"It controls the senior Demons." She coalesced into human female form again. "It has never been invoked in my memory. What possible pretext could there be to use that?"

"The Demon Earth has disappeared. We think he's been abducted. We need to rescue him."

"Rescue him! Good riddance!"

"His magic of gravity is fading. That will affect Xanth."

Dara's floating form abruptly sank to the floor, as if feeling gravity's effect. "I suppose that's true. But the Swell Foop—that's a really scary business."

And demons did not readily scare. "Will you help us search for the Ring of Earth?"

She sighed. "I suppose I have to. But I want you to know that this is not what's normally expected of a Designated Wife."

"Surely not," Che agreed. "We think it must be somewhere in the castle. I fear we shall have to search everywhere."

"Have you any idea how much idle junk is crannied away in obscure nooks?" she demanded rhetorically.

"I fear we are about to find out."

"Indeed we are. Well, let's get to it."

They got to it. They divided the castle into quadrants, and each of them—Dara, Wira, Zyzzyva, and Che—took a quad. This promised to be a horrendous bore.

Che had the rear storeroom. It was jam-packed. Fortunately the jars of jam were dated, and none of them were more than fifty years old, so he didn't have to open them. The first other thing he spied was a rack covered in fur coats. He lifted it—and discovered that it wasn't a dead rack but a live tree. It was growing the coats. It was a fur tree. But there was no Ring with any of the furs.

The next thing was a pot of paint. He picked it up, and it bubbled angrily, spattering hot drops on his hand. It seemed to be in a vile mood. He looked at the label: TEMPERA. That explained why it was so temperamental. But there was no Ring with it.

He found a dried flower. He sniffed it—and suddenly had an urgent call of nature. He galloped to the garden before he exploded.

A cloud appeared before him. "What's up, centaur?"

"You already know, Dara."

The cloud formed into a male figure. "I'm not Dara. I'm her son Dafrey. Humfrey's first son."

Che was surprised. "I took you for a full demon. Aren't you half mortal?"

"I've learned some illusion in the past hundred and fifty years. I can't really become a cloud. What are you doing?"

"I'm searching for the Ring of Earth. I could use some help."

"Sure. That promises to be interesting."

Dafrey accompanied Che back to the storage room. "Do you know what this is?" Che asked, showing him the dried flower.

"That's a begonia. It makes you have to go in a hurry."

"No wonder I had to hurry! I didn't recognize it."

They continued searching, but there was no Ring to be found. They returned to the kitchen to find the others there, similarly frustrated. "We could search for years," Zyzzyva said. "There's just too much junk here."

"This seems hopeless," Che agreed wearily. "It's too well hidden."

"Maybe you just need to think more like a Ring that doesn't want to be found," Dafrey said.

"Think like a Ring?"

"Yes. If you were a Ring, and you wanted to stay hidden forever, where would you hide?"

"Under the Good Magician's dirty socks," Wira said.

They all burst out laughing. Humfrey was notorious for being unable to keep up with his socks. His fourth wife was Sofia Socksorter, a Mundane woman he had married in an effort to get on top of that situation. But when she had eventually grown old and returned to Mundania, the socks had quickly gotten out of hand again. Now she had an afterlife as a sometime wife, but whenever she was off-duty the dirty socks piled up. There were piles that had lain seemingly undisturbed for decades.

Then, almost together, they began to sober. "I wonder," Che said. "Who would ever look under a dirty sock?"

"No one," Zyzzyva said. "Even a zombie would have trouble with the smell."

"I think we had better look," Dara said. "Let's spread out again, this time collecting only socks."

They did so. And in only another hour, Che picked up the last sock in the last crevice of the last chamber in his quadrant, and saw an earth-colored Ring.

Could it be? He picked it up. It seemed to be made of clay, but was well formed. "How can I verify it?" Che asked uncertainly. "It could be a mere incidental trinket."

"Father will know," Dafrey said.

They returned to the kitchen. "I may have found it," Che announced loudly.

In time ranging from two-thirds of a moment to one and a half moments, they were there. "That's it?" Zyzzyva asked, frowning.

"May I touch it?" Wira asked.

Che gave it to her. She tried it on her middle finger, and it fit well. "It's a nice Ring," she said, slipping it off and passing it to Dara, who had just popped in.

"That's it," the demoness agreed, squinting at it. "See, it says RING OF EARTH inside."

"But an imitation Ring could say the same," Zyzzyva pointed out.

"We'll test it, then. Put it on, Che." She handed it back to him. "But be warned: Once you don it, you won't be able to remove it until its task is done. That may be a burden."

"A burden?" he asked, slipping it on his little left finger, where it settled comfortably.

"You now have dominion over all the land-bound animals—the creatures of the earth. That's a considerable responsibility."

"I do?" he asked, surprised.

"Test it," she suggested. "Give them a directive."

Smiling, he did so. "Bow down to my left forehoof."

Immediately Zyzzyva and Wira got down on the floor, facing his hoof. Dafrey got halfway down.

"You're teasing me," he said, embarrassed.

"No," Wira said. "I am compelled."

"So am I," Zyzzyva said. "And I am not pleased."

"But why doesn't it affect Dara? And what's Dafrey doing?"

"I am not a creature of the Earth," Dara said. "I am compelled only by the Ring of Fire, which is not here. My son is half human, therefore half land-bound, so he bows halfway. But you can test it more directly: Try to remove it."

Che did. The Ring, though not tight, absolutely refused to budge. It was locked on his finger.

"Are you going to let us up?" Zyzzyva inquired with more than a trace of annoyance.

Oh. "Yes, of course. Please rise."

They got up and dusted themselves off. But Che wasn't satisfied. "If the Ring of Earth gives its wearer such power, why didn't it affect Wira when she tried it on? Why didn't it stick to her finger?"

"Because it belongs to the one who finds it," Dara said. "For the duration. You accept the commitment of it by donning it. For Wira, it was just a ring."

"But a nice one," Wira said.

"I thought I was just looking for it, to bring it back," Che said. "It is really Cynthia's mission, to find the Swell Foop."

"And yours to help her," Zyzzyva said. "Let's go." She climbed onto his back.

"Uh, yes. Thank you, Dara, Dafrey, and Wira. I sincerely appreciate—"

"Oh, cut it short," Dara said. She slapped him on the flank. Startled, he bolted out the door, and was soon in the garden court, where he flicked them both with his tail, spread his wings, and took off.

"I'm not sure I like this," he remarked as he gained elevation.

"Too bad," Zyzzyva said unsympathetically.

5
RING OF IDEA

J ustin watched Breanna depart with King Xeth. He wasn't totally easy about this, because Xeth had once wanted to marry Breanna, but he chided himself for even thinking of having doubt. After all, there was no question of Breanna's loyalty to him or Xeth's to Zyzzyva. Maybe it was that ever since his conversion from tree to young man, Breanna had been with him, and he wasn't used to being apart from her. He had been a tree for so long that he was hardly comfortable with the man state, but she had supported him throughout. They were about to be married, and though she liked to pretend that she was forcing him unwillingly into it, he truly wanted it.

But now he had to find his own zombie and search for a Ring of Xanth. According to King Xeth, all the Ring zombies were here, so he had merely to choose one and go find the Ring. He hoped it turned out to be that simple.

He turned to the nearest zombie, who was not far gone as zombies went. He had met most of the zombies in the course of the past year, and come to appreciate their qualities, but did not know this one personally. He was not part of the Castle Zombie contingent. "Hello."

"Hullow," the zombie responded.

"I am Justin Tree. Who are you?"

"Unpun."

"Unpun, do you know where a Ring of Xanth is?"

"Yeth."

"Which one?"

"Ring of Ider."

This would require some finesse. "Please spell that."

"Eye Dee Eee Ay."

"Ah, the Ring of Idea. That will do. Take me there."

"Canth."

"Can't? Why not?"

"Complishated."

"It is complicated to explain?"

"Yeth."

Justin considered. The brains of zombies were notoriously poor, and simplicity was best. But he saw no ready way around this complication. "Then we shall just have to figure it out as we can. What makes it complicated to explain?"

Unpun started talking, with many confusingly slurred words. Justin focused, got clarifications on words, and managed to piece out the story.

Unpun was once a living young man with the talent of making puns disappear. He kept company with a young woman named Punny, whose talent was creating puns. They went everywhere together, their talents nullifying each other. They were not consciously controlled talents; it was just that wherever Punny went, puns grew in her wake. Wherever Unpun went, puns were destroyed. So as long as they were together, their wakes overlapped, and the pun ratio of Xanth was fairly constant. Of course some of her new ones got away, and he canceled some that had existed before, but overall there was no problem.

Then they encountered a bad situation. Justin was unable to clarify whether it was a dragon or some other monster. It attacked, threatening to gobble up Punny, because she was delectable, and Unpun tried to protect her. So it turned on him instead, and with one chomp killed him.

Punny was distraught, but nothing she could do could bring him back to life. She could not create puns consciously, and even had that been possible, what pun would suffice for something as unfunny as this? So she did the next best thing: She brought Unpun's body to Castle Zombie and begged the Zombie Master to zombie him, so that he could have at least half a life. The Zombie Master did so, but Unpun could no longer make puns disappear. There seemed to be no fixed rule with respect to talents and zombies; some zombies kept their talents, some had partial talents, and some had none.

"I wonder why that is," Justin remarked musingly. "One would think that the process would be consistent."

"Don'th know."

"Could it be that some are fresher than others? How long were you dead before getting zombied?"

"Threee daysh."

"So have any zombies of that duration of death retained their talents?"

"Yesh, a numberr."

"So that's not it. Does the nature of the talent have bearing?"

"Noo."

"But there must be some reasonable rationale."

"Nooo."

Justin gave it up, frustrated; this was, after all, peripheral to his quest. "So what happened after you became a zombie?"

It turned out that Punny did not want to continue without Unpun. For one thing, there was now no nullification of all the puns that grew in her wake. She had to keep moving, or they soon surrounded her, making life unbearable for her and anyone near her. She had depended on Unpun to keep them under control, and now they proliferated impossibly. For another, she loved him, and had no joy of life alone.

"But why didn't you stay with her, as a zombie?" Justin asked. "She did not have to be denied your company."

"Nooo," Unpun said, pained.

It turned out that when Unpun lost his life, and his talent, he also lost his sense of humor. He did not find it funny, being a zombie, and he did not feel like laughing at anything. But Punny was increasingly surrounded by puns. He could not get close to her without stepping on them. Every time he touched one, it forced him to laugh, and it really hurt him to laugh. He couldn't endure it. So he was unable to approach her.

"That's an intriguing reversal," Justin remarked. "Zombie fleeing maiden."

But Unpun did not appreciate that form of humor, either.

The regular folk of Xanth normally took puns in stride, and even expected to encounter a certain number regularly. But the density around Punny was far too intense for anyone who wasn't a masochist. Punny lost her friends; the stench of bad humor was just too much for them. Finally Punny fled Xanth, seeking refuge on Ida's moon Ptero. She left her body in a safe place for the duration, and her soul went to reside in one of the few places where puns were welcome in any concentration. There she remained, patiently awaiting rescue from her fate.

"That is certainly interesting," Justin concluded. "But I remain uncertain how it explains why you can't guide me to the Ring of Idea." For that was, after all, the point of this association.

Unpun explained, slowly and confusingly, and finally Justin understood. Punny's job on Ptero was to safeguard the Ring of Idea, so that it would be there when it was needed. That meant that the Ring too would be surrounded by puns. Unpun would be unable to approach it, or even to direct anyone else to it, as long as it was in Punny's possession.

"But why did she take that job, then?" Justin asked, righteously perplexed. "She surely didn't have to. Didn't she know that would prevent you from guiding anyone to it when the need came?"

"Yesh."

As usual, it was necessary to question further, slowly unraveling the details. It seemed that Punny wanted Unpun to recover his sense of humor, so that both of them could be happy again. The only way he could possibly do that was to be returned to full life. That could be accomplished by the holder and wielder of the Ring of Idea. So Punny made sure to be there when the holder came, so she could ask him to do that for Unpun.

"The Ring of Idea can do that?" Justin asked, amazed. "It can restore you to full life?"

"Yesh."

"That is amazing. I never heard of life being fully restored after death. What an idea!"

"Precishly."

It took Justin a moment to assemble that thought. Restoring life after death was a fantastic idea, so it fell in the province of the Ring of Idea. "And that is why you know where the Ring is!" Justin exclaimed, finally making the connection. "Because you know where *she* is. Yet you can't guide me there."

"Yesh. Yesh," Unpun agreed.

"What an irony!"

"Yesh."

"But you know I do have to find it, and you surely want me to succeed."

"Yesh."

"So we shall just have to figure out how you can help me get that Ring."

"Yes," Unpun agreed. But the zombie did not look confident.

Justin pondered half a moment. "First, of course, we shall have to travel to Castle Roogna."

"Noo."

"No? Why not?"

"Bad direchion."

"But that's where Princess Ida is."

"Nooo!"

"It certainly is. Breanna delivered our wedding invitation there only a few days ago. We would have heard if she had moved."

"Noo."

"But I tell you—" Justin broke off, catching on. "You can't guide me there! So you had to protest when I called out the correct route."

"Yesh," Unpun agreed, abashed.

"Very well. We shall go to Castle Roogna. You know it's best, don't you?"

"Yesh," the zombie agreed faintly.

But at that point Justin discovered another problem. "We need to get there quickly. Walking will take days. But what else is there?"

"Nozing."

Justin looked around. His seventy-seven years as a tree had given him a certain insight into the vegetative realm. He spied several orange-yellow cloudberries that must have fallen from passing clouds. They weren't vegetables, of course, but he had seen them before. "These may do."

"Whath?"

He went to pick up two of the berries. "If we eat these, they will make us float like clouds. Then we can float to Castle Roogna."

"Noo."

"Now Unpun, you know we have to get there," Justin said reasonably.

"Wonth worrk."

"Won't work? Why not?"

"Winnd wrongg."

Justin looked up. Sure enough, the clouds above were moving in the opposite direction they needed to go. "Why, you are correct, Unpun." He didn't want to add that he had assumed the zombie would not be very smart, because most weren't. That was because of their rotten brains.

"I nnew a punn would noth do."

And a cloudberry was a pun. Unpun had seen right through the humor, having no sense of it, and caught the flaw in the plan. They would have to find another way.

Justin looked around again. This time he saw hoofprints. He had developed a fair eye for prints too, as many creatures had passed by his tree in the course of those decades. He recognized these: "Peek," he said.

"Whath?"

"I see the hoofprints of Peek. She's a ghost mare. She and her family passed my tree many times. They are nice ghost horses. I'm sure they'll help."

"Where?"

"Oh, those prints are fresh. They are close by. I'm sure they'll hear me if I call." He put his hands to his mouth and called: "Pook! Peek! Puck! It is I, Justin Tree, in man form."

In three-quarters of an instant three pooka appeared: the ghost horse family. All of them had chains wrapped around their barrels. The chains were necessary to keep the horses solid, since they were ghosts. Pook was the stallion, shaggy and wild-looking. Peek was his mate, with beautiful eyes. Puck was their colt, much smaller and cuter; it would take him centuries to grow.

"Hello, ghosts!" Justin said cheerily. "Remember me from my days as a tree? Breanna of the Black Wave made me change back to man form, and we expect to marry soon. But first I have an errand to do at

Castle Roogna. I would be much obliged if you would carry me and Unpun Zombie there."

They hesitated, understandably, so Justin explained. "We need to fetch the Ring of Idea, to help save Xanth from a loss of gravity. To do that we must see Princess Ida, and visit her moon of Ptero. So it is essential that we reach Castle Roogna rapidly."

The three ghost horses shared a glance. Then Pook nodded. They would help.

"Thank you," Justin said. "Unpun, you may ride Peek. I shall ride Pook." He went to the pooka stallion.

"Buth I donth know how," the zombie protested.

"Have no concern," Justin said. "You would never be able to stay on a ghost horse without its consent, and you will not be able to fall off if one agrees to carry you. Peek is very nice; she will safeguard you."

Still Unpun hesitated, until Peek shot him a pretty-eyed look; then he went to her and climbed awkwardly onto her chains. Justin did the same with Pook. He expected the chains to be uncomfortable, but they weren't; they made a reasonable saddle.

Suddenly the two ghost horses were off like the wind, which was not surprising, considering their nature. Little Puck raced along behind them, every so often kicking up his hind feet. Justin had no trouble remaining mounted; Pook was indeed keeping him secure. That was one advantage of riding a magical beast.

But even at the speed of the wind, their travel was not instant. The landscape of Xanth passed around them, field and forest, hill and dale, country and village, plain and lake. They passed individual settings so quickly that they did not have time to move; they seemed like a series of pictures, frozen flashes. Surely the rapidly moving horses seemed like mere blurs to those they passed.

Pook angled his head so as to send a one-eyed glance back at Justin. Oh—he wanted to know more about their mission, and the news of the day, in exchange for the ride. It was customary.

"It seems that Cynthia Centaur went to the Good Magician Humfrey to inquire whether her offspring would breed true to the winged centaur line," Justin said as Peek and Puck drew closer to listen. "The answer was affirmative, but the Service required entails the saving of the Demon Earth, who it seems has been abducted, surely by some other Demon.

The only way to accomplish that is to obtain the Swell Foop, which is a—" He hesitated. "Actually, I don't know what it is or what it does or how it works. But it is surely a very powerful instrument, as it requires the massed effect of all six Rings of Xanth to locate and control it. Thus Cynthia is being assisted by Che Centaur, and by Sim the Simurgh's chick, and by Breanna of the Black Wave, and myself. We are on five separate missions to obtain the Rings."

Peek sent him a sidelong glance, which was convenient for her to do because she was now running beside Pook. The pooka did not talk, but they understood perfectly, and their glances could convey much.

"Why, you are correct," Justin said, surprised. "There are five of us— seeking six Rings. We are missing a Ring holder! That is surely a complication, unless someone else volunteers." He shook his head. "Oh, dear, I fear this will delay my marriage to Breanna. She will not be pleased." In fact she would probably generate such a black cloud of ire that Castle Zombie itself would shake on its mushy foundation. It was enough to make a man wonder whether they shouldn't have eloped.

In such manner their journey to Castle Roogna passed. In due course they spied its orchard and moat and turrets and all. The ghost horses deposited them at the drawbridge, went to sniff noses briefly with Soufflé the moat monster, then were gone in a ghostly stir of invisible air.

Justin and Unpun introduced themselves to Soufflé, who was all the guard the castle needed on a quiet day like this, and walked on into the castle. No one met them; they were unannounced, and the castle ghosts had probably been reassured by the presence of the ghost horses. Had they been hostile intruders it would have been another matter; the castle had its own ways of dealing with those.

They found Princess Ida's little chamber. She was entitled to much fancier lodgings, but preferred to live simply. Her talent was the Idea; whatever she believed would come true, did come true, if suggested by someone who did not know her talent. Most folk did know her talent now, so it didn't get much exercise. But she also had Ptero, and that made all the difference. That was her moon, whereon all the characters who ever existed, or would exist, or might exist, stayed, waiting their turns for lives in regular Xanth.

"Why, hello, Justin," Ida said, rising from her simple chair to greet them. A ball the size of a cherry bomb circled her head. It hid shyly behind her hair the moment Justin looked directly at it. "But I don't think I know your friend."

"He is Unpun Zombie. He knows where—"

"Oh, Punny's friend!" she said. "She came here last year, hoping to wait until there came a way to restore him to full life."

"Yeth!" Unpun agreed.

"And have you found a way?"

"We have, perhaps," Justin said. "We have come for the Ring of Idea."

She looked at him with surprise. "What use could you have for that?" Her moon was evidently curious too, for now it swung back into sight.

"We need it to obtain the Swell Foop. Unpun says that Punny has it. When I get it, I can use it to restore Unpun to life, so that he can resume dissipating puns. That seems straightforward."

"Yes, it surely is," she agreed. Justin knew then that it was true, for Ida did not agree to things she did not believe, and what she believed was true. It did not matter, in this case, that Justin knew her talent; he was not originating the concept, merely repeating what he had learned from Unpun. The zombie evidently did not know.

"We shall need to go to Ptero to find it."

"I will help you go," she agreed. "Lie down on those cots." She indicated two beds in the chamber. Perhaps their visit had not been entirely unexpected. She brought out a bottle. "Sniff this soul remover; it will release your souls for the journey."

"Buth I can'th go there," Unpun protested.

"Yes you can," Justin said immediately. "You must lead me to Punny."

"Noo!"

"If he does not wish to go—" Ida said, concerned. Her little moon clouded over; evidently it did not like stress.

"He does want to go," Justin said. "It's just that he can't stand all the puns that have accumulated around her. So I must be guided by his objections. It's the only way."

"That is sad," she said. "I wish I could help."

"Comth with me," Unpun said.

"I will sit beside you and hold your hand," she said, doing so. "But I can't—"

"Comth with me!" the zombie repeated. "You are a nize woman. I like your touch."

"But Unpun, I can't—"

"Yeth you can!" Now the zombie was echoing Justin's response to him. "Your touch gives me strength." Indeed, he was speaking better now. "Come with me to Ptero! I can handle it then."

Ida looked at Justin, startled. "Do you suppose—?" Her moon paused momentarily in its orbit, similarly surprised.

Justin was as startled as she was. Everyone knew that Ptero was the one place Ida could not go. But was it true? "We just assumed," he said. "But where was the proof? Unpun needs your company." The zombie clearly believed it was possible. He did not know of the limitation on her talent. Maybe she *could* go to her moon.

"But Ptero orbits me," she said. "How can I go?"

"It is only the soul that travels," Justin said. "Your soul can go, while your body remains here, just as ours do."

"Come with me," Unpun repeated.

"I believe—I believe I will," Princess Ida said, her smile radiant. It illuminated the little moon, banishing the last of its clouds. "I have always wanted to visit my worlds, but never thought—"

"Doubt is death," Justin said. "We'll all three go. Lie between us, and hold our hands." He spoke as positively as he could, because he wanted Ida to have this chance to do what she had always wanted. As long as Unpun believed she could, she *could*. They had to seize the moment.

Ida moved another cot between them, and lay on it. The moon adjusted its orbit so that it would not bang into the bed. They held hands. "Now orient on Ptero," she said. "After sniffing the bottle. You will be disoriented at first, but when you see Ptero you will know where to go." She passed the bottle to Justin, who sniffed once and lay back.

He found himself riding out of his body. In a moment he saw the other two doing the same. They were both rather shapeless. "This way," he called. "Take my hand." They were holding hands in their bodies, but not with their souls.

The other two vapors floated toward him, extending pseudopodia. Justin extended his own and realized that it was the branch of a tree; he had unthinkingly reverted to that form. He revised it to man form, caught

Ida's hand, and she caught Unpun's with her other extremity. Both of them were starting to shape into images of their physical selves.

"Oh, this is weird," the Ida form said voicelessly. "I never did it before, myself."

Justin saw the moon of Ptero orbiting the reclining head of the physical Princess Ida. "This way," he said, and urged them toward it. Travel was mostly a matter of thought, in this condition.

"We must make ourselves small," Ida said.

Oh. Yes. Of course. Justin focused on smallth. Now the moon began to grow, becoming a world. It was no longer cute or shy; it was significant. They were flying toward it, and the closer they got, the larger it loomed. Then it seemed that they were falling toward it. The fall accelerated as the world of Ptero loomed huge.

"We need to slow!" Justin said, alarmed.

"Just focus," Ida said.

They focused, and their descent slowed. They came to land on a level plain surrounded by faint haze.

"Oh, this is wonderful!" Ida exclaimed. "Just the way others have described it to me!"

"Blue haze?" Justin inquired dubiously.

"That indicates cold north," she said. "South is red-hot."

Justin looked the other way, and saw that the haze in that direction was indeed reddish.

"What's the green?" Unpun asked. His slight impediment of speech had entirely disappeared; maybe it was an effect of soul travel. Justin had not realized until this trip that zombies even had souls. Breanna would have chided him severely for that ignorance.

"That is To," Ida said. "That is, the Future. West. And East is From, the Past. It is such a beautiful system."

"But surely when one proceeds any distance, the mists will lose their effect," Justin said. "For example, if one goes north, he will be entirely in blue haze."

"You are being reasonable," Ida said. "This is not a reasonable world. I am told that the colors hold regardless of location. Furthermore, age changes as folk move east or west. This may make travel awkward."

"Is this physical or chronological age?"

"Chronological. That usually means physical as well, though I can't be sure how it will affect your appearance. I hope your destination is within your range."

"I don't know." Justin had not thought of this aspect. He turned to Unpun. "Exactly where is Punny?"

"I can't—" the zombie began. But Ida took his hand, and he reconsidered. "She is in the Pun-kin Patch of a Comic Strip. I can't possibly go there."

"Because of your age, or because of the humor?"

"The humor. It must be within my age range, because Punny was no older than I, and she got there."

"Well, then, Ida and I will go, and then return here for you," Justin said.

"Is that wise?" Ida asked, puzzled. Her moon looked puzzled too; Justin realized that it had accompanied her here. He would have to think about the significance of a moon appearing on the surface of itself, but not until he was not standing on it.

"Oh, yes," he said, for he had something in mind.

"Yes," Unpun said.

"Then it is surely all right," she agreed. That made it so, for Unpun did not know this aspect of her talent.

"Now we shall need to get there," Justin said. "It is in walking distance?"

"No," Unpun said.

"Is there some way to gain transport?"

"Yes," Ida said. "I understand that visitors to Ptero normally arrive in Centaur country, and may gain the help of centaurs by trading favors."

"Favors?"

"It is a barter system."

"But what do we have to barter?"

"Your talent is, as I remember, voice projection. Could that be entertaining?"

"Why, I suppose it could," he said, startled.

"And perhaps I will be able to provide interesting information." She glanced at Unpun. "But I'm not sure what—"

"He is covered," Justin said quickly.

"I am?" Unpun asked.

"To be sure. Now how can we find a centaur?"

"I understand it is merely necessary to announce your desire to trade."

Justin shrugged. He faced the blue mist and spoke loudly. "We are three visitors to Ptero who would like to exchange favors with centaurs. One of us is a zombie."

Suddenly there was the sound of the beating of hooves. Three centaurs galloped out of the north. They came to a halt before the visitors. "Shall we exchange introductions?" the male inquired.

"By all means. I am Justin Tree, this is Princess Ida, and this is Unpun Zombie. We are from Xanth proper."

The centaur nodded. "I am Cassaunova Centaur, this is Cassaundra Centaur, and this is Catarrh Zombie Centaur."

"Those are interesting names," Justin said.

"I have the ambition to be every filly's lover, but lack the ability," Cassaunova said.

"And I have no power of prophecy, but others think I do," Cassaundra said.

"I lost my talent when I became a zombie," Catarrh said. "It was not a nice one anyway."

Justin decided not to inquire. "We wish to go to the pun-kin patch. Can you convey us there?"

Cassaunova glanced at the other centaurs. "We can, but would prefer not to. That is in one of the worst of the comic strips. The puns are ferocious."

"They would be," Justin agreed. "Nevertheless, we must go there. Our mission is rather important."

Cassaunova turned to Cassaundra. "Do you foresee a problem?"

"There you go again!" she exclaimed. "I *have* no power of—"

"I'm sure he meant it figuratively," Justin said quickly. "He does not wish to make an exchange of favors that might cause you distress."

"Exactly," Cassaunova agreed as quickly.

"Oh." Cassaundra seemed momentarily flustered. "No, no problem other than distaste. The puns are so thick there it's hard to avoid stepping on them. Have you ever had to scrape a squished pun off your hoof?"

"I'm sure it's a horrible experience," Justin said. "But as it happens, our mission relates. We may be able to commence alleviation of that situation."

She glanced sidelong at him. "You seem to be a fair hand at expression."

"That has on occasion been intimated."

She glanced at the other two centaurs. "Let's do it. They should be interesting to converse with."

Cassaunova nodded. "Turn we now to negotiation. We offer to transport the three of you rapidly to the pun-kin patch. What favors do you offer in return?"

"A modicum of entertainment, perhaps," Justin said, projecting his voice so that it seemed to emanate from behind the centaurs.

All three turned to look, but of course there was nothing there.

"My talent is projection of my voice," Justin said, this time projecting it to a spot over their heads. "I thought it might amuse you." Then he made a dirty sound behind Catarrh's tail, and an ugh sound from before Cassaunova's face, as though he had spoken it.

The male centaur smiled. He of course had no foibles about natural functions, but appreciated the humor. "I will carry you, if you continue that entertainment while we travel."

"Agreed."

"You act as if something funny occurred," Unpun said sourly.

"It did," Cassaundra said.

"Oh. Thank you for informing me."

The filly turned to Ida. "You strongly remind me of someone. Have we met before?"

"Have you encountered a woman with an orbiting moon?"

"Not directly, but I do know of one. But her moon is in the shape of a four-sided pyramid. Yours is spherical."

"That would be that version of me who exists on this world. I understand that each version has a satellite of different shape."

"That surely accounts for my thought," Cassaundra agreed. "What favor are you prepared to exchange for transport?"

"I thought I might provide information on the relation between Ptero and Xanth."

"We already know that Ptero is a derivative of Xanth," the centaur said. "We are the souls of all creatures possible."

Ida nodded. "Perhaps I have no information of interest to you. I had not anticipated this, because I had never expected to be on this world. I had no ideas about participating in it."

Cassaundra considered. "I wonder whether your moon can help. It is of course the soul of our own world, Ptero; we normally are unable to see it as a sphere. It is responsive?"

"Why, I don't know," Ida said, as her moon hid behind her head. "On Xanth it is, but there it is *this* world. I don't know how perfectly its soul duplicates the original."

"Surely as competently as our souls duplicate our larger existences," Justin said.

"Let's find out," the centaur said. "Soul-Ptero, come forward."

The moon swung hesitantly to the centaur's side.

"Do you emulate your larger self perfectly?"

The moon bobbed up and down.

"I take that as yes," Cassaundra said. "Can you answer questions?"

The moon bobbed again.

"Are your answers accurate?"

A third bob.

"Better try a negative," Cassaunova murmured. Justin knew why: The bobbing might be mindless.

"Are the creatures on your surface different from those of our world?"

Now the moon swung from side to side, indicating no.

"Do you know the outcome of your group's mission here?"

Another side swing.

"If that mission fails, will all be well?"

The moon turned dark and blistered as it swung.

That made them all take note. It indicated destruction.

"And if the mission succeeds?"

The moon turned bright and alive again.

Cassaundra nodded. "I believe I will accept this demonstration as a sufficient exchange favor. I will convey you to your destination."

Now Catarrh Centaur addressed Unpun. "You are a zombie, like me. What favor do you offer for your transport to the pun-kin patch?"

"None," Unpun said. "I don't want to go there."

"Why is this?"

"Because my love is there, making awful puns, polluting the region. I lost my sense of humor, and can't stand to be among them."

"I should clarify that his humor would be recovered, if our mission succeeds," Justin said. "If he returns to life, he will resume abolishing puns. That is his talent."

All three centaurs were interested. "He could thin out the dreadful glut?" Catarrh asked.

"Yes," Justin agreed. "But as it is, lacking his humor, he doesn't want to go near that glut."

"We appreciate his position," Cassaunova said.

"Yet we also appreciate the need to restore this man to life and talent," Cassaundra said.

"For the good of our realm, I will convey you to the pun-kin patch," Catarrh said to Unpun.

"No!" Unpun walked away.

"I did not ask your agreement," Catarrh said, walking after the zombie. He picked Unpun up and set him on his back.

Because of the position, Unpun was mounted facing back. "I won't go."

The centaur started walking. Cassaunova and Cassaundra quickly helped the other two mount facing forward, and paced the other. They ignored Unpun's continued protests. It was evident that the zombie lacked the ability to dismount without help, so he was stuck.

"Nicely accomplished," Justin murmured.

"We are not stupid," Cassaunova murmured back, in a polite understatement. No centaur was slow, let alone stupid.

The centaurs galloped not east or west, but north, so age was no problem. That was a private relief to Justin, for though he was technically over a century old, so was proof against much problem of youth, he wasn't sure of the others. Also, he had been a man for only the past two years; would he revert to being a tree beyond that point? That would surely complicate things. It was better simply to remain their present ages.

Justin projected his voice. "Hello, party," a passing fudge nut tree seemed to say.

"That's so clever," Cassaundra said with a brief laugh.

"Thank you," a green ant hill said in Justin's voice.

Then they passed a mean-looking tangle tree. Its tentacles quivered expectantly, for their path was uncomfortably close to it. "Oh, I am about to fall into that tree!" Justin's voice said right behind it. The tree's tentacles whipped around to the rear, grabbing at air, as their party got by. It had been deceived for just that time necessary to secure their safety.

"Admirable," Cassaunova said.

A stray thought occurred. "I am, as you know, new to this realm," Justin said. "So this may be a stupid question."

"Stupid questions we are prepared to deal with," the centaur said. "It is stupid answers that disturb us."

"Since everything imaginable exists here on Ptero, are there duplicates of the three of us?"

"Certainly. But we don't encourage meetings, as they can lead to paradox."

"Paradox?"

"You of Xanth proper are not supposed to know your futures, unless you patronize some approved divination or other magic. If you travel into your own future here, where time is geography, you may learn things you should not."

"That is a reasonable proscription," Justin agreed regretfully. He had been curious about the outcome of their present mission, but one whiff of paradox might spoil an otherwise acceptable outcome.

"I have answered a question, perhaps unsatisfactorily," the centaur said. His tone was low, so that his voice did not carry far.

"And I should answer one in return," Justin said, remembering that nothing was done here without an exchange. "With whatever acumen is feasible."

"Have you any insight on interpersonal relations?"

"Very little, I fear. I was a tree, until I met Breanna of the Black Wave. She soon took me away from all that."

"I would like to have more of a relationship with Cassaundra, but she doesn't take me seriously. We gallop together, but go no farther, as it were."

"She assumes that your ambition with respect to every filly makes her merely one of an innumerable number."

"Precisely. But I would settle for her, were she inclined. She is a nice person."

"Perhaps I can help. I shall speak to Ida, with your permission."

"I have no objection."

Justin projected his voice to Ida's ear. "This is Justin," he whispered. "Cassaunova would like to have a serious relationship with Cassaundra, but she does not take him seriously, because of his reputation. If she would like such a relationship, she should perhaps take the initiative. It would be helpful if you discussed this prospect with her."

Princess Ida glanced across at him and nodded.

"I spoke to Ida," Justin said to Cassaunova. "She will converse with Cassaundra, suggesting that she take the initiative. I can't promise that anything will come of this."

The centaur shrugged. "If Cassaundra approaches me, she shall find me receptive."

After a reasonable interval the centaurs slowed. "We are nearing the border of our region," Cassaunova said. "We must pass through a comic strip to enter the little machine region, which in turn borders the one we seek."

"Little machines?"

"A young woman makes them from inanimate objects. They are peculiar as machines go, and other machines do not approve of their origin, so they are isolated from the main machines."

"But first we must cross the comic strip," Cassaundra said with a delicate shudder.

"Indeed," Cassaunova agreed. "It may be best to plunge through it rapidly."

"What can be so bad about a comic strip?" Justin inquired.

He saw the two centaurs exchange a glance, to which the female added half a smile. It lit half her face, making it prettier. "On reconsideration, let's walk through this one," she suggested. "So they can experience it more fully."

Cassaunova nodded and led the way. He stepped across a faintly shimmering line on the ground.

A strange man appeared "Get your cures here," he said loudly. "Very reasonable prices. Offer will not be repeated."

"Why, I could use a cure," Cassaundra said.

"Sorry, no females need apply," the man said. "My cures are only for men. I'm a man-i-cure."

"Oof," Justin said involuntarily. "What a pun!"

Then he received a rough poke in the side. He jumped, and saw that he had brushed up against a big knobby plant. No—it was reaching out to poke him and the centaur.

"Poke weed," Cassaunova said. "Can't be avoided in this nefarious strip."

Another obnoxious pun. "Let's move on," Justin said somewhat shortly.

A bird flew up before them with a great racket of wings. It was green, and seemed to be made of strung-together green beads. One of the beads flung loose and landed in Justin's lap. Suddenly he felt the urge to urinate. He quickly brushed it off, and the urge abated. "What was that?"

"A peacock," the centaur explained. "A bird made entirely of peas."

"Oof!" Justin repeated. There was more to that pun than met the eye.

They came to a path running down the center of the comic strip. It was wide and smooth. "This seems nice to travel," Ida said.

Cassaundra shook her head. "We must cross it quickly."

Before anyone could ask why, several weird things came zooming along the path. They seemed to be human beings on wheeled devices that they impelled by the use of pedals. But instead of proceeding in single file, they were constantly crashing into each other. Some were sitting facing back, while others were resting on their heads, with their feet in the air and using their hands to pedal. All of them had crazy looks on their faces. "Get out of my way!" one yelled at another as he veered into the other, making them both crash.

"No, *you* get out of *my* way!" the other retorted, getting back on his machine and deliberately colliding again.

There was a growl from below. The path, evidently annoyed, heaved up and hurled both cyclists forward. But as soon as they got their wheels under them again, the two resumed their reckless behavior.

"What on earth is going on?" Justin asked, appalled.

"This is a cyclepath," Cassaunova explained. "All the cyclers on it are crazed. They are positively cyclepathic."

"Oof!" This time it was Unpun. "I can't stand it!"

"Fortunately you are sitting," Catarrh said with a rotten smirk.

"The path seems none too pleased, either," Ida remarked.

"Oh, that's just road rage," Cassaundra said.

All three visitors groaned.

"Do you think they have seen enough?" Cassaunova asked her innocently.

"Yes, more than enough!" Justin said.

"Then let's leap out of here." The three centaurs meant that literally; they leaped across the cyclepath and again to the far side of the comic strip.

The terrain beyond was pleasant enough, especially as it was pun-free. But scattered across it were assorted small objects that turned out to be machines. Some looked like stones, but they put down stony legs to move out of the way. Others looked like sticks, until they clicked open wooden eyes. Still others were more complicated, doing all manner of obscure tasks. A number were building a little house.

The centaurs drew up before that house. "Three greetings, Lyn!" Cassaunova called.

A little machine cranked open the door and a young woman stepped out. "Why, hello, Cass," she said. "Are you still romancing all the girls?"

"Well—"

"No, he isn't," Cassaundra said.

Both Cassaunova and Justin paused for a moment. Was that an initiative?

"Then to what do I owe this rare visit?" Lyn inquired.

"We are merely crossing your region," Cassaundra said. "We thought we should stop by, in case you have objection."

"Are you planning to do any damage?"

"No, of course not." Then the centaur filly reconsidered. "Unless you consider the abolition of some puns to be damage."

"By no means! Puns are overflowing the pun-kin patch and polluting the land. Something needs to be done before we all perish of groaning."

"This backward fellow is Unpun," Catarrh said. "We hope to help restore him to life and humor, so that he can resume the destruction of puns. That is his talent, in life."

"Oh, Unpun, I could kiss you!" Lyn said. Then she reconsidered. "After you are no longer a zombie, of course." She smiled, hinting that this was not completely serious.

"Of course," Unpun agreed sourly, finding no humor in the situation.

"We must be on our way," Cassaunova said. "I trust you will wish us success."

"Oh, I do, I do!" Lyn agreed. "I hate it when puns gum up the works of my machines. I had a nice harvest reaper, until a pun made it a weeper and it cried until it rusted."

"A very sad event," Cassaundra agreed, though a trace of a smile hovered near her mouth.

"Completely unfunny," Unpun agreed.

They resumed travel, and soon enough came to another comic strip. "Now we shall have to enter this and search for the pun-kin patch," Cassaunova said. "The experience will not be pleasant, but must be endured."

"I have no intention of enduring it," Unpun said. "You enter the strip; I'll wait here."

"Of course," Cassaunova said, nodding at Catarrh.

Then, together, the three centaurs jumped into the comic strip. Unpun's scream resounded throughout the welkin, shaking the very sky.

A figure loomed before them. It wore a robe covered with planetary symbols. "Ah, I see you are in the proper mood for your horror-scope," it said. "Your fate is bound to be horrible. Let me cast your fates—"

They walked on by, but there was another figure there. She looked very sweet. "My name's Candi. Have something for your sweet tooth." She held out a box of candy.

"That does look nice," Ida said.

"Don't touch it!" Cassaundra said. "It will turn your teeth into candy. That's what a sweet tooth is, in the comic strip."

"Oh," Ida said, taken aback.

They went on by the sweet girl, and encountered an elder man. "Here are your berries," he said, showing an assortment of yellow, red, green, brown, black, and blue berries. "They will make you wise."

"They will also make you old," Cassaunova said. "Those are elder-berries."

"What an awful idea!" Justin exclaimed.

"Well, this is the world of the idea," Ida reminded him. "And the section of it to make them foolish."

"We still have to locate the pun-kin patch," Cassaundra said. "These are mere distractions."

"I think we have no choice but to keep looking."

They looked. "There's something," Justin said. It appeared to be a giant flower.

They went toward it, but the closer they got, the smaller it became. By the time they reached it, it was tiny. "What happened?" Ida asked.

"Now I recognize it," Cassaundra said, disgusted. "It's a shrinking violet."

Unpun groaned again.

Something came running toward them. It was a giant eyeball with long skinny legs. It stopped and gazed intently at them. "What is this?" Justin asked.

"I'm not sure," Cassaunova said. "I haven't seen this particular pun before."

"It is the eye of the beholder," Unpun said. "I find no humor whatsoever."

"That is your irony," Cassaundra said.

"You should not have said that," Cassaunova said warily.

She put a hand to her mouth. "I forgot where I was! Maybe they didn't hear."

"They heard."

A group of small metal forms floated toward them. "We had better get out of here!" Cassaundra said, alarmed.

The centaurs leaped—but turned back toward the center of the comic strip. "Too late," Cassaunova said despairingly.

"Why didn't you leave?" Justin asked.

"We can't. Those are iron E's—they reverse whatever we try to do."

"Ironies!" Justin exclaimed. "Lovely."

"But won't they interfere with our mission?" Ida asked. "We can't accomplish it while being constantly reversed."

"Not so," Justin said. "They will enable us to readily accomplish it."

The others looked at him, evidently uncertain of his sanity. "You are aware of something we are not?" Cassaunova inquired.

"Merely common sense. We must strive our utmost to avoid the punkin patch."

"To *avoid* it?" Ida asked.

"Yes. We must get far away from it immediately. Now run; flee it."

"As you wish," the centaur said dubiously.

They tried to run out of the comic strip—and there before them was a big pumpkin patch. Or rather, the pun-kin patch. They had found it.

"Irony!" Ida exclaimed. "The opposite of the stated intent! I forgot."

"Irony brought us here," Cassaundra agreed, surprised. "We all missed it."

"Merely common sense, as I said," Justin said, a trifle smugly. "There is generally a way to accomplish one's goal, if one takes the correct approach."

"But where is Punny?" Ida asked.

They all looked, and saw only pun-kins of all different sizes. No people.

"She isn't here," Justin said, disappointed.

"But she must be," Ida said.

Then Justin got another idea. "Unpun."

"Leave me out of this!"

"Where do you want to go?"

"That way," Unpun said, pointing.

"So it must be the opposite way," Justin said. "Another kind of irony." He marched the opposite way.

But all he found was a pile of funny papers surrounded by tiny pun-kins. No woman.

Unless—

He picked up one of the funny papers. There was the cartoon figure of a woman. "Hello, Punny!" he said.

"Oh, you found me," the cartoon picture said. "I was trying to hide, because my life is not worthwhile without love."

"Your love is here," Justin said. "Give me the Ring of Idea, and I will restore him to you."

"But he's dead!"

"The Ring will restore him."

"So it can," the picture agreed. "But only if wielded by the chosen user."

"I believe I am that one."

"Oh. In that case, try it." The figure lifted her hand, where a Ring was marked.

Justin somewhat dubiously put his fingers to her paper hand and touched the Ring. To his surprise it came free, and was a regular physical Ring. He put it on his little left finger, and it fit comfortably.

But was it the real Ring of Idea? Did it have the phenomenal magic power attributed to it? He needed to be sure. "Unpun, let's see what this can do," he said.

For once the zombie did not balk. Justin approached him. "I am not sure of the protocol of operation," Justin said. "Do I invoke it, or what?"

"Just think of the Ring as you speak," Ida said. "Will it to make your idea real. Unlike my own talent, you can originate your ideas for reality yourself, knowing the Ring's power. It can make anything happen in this realm, and is not without impact in Xanth proper. Do not abuse its authority."

"I wouldn't think of it," Justin said. "But I think restoring Unpun to life should not represent an abuse."

"Definitely not," Cassaunova said, moving a forefoot to avoid a punkin that was sprouting beneath it.

"Very well." Justin thought of the Ring of Idea, and spoke. "Unpun, return to full life and humor, your talent complete."

Just like that, Unpun straightened up, his ragged clothing mending, his face and body becoming halfway handsome. The pun-kins around him sagged as if cooked, shrinking to mottled buttons. His talent was manifesting.

"Oh, Unpun, you're back!" Punny exclaimed, stepping out of the funny paper and becoming fully real. Except for her little hat, which remained paper. She ran to hug him.

"I'd rather have a paper doll," Unpun said, holding back.

"You can't be serious!"

"Of course I'm not serious!" he said, laughing. "You look hilarious in that stupid paper hat." But as he spoke, the hat warped and fuzzed out.

"It must have been a pun of some kind," Punny said as she kissed him. "Oh, Unpun, let's go back to Xanth now."

"Of course."

Cassaundra turned to Cassaunova. "Isn't that just the most romantic thing?" she asked him.

"Yes."

She kissed him. "Let's carry these good folk wherever they're going, then see whether we can devise something similarly romantic."

The male centaur glanced at Justin. "By all means."

"We can depart from here," Ida said. "But there is something I must clarify first."

"There's a complication?" Punny asked, alarmed.

"Only a small one. What you just gave Justin is merely the soul of the Ring of Idea. There are no physical things here, merely their souls. The physical Ring is in Xanth, and it must be found so that Justin can wear it and use it."

"Another search?" Justin asked, discomfited.

"I'm sure you can readily find it, now that you have its soul. Simply maintain your awareness of it as we return."

"Gladly." Justin turned to the centaurs. "I thank you for your kind assistance, and—" He broke off, for they weren't listening. Catarrh had already departed, and the other two were kissing again.

"I think you started something," Ida said.

"Perhaps so," Justin agreed, thinking of Breanna. How he wanted to be back with her!

"Shall we return?" Ida inquired.

"By all means," Justin agreed.

"My body is in a closed chamber next to Princess Ida's room," Punny told Unpun. "I will come to join you the moment I wake."

"Now let your substance expand into mist," Ida said. "And orient on my body in Xanth."

Justin concentrated on diffusion, and soon felt himself dissipating. He expanded right out of the pun-kin patch, the comic strip, and the region of the surface of Ptero. He floated hugely over that world, like a cloud, and saw three other clouds similarly forming: Ida, Unpun, and Punny.

He looked around, and saw the gigantic head of Princess Ida, about which this whole world orbited. He went for it, still expanding. The other clouds paced him.

They came to their sleeping bodies. Three were in one room, and one in another room. But where was the Ring?

Then he felt a tingle at his diffuse finger. The soul of the Ring knew where its body was. That would guide him.

They reached their bodies and dived in. It took two and a half moments to recover full alertness.

"Oh, that was wonderful!" Princess Ida said. "For the first time I experienced Ptero myself! I must do it again soon."

Unpun stirred. "I must find Punny."

"And I must find the Ring of Idea," Justin said.

"This way, I'm sure," Ida said, opening a door.

In the chamber beyond was a young woman just sitting up. Unpun hurried to help her. Justin focused on his finger, and it guided him to the pallet on which the woman sat. Underneath it, in a clump of dust that had evidently been undisturbed for a long time, was the Ring. He picked it up, brushed it off, and put it on.

"Now do me physically," Unpun said, and Justin realized that he was a zombie again. So he quickly repeated his directive, with the Ring in mind, and Unpun made the same transformation he had on Ptero.

"Thank you," the fully living Unpun said.

Justin nodded. But privately he was amazed at the power of the Ring. It could actually restore a zombie! That was surely not the limit of its power. Yet it was one of six required merely to locate and control the Swell Foop. What a device that must be!

6
RING OF WATER

C ynthia saw the others pairing off and departing, so she
    looked for her own zombie. She spied one sitting in a
    pool of stagnant water. She was female, according to
her upper torso, but her legs seemed to be fused. A zombie mermaid!

Cynthia was mildly partial to crossbreeds, having become one herself, so she approached this one. "You know of a Ring of Xanth?"

"Yez."

"I am Cynthia Centaur. Who are you?"

"Zilche Zzombie."

"I was once human. You were a mermaid?"

"Yez."

"What Ring do you know of?"

"The Ringg of Washer."

"The Ring of Water," Cynthia repeated, getting it straight. "Where
is it?"

"Ze pulsh ze zing."

Cynthia had to ponder that for much of a moment. Then she got it.
"The pool's the thing?"

"Nosh eggazly."

Cynthia pondered again. "Or more precisely, the Brain Coral's Pool," she concluded. "The Brain Coral might reasonably be construed as governing the Region of Water, so that makes sense." She looked down at the zombie. "But that's still very general. I will need your help to locate its specific site. I will have to carry you. Let's see how that can be done."

She looked around, and spied some netting. It had probably been used to bring the mermaid here. She picked it up and fashioned it into a bag. She tied the bag to her body, so that it was against her right side: The mermaid could ride side-saddle. It would have to do.

"I will carry you to the pool," she said. "The trip will not take long, so your tail should not get too dry." She put her hands under Zilche's arms and lifted her up to the net bag. The zombie fit there comfortably enough, assuming that zombies were capable of discomfort.

Then Cynthia flicked them both, spread her wings, and took off. In a brief duration and two moments she was flying above the trees. She oriented, and headed for a little-known mountain.

"Wwhare?" Zilche asked.

"Oh, you are wondering how I expect to reach an underground pool by flying through the air? That is an excellent question. You see, I was confined in the Brain Coral's Pool for seventy-two years, ashamed of my condition, having been human for the first sweet sixteen years of my life. For most of that time I was unconscious, by my own choice, though on occasion I did circulate and make some friends among the other detainees. I noticed that there was an air pocket above the pool, and I wondered how it remained fresh. So later, when I was studying centaur information, I researched that, and learned that there is an air pipe leading from the pool to the surface. Very few folk know of it, but I ferreted out its location, and now I shall use it to descend to the pool." She was rather pleased with herself for finding a use for what had seemed to be useless information.

The flight was not as easy as she had hoped, because she encountered cross winds. They irritably buffeted her back and forth, so that she had to descend to tree level to avoid them. She came perilously close to a tangle tree, and even brushed its tentacles, but they did not grab her. That was a relief, but odd.

Then she saw that there were no bones around the tree. It was a faux tangler—an imitation, innocuous, but safe from predation because of its

protective camouflage. Good for it! She made a mental note of its location, because if she ever needed a safe place to sleep in this area, this
was it.

Then she saw a sign: SUN GLARE AHEAD. Sure enough, in a moment
the sun formed a face and glared villainously at her. Fortunately that
didn't last; once she got past that section, the sun returned to its normal
favor.

She had gotten past the cross winds, so was able to rise back above
the forest. That was really more comfortable. Had she had the magic
talent of her friend Daniel, she would have been able to talk to the wind
and have it obey her wish. But of course she would never trade that for
her ability to fly.

They flew over one of her favorite regions: the retreat for centaur
crossbreeds who were excluded from association with normal centaurs.
They had made their own home, and their population was growing. There
were centaurs with the bodies of felines, deer, zebras, oryx, and others;
there seemed to be no limit to their variations, and each was beautiful
in his or her own right. She waved and dipped her wings, and several
of them waved back; they knew she accepted them.

She came to the obscure mountain, and circled until she spied the
truly obscure peak that concealed the pipe: Pipe's Peek. She descended
rapidly toward it.

"Crazsh!" the zombie exclaimed, alarmed.

"By no means. Pipe's Peek is illusion, invisible from the air." She
continued her descent, dropped into the surface of the mountain, and
passed through the illusion into the air pipe. Now they were in a vertical
tunnel, still dropping. Little illusion glow-worms lined its sides, so that
it was easy to follow; the Brain Coral had taken this intelligent precaution to ensure that the air did not get lost.

Way, way down in the depths the air pipe opened onto the deep
subterranean lake that was the Brain Coral's Pool. Cynthia felt two tin-
gles and a twinge of nostalgia for this familiar locale. She had come
here for oblivion when she thought herself transformed into a monster.
But seven decades of consideration had reconciled her to her situation,
and now she was happy to be a winged monster, and wouldn't trade it.
In fact, straight human people seemed somewhat inadequate, with their
small physiques and lack of wings, not to mention their limited intellects

and hang-ups about natural functions. But of course she wouldn't say that to any of them; it would not be polite. After all, some of her best friends were human. She thought of Magician Trent, and that brought two-thirds of a tremor of wistful longing. She had had more than half a crush on him at one time, as had her friend Gloha Gobliness; he was a fine man, and extremely attractive in his rejuvenated state. Oh, she loved Che Centaur, she truly did, but if by some misadventure she were ever to find herself fully human again and alone with Trent, in some dark cave with survival uncertain, and no one would ever know . . . she would refuse responsibility for any consequences.

She landed on a little rocky beach and folded her wings. There stood a handsome oxlike antelope with a big nose. "Cynthia!" he exclaimed, recognizing her.

She sighed inwardly. This was another friend, Watt's Gnu, who was nice enough, but very nosy. He always had to learn of everything that had happened in the past day, and would not relent until he had it. But he didn't remember anything beyond a day. She didn't have time for that right now. So she did something a trifle unkind. "My friend Zilche will catch you up in just a moment." Then, to the mermaid: "Just tell him all about our mission."

Now how would she locate the Ring of Water? It would be useless to search for it by herself; the pool was larger than it seemed, and crowded with guests (few could leave by choice, but they weren't exactly prisoners), many of whom would not care to cooperate. The Sea Hag, who had escaped the pool last year, was not the only obnoxious denizen in cool storage there. She could search for half of forever before finding it. So she would have to ask someone. The Brain Coral itself was not much of a talker, but she had friends here. Who would be likely to know?

A watery bulb flashed over her head. "Jackson!" she exclaimed. He was the official inventory taker for the Brain Coral, so knew where everything was.

In a moment a head broke water. "Cynthia!" he exclaimed. "Are you giving up on worldly Xanth?"

"Jackson! How are you? No, I'm here on brief business."

"Pleasure before business," he said. "Come in and give me a hug, you fantastic creature."

"Gladly." She set Zilche in the shallow water, where she could be comfortable while talking with Watt's Gnu, then waded deeper until she was chest deep. It felt good against her hide, because of its preservative quality. Jackson swam up to join her. He was a merman, with a history roughly similar to hers: He had been fully human, but had swum in a dangerous section of a river and been swallowed by a big fish. But the fish had a hunger bigger that its stomach, and was able to swallow only the lower half of the man. By the time it realized that, it had already digested Jackson's feet. Jackson could neither die nor escape. Finally they compromised, agreeing to merge, becoming a merman. Unfortunately the natural merfolk did not accept Jackson as one of them, considering him at best an imitation. Some species were like that; in fact, the centaurs were as purebred snotty as any, but by no means the only ones. Frustrated, isolated, he swam to the Brain Coral's Pool for storage until the issue could be resolved. Jackson had liked it, and had taken a job there.

They hugged, and Cynthia even added a chaste kiss. She understood as well as anyone what it meant to be neither fish nor fowl. They had been friends for decades, before she left the pool.

"You don't seem to have aged a bit," Jackson said. "I would swear by the feel of you that you are still sixteen, physically."

She released him and glanced down at the human portion of her torso. She had filled out rather well, if she did say so herself. "That's not surprising. I was rejuvenated to the physical age of eight, after I left here. That was eight years ago, so I am physically sixteen now, again."

"Why would you want to become eight?"

"To be suitable for Che Centaur. It is working out well. One year we shall marry, and our foals will breed true." She knew it was foolish, but she felt a small flush of pride at being able to make that statement. "Winged centaurs."

He glanced appraisingly at her body. "I'm jealous of him."

"Thank you."

"Now what is your business?"

"I need to find the Ring of Water. I believe it is somewhere in the pool."

"No."

"I beg your pardon?"

"There's no such Ring here. I have inventoried everything, so am in a position to know. If you would like some opti or pessi mist spray to make you feel positive or negative, we have that. We have a fine brain eyeball, or a show-and-tell-a-vision box that lights up with a person's idea. We have a fine scarf that wraps around a person's neck and keeps it warm, though it eats too much."

"The scarf eats?"

"Voraciously. It has a high metabolism. It just gobbles food down in whole chunks, so that the person wearing it can hardly get a bite. That's why the scarf wound up being stored here despite its usefulness. We have many things. But no Ring."

"But there has to be! Zilche said—"

He glanced at the zombie, who was happily swimming nearby, having caught Watt's Gnu up. The water was good for her too. "What did you say, Zilche?"

"Ze pulsh ze zing."

"See?" Cynthia said. "The pool's the thing."

"That is not what I heard."

"Well, she is a zombie. Her pronunciation—"

"She said, 'The play's the thing.' Right, Zilche?"

The zombie nodded.

Cynthia was dismayed. "But that makes no sense! The Ring of Water should be in water, and it is natural that the Brain Coral would be in charge of it."

"Perhaps so, but the domain of water is hardly limited to the pool. There's the entire Region of Water."

"The Ring has power over that, so I don't think it would be there. My impression is that the Rings are somewhat apart from what they control, though I could be in error."

Jackson spoke again to the zombie. "Zilche, what play?"

"Ze cursh ffiendz pulsh."

"The curse fiend's play!" Cynthia exclaimed. The word "pulsh" still did not sound much like "play" to her, but the rest was clear enough. "I don't want to go there."

Jackson shrugged. "You are welcome to stay here."

She laughed. "No, I must be gone. Please relay my greetings to all my friends here."

"I shall. But you have many friends. Which ones were you thinking of?"

"Miss Erry, who loves company but somehow manages to alienate most folk. Miss Steppe, with her painful talent of falling down. And of course the relatives of MareAnn: SpartAnn, TrojAnn, HellAnn—"

"I will notify them all."

She hugged him again, then splashed out of the pool. "Come on, Zilche; we're off to the curse fiend's castle."

"She's a mermaid!" Jackson exclaimed, as if just realizing. "I had thought of her as a zombie."

"Zombie mermadz," Zilche clarified.

He studied her more closely. "You must have been a rather pretty creature, in life."

Zilche did her best to blush while trying to brush out her tangled hair. "Nod spezaly." She inhaled, accenting a well-formed bare bosom.

"Modest too. I like that."

"We have to go," Cynthia said impatiently.

They ignored her. "Zo handzum merrmum."

"Well, I'm only a half-reared merman. The real ones—"

"Handzum," she repeated, firmly for a zombie.

Jackson considered. "Do you know, the Brain Coral's Pool has some curative properties, to enable folk to remain healthy for decades or centuries while in storage. I have felt much better since settling here, despite having no companion of my type. I think you could be restored almost to the qualities you had in life, if you cared to reside here."

Zilche's eyes widened. "Zo wandz?"

"Well, yes, I want, if you should be interested."

Cynthia realized that the composite man and the undead mermaid had much in common. Both were outcasts of their kind. But she didn't have time for this. "Zilche, we have a mission to accomplish. We have to go."

The zombie nodded reluctantly. "Maabee ey come bakz?"

"By all means come back!" Jackson agreed eagerly. "When your mission is done."

"All right!" Cynthia said. She reached down into the water, set the zombie into the net, flicked them both, spread her wings, and took off. Jackson waved, and Zilche waved back. "Bakz!" she promised. To that

Cynthia could agree; she would be glad to bring the zombie back here, once she had the Ring of Water.

Then, as an afterthought as she spiraled back up the air pipe: "I apologize for misunderstanding you, before."

"Pulsh—plush—playsh," Zilche said, trying to clarify her expression. Evidently she had difficulty with the *P L* combination. "Zhakzon nize."

"Yes, Jackson is nice. It never occurred to me that he could be lonely for his kind."

"Zlonly," the zombie agreed with feeling.

They passed through the illusion of Pipe's Peek and climbed higher into the sky. Then she oriented on Lake Ogre Chobee, where the curse fiend's castle was. She dreaded the coming encounter, but it seemed it was necessary. The curse fiends were not necessarily friendly to outsiders.

In due course she spied the lake. The ogres were no longer there, having long-since migrated to the Ogre-fen-Ogre Fen, but the name lingered. Folk remembered ogres for a long time, unsurprisingly.

The turrets of the curse fiend's Gateway Castle came into sight. Cynthia nerved herself and glided down to a landing on a high plaza.

There was an attractive garden there, with assorted musical plants. Blue bells rang, golden horns tootled, tubers oompa'd, and a plant with a root shaped like a red heart kept the beat. It was of course a heart beet.

A dour man appeared. The curse fiends were always alert to intrusions. "What is your business, centaur?" he demanded gruffly.

"I am on a mission for the good of Xanth. I must locate the Ring of Water."

"We know nothing of this. Kindly depart."

This was exactly the welcome she had anticipated. "I must not depart without that Ring. I shall need to search for it."

"You are refusing to depart our premises?" the man asked, beginning to swell up as if about to deliver a curse.

But Cynthia had not been completely asleep in centaur school. She knew how to finesse this. "You are against the good of Xanth?"

It did set him back a quarter step. "That depends on definition."

"The Demon Earth has been abducted, and in his absence the magic of gravity will fade. Xanth needs some gravity. Without it Gateway

Castle would lose all the water surrounding it and become a structure on a muddy plain. Your definition favors this?"

He became defensive. "How do we know you speak the truth?"

"Have you ever known a centaur to speak other than the truth?" Of course she was not a natural centaur, but he wouldn't know that.

"Your information could be inaccurate."

She merely stared at him.

After a moderately generous moment, he gave way. "Where is this Ring?"

"I don't know. I said I will have to search for it."

"We cannot let you do that unsupervised."

Cynthia sifted through her memory. Che's mother had once traveled to the Vale of the Vole with a curse fiend woman whose every third curse turned out to be a blessing, making her unpopular with her kind. Was it possible she was still here? She had been old when Chex knew her, a generation ago. What was her name? "Dame Latia!"

"You know the old crone?"

This did not sound promising, but it remained her best chance. "Indirectly. Is she available?"

"Naturally not."

What did that mean? Was the woman so old and frail she could not do anything? Cynthia realized that she would have to finesse again. "Suppose you query her?" That was technically a question, rather than a demand.

He countered similarly. "Why should I bother the crone?"

"Suppose you inform her that a winged centaur would like to see her?"

"Suppose I don't?"

"I wonder what her reaction would be, when she learns you didn't?"

He pondered that for an instant short of a moment. "Wait here." He retreated through a doorway.

"Nize," Zilche remarked.

"Nice? But I know nothing about Dame Latia. She's the only curse fiend I have heard of. It was just a wild chance that she was still alive, let alone available."

"Zhe Mazizdath."

"She's what?"

"Mazizdath."

Cynthia still couldn't get it. "Well, I hope that's not mischief."

The door opened. "The crone will see you," the curse fiend said distastefully.

"Excellent," Cynthia said, as if this had been a certainty all along.

The door looked too small for Cynthia to pass, but it expanded as she approached, as did the stairway beyond it. It was evident that the curse fiends were pretty good craftsmen.

They were ushered into a very plush chamber. "Here are the intruders, Crone," the man said.

"Thank you, Functionary," a cracked old voice replied.

It was indeed a very old woman. She sat on a plush pillow on an extremely ornate chair. She was the ugliest human person Cynthia had seen anywhere.

Cynthia stepped forward. "Dame Latia?"

"The Crone," the woman agreed. "Ah, you are not Chex."

"I apologize if I misled you. I am Cynthia, her foal's fiancée."

"My, time has certainly passed! Tell me of her life events since I knew her."

"She matured and married Cheiron. Their first foal was Che, who became the tutor to the Simurgh's chick Sim. They have other foals, and are quite satisfied with life."

"I am so glad to hear it. Chex was a good person, though no older than you are now." She squinted at Cynthia. "You look to be about sixteen."

"Yes, Dame." And the old woman looked to be over a hundred. "Actually, she was younger when she visited the Kiss Mee River. She was fully mature by age ten, because of her winged monster sire."

The woman peered at her. "There is reason you do not call me Crone?"

Cynthia was on the verge of being slightly flustered. "I do not wish to be offensive."

"You know nothing of me since I shared adventures with Chex and her friends Esk Ogre and Volney Vole?"

"That is true, Dame. I—I needed to invoke a name to gain admittance to Castle Gateway, and yours was the only one I knew. Because Chex mentioned you as a good person. I apologize for my ignorance."

"And your companion, the zombie mermaid?"

"Mazizdath," Zilche said.

"I am unable to fathom that word," Cynthia said, embarrassed.

Latia addressed the zombie again. "So you know, but she does not?"

"Yez."

"How delightful! It is such a pleasure to encounter innocence."

"Innocence?" Cynthia asked, not totally pleased.

"I will explain. Thanks in significant part to Chex and her friends of the time, we had a successful mission, and I returned to Gateway Castle with elevated status despite my infirmity of talent."

"Infirmity?" Cynthia asked, still muddled. Actually, she knew what Latia meant, but remained distracted by this mysterious reference to innocence. What had she failed to comprehend?

"We curse friends all have the same talent: cursing. This manifests in different ways, but generally means mischief for those we curse. Unfortunately my cursing is flawed; one curse in three turns out to be a blessing. My associates wanted to be rid of me, for my visage even then was so ugly as to curdle water. But after my success, that was not possible, and in due course seniority enabled me to assume the role of Magistrate."

"Mazizdath," Zilche agreed.

"Magistrate," Cynthia echoed, finally seeing it. "But isn't that a significant office in your society?"

"Yes. Equivalent to Queen, in the human society."

"Oh!" Cynthia cried, appalled as she realized the nature of her ignorance. "And I demanded to see you! I didn't know!"

"Yes, so we have ascertained. You are the first in some time to come to me asking a favor without knowing my office. I like that."

"But the guard called you a—a—"

"Crone. Not a—*the*."

"I—I don't—"

"Ze Crone rulz," Zilche exclaimed.

"The Crone rules," Latia agreed. "It is no longer a term of disrespect, but my title. There is only one Crone in the Gateway Castle at present."

"I had no idea! I would never have—"

"I know, dear. I liked Chex, and I like you; you will surely do right by her foal. Now let's see to your mission. You seek the Ring of Water."

"Yes, Dame—I mean Crone."

"I had no idea it was here, but zombies lack the wit to prevaricate. We surely do have it. We shall undertake a search for it."

"Thank you, Crone." Cynthia felt weak in all four knees. This had seemed so doubtful, and grown worse, yet suddenly had turned out so well.

Latia picked up a little bell and rang it. Immediately a uniformed man appeared. "Yes, Crone."

"Institute a thorough search of the premises. You are looking for the Ring of Water. This is a band of exceeding power, I suspect not made of water." Latia allowed a smile to crack the lower portion of her face. She had made a funny. "We do not know its precise appearance, other than the form of a ring. So bring all rings you find here for inspection."

"Yes, Crone." He disappeared.

"Now while they search, would you like to see a play? We are always in need of pre-tour audience reaction by persons who have no familiarity with the productions."

Cynthia realized that it would not be courteous to decline, though she was not at all sure she wanted to waste time in such manner. "If you wish, Crone."

"This way." Latia got off her cushion, which Cynthia now realized was padding on a throne, and led the way out of the chamber. Obviously the woman was not much for ceremony, and she was quite spry for her age.

They went down another flight of stairs. There was a window, and Cynthia saw that beyond it was water, with fish swimming by. This was below the surface of the lake!

"You must admire this," Latia said, indicating a massive glass wall.

They peered out. There was a monstrous whirlpool, swirling down to unknown depths. "This is what keeps Lake Ogre Chobee shallow," Latia explained. "Its extra water pours into the depths, concluding at the Pool of the Brain Coral."

"Oh, this is the other end of the underground river!" Cynthia exclaimed. "I had not realized."

"Few do. But we do regard ourselves as guarding the gateway to the underworld."

They followed her to a larger chamber. There were several chairs, and a fair-sized tank of water. "For your friend," Latia said, indicating it.

Cynthia set Zilche in the tank, and the mermaid swished her tail gratefully.

The stage curtains parted to reveal a group of actors holding various objects. One stepped forward. "The name of this play is *Charades*. It is interactive. We shall present each concept for ten seconds, and if any member of the audience fathoms it, the audience scores a point. After that time, the answer will be given, and the audience will lose a point. At the end of the play, the score will determine whether the players or the audience won."

"I am not familiar with this play, so I will be a part of the audience," Latia said. "Thus we are three."

The first player stepped forward. She wore nothing but a tight body stocking. It occurred to Cynthia that any males would have found that interesting, for the actress was of a shapely disposition. She lifted a suit from a hanger, and put on trousers over her bare-seeming legs. Suddenly water splashed out; the trousers must have been filled with it. Then she put on a jacket, and bubbly water poured out from around her arms. "I am becoming quite clean," she said, "as this apparel washes me. What is it?"

A suit that washed its wearer? Cynthia drew a blank.

"Bazing zuit!" Zilche said.

"A bathing suit," the actress agreed. The number *1* appeared on a plaque marked AUDIENCE.

A man stepped forward. He carried a cudgel that was shaped roughly like a volume, with visible pages. "I will pulverize ignorance!" he declaimed, swinging the tome around. "What do I have here?"

"Why, I believe that is a book club," Latia said, and the audience number went to *2*.

A third actor brought out a large bowl. In it was a ball that rolled around and around of its own accord. Cynthia tried to figure it out, but had no success, and neither did the others. "A bowling ball," the actor said. The *2* became a *1*. They had lost a pun.

"I don't think that quite works," Latia said. "It is a ball in a bowl, but not bowling it over."

"I agree," Cynthia said.

Another actor stepped forward. She had a bell, but when she rang it, instead of ringing it went "Mooo!"

"A cow bell!" Cynthia said, finally getting one.

The next actor was in the shape of a huge foot. It hopped up to another actor who was evidently feeling ill. "Take two pills and call me in the morning," the foot said.

"Fooz docthor!" Zilche said.

"A foot doctor," the actor agreed, and the score went to 3.

Stage hands laid down a blue sheet with waves painted on it. Then an actor dived on it, as if thinking he would swim. Instead he bounced off the surface. "What is this?" he asked, seemingly bewildered.

Cynthia had had enough. "Please, I must search for the Ring," she murmured.

"Hardz wazer!" Zilche said.

"Hard water," Latia agreed. "I must say, you are sharp at charades, Zilche."

"Zank zhu."

"This mission is important," Cynthia said, moving toward the door.

Meanwhile, onstage, an actress donned a light coat. Then she started doing nasty little things to other actors.

"It must be something about the coat," Latia said, mystified.

"Meenz Zpiritedz," Zilche agreed, also struggling.

"It's a petticoat," Cynthia called back as she left the room. "It makes its wearer think petty thoughts and do petty things." Then she trotted off, her absence surely not even noticed. She was glad to get away from those awful puns. Maybe it took a mind pickled by great age or zombyism to sit still for all that.

One side of the hall was the great glass wall; surely no Ring hidden there. The other side was lined with doors. She peeked into the next chamber. Curse fiends—curse friends, as they called themselves—were busily searching everywhere. Good enough.

She walked on, checking other chambers. All were busy, until she came to one that was empty. It was evidently a theater that was not currently in use; stage props were stacked everywhere. She saw five statues of men and women set in a circle facing inward. "Circle of friends," she murmured, then reacted. "Horseflies! I'm still fathoming puns!"

Could the Ring be here? She saw no particular reason, as it could be anywhere in Gateway Castle. But it occurred to her that if she was destined to be the one to find and wield this Ring, then she would somehow be led to it. Perhaps there would be a psychic rapport.

She looked around, seeking rapport. Her eyes fell on a folded blanket. She picked it up, and saw that it was made from many little dots, each with four tiny hands that clasped the hands of other dots, forming an array that in its larger scope became the blanket.

"A dot matrix," she murmured, and winced as she realized she had done it again. "Founderhoofs! I've got to rid my brain of these puns so I can find the Ring!"

She closed her eyes and tried again. She tried to clear her mind of all punnish thoughts, focusing only on the Ring. And it seemed to work. The image of a circle formed, white and bright. Could she have found it?

She opened her eyes. There was the circle: a large ring of smooth white wood set on a box. Could that be it?

She walked to it—and caught the smell of manure. Suddenly she recognized the structure: It was one of the human refuse devices. A person would sit on it and deposit a clod of manure, then depart. Humans were exceedingly uptight about natural functions, and tried to conceal them whenever possible. Hence this unwieldy mechanism. When repeated uses filled the box, it would be emptied into a latrine pit. So this was just a stage prop, or, worse, a real toilet for stage hands to use. She had thought this could be the marvelous Ring of Water?

Disgusted, she searched elsewhere in the chamber. There were props galore, but no Rings. Obviously it wasn't here, or was so well hidden she could not find it. Maybe her notion about being somehow attuned to it was vain. Maybe she simply was not destined to be the user of this Ring. After all, she had more or less randomly come to Zilche, and assumed that she could locate the particular Ring the zombie knew about. That was a very tenuous connection.

Still, the Good Magician had given her a mission to perform, and this Ring was an essential part of that mission. If she was not to be the one to find it, then who else was?

"No one!" she exclaimed. "This *has* to be my Ring to find."

So where was it most likely to be? Apparently it was so well hidden that all the curse fiends could not find it. So it must be in the least likely place. What was that?

"The toilet," she said with wry humor.

Then she paused, gazing at the human privy box. Wouldn't that be fitting!

She walked back to the box. She put her hand to the white wooden ring and picked it up. "Ring of Water, I claim you," she said.

There was a flushing sound, and the Ring dissolved, becoming fluid. It was flowing away! But then it coalesced, forming a translucent Ring around her left little finger.

She had found it. Now what was she going to do with it?

There was just a tiny weak hint of maybe a doubt in her mind. Was this the Ring of Water—or was it merely an imitator? She needed to find out before she called off the search.

She took the Ring out to the hall and gazed through the thick glass. This was supposed to have power over all the water creatures. She would find out.

"If there is any big sea monster in range, come to me," she said. But of course this was foolish, as she was in the castle and couldn't be heard beyond it. She would have to find a better test.

Then a shape loomed in the dark water of the whirlpool. It was a huge serpent! It spread itself against the glass, so as to avoid being sucked down into the vortex below. Its head swung around to gaze at Cynthia. The thing was enormous. Each eye was almost the size of Cynthia's head.

Embarrassed, she reversed. "Return to safe waters," she said.

The serpent nodded, then slithered around and upward, escaping the deadly pull. Soon it was gone.

Cynthia turned to discover Latia there. "So you found it," the Crone said.

"So it seems. I wasn't sure, so—"

"Of course. I will call off the other searchers."

"Thank you," Cynthia said faintly.

"We haven't seen that monster in twenty years. I had feared it was dead."

"Just busy elsewhere," Cynthia said. "I shouldn't have bothered it."

But Latia was already turning away. Out of sorts, Cynthia returned to the play chamber.

"Jach and Jillz rabbits!" Zilche exclaimed, responding to the play. The rabbit actors hopped offstage. Jackrabbits and Jillrabbits—of course.

Cynthia paused, not wanting to disturb the zombie's enjoyment. But she found the dramatized puns increasingly hard to take. She saw an actress jumping from one panel to another, and didn't get it until she saw that the panels had printing: CONCLUSION. Jumping to conclusions. Groan.

An actor came to stand at one side of the stage, and a mean-shaped cloud floated at the other side. It rumbled menacingly.

"Hello, Fracto Cumulo Nimbus," the man said.

The cloud turned darker.

The actor drew out a small package. "What, you want my C-ration?" he asked. "You can't eat it."

The cloud swelled, and a painted wooden lightning jag flew from it, followed by an explosive boom of thunder.

"Oh, very well; I'll cast it to you." The man tossed the package into the cloud.

The cloud took it in, then abruptly its rumble became a high-pitched squeal. It shrank as it fled.

Despite herself, Cynthia was intrigued. Food that denatured a cloud? It had to be a pun of some kind.

"Casth rachon!" Zilche cried. And of course she had gotten it: C-ration, cast to the cloud: cast-ration. It had unmanned Fracto, as it were.

Enough of this. "I found the Ring," Cynthia said, showing the band on her finger.

"Ouch! I zhuld havz lookedz!"

"No, that's all right. I think it was something only I could do. Now I must return to Castle Zombie."

Fortunately the play was wrapping up. All that remained were two actors made up as cats who were joined together by their common tail. "Ziameze catz!" Zilche exclaimed, getting it. She was actually quite good at charades, as Crone Latia had noted.

Zilche gave her report on the play, and the actors listened appreciatively. There would be some changes made.

Then they bid adieu to Crone Latia, and departed Gateway Castle. "I presume you wish to return to the Brain Coral's Pool," Cynthia said.

"Yez, pleze."

"With pleasure. I am glad you found something worthwhile in exchange for your assistance."

"Yez," the zombie agreed dreamily.

Cynthia returned Zilche to the pool, where she was welcomed, then set off for Castle Zombie. Alone, she had more occasion to ponder. A Ring that could summon a monster not seen in twenty years, and control other creatures of the sea—such amazing power! Yet it was only a little part of what was required to control the Swell Foop. What awful potential did that other device possess?

7
RING OF AIR

Sim looked for a suitable zombie, and quickly found it: a large bird. He promptly went to it. "Do you—" he squawked.

"What the ZZZZ do you want, you rotten excuse for wings?" the zombie screeched.

Oh, no! It was a zombie harpy! "Nothing," he squawked quickly.

"Oh, no you don't, Birdbrain! You're looking for a Ring, aren't you!"

What was worse, she understood him. He couldn't plead confusion. He was stuck for it. "Yes," he squawked. "I am Sim Bird."

"And I'm Garnishee Zombie," she screeched. "I know where the Ring of Air is."

"Then we had better fetch it," he agreed with regret.

"You won't like where it is," she screeched with malign satisfaction.

"Where is it?"

"Castle Maidragon."

Sim did a quick sort through his comprehensive avian memory. "The castle the three princesses made last year for Becka Dragon-girl."

"You got it, pipsquawk."

"Why shouldn't I like that? It's a very nice castle, and she's a nice girl."

"You'll be soo-ree, poop-for-brains!"

"Is it really necessary to be so offensive?" he squawked.

"Of course it is, stink-feather!" she screeched. "I'm a zombie harpy with a rotten disposition. It's my spoiled nature to be fowl-mouthed. Or hadn't you noticed, dullard?"

Sim knew himself to be dull neither in feather nor mind; in fact, he was the prettiest and smartest young bird in Xanth. Nevertheless, this ugly creature was beginning to get to him. So he drew on his mental power to handle it, making her seem to be a lovely bird with an endearing manner. Reversing impressions was a straightforward perceptive exercise that could be useful on occasion.

"Thank you for the clarification," he squawked.

"You are welcome, beautiful chick," she murmured dulcetly.

Mildly startled by his success, he glanced at her. She now resembled the historical figure Heavenly Harpy, the loveliest harpy ever. Her wings were shapely, her feathers bright, her face beautiful, and her bare bosom would have freaked out a human male. Sim realized that he had underestimated his own powers of reverse imagination.

"Let us go," he squawked.

"With pleasure," she agreed sweetly. "Though I must confess I feel slightly odd."

Was she catching on? "That's quite all right."

They spread their pretty wings and lofted upward. When they were at cruising elevation, they looped about and oriented on Castle Maidragon, which was not far as the crew flowed. Oops, his reversal was extending too far, messing up even his thoughts. As the crow flied. Flew. Whatever. Shades of the Demoness Metria!

He pumped his wings and zoomed onward.

"Please!" the dulcet voice came from behind. "I am unable to keep up with your magnificent strokes."

Oh, of course. No ordinary bird could pace Sim as he flew, and harpies were clumsier than birds, and zombies worse yet. He looped back, slowing his pace so that she could fly abreast.

Then, curious what she had really said, he did a spot mental translation: "Creep!" she had screeched. "Get your tail out of gear, stupid!"

On the whole, he preferred the euphemistic mode.

As they flew, slowly, he thought of something else. "How can the ageless Ring of Air be in a castle that was constructed only a year ago?"

"I fear that in heaven I am not required to know," she replied gently enough. But a tall branch of a tree they were flying over abruptly wilted, and he realized that it was not heaven she had actually invoked.

"Who controls that Ring?"

"Why, that is your illustrious mother, the Simurgh." A passing flock of whitebirds lost elevation as its V formation melted into an XXX formation. Exactly what twist had she given to the concept of "mother"?

"Then this must have occurred with her acquiescence," he squawked.

"She surely indulged in an eloquent preening," she agreed. A nearby cloud turned red, though it was neither sunrise nor sunset.

"Perhaps I can figure it out," he squawked, for he always liked a good riddle.

"You may do whatever you like, with whatever appendage is convenient, handsome avian," she agreed. A dark swirl of smoke appeared near her mouth, as the heat caused the air to burn explosively.

"I suspect it is this way," he squawked. "Castle Maidragon was made magically by the Three Little Princesses—Melody, Harmony, and Rhythm—in their adult guise as exists on the world of Ptero. Any single princess is a sorceress with great power of magic. Any two princesses working together square that power. When all three work together, that power is cubed. Therefore they brought a phenomenal focus of magic to bear on the project. This enabled them to conjure an entire castle from nothing, and to stock it with all manner of relevant artifacts. They must have liked the notion of having something invaluable in its storage vault, so conjured the Ring of Air from its natural location in the floating Nameless Castle. Perhaps Nimby and Chlorine were otherwise occupied at the time and so were not aware of its departure."

"Nimby and Chlorine were making love," she agreed. More smoke appeared, rising in a roiling ball that soon formed a mushroom-shaped cloud. The average harpy put a rather negative interpretation on that particular process.

Fortunately the highest pennant of Castle Maidragon now came into view. "We are almost there," he squawked, relieved.

She sent a sidelong glance his way. "But we were just beginning to speak of love," she murmured. "Must we end it so soon?"

He wasn't sure what she had actually said, but a nearby swarm of gnasty gnats abruptly collapsed into a heart-shaped swoon. That was more alarming than a smoke ball. Perhaps it was time to end his mental reversals, so he would not be confused when they entered the castle. He performed the mental correction.

"As soon as I obtain the Ring, our association can dissolve," he squawked.

"Too bad for you, puckerbeak!" Garnishee screeched. "You'll never know what a really hot piece of tail is."

Sim was destined to know all things, eventually, but he thought that he could afford to wait a century or two for that particular information.

They glided down toward the castle. A dragon appeared, and flew up to intercept them, stoking its fire. It had batlike wings, bright green purple-tipped scales, and an aggressive stare.

"Watch it, hotbox!" the harpy screeched. That hardly helped.

The dragon brought its snout around, readying its fire.

"Becka!" Sim squawked. "It's me, Sim!"

The dragon did a double-take, then nodded. It looped around and led the way down to the castle with a fine spiral.

When they landed, the dragon transformed into a human girl of about sixteen with blonde hair and brown eyes. "Sim!" she cried, running forward to hug him. "What are you doing keeping company with a zombie harpy?"

"I have to find the Ring of Air," he squawked. Because she knew him, she understood him. "Garnishee Zombie-Harpy knows where it is. She says it is at Castle Maidragon, so we came here."

Becka turned to the harpy. "Hello, Garnishee."

"Go ram a red-hot poker up your—"

"Harpies are hostile by nature," Sim squawked, drowning her out for the moment. "They don't mean anything by it."

"Yes we do!" the harpy screeched. "We mean it literally!"

"That's all right," Becka said. "I speak their language." She turned again to the zombie. "Up yours first, sidewise, twice, snotbrain!" she screeched.

Sim's beak dropped. Garnishee's eyes widened. "You're one of us!" she screeched, embracing the girl with her dirty wings.

Becka turned dragon just long enough to extricate herself, then went back to girl form. "No, I was possessed by the Sea Hag for a while. I learned something. None of it good, but I remembered."

"The Sea Hag! She is our goddess!"

"I'm sure. I never encountered a meaner spirit. Now where do you say this Ring is?"

"In the Forbidden Chamber."

There was half a silence. Then Becka turned to Sim. "That's a problem."

"I know it," Sim squawked. "She said I'd be sorry. I thought she was just being mean."

"I *was* being mean," Garnishee screeched indignantly.

"You mean it's not really there?"

"Of course it's really there. Now what are you going to do, smart behind?"

"I could get annoyed, if I really tried," Sim mutter-squawked. "It is not safe to open that door."

"It certainly isn't," Becka agreed. "Well, come on in, and we'll think about it. I don't receive compatible company often."

"Compatible!" Garnishee screeched, outraged.

"You excluded, of course, stench puss."

"That's better," the zombie agreed, mollified.

They crossed the drawbridge and entered the castle. It was well-kept inside, with all its halls, chambers, stairways, and incidental turrets clean. There was a smell of chocolate about it.

"What's that stink?" Garnishee demanded.

"The princesses liked to make little castles out of chocolate," Becka explained. "Then they would eat them. This is a real castle, but some of the blocks are chocolate. I don't know whether they forgot, or maybe it was just mischief. I try not to nibble on the blocks as I go by."

"What an ant warren," the zombie remarked, impressed.

"Yes, there are many by-paths," Becka agreed. "I love exploring them, though I am pretty well familiar with the castle by now. Sometimes I play a game, to see how many ways I can get from here to there without crossing any of the other routes. I don't suppose you folk will be staying the night?"

"Why should we stay even a minute, pee-hair?" Garnishee demanded.

Sim would have bitten his tongue, if he had teeth. The harpy never lost a chance to fashion an insult from innocuous material. The girl's hair was yellow, but not that shade.

"Just for nuisance value, buzzard-claw," Becka retorted.

"Flattery will get you nowhere," Garnishee screeched, obviously flattered.

"Let's explore options," Sim squawked. "As I recall, the Forbidden Chamber contains the Random Factor, who does unpredictable things to any folk opening that door."

"Such as exchanging their souls," Becka agreed. "And he doesn't seem to do the same thing twice, so the victims are stuck with whatever it is. It was really weird when he switched Princess Melody's soul for the Dastard's. She became worse than he was."

"That sounds nice," the zombie screeched, walking around.

"I wonder," Sim squawked. "You had a good view of the proceedings, as I remember."

"Yes. I *was* the castle, at the time. The princesses had transformed me into the castle. I was aware of every part of it."

"So you would know if there were any other chamber, perhaps containing a counter to the Factor."

"There isn't."

"What, then, is left?"

"I don't know. All I do know is that if you open that forbidden door, the Factor does something random that will probably mess you up. It's not safe to risk it unless you know exactly what you're doing."

"Factor," Sim repeated. "That can be taken as a mathematical term."

"Oh? How is that?"

For the first time, Sim appreciated the math lessons Che had forced on him. "A factor is one of two or more numbers or algebraic expressions that are multiplied together to produce a given result. For example, the number *12* may have factors *2* and *6,* or *3* and *4,* or *2* and *2* and *3.* Factoring is the effort to discover what numbers can be multiplied together to make the given number."

"Can all numbers be factored?" Becka asked.

"Not evenly, no. Numbers that can't be factored are called prime numbers. Such as *7*—it can be divided only by itself and *1.* Some primes are very large, and it is not at all easy to discover whether they can be factored, but until that possibility is eliminated, they can't be verified as primes."

"Say," she said. "Suppose you asked the Random Factor to factor a prime number? Would he do it?"

"Well, he couldn't factor a prime number, as I said."

"But would he try?"

Sim looked at her. "He would be very frustrated, if he didn't know it was prime. In fact, he might be out of commission for a while."

"And could you get the Ring of Air while he was distracted?"

Sim considered. The more he considered, the more promising it seemed. "I believe this is worth a try," he squawked. "Thank you."

"Just trying to help," she said, pleased.

"What do you think, Garnishee?" he asked. "Should we gamble on opening that door and feeding the Factor a riddle?"

There was no answer.

"Where is she?" Becka asked.

"She was here not long ago. Until we started talking about the Factor."

"You don't suppose she—?"

"I hope not!" he squawked. "That could be mischief!"

"Zombies are somewhat literal-minded."

"We had better check!"

They ran for the depths of the castle. Becka led the way, knowing it best. They sped through halls and almost tumbled down stairs. They came to the nethermost region just as the zombie harpy was reaching for the doorknob.

"No!" Sim squawked, half spreading his wings in an effort to intercept her. Becka was right beside him.

But Garnishee opened the door before they could stop her. They collided with her, and all three fetched up in a heap before the open doorway.

There was the dread Random Factor, looking like a giant golem. He gestured toward them.

Then they were in a doorless chamber with sheer walls and a decorated floor. There was nothing else.

"That was fun," Becka said, climbing out of the pile.

"A terrific experience," Sim squawked, drawing his left foot out of the zombie's mouth.

"A real joy," Garnishee agreed, untwisting a tangled arm.

"I could do it a million times," Becka said.

"And die a thousand deaths of mortification," Sim agreed, shaking out his wing-feathers.

"For a billion years," the zombie said.

Becka glanced at the door, which was now closed. "Let's get out of here before our friend does us another favor."

"The Factor is very accommodating of individual needs," Sim squawked.

"Especially considering how well we are acquainted," Garnishee said.

There was something odd about their dialogue, but Sim couldn't quite place it. He looked around. "There is no obvious exit. This chamber is like a prison."

"Or like a playpen," Becka agreed.

"Like a disaster," the zombie screeched.

"Something is wrong," Becka said. "We are not acting normal. It's not just this chamber."

"The Random Factor put us here," Sim squawked. "He affected us somehow. I suspect we won't be able to escape until we figure out what it is and how to counter it."

"I just want to get out of this place," Becka said. "Maybe if somebody boosts me up, I can get a hand on the top and climb over the wall."

"Perhaps I can fly out," Sim squawked. He spread his wings and tried to fly, but the chamber turned out to be too small for him to take off. He crashed back to the floor, rumpling his feathers. "Apparently not."

Becka helped him get back to his feet. "That's all right. You tried. And I guess if you can't fly out, I wouldn't be able to do it in dragon form, either."

"I think we shall have to figure it out mentally," Sim squawked. "Then perhaps the physical aspect will abate."

"All we're doing is standing here talking," Becka said.

"This thing is out to get us," Garnishee screeched.

"It's balking our efforts to escape," Becka agreed.

"And it's going to keep after us until we stop it," Sim squawked. And felt another twinge or two. Why were they so busy agreeing with each other?

"It's a monster," the harpy screeched.

"A giant worm, with us in its stomach," Becka agreed.

"A malign god playing with us," Sim agreed. "I think it is affecting the way we speak."

"You think so, beak?" Garnishee screeched.

"This is interesting, rainbow feather," Becka agreed.

"Indeed, brown eyes," he squawked. Then a bulb flashed. "Synecdoche!"

Both others stared at him. "Would you translate that, please?" Becka requested.

"Gladly. I believe I have figured out the riddle of our dialogue. Synecdoche is a figure of speech, wherein one employs the part for the whole, the special for the general, or vice versa. All three of us just used it: Garnishee called me beak, you called me rainbow feather, and I called you brown eyes. These are all parts of us, but we understood them to mean our persons. We have been speaking in figures of speech—when one of us does it, the others do too."

"But you're not doing it now," Becka said.

"I will demonstrate. I will use another figure of speech, metonymy, wherein a thing is named for one of its attributes, or names of related things are exchanged. See if you can avoid doing similar, dragon."

"Why should I, genius?"

"Yes, why should she, iridescence?" Garnishee screeched.

Then both of them paused, their glances nearly colliding. "We did do it," Becka breathed.

"I will try another. This time an oxymoron, wherein opposites are paired. I'm a smart dummy."

"And I'm a clean harpy," Garnishee screeched.

"I'm an ugly cutie," Becka said.

There was another pause as they recognized the syndrome.

"When one of us uses a figure of speech, so do the others," Becka said. "We can't help it."

"That's why we've been talking funny," Garnishee screeched. "But how do we stop it?"

"I suspect identification of the syndrome is the first step," Sim squawked. "And refusal to use any figures of speech must be the second. Identifying and refusing them all may nullify the spell."

"But we don't know anything about figures of speech," Beck said.

"Fortunately I do," Sim squawked. He rolled back his eidetic memory. "When this sequence started, we all used irony, pretending this was fun. Irony is the expressed reversal of one's real feeling. Then we used hyperbole, which is a gross exaggeration. Then we used irony again, and then simile, which is an explicit comparison. All figures of speech."

"Then we tried to escape physically," Becka said, reeling back her own memory. "And couldn't. And Garnishee said this thing was out to get us. Was that a figure of speech?"

"Certainly. That was personification, attributing an animate motive to an inanimate thing."

"Then I said it was a monster," Garnishee screeched. "What was that?"

"That was metaphor—an implied comparison. Then we got into synecdoche, as I said."

Becka nodded. "And finally oxymorons. It's a good thing my friend Mistress Man isn't here; she makes them literal."

"That must be some sight!" Garnishee screeched appreciatively.

"It can be," Becka agreed. "She's a pretty ugly stupid genius. Oops!"

There followed another relaxed siege of oxymorons as the others trailed the preceding example.

"So how do we stop it?" Becka asked when it cleared.

"I'm not sure," Sim squawked. "But I suspect that if we refuse to use any more figures of speech, the effect will fade."

"So we should shut our mouths, like good little—" Garnishee stifled herself in mid-simile.

"Exactly," Sim agreed. "Perhaps it will suffice simply to be silent for a sufficient period."

They were silent. Slowly the walls of the chamber faded, and the castle hall reappeared. The spell was wearing off, because of disuse. They had vanquished it.

"What can the Random Factor do to us, worse than that?" Becka asked.

"Well, there's one way to find out," Sim squawked. He walked to the door.

"No!" Becka cried, but she was too late. Sim got a wing behind the knob and managed to twist it and draw the door open.

There was the Random Factor, gesturing.

Suddenly they were standing in a deep forest. Something stirred just ahead of them. It was huge and green. In fact, it was a big tangle tree.

"Get out of here!" Sim squawked. But like Becka, he was too late. Myriad tentacles flicked out and coiled around all three of them. They were hauled into the main foliage of the tree.

"Here's another fine mess you've gotten us into!" Garnishee screeched.

"I'll turn dragon and get us out," Becka said. She changed form— but the dragon was just as securely bound as the girl had been. She exhaled fire, but the tentacles wrapped around her snoot, closing it.

"I'll curse us out," Garnishee said. She let fly a torrent of expletives that browned the tentacles holding her. But then another flicked in and circled her head, holding her mouth shut.

Sim did not like pulling rank, but this was an emergency. "Have you any idea who I am?" he demanded of the tree in an outraged squawk. "My mother is—"

Then a tentacle whipped around his beak, closing it.

All three of them were caught and gagged. They could neither fight nor protest. Meanwhile, the tangle tree was opening its huge wooden maw, considering which of them to eat first.

It decided on Sim. It carried him inward. He tried to struggle, but succeeded only in jostling loose one feather. The wind caught it and blew it away. He tried to squawk in protest, but all that emerged was one muffled peep. The maw loomed hugely, dripping digestive sap.

Then it halted. Sim dangled just beyond the wooden teeth, unable to fathom the delay.

A huge hairy ham-hand appeared. It grabbed the twisted tentacles holding Sim and squeezed. They quickly became green pulp, and Sim dropped to the ground, the severed tentacles writhing off him like headless snakes.

Someone had rescued him! Sim turned to look at his benefactor— and saw an ogre.

But beside the ogre was a lovely young nymph, and she was holding a little boy. The boy had aspects of both ogre and nymph; they were evidently a family. But why had they intervened to save Sim?

Then he saw the feather in the little hand of the boy. Like all of Sim's feathers, it scintillated with twice the colors of the rainbow. Evidently it had blown their way, and the child had been intrigued by it. So they had come to see what was what.

"My, you are a pretty one," the nymph said somewhat shallowly, as was typical of her kind.

"I am Sim," he squawked. "I thank you for rescuing me from the tangle tree."

The ogre shrank into the form of a man. "I am Smash Ogre," he said. "This is Tandy Nymph, my wife, and Esk, our son."

Sim was for the moment squawkless. He knew this family—but the adults were in their late fifties, and the child was in his late thirties and married to a brassie woman. How could they be so young?

Unless—

"What year is this?" Sim squawked.

"Why, it is the year Ten-sixty-six, of course," Smash said.

Sim's smart mind clicked through ancient dates. That was two years after Smash and Tandy had married, and one year before Magician Dor married Princess Irene. "We got displaced in time!" he squawked.

"Yes, Smash caught you just in time," Tandy agreed. "I thought it would be a shame to see such a beautiful bird eaten, so I asked him to do something about it."

And so, either by pure chance, or to spare future Xanth a paradox, the ogre family had come just in time to rescue him. But how had they traveled backward in time? Probably the Random Factor had simply fed them into a magical wormhole that popped them out in a random time. That was certainly an effective way to get rid of them.

Sim realized that they were still standing amidst the quivering tentacles of the tangle tree. "You can cow a tangler just by your presence?"

"Well, Smash is a real ogre when he gets worked up," she said. "And I can throw a mean tantrum when I get worked up. The tree knows that, so it leaves us alone. A cow wouldn't scare it, but an ogre family can. We wouldn't have interfered, except for the feather."

Little Esk waved the bright feather, liking it.

Sim realized that he had been uncommonly fortunate. The Random Factor had sent them back thirty-five years, to a time before any of them had existed. It could have been worse, if the ogre family had not seen the feather.

But the others were still tied up. "Would you do me a favor?" he squawked. "I have two companions who are also caught by the tree, and I would like to save them."

They considered. "Are they worth saving?" Tandy asked.

"Certainly. One is Becka Human, who—" He realized that it might not be expedient to identify the girl. The complications of Castle Maidragon and the Random Factor would be anachronistic at best. "The other is—" He stalled again. Since when was a harpy worth saving?

"Har-pee!" little Esk exclaimed, spying the dirty bird.

"Yes, that is a harpy," Smash said. "They can wilt foliage with their swearing."

"Gee!" the child said, smiling.

Sim tried to make the best of this. "They can also make a nymph blush. I'm sure she will be happy to demonstrate, if you wish."

Smash walked to where the harpy was hanging. "Give," he said, not loudly.

The tentacles let go. Garnishee dropped to the ground, bashing her tail. "**XXXX!**" she swore. Sure enough, Tandy blushed, and the grass wilted. Little Esk clapped his hands with delight.

"And my other companion is a nice young woman," Sim squawked.

Smash walked to where Becka hung bound. "Give."

But this time the tree balked. This was, after all, the most delectable of the three. It did not want to give up such a morsel. Instead it started swinging Becka toward its maw.

Smash swelled up into full ogre stature, but Tandy acted first. She nestled Esk in the crook of her left elbow, and made a throwing motion with her right arm. Sim didn't see anything leave her hand, but suddenly the tentacles around Becka straightened out as if electrified, and so did Becka's hair as she dropped to the ground. The tantrum had struck.

"Uh, thank you," Becka said, disheveled.

"The pretty bird asked," Tandy said.

"Maybe we can do you a favor in return," Becka said.

Smash shrugged as he returned to man form. "Probably not. The only thing we lack is knowledge of our son's magic talent."

Sim strained his copious memory, but apparently that bit of information had not yet been entered into his database. "We will try to figure it out," he squawked.

"Oh, thank you!" the nymph exclaimed, throwing him a kiss with her fingers. It smacked against his beak, sinking in pleasantly.

They walked to the ogre's den. By tacit agreement, none of the three time travelers spoke of their origins. Instead they focused on little Esk.

"It may not be a fancy talent," Beck said cautiously.

"That's all right," Smash said. "We're not fancy folk. We just want to know, whatever it is."

Tandy set Esk down in his playpen, where he tried to break out but lacked the strength. So obviously he wasn't much of an ogre in terms of strength. He was looking around brightly, so he wasn't much of an ogre intellectually, either; ogres had always been justifiably proud of their stupidity. He was a halfway-middling handsome lad, so wasn't suitably ugly, either.

So what could his talent be? He had to have one, because every person with any human component did. Some talents were so simple as to be hardly worth it, like forming a magical smudge on a wall or changing the color of one's own urine. Others were so powerful as to be scary, such as transforming others into other forms, as was the case with Magician Trent. Most were in the broad, dull, middle range, such as, well, Becka's ability to turn girl or dragon.

"Maybe he can change form," Sim squawked.

"Try this," Becka said, and turned dragon.

Esk tried, but did not manage to change into a dragon.

"It doesn't have to be a dragon," Sim squawked. "It could be to anything else. A crow, an ant, even a plant." But still no luck.

"Or an intellectual talent," Becka offered. "Such as having magical intuition, knowing about things better than others do." But if Esk had that, he didn't show it. "I guess that's limited to women," Becka added intuitively.

"Still, there could be other intellectual talents," Sim squawked. "Like maybe being able to decipher any code." He tried to think of a code that a two-year-old might tackle, but for once his super bird brain failed him. In any event Esk was looking blankly at him, so that probably wasn't it.

"Or to intimidate anything," Smash suggested hopefully. He made an ogre face. A low-flying cloud saw that, and hastily scudded out of the way, intimidated, but Esk just yawned. He didn't seem to be much on intimidation, either way.

"Or to hide anything so not even Jenny's cat can find it," Garnishee screeched.

"Who is Jenny?" Tandy asked.

Oops—Jenny would not exist in Xanth for another three decades. "Just someone with a clever cat," Sim squawked.

"But he's not good at finding things," Smash said. "He loses his marbles all the time."

"Enough of this feline-footing!" Garnishee screeched. "If he doesn't show a talent this instant, I'll kiss him."

Esk gazed at her with horror. Small wonder; it was a dire threat.

"So where's your magic?" the zombie harpy screeched, leaning down over the playpen to kiss him.

"No," Esk said.

"Well, maybe not," she agreed. "Maybe I'll just stroke you with my fowl wing." She stretched forth a wing.

"No."

"Or not," she agreed. "Maybe I'll just tell you a nice nursery story of bloodshed, mayhem, and betrayal. Once there was a sickly sweet pretty little princess who loved a hateful ugly troll who wanted only to butcher and cook and eat her. So she sneaked out—"

"No."

"Well, it's not much of a story, because she escapes, and after that she listens to her parents. Still, it has a nice wrinkle when she falls naked into a den of starving nickelpedes and—"

"No."

"Stop stopping me from telling my story!" she screeched, frustrated. "I haven't even gotten to the part where the harpies catch her and make her clean out their hutches with her tongue, and—"

"No."

"But—"

A lightbulb flashed over Sim's head. "He can say 'No'! That's his talent."

The others looked blank. "Anyone can say no," Tandy said. "It's an easy word."

"But he means it. Try doing something he doesn't like."

"Well, he doesn't like a bath. Of course it hasn't been convenient recently."

"Because he said no," Sim squawked. "Try it now."

Tandy brought out a tub. "Time for your bath, Esk," she said.

"No."

"You're right, it's not time," she agreed. "In fact, it's never time, these last few weeks." Then she paused. "It's true! He's been doing it all along!"

"That could be another reason the tangle tree stopped," Becka said. "Maybe he told it no."

"Yes," Esk agreed smugly.

"We've found your talent!" Smash cried. "And it's a good one." Then he considered. "I wonder if it works to stop other things you don't like, such as being confined in a playpen."

A little bulb flashed over Esk's head. He took hold of the playpen bars again. "No." And pushed on through; they had not been able to balk him.

"I wish you hadn't thought of that," Tandy murmured.

"I'm an ogre. I do stupid things."

"So you do." She kissed him. "Like loving me. I'm glad the night mare brought me to you."

"Me too," Smash agreed. They embraced. Little hearts appeared, circling them. She had evidently forgiven him.

Esk paused in his exploration of the great outside, turning slightly green. He was jealous of too much affection that wasn't shown directly to him. He opened his mouth.

"Better not," Becka said in a singsong voice. "Where will you be, if they stop loving each other?"

Esk thought about that long and hard. Finally he nodded, and went on with his explorations. He forged toward a nettle bush. It readied a nettle for him, but changed its mind when he told it no.

"I think we have repaid them for rescuing us," Sim squawked. "Now how do we get home?"

"You can't just walk home?" Smash asked.

"It was a very devious route," Becka said. "I think we can't return the way we came."

That stumped them, until Tandy thought of something. "How about reverse wood?"

"Well, that does not reverse time," Sim squawked before he thought.

"It reverses things all the time," Smash said. "We have some we use against hostile magic. You are welcome to borrow it."

"I wonder," Becka said, "if it could reverse the Factor's spell."

"Why not?" Garnishee screeched.

"Then again, maybe it wood. I mean would," Sim squawked, reconsidering. "Certainly we could try it."

Smash brought out a little bundle of chips. He carried it carefully by a string so that it did not touch him. "You do have to be careful with this stuff," he said. "You never can tell what it will do. But usually it reverses the effect of magic."

"We'll try it," Sim squawked.

Smash dropped the bag. It fell open, letting chips spread out. They stood around it, then each person picked up a chip at the same time.

Suddenly they were going backward. They were reversing what they had just been doing. Soon they were running backward toward the tangle tree, and getting caught up in it. "!eyb-eyB," Esk cried, waving a chubby arm as the ogre family retreated from the tree. At least, that was the way Sim heard it.

Before (or after) long they were standing before the tree, and then they were back in Castle Maidragon, and Sim was closing the door with his wing. They were back, and the reverse wood was gone.

"We're back," Becka breathed, visibly relieved.

"That was scary," Garnishee said, for once forgetting to screech. "Let's not do it again."

"But I haven't gotten the Ring of Air," Sim squawked. "I can't depart until I have completed my mission."

"Look, you blithering moronic fool of an idiot!" the harpy screeched. "That randy factor changes our bleeping reality every time we open that door! Are you too dim to get the message? DON'T OPEN THAT DOOR!!"

Becka nodded agreement. "When Princess Melody and the Dastard opened that door, there was inferno to pay. She lost her soul."

"I remember. I know it is dangerous. But I have to get that Ring."

The girl and the harpy exchanged a look of rare mutual understanding. "Maybe you should get out of range before the next siege," Garnishee screeched quietly to her. "After all, you're responsible for the maintenance of Castle Maidragon."

"And all things in it," Becka agreed. "But I don't think I can desert a visitor in need, especially when his errand is important. So I think I will just have to take the risk, though it terrifies me."

"It scares the undead poop out of me," the zombie harpy agreed. "But what's gotta be done, gotta be done."

Sim realized that these frightened females were in their fashion supporting him. They were showing true courage and honor. He was frightened too, but they were shaming him into courage of his own.

Courage and honor. Suddenly he had a notion. "I think the Random Factor has the Ring of Air," he squawked. "And that all I have to do is take it from him. All I have to do is reach him and demand it. Because I am the designated Ring Holder. I believe I can do this alone, so you ladies need not expose yourselves to further mischief."

"Ladies!" Garnishee screeched derisively. "I'm a *harpy*! Well, actually, a zombie. Not a lady."

"And I'm a girl," Becka said. "Actually, a dragon. Not a lady."

"It requires more than lineage or age to make a lady," Sim squawked. "It takes character. Both of you are filling the role. But there is no need for you to risk yourselves further. Go elsewhere in the castle while I brace the Random Factor again."

This time they didn't bother to exchange glances. "No," they said almost together. "You may need us."

Sim nodded. "Then I hope I do not bring disaster upon you both. I must brace the Random Factor and take the Ring from him, whatever the cost."

"My turn," Becka said. She opened the door. This time she put her foot in place so that the door could not automatically close.

The Factor was there. He gestured. Sim suffered a moment of disorientation. Then the scene clarified. He was standing in the doorway, his foot bracing it open. The Factor remained in place, unmoving, evidently waiting for them to open the door again, not realizing that it hadn't closed.

There was a squawk behind him. Sim looked—and saw himself, with a crazed look on his beak. Beside him stood Garnishee, looking quite startled.

His foot was in the door? Sim glanced down, and saw a nicely formed human leg with a delicate slipper. *He was in Becka's body!*

"I think I know the source of your confusion," he said. "We have exchanged bodies. I am Sim."

"I am Becka," the zombie harpy said.

"I am Garnishee," Sim's body squawked.

"Because Becka had the wit to brace the door open, it can't close," Sim said. "It seems that the Random Factor's actions are triggered by the opening of the door. It can't open because it hasn't yet closed, and the Factor is in stasis. We are for the moment in command of the situation."

"In the wrong bodies!" the harpy body cried.

"I think that can be rectified in a moment. Please, one of you come brace this door open so I can go to the Factor."

They didn't question this. Both came forward and wedged their bodies into the doorway, forcing the door farther open. When Sim was sure it was secure, he removed his—Becka's—foot and walked up to the still figure. "I have come to take what is mine," he said. He looked at the Factor's hands, and sure enough, there was an air-colored Ring on one little finger. Sim used Becka's hands to hold the Factor's hand and pry off the Ring. He put it on his—her—own little finger, where it fit nicely. "Thank you."

"Did you get it?" the harpy body called anxiously.

"I did." Sim approached them. "I am uncertain how to use this Ring, so may fumble at first, but please bear with me." He lifted the hand bearing the Ring. "O Ring of Air, I invoke you," he said. "You command the creatures of air. We are three creatures of air—a harpy, a winged dragon currently in girl form, and a big bird. Return us to our proper bodies."

There was another brief disorientation. Then he found himself jammed next to the zombie harpy, wedging the door open. Before them stood Becka. "You did it!" she said. "But I think I have something of yours." She removed the Ring from her little finger and handed it to him.

"But I don't have a finger," he squawked.

"You have a toe, dummy!" Garnishee screeched.

True. Sim lifted his left foot, and Becka slid the Ring over the claw and onto his smallest toe. The Ring settled comfortably into place, exactly the right size. "Thank you," he squawked.

"Let's just get out of here," Becka said anxiously.

"You two get out; I will hold the door."

They didn't argue. They squeezed by him into the hall. Then Sim squeezed through too, leaving only his foot in place. Then he jerked out that foot, and the door swung closed. They were safe and in their own bodies.

"That Ring has a lot of power," Becka said.

"Yes. And now my portion of this mission is accomplished. I will take the Ring and meet with the others."

"And I'll return to Castle Zombie," Garnishee screeched sadly.

"You don't wish to go?" Becka asked.

"Well, it wasn't much of a life being a harpy, and it's not much of a death being a zombie. All that kept me going was my role as a locator of a Ring of Xanth. Now that's done and I have no further use. Some other zombie will do it once it gets hidden again, so that no living person will know where it is. It was sort of fun being part of an adventure. Now there's nothing."

"You know, you're a winged monster," Becka said. "So am I, in my other form. Sometimes I would like to fly far, like maybe to see my father Draco Dragon, but I can't because that would leave Castle Maidragon unattended. But if there were someone else to watch it—"

"I don't understand," the harpy screeched.

"Yes you do," Sim squawked. "She is asking you to stay here and help guard the castle from intruders. That would be a useful task, so you would have something to give your half-life meaning."

"But nobody wants a zombie nearby." She was plainly touched, as she forgot to screech again.

"Well, maybe I had a little prejudice against zombies," Becka said. "But I have gotten to know you, and we have worked together to help find the Ring of Air. I think I could stand you, and I could use some help. It gets sort of quiet here, between visitors."

"It's never quiet around a harpy!" Garnishee screeched.

"Precisely."

Sim saw that they had worked it out. "I can find my own way back," he squawked.

They escorted him outside. He spread his wings and took off, satisfied in more than one respect.

8
SEARCH

Breanna of the Black Wave ran to hug Justin Tree as he returned with his Ring. "I got mine; you got yours!" she exclaimed happily. "Now we'll get married."

"I fear not yet," he said.

"Not yet?" she demanded dangerously, a black cloud forming over her brow. "Just as soon as the others return, we'll have all the Rings."

"It seems that there are six Rings of Xanth, and only five members of our party. We will be short one Ring."

"Short one Ring!" she repeated. The black cloud swelled up dangerously, emitting a warning peal of thunder. Castle Zombie shook on its sloshy foundation.

Cynthia Centaur trotted up. "He is correct," she said. "There are six Rings. There must be one more zombie, and none of us can go for a second Ring."

Lightning jags poked out from the cloud. "*What* zombie?" Breanna demanded, swinging her dark gaze around.

A zombie horse perked up his ears. A dreamlet formed, showing a slightly sloppy speech balloon. "That would be me," the balloon wrote.

"I don't remember you, horserump," Breanna said. "Who are you?"

"I am Palus Putredinus the zombie night colt, knower of the Ring of Void. No Ring Seeker has approached me."

Breanna realized that they had all overlooked the obvious: They needed a sixth person. The job was not yet done. "Do you have any idea who that Ringer might be?" she asked, her cloud dissipating as she accepted the inevitable further delay.

Another speech balloon dreamlet appeared. "Only that this person must be a dreamer, for this Ring controls all dream things."

Breanna looked around. All the others were now present, with their Rings. All looked blank.

"Then I guess it's up to me," she said. "We'll go ask the lord of dreams, the Night Stallion."

"But Breanna, you know you can't seek a second Ring," Justin protested.

She grabbed him and planted a hard kiss on his mouth. Then, as he stood stunned, she answered: "I'm not seeking a second Ring, wood-for-brains. I'm seeking the identity of the sixth Ring holder. That's the one who will seek the Ring of Void."

"But I can't go there," the zombie night colt speech-ballooned.

"Why the bleep not?" she demanded. "It's your bleeping Ring, Putre!"

"That is a moderately complicated story."

"Tell it as we travel," she said. She vaulted onto his back. "If you can't go all the way there, you can at least deliver me to the next-door address." She slapped him on the flank, and he bolted. It was in the equine book of rules that they had to bolt when flanked.

The colt leaped forward. Breanna saw the surprised faces of the others. Then they were gone, as the horse galloped through the forest. That was literal, for he was a creature of dreams; only the fact that he was a zombie made him solid enough to support her, and only because she had a certain authority over zombies.

"It is like this," his dreamlet speech balloon wrote. It was easy to read, because it actually appeared in her head, only seeming to be in front of her face. "Some time back, Mare Imbrium salvaged half a soul, and failed to turn it in to the Night Stallion. This gave her a conscience, and she was no longer able to properly punish sleepers with bad dreams. So she became a day mare, carrying good daydreams, and later a tree nymph."

"I know all that," Breanna said. "Mare Imbri's my friend."

"But perhaps you do not know this: During her tenure as a day mare, bringing nice dreams to good folk, she had a relationship with the Day Stallion and took delivery of a foal. Thus it was that I traveled from the realm of Ptero to the realm of dreams. Unfortunately there is little place for male equines in the dream realm; they are routinely abolished. She tried to hide me, but in time the Night Stallion discovered my existence and struck me with a dream bolt and destroyed my life. But Imbri had given me part of her soul, so I didn't fade out entirely. She really respects the power of a soul. She took my remnant to the Zombie Master, and he not only zombied me, he made me the knower of the Ring of Void. That protected me from further assault. But the Night Stallion harbors a grudge, and should I ever come into his domain, he will strike me again and this time certainly destroy me, and some other zombie will inherit the knowing of the Ring."

Breanna realized that the zombie had a case. "I never knew Imbri had a foal."

"She does not bruit it about, for fear it will bring me mischief. We never thought a need for the Ring would come so soon. Now I must do my duty, but I must try to avoid the Night Stallion."

Breanna pondered, then came to a decision. "No. I'm in a hurry and I need your help, and the Ring Holder will need it too. This mission is too important to let it get hung up because of a hang-up by the Night Stallion. I will try to protect you."

"There is no protection from the lord of dreams. Not for a dream creature."

"This may be an exception. Let's give it a try."

"I am not able to defy you, for you are becoming mistress of zombies. But I fear you are leading me to destruction."

"Well, I hope not. Take me directly to the Night Stallion."

Putre shuddered, but then veered to the side where a hypo-no gourd was growing. He made a special leap, right into the gourd. That seemed impossible, but she saw it happen; they passed right through its expanding peephole. Suddenly they were in some kind of cave—and there before them stood the Night Stallion. She recognized him immediately, though she had never seen him before; he was a magnificent horse of another color.

This was of course a dream, but it seemed uncannily real, the way dreams did. So she dismounted and plunged in. "Hello, Trojan. I am Breanna of the Black Wave. I have come to—"

"What is this miscreant doing here?" Trojan demanded. He seemed to be speaking, but probably he was just projecting his thoughts into her mind. It hardly mattered.

"This is Putre, who brought me here. Leave him alone. Now about my mission—"

"I will destroy him!" The Night Stallion brought his terrible gaze around to bear on the colt.

"No you don't, Trojan!" Breanna said. "I said I'd protect him, and I will. Let him be."

The gaze swung like a cannon to bear on her. She would never admit it, but the Night Stallion was a terrifying apparition. "By what power do you seek to oppose my will in my domain, black girl?"

"By the force of logic, and the need of Xanth," she said more stoutly than she felt. "And by this." She lifted her left hand to show the Ring of Fire on her little finger.

Trojan stared at it. As if in response, the Ring sent out a coruscating little loop of fire.

"That is the Ring of Fire," Trojan said. "How came you by it?"

"It's a long story, Stallion. Why don't you just take my word that we also need the Ring of Void, and let it go at that?"

"Then again, perhaps it is a fake." Trojan swung back to Putre. His eyes turned deadly.

Help, Breanna thought to the Ring.

There was a cloud of smoke. In a moment it coalesced into the Demon Professor Grossclout. "It is the Ring," the Professor said through his glare. "This girl has important business. Sim Bird is part of it, by leave of his mother and nanny; indeed, he holds the Ring of Air."

Trojan paused, then nodded. The Night Stallion, like all the major figures of Xanth, was sworn to protect and support the Simurgh's chick. "So I see. I will postpone this matter for the duration."

"Thank you." Grossclout faded out.

Breanna was impressed in spite of herself. Evidently the Demon Professor had been watching, or was attuned to the Ring of Fire, or both. Certainly he had made the difference; no one had ever defied him and survived to speak of it. Except maybe D. Metria, but she didn't count.

"So what is your business?" the Night Stallion inquired, suddenly ignoring Putre.

"The Demon Earth has been abducted, we think, and we need to get the Swell Foop to rescue him."

The dark horse gazed at her for more than an instant. "You already have the other Rings of Xanth?"

"Yes. One person per Ring. But we need to find out who is to go after the Ring of Void, and we think you are the one who will know."

"This may be complicated. You were supposed to have six persons in your Ring group."

"We forgot," Breanna said, embarrassed.

"Normally you would fetch the Six Rings of Xanth, then select one of your number to fetch the Foop."

"We'll still do that, once we have the sixth Ring."

"No. Normally your sixth member would fetch that Ring."

"I know that," Breanna said, getting edgy. "First we have to *find* that sixth member. That's why I'm here."

The Stallion flashed her a glance of impatience. "Because you did not bring a sixth member, who would have oriented on the sixth Ring, you have forfeited that choice. Now you must orient directly on the Swell Foop."

"I don't understand."

"Fortunately I do. Your sixth member must select himself by naming the Swell Foop. Then you must recruit him for the mission, and he must fetch the Ring of Void. Because of your prior dereliction you will not be able to discuss this in advance; you must have that particular person, or all is lost."

Breanna gulped. "But what if he doesn't want to do it?"

"That is why it would have been better to have had six in your group at the start; you would have known that all were committed. Now you must take the chance that your designated sixth member is not committed. The Rings respond to the sense of mission; that is why each of you had no trouble taking them, once you located them. This new person must develop that sense of mission. You must gamble on your persuasive abilities."

Breanna thought of Justin. "I can be persuasive when I have to be."

The Night Stallion looked down his long nose at her. She didn't like that, because it made her feel exactly as stupid as she thought she was. "The designated sixth may not be romantically inclined. In fact, he can be any creature. Suppose he is a dragon? An ogre? A cockatrice?"

This was looking worse. "I'll summon a demon if I have to, to help persuade him."

"You may have to. In fact, he may *be* a demon. I hope you succeed."

"Yeah, sure," she said wryly. Actually, she was pretty sure it wouldn't be a demon, because demons weren't mortal.

"I have no interest in seeing Xanth destroyed by lack of gravity."

"For sure. We've got too many puns already."

He did not smile. "Now we must explore the dreams of the universe. The first who names the Swell Foop will be your designee."

"Got it," she agreed, gulping again. Why *hadn't* they thought to have a compatible sixth member? She had any number of friends who would surely have served. Now they had to take whatever fate offered, and it might not be fun at all. A cockatrice, whose very glance was poisonous? Anything but that!

"I am instituting the search of dreams. I regret that I am unable to search waking thoughts; those are not my department."

"Wait half a moment! How about day dreams?"

The Stallion paused half a moment. "Those belong to the Day Stallion."

"But we've got a representative here. Putre is the foal of the Day Stallion."

Trojan glanced at the zombie colt, who had been very quiet since obtaining his reprieve. "Very well; a broader search is best. Let him add his input, and it will include day dreams."

Breanna patted Putre on the shoulder. "See—you're useful already."

"Thank you," his speech balloon wrote.

The search started. The chamber faded out, and they seemed to be in the center of a swirling universe. Voices came from near and far, all saying the same two words, but not together. "Swell." There were thousands of those. "Foop." There were only a few of those. It had to be the combination, in the right order.

The search ranged out, extending to the very fringe of Xanth. Then it fixed on one "Swell Foop!" A picture of the speaker formed: Cynthia Centaur, snoozing during the wait for Breanna's return, dreaming of her mission. That was no good; she was already committed to the Ring of Water.

The search resumed. Now it went beyond Xanth, into drear Mundania. Breanna's heart sank to the bottom of her chest. That was all they needed: a Mundane! Not that all of them were bad; she rather liked Edsel and Pia. But neither of them could do this; they were too busy with the environment, not to mention their new baby.

"Swell foop!" A second strike. The picture formed, establishing the context.

It was a girl of about fifteen, having a daydream. "I want it all in one swell foop, I mean fell swoop!" she exclaimed, laughing.

The swirling background faded. "There is your designee," the Night Stallion said.

"But she was only joking, making a play on words," Breanna protested.

"That does not matter. She dreamed the words."

"But I don't even know where she is. Mundania's a pretty big place. I ought to know; I lived there once."

"I can locate her," Putre's balloon wrote. He concentrated. "She is Jaylin, in Hawaii, Mundania."

"Hawaii! That's halfway around the world from the Xanth portal!"

Trojan nodded. "You had better get on it, before gravity fades."

Breanna sighed. "A trip to Mundania! That's all I needed, on my wedding day." But she knew it had to be done. "I'll have to get Mundane help. I don't even have a Mundane identity anymore."

"I suggest you gather some magic dust to take with you. The Rings of Xanth are self-powered and will work anywhere, but for any other magic you will need more. That may enable you to invoke a spell in an emergency."

"For sure! Thanks." She turned to Putre. "Let's go."

"I will tell the Day Stallion to send a mare with a dream of your coming," Trojan said.

That set her back. "A dream to whom?"

"The Baldwin family. They live near the portal."

"Oh—Sean and Willow," she said, remembering. "Yes, that makes sense. Thanks."

The zombie horse carried her rapidly out of the dream and on to

Centaur Island, and to the portal there. He knew about it because the day mares used it for day dreams destined for Mundania; Mare Imbri had told him. That was as far as he could go; he would have no reality in Mundania. "Thanks," she said. "You've been a big help so far, and we'll need you later to find the Ring."

"I will be here," he agreed. "But first, you must fetch some magic dust."

"That's right! I had forgotten." She foraged, putting some dust in the change purse of her handbag, which she no longer used for change. She should have thought to get some of the really intense dust from the Region of Madness, as that had many times the potency of dirt here at the fringe of the peninsula. But it could be complicated getting out of the Region of Madness with one's sanity, no pun. This would have to do.

Then she passed through the portal and was in Mundania. She looked back, and saw that she had just stepped out of a picture hanging on a wall. That was interesting! But she didn't have time to admire the effects; she needed to get her mission done.

She was in a house, and it seemed to be empty at the moment. That was all right; she wasn't here for any social call. She made her way outside.

"Yo!" a young man called. He had green eyes and blond hair, and looked to be about seventeen.

"You know me?" she inquired cautiously.

"Never saw you before in my life, dusky maiden," he said cheerfully. "But if you're from Xanth, I'm here for you."

Still she hesitated, not trusting white-skinned Mundane teens. "Who are you and what do you want from me?"

"Fair enough. I'm David Baldwin. I was listening to music, just sort of drifting, and this notion came to me about a beautiful black sweetheart coming from Xanth to travel somewhere with me. After what my brother Sean found in Xanth, I just had to follow up."

"What did your brother find in Xanth?"

He shook his head. "I've told you more than enough to identify me. Now you tell me enough to identify you."

She considered, and concluded that this was fitting. Obviously he knew of Xanth, and had received an advisory daydream. "I am Breanna of the Black Wave, and your brother found Willow, the flying elf, and they fell in love. Now they visit Xanth and fly together. And that's not all. He has seen her—" She paused, waiting for his response.

"Panties!" he exclaimed. "Okay, honey, you're for real. Get in my car."

It had been a long time since she had been in a Mundane car, but memories were flooding back. Mundania did have its advantages, she had to admit.

David started the motor and drove out onto the highway that connected the chain of islands that was all that remained of Centaur Isle in Mundania. She saw the enormous sea on either side, and was duly impressed. "These are the—the Keys," she said, with another effort of memory. "Only they don't lock doors. And the portal is on No Name Key."

"Right. Many folk think it doesn't exist. But it does. When we crossed, it was right here, in a storm."

"A storm," she agreed. "Hurricane Happy Bottom."

"Only on this side it was Tropical Storm Glad Ass—I mean Gladys. It was weird at first; we looked out and saw a centaur. It took the parents some time to believe it, even with it right there before their eyes. But Mom took note when the first female centaur trotted up. I was twelve; I'd never seen architecture like that before. Not in living flesh, I mean."

Breanna was remembering the restrictive attitudes of Mundanes toward things like bare breasts. It was all coming back. Centaurs had no hang-ups about body parts or natural functions. "Nymphs and trotting centaur fillies—your mother would have had a fit."

"Yeah, she did. Didn't show it, though. But by the time we got home, she was getting used to Xanth." He glanced sidelong at her. "So are you going to show me yours?"

She understood him perfectly. But she needed his help, so she set him down politely. "I am betrothed, and soon to be married to the man I love. I am here purely on business."

He tried manfully to mask his disappointment. "So the part of the dream about traveling with me—it's like riding in my car. Nothing else."

"You got it, David. But if it's any consolation, my mission is extremely important, and you might consider it a privilege to be a part of it."

"What I'd like is a pass to Xanth, the kind that Sean got."

"I'll see what can be done."

"Thanks. So exactly what *is* this mission?"

"I don't know how much I should tell you. I guess it depends on how much you're going to help."

"And how shut I can keep my mouth? You know, we don't talk much about Xanth, outside of the house, because nobody'd believe us, and anyway we don't want to get Willow in trouble. But my little sister Karen sure would like to go there again, and so would I. Why don't you tell the parents, and then we'll see who helps you how much."

"Fair deal," she agreed.

In due course they left the highway and the sea, and proceeded through the complicated city of Miami. At last they came to the Baldwin home. David ushered her inside. "This is Breanna of Xanth," he announced. "She's here on business, and needs our help."

"You're in the Xanth Xone!" a girl of twelve exclaimed. She had red hair and blue eyes and seemed to be full of energy. That would be the little sister.

"Yes, I have a leaf in the Magic Mesh of the O-Xone," Breanna agreed. "It's sort of an interface with Mundania."

"I am Jim Baldwin," the man said. "This is my wife Mary, and our daughter Karen. Sean and Willow live separately, and you have already met David. How can we help you?"

Breanna told them enough of it so that they understood the importance of her mission. "So I have to go fetch Jaylin in Hawaii. I'm not sure how to do that. I was nine years old when I left Mundania, and I have no money or identification. But I have to get this done, because if gravity starts fading—"

"We understand completely," Jim said. "I think it will be best if David takes you there. He likes to travel, and it will be good experience."

"With such a nice young woman," Mary murmured. "From Xanth."

"Mom, she's got a fiancé," David said, pained. "She's not like Willow."

"She has no wings," Mary agreed.

Breanna usually had something to say on anything, but she was blank for the moment. This family wasn't aware of color? Maybe it was being studiously polite. But she had better make sure. "It's been half my life, but I have some pretty clear memories of Mundania. In my day a white boy did not travel much with a black girl. Has that changed?"

"Not enough," Jim said. "The identification may be the greater problem, however. But I think it can be managed, if the parties are circumspect."

"Like pretending I'm a foreign princess and he's my translator?"

They all laughed, but not with any force. "You willing?" David asked.

"Yes. Anything to get this job done efficiently and get home in a hurry."

"Then let me set you up," Mary said.

She took Breanna to her bedroom where she quickly adapted a black dress and jacket and cap to fit. "Your fiancé," she said as she worked. "Would we know of him?"

"I don't know. He was a tree when you were in Xanth." She explained about Justin Tree and their relationship.

"Why, that's charming," Mary said. Then she got down to serious business. "David and Karen long to return to Xanth, at least for a visit, but only Sean has a pass. Do you think, if your mission is successful—?"

"I know a woman called Chlorine. She has Nimby's ear. You know about Nimby?"

"We traveled with them both. He is a donkey-headed dragon—and rather more, we learned later."

"Much more. I think maybe they'd go for it. I'll ask."

Mary nodded. "Thank you. It would mean so much to them. It's the kind of thing money can't buy, literally."

"For sure. Speaking of money—"

"We will cover the air fare and incidental expenses. As you say, your mission is important."

"Yes, it is. You're being very nice to take it on faith."

"We did visit Xanth," Mary reminded her gently. "We became believers. David and his cat Midrange had a small additional part in the matter of Nimby's visit to Mundania two years ago."

"That's right!" Breanna agreed, remembering. "Still, maybe I can give you a little bit of evidence, so you know I'm not a fake."

Mary demurred, but as with the laugh, not with force. That meant she did have some doubt.

Breanna lifted the Ring of Fire. "Can I have a little demo, please?"

A bit of smoke curled up from the Ring. It formed into the head of a tiny demoness. "I thought you'd never levy," she said.

"Never what?" Breanna asked.

"Exact, claim, impose, require, beseech—"

"Ask?" Mary suggested.

"Whatever," the demoness agreed crossly.

"Metria!"

The demoness looked at her. "Have we met?"

"We met your alter ego Mentia five years ago. A most seductive creature. She told us of you."

"She would," Metria said darkly, but she was evidently satisfied. She turned to Breanna. "How are you doing?"

"I am becoming a Mundane princess so I can associate with a white boy without getting the vigilantes on my tail."

"I don't understand."

"That's because you're not Mundane. I just wanted to show Mrs. Baldwin that I'm really from Xanth."

Metria turned her gaze back to Mary. "She's really from Xanth. You have my demonly word."

"I believe it," Mary said.

"I'd rather have made some mischief, but Grossclout put me under strict orders. I'd better not use up any more toxic waste."

"Any more what?" Mary asked, startled.

"Magic dust," Breanna said quickly. "I have just about enough to make the Ring work, in case I need it."

"See that you do," Metria said. "I want to see more of Mundania."

Then Breanna remembered. "Actually, the Rings are self-powered. But you never can tell when some extra magic would help, away from Xanth. That reminds me: When you return to Xanth, ask Chlorine if David and Karen Baldwin of Mundania can have passes to Xanth. The family is really helping with the mission."

"Will do." The little head fuzzed, became an even smaller figure of a bare voluptuous woman, and faded out.

"She hasn't changed," Mary said. "Thank you for showing me."

"I didn't know Metria was the one on duty, or that you knew her. I just wanted a demonstration."

Mary laughed. "You said 'a little demo'! She must have taken that to mean a small demon."

Breanna knocked her forehead with the heel of her hand. "She would!"

"Well, I think you're ready, princess. Jim will have the e-tickets set up."

"The what?"

"A recent development. We no longer need physical tickets for airplanes."

"Just as well David's going with me," Breanna said ruefully. "I'm sure not up on the latest."

"We suspected that would be the case."

Breanna found herself liking this family.

Soon they took her to the airport. Sure enough, they were listed for passage. David showed his identification, and showed a blank card for Breanna. She invoked the Ring of Fire, and the demoness made it look like a valid ID. They were allowed to board the plane.

Except that they had to wait an hour in a gradually filling waiting room. Then came an announcement: The flight was delayed half an hour.

"Something wrong?" Breanna asked, alarmed.

"Routine," David reassured her. "These days they figure it's an error if a flight travels on time. I hope we don't miss our connecting flight."

"Connecting flight?"

"On such short notice, we had to take what we could get, the zigzag express. We'll change planes in New Orleans, Dallas, Phoenix, and Los Angeles. Some of those connections are pretty tight. We'll be lucky to make our schedule."

"Oh." Breanna wasn't pleased, but this was, after all, Mundania. She was remembering why she was glad to have left it. "Well, whatever. Just as long as we get there."

"We'll get there. I just can't say when."

But after half an hour, the plane was in, and they did board. Their seats were in the rear, and not together. "Maybe we can trade with someone," David said.

"It's okay. Don't get off without me."

He smiled. "I won't, Princess Bre."

That was right: She was a foreign princess, garbed in black. She took her seat, which was by a window. She liked that; she always liked to see where she was going. She buckled up. There was no leg room to speak of, and hardly any hip room; she was not a large person, in fact she was on the smallish side, but she would not have cared for a tighter fit.

A large man sat next to her. His thigh and elbow overlapped her space, and his extra bag overlapped her foot room. This was annoying, but she wasn't here to quarrel, so she bore with it.

The plane took off and forged up into the clouds. She was fascinated; this was like being carried aloft by a roc bird! It passed through a cloud with a faint swishing sound, and emerged above it. From here the clouds were huge vertical masses of mist, rather than the pretty muffins they appeared from the ground. Unlike Xanth clouds, they were not cup-shaped, with the cups filled with water; there was a more complicated mechanism for rain.

She became aware of something. The hand of the man next to her was touching her thigh. Her voluminous dress covered it, but still his fingers were somewhat too familiar. She realized that she was stuck in this little seat, cut off from escape. She didn't want to make a bad scene, but neither did she want to be handled by a stranger.

She lifted her Ring to her mouth. "Metria," she murmured.

"Got it," the Ring replied in the demoness's voice.

Breanna let her arm fall across her lap so that her left hand was on her thigh near the man's hand. She nudged it closer, without actually touching.

In a moment his hand moved. It touched hers. A spark jumped from the Ring.

"Ooof!" the man grunted, jerking his hand away. It must have been quite a shock.

Breanna turned wide innocent eyes on him. "Is there a problem, sir?"

"No, no, of course not," he muttered.

And by some odd coincidence, his hand did not stray again. "Thanks, Metria," Breanna said subvocally.

The Ring turned warm for a moment, just a pulse of acknowledgment.

Nut and cracker snacks were served, and drinks. Breanna enjoyed her first Mundane fizzle water in nine years. This trip really wasn't bad, so far.

The plane made up time on the flight, and was only fifteen minutes late landing at New Orleans. Breanna rejoined David, and they got off and hurried to the gate for the flight to Dallas. They just made it. This time they had seats together. "What did you do to that guy?" he asked.

"Just burned him with the Ring of Fire," she said. "Nothing serious."

"I'll bet," he agreed, smiling.

But now there was weather. The plane went around it, but then was late, and was put in a holding pattern around Dallas. By the time it landed, they were an hour late, and had missed their connecting flight.

"We'll take the next one to Phoenix," David said.

The clerk checked his listings. "In twelve hours."

"Twelve hours! There should be a plane every two hours."

"All booked solid," the man said. "You should have taken the one you were scheduled for."

"Our plane didn't even land until that one had taken off."

The man checked his computer listings. "True. In that case, we'll put you up for the night, compliments of MundaniAir. We like to have satisfied customers."

"Satisfied cus—" But he broke off, for Breanna's hand was on his arm, cautioning him. "Okay. Thank you," he said insincerely.

Actually, the hotel room wasn't bad. It was small, but had a TV set with cable and an Internet connection. "Say—can that thing reach the Xanth Xone?" she asked.

"Sure, if you have the magic code."

"I have it."

He used his credit card to go online, then turned it over to her. She typed the magic code and entered the Xone. Then as an afterthought she turned to David. "Put your hand on my shoulder, so you have contact. Then you'll be there too."

"Thanks!" He clasped her shoulder.

A lovely woman appeared on the screen. "Why, hello, Breanna," she said. "Back so soon?"

"Hi, Mouse Terian," Breanna said. "No, I'm calling from Mundania."

"And who is your handsome companion?"

"I'm David Baldwin," David said.

"I'm sure you are." Terian gazed at him speculatively.

"Hey—we're talking in sound!" he said, realizing.

"We're in the Xanth Xone," Breanna reminded him. "We're in three dimensions too."

"We sure are," he agreed, gazing raptly at Terian's décolletage, which was somewhat more revealing than she pretended to realize.

"I'd like to leave a message for Justin Tree," Breanna said. "Can you get it to him?"

"Where is he now?"

"At Castle Zombie."

"I will relay the message there."

"Thanks. Just tell him I'm delayed in Mundania, but I'll be back as soon as I can. Tell him not to get fresh with any zombie nymphs tonight."

Terian smiled. "I shall." She glanced again at David, then faded out. The screen went blank.

"Wow!" David said.

"Don't get your hopes up," Breanna warned him. "Not only is she committed to Tristran Troll, she's a literal mouse."

"The kind that squeaks?" he asked, astonished. "She sure looked human."

"She assumes that form when dealing with humans. I understand her kisses are divine. But she really is a mouse. Com Passion's mouse, in fact."

"Well, it was nice meeting her, regardless. Anytime she wants to breathe in my direction, I'll look."

"I figured you deserved something for letting me use your connection." Breanna looked around. "I'm tired. I'd love a good shower, a meal, and a night's sleep."

"Oops," he said.

"Oops?"

"I just realized: There's only one bed. Well, I'll sleep on the floor."

Breanna pondered half a moment. "Can you keep your hands to yourself?"

He understood her as readily as she had understood him when he asked about seeing her panties. "Yes, when I have to. And I guess I do."

"You do. Then we'll share the bed. I won't tell Justin, and you won't tell your mother."

"Agreed." He glanced at the phone. "I'll make a reservation for dinner while you take your shower."

She went into the bathroom, stripped, and got into the shower. It was a glorious experience after the day of travel. Then she grabbed a towel, rubbed herself dry, tossed it aside, and stepped into the bedroom to fetch her comb. She had left it in the bag Mary Baldwin had thoughtfully provided her, along with a change of clothing.

David was sitting by the phone, staring at her, jaw dropped. "Oops," she repeated. "My error." She turned around and went back into the bathroom to recover the towel.

"I'm sorry," David said, blushing. "I didn't mean to peek. I assumed you would be clothed."

"Not your fault. I just forgot I wasn't with Justin." But as she spoke, she wondered. She was secretly rather proud of her body; she might not have the figure of a nymph or the frontal oomph of a filly centaur, but she did have the female stuff. Had she really forgotten, or had she wanted to flash him? She had flashed Justin in times past, theoretically by accident. She had flashed her panties at both Justin and Edsel two years ago, just to show Pia how it was done. This time she had given David solid frontal and backtal views. Maybe it was in her nature.

They went to supper, and it was fun eating well in a nice setting, even if several other diners did let fly a few covert stares. It was that black/white thing, she knew; they thought they were an interracial couple. Well, tough beanbags! Let them think what they wanted.

Back in the room, David showered while she watched the Mundane news on the television. There were wars, floods, fires, earthquakes, and some negative items. Also a piece about rescuing a lost cat.

"Say, didn't you have a cat?" Breanna asked as David reappeared, suitably garbed.

"Oh, I still have him. Midrange. He helped Nimby and got a pass to Xanth."

"That's right! We helped with the magic dust at the Xanth end."

"So now Midrange takes Tweeter to Xanth on visits. I'm sure they enjoy it. But when they return to us, they can't tell us what they did there. It's frustrating."

"For sure." She paused, then looked at the bed. "Which side do you want?"

"Are you sure this is—?"

"Long as you stay on your side, I'll stay on my side."

"Okay. I'll take the left side."

They got into their sides and settled down for the night. Breanna really was tired, in mind more than body. She was soon asleep.

She woke in the morning, refreshed. David was still asleep. He had stayed on his side; he hadn't cheated. She appreciated that.

They had breakfast, then checked in in time to catch the plane to Phoenix. This one ran on schedule, and made the connection with the flight to Los Angeles.

The flight to Honolulu was the long hop. The airplane was large, ten seats wide, with two center aisles, a movie, and a meal. But there was an extra charge for earphones to receive the movie sound. "Is it worth it?" she asked.

David frowned. "It's *Incredible Hulk Vs. Little Shop of Horrors IV,* so I doubt it. I saw the first two and didn't bother with the third. The earphones are germy too. Anyway, just looking at the screen without the sound can be just about as interesting. You can fill in your own dialogue."

"Fine with me," she agreed.

They watched the silenced movie. It started with a medium-small man evidently traveling somewhere. He carried a small black bag, and there was a stethoscope dangling from his neck, so he had to be a doctor. He entered a public lavatory—and there were three toughs with knives. They threatened him, wanting his money. He gave them that, but when they went after his black bag, he resisted. When he tried to escape, one caught him and threw him against the wall. They didn't even bother with the knives; they started beating on him with their fists. He was getting mauled.

The Ring of Fire opened an eye. "Wow!" it murmured. "Some fiasco." It seemed Metria was watching too, and she probably had the right word this time.

"This is G-rated," David remarked, disgusted. "If there's any sex, or a bad word, it's R-rated just like that, but a little healthy violence is considered okay."

"This is Mundania," she reminded him unnecessarily.

"That's why I want to visit Xanth again."

"To see the nymphs and bare-breasted centaur fillies?"

"You know it's so. If I could catch and tame a nymph—"

"They don't have much mind. All they're good for is just one thing."

He glanced at her. "What's your point?"

She laughed. "I hope you catch one."

After the doctor had taken enough of a beating, he became annoyed. Then he swelled up hugely, bursting out of his shirt, and became a giant green man. He laid about him, quickly smashing the three thugs through the walls.

"I didn't know they had green ogres in Mundania," Breanna said, intrigued.

"We don't. This is faked up. Wait till you see the little shop of horrors. There's a plant like a tangle tree."

"The green against the greens," she agreed appreciatively.

By the time the doctor got to the shop, the meal was served. The plate contained a mass of something yellowish and a sickly salad drenched in oil. Breanna tasted it and made a wry face. "What is this stuff?"

"Inedible bulk vs. a little slop of humongous," he quipped, smiling. "Standard fare on flights."

"Thank you so much for clarifying that. Now I can really enjoy it."

"If you do, you'll be the first to achieve that fate."

She had to laugh. That helped.

When they finally reached Hawaii she was thoroughly tired of sitting, and her stomach was not at all certain that "inedible bulk" was a joke. But they set down safely.

"I gotta get to the men's room," David said, embarrassed. "I knew I shouldn't have eaten that stuff."

"Me too," she agreed.

They hurried to the rest rooms and took the separate doors. Breanna finished her business efficiently and stood, looking for the flush handle on the toilet. There was none. She stood—and the toilet flushed of its own accord, startling her. There must be a little magic in Mundania after all.

She washed at a sink, the water flowing the moment her hands came near and stopping when they were removed. Definitely magic!

The Ring warmed. Breanna put it to her ear. "Yes?"

"David's in trouble in the men's room," Metria said.

"I can't do that particular thing for him."

"Robbers. Like the movie."

Oh. And David couldn't turn into a green ogre. "Can you help?"

"If you touch the Ring to someone. But I don't have a lot of power. Better to save it if possible."

"Okay." Breanna dashed out of the women's room and into the men's room, heedless of propriety, her mind whirling. By the time she made the scene she had a crude plan. She would have to make like the green ogre, in her fashion. She opened her black robe partway and flounced out her hair, forming a wild expression. She knew she didn't look much like a maenad, one of the killer wild women of Mount Parnassus who ripped men apart and drink their blood, but this was the best she could do, on short notice.

Two big men had David backed up against the wall so that he couldn't escape. It was clear that if he didn't give up his wallet soon, he would lose more than that.

"There you are!" Breanna cried, pushing by the nearer man to reach David. "What do you mean, keeping me waiting like that?" She slapped him resoundingly across the cheek, glaring balefully around. The men were staring, amazed to see her in this room. "But I'll forgive you this time." She grabbed his head and planted a hot kiss on his mouth. "Now come *on*; we've got business ahead." She took him by the hand and headed for the door, hauling him along.

By the time the two toughs finished staring, the travelers were back in the main concourse, safe from further molestation. "You're a wonder," David said shakily.

"I had to get you out of there before you lost your credit card," she said. "I still need your help."

"That too."

She laughed. "Kisses you can have. Just not the rest."

"Yeah." But she suspected that he had a certain hankering for the rest too. That pleased her. It was illicit fun impressing an impressionable boy.

"Now to zero in on Jaylin," she said briskly.

"What's her address?"

"I don't have that."

He stopped walking. "You what?"

"The dream vision didn't give that detail. But we know it's Hawaii. She's here somewhere."

"Breanna, there are tens of thousands of people here! We need an address."

"No we don't." She lifted the Ring of Fire. "Which direction?"

David looked halfway fit to be tied.

A little arrow speared out from the Ring, pointing the direction. "That way," Breanna said.

"So nice to have that clarified."

They found a map on the wall. "Southeast," she said. "A fair distance."

"That would be the main island of Hawaii."

"For sure. Get us there."

"We'll have to take a commuter flight."

"Whatever."

Still, he hesitated. "Are you sure this is right? That we aren't wasting our time and money?"

Breanna wasn't sure, but saw no alternative but to plow ahead. "How can I convince you? Do I have to kiss you again?"

Her bluff worked. "No! That wasn't what I meant. It's just that—"

She stepped into him and kissed him. When she released him she saw his green eyes turn momentarily black, reflecting her image. "No problem," he gasped, and set off for the ticket office.

The little commuter plane seemed like a toy compared to the huge airline they had come on, but it buzzed up into the air and got them two hundred miles to Hawaii island without crashing. Breanna was relieved.

They landed at Hilo in the evening. She checked the Ring for direction, and it sent them south. Breanna was relieved again; it meant they hadn't overshot the mark.

They took a taxi south, and Breanna checked the Ring frequently, zeroing in as the direction changed. The taxi driver looked doubtful as they kept asking him to change direction, but David gave him a good tip and he played along.

At last they came to a particular house that had to be it. They got out of the taxi, and it sped away, evidently glad to be rid of these odd customers.

Now they were here. Their quarry was inside the house. What were they to do next?

9

RING OF VOID

Jaylin was home alone for the moment; the folks were out on business. She was fifteen, and of course bored with the routine; it came with the territory. Naturally she had more homework than she cared to do.

She looked in the mirror, and saw an image that others said was just like that of her mother at that age, with nice black hair. In fact, some said she looked more like her mother than her mother did. Jaylin knew why: Her mother was old, dangerously close to thirty-five, so was losing it.

"Isn't that right, Nikko?" she inquired. Nikko wagged his tail in agreement. He was very agreeable.

There was a knock on the door. Nikko barked. Probably a salesman; she would get rid of him soon enough.

But when she went there, she saw an odd couple indeed: a young white man and a young black woman garbed completely in black. He looked like a typical mainland American teen; she looked like a foreign princess. Whatever they were selling must be pretty exotic. "Yes?" she said politely. It was always best to be polite to strangers, lest they suffer an extemporaneous fit of road rage or something and blow up the town.

"Hello, Jaylin," the princess said.

That was another surprise. "Do I know you?"

"Not yet. But we must talk to you about something that is very important. May we come in?"

"No!" Jaylin said more sharply than she meant to. Letting strangers in was a good way to get robbed or worse.

"Well, will you come out and talk, then?"

"No." This was becoming nervous business.

"Then I guess we'll just have to talk right here. I am Breanna of the Black Wave, from the Land of Xanth, and this is David Baldwin of—"

"You're joking!"

"No, I'm serious. We—"

"Did my classmates put you up to this? Pretending to be one of the fantasy people I read about?"

"I'm not pretending. I really am—"

"Your talent is seeing in blackness. You want to marry Justin Tree."

"For sure!"

"So what are you doing here? That doesn't look like Justin Tree to me. Not enough foliage."

"I'm not Justin," the man reminded her. "I'm David."

"So now she's two-timing Justin?"

"Justin and I were supposed to be married yesterday," the black woman said hotly. "But something came up, and now we need to recruit you."

"A likely story. The joke's wearing thin, and I have homework to do. So if you don't mind—"

"We do mind," the woman said. She lifted her left hand. "Metria."

Smoke rose off the Ring. It formed into the head and upper torso of an inordinately shapely woman. "It's true," the bust said. "We need you for the sortie."

"The what?" Jaylin asked.

"Raid, charge, foray, attack, sally—"

Jaylin burst out laughing.

"Mission," Breanna said quickly. "It's not at all funny."

"Whatever," the little demoness agreed crossly, dissipating into mist and drifting away.

"Oh, I wasn't laughing at you," Jaylin said. "It's just that—never mind. How do you do that trick?"

"It's no trick," Breanna said. "This is the Ring of Fire, and it controls all demons. Metria is a demoness, so it can summon her, even here. We need you to fetch the Ring of Void."

"The what?"

"It's complicated to explain. First we have to get you to listen."

Jaylin considered. It could be a joke, but that trick with the Ring was impressive. She would like to have a Ring like that, and be able to conjure up a little holographic image of a bare-breasted demoness. There were any number of people that sight would freak out. So she compromised. "Give me that Ring, and show me how it works, and I'll listen."

"I can't give you this Ring; I'm its designated holder. But you can have a Ring of your own, at least for a while, that's just as powerful."

"Oh? How?"

"You'll have to come to Xanth with us, and—"

"I'm not going anywhere with you! In fact, you'd better get out of here before my folks return." Oops—she had just inadvertently blabbed that she was alone in the house, except for Nikko, who really wasn't much of a guard dog.

"Maybe you can borrow this Ring for a moment," Breanna said. "I'll see if it will let me lend it." She put her fingers to it. To her evident surprise, it came loose. "I guess it will. This must be mission-related." She handed it to Jaylin.

Jaylin took it. It seemed quite ordinary. She put it on her little left finger, and it fit comfortably. "So how do I do the trick?"

"Just say her name."

"Demoness Metria," Jaylin said.

The Ring warmed on her finger. Smoke formed. The little head and torso reappeared. "I'm just doing this as a demon-stration," she said. "I really don't have to answer to you, Mundane."

Fascinated, Jaylin poked a finger at the figure. It passed through the belly without resistance. "If you were a man, I'd make you marry me before I let you do that," Metria said severely. Then she returned to smoke and swirled away.

Taken aback by the implication, Jaylin didn't know whether to laugh or blush. This was beyond any trick she knew of. But could it really be magic? "Okay, come on in and I'll listen. But that's all." She removed the Ring and returned it to Breanna.

"Thank you." Breanna and David entered the house and took seats in the living room. Then she started explaining, and Jaylin was amazed despite her reservations.

"There really is a Demon Earth?" she asked. "And he's gone?"

"And gravity's not long for this world if we don't get him back soon," Breanna agreed. "Everything will float away."

Jaylin found herself believing. "That really *is* serious. And I have to fetch the Ring that controls the Void?"

"And all the things of dreams, including the night mares," Breanna agreed. "Each Ring is phenomenally powerful in its domain."

"All because I daydreamed I said swell foop?"

"Yes. That was how you related to it, after our mess-up. So now it will accept you as its holder and user, and no one else. We have to have you."

"And you don't even know where it is?"

"We don't. But Putre will help you find it."

"Putre?"

"I guess I forgot to cover that part. He's a zombie night colt. Like a night mare, or a day mare, only he doesn't carry dreams to sleepers, or even daydreams. He's sort of shut out of the system."

"The poor thing!"

"Well, it's a sexist realm, and in this case it's the males who lose out. He's really nice enough, and he was zombied quite fresh, so it doesn't show at all. You can ride him; I did."

To ride a magic horse! This mission was becoming more attractive. But there was a formidable constraint. "Mother would never let me go."

"Bleep! I never thought of that," Breanna said.

"Maybe I can help," David said. "What we need is a cover story. Like—like maybe Jaylin and I met in an Internet chat room, and now she wants to visit Florida. My folks would go along with that."

Jaylin eyed him. He was halfway handsome in his fashion, but this was a big step. "Go with you to Florida?"

"It's just the story," he said quickly. "I don't mean we really are— that is, like, going together—it's just a way to make it look all right." He stopped, evidently flustered.

Jaylin reconsidered. David—she remembered him now. He had been a character in a prior novel, twelve years old and a brat. But he was seventeen now, and was not unpersonable. This could be interesting. "And Breanna is the chaperone?"

Now Breanna looked startled. "Of all the things I never thought to be! An enforcer of the Adult Conspiracy. But I guess I could choke down the bile and do that. For a while."

In fact, Jaylin was getting to like these people. "Okay, you convince Mom, and I'll go. It sounds like more fun than school."

Just in time, for now the parents returned. There followed a somewhat wary interaction, and the outcome was in deep doubt, until two things tipped the balance. The first was the Ring: Breanna touched Jaylin's mother with it, and murmured "believe," and suddenly, irrationally, she accepted the concocted story. That was some magic!

The second thing was the call to the Baldwin family in Florida. David's mother was quick to catch on, and to say that any friend of David's was welcome to visit them; Jaylin could borrow Sean's old room, and there would definitely not be any unsupervised fraternizing.

"She means it too," David said glumly. "That's why Sean had to move out, if he wanted more than a brotherly relationship with Willow."

It was evident that the two mothers saw eye to eye on such matters. That was oddly reassuring. This was definitely a case where Jaylin wanted not too much freedom. Yet.

But the hurdles were not over. "We can't afford a ticket to Florida," Jaylin's mother said.

"We'll get one," Breanna said. This too Mom accepted. That was evidence of the continuing effect of the magic. If Jaylin hadn't been convinced before, the effect of the Ring of Fire on her mother would have done it.

David and Breanna shared some food with the family, borrowed pillows and a blanket, and camped out on the back porch for the night. Jaylin caught herself getting jealous, then had to laugh at herself: She was already getting proprietary about David, though their relationship was only pretense. For now. Anyway, Breanna was set to marry Justin Tree, and she was definitely not the cheating type. So David was available—if Jaylin was interested.

In the morning they took a taxi to the airport. Then Jaylin remembered the ticket. "You did manage to get one for me that's on your plane?" she asked Breanna.

"No. I still have to take care of that detail."

Both Jaylin and David looked at her, frowning. "Maybe they'll have an extra seat and maybe they won't," David said. "I think these flights are usually pretty well filled. Even so, I'm not sure my credit card isn't already maxed."

"I checked with Metria. She says she'll take care of it."

"But she's in Xanth! She can talk to us in miniature, but she can't conjure up a valid MundaniAir ticket."

"She's a pretty canny demoness. I have confidence in her."

David looked just as doubtful as Jaylin felt. But what was there to do except find out what the demoness had in mind? If Jaylin got stuck at the airport, she'd simply call home, and her mother would be more than glad to bring her back.

They reached the airport and went to the waiting room for their flight. Breanna held up her ring hand. "Okay, Metria," she murmured. "Put out." Then she held the Ring to her ear. "Wow! Which one?"

The Ring must have told her, because Breanna led the way to a heavyset middle-aged woman seated on a bench. "Mrs. Crumpet?"

The woman glanced up, surprised. "Yes?"

"I'd like to make a fair trade. You have a ticket to Miami, Florida. I have a friend who needs it. I hope we can deal."

"I don't understand."

"Please touch my hand."

The woman looked as if she were about to protest, but then she shrugged and touched Breanna's extended hand. Her fingers brushed the Ring of Fire. "I believe you," she said, surprised again.

"Mrs. Crumpet, you have an aneurysm that will kill you if not dealt with soon. The airplane is going to have a brief lapse of pressure that will be uncomfortable for others but lethal for you. You must not board that plane. Instead you must go to the hospital and have it checked. It will probably mean surgery, but it will save your life and give you a good many more years. Is this information a fair trade for your ticket?"

The woman stared at her. "Where—?"

"The car—carrot—I don't know the medical term, but it's about here on you." Breanna put one hand to the side of her own neck, below the chin.

"The carotid artery?"

"That's it. The left one."

"I thought that was just a sore muscle."

"No. It's a weak blood vessel."

The woman considered further. Then she delved into her purse, brought out a ticket, and gave it to Breanna. She got up and walked away.

Breanna gave it to Jaylin. Jaylin looked at it. It was a ticket to Miami. At that point she began to be a little afraid.

"Is it true?" David asked, sounding awed.

"Yes. We have just saved her life."

"But how did the demoness know?"

"She went to a woman whose talent is to look forward in time and see the result of a decision. Her name is Ashli. She spent all night looking long-distance at every passenger on this plane, until she found one who was going to die on it. It was her decision to board the plane that made her fate."

"That seems like an awful lot of work by Ashli just to help someone she'll never know," Jaylin said.

"This is an awful important mission. If we don't save the Demon Earth, gravity will fade and all of us will suffer and maybe die within a month."

"Why not just tell the government and have it look for the Demon Earth?"

Breanna just looked at her, and Jaylin felt stupid. Of course the government wouldn't pay attention. It never did. Even if it believed in magic, which it surely didn't, except when it came to financing the economy. "I withdraw the question."

"This is Mundania," David said. That covered it all.

They boarded the plane without incident. Jaylin was able to trade seats with another passenger so she could sit with David and Breanna.

About an hour into the flight there was a bump in the air, and a sudden loss of cabin pressure. They gasped, but in a few seconds the pressure was restored and they were all right. "Loose hatch," the captain's voice came over the speakers. "The automatic seal caught it. We apologize for the inconvenience." He sounded as if this were routine.

Jaylin began to be a little more afraid. If a woman far away in Xanth could foresee this happening, and in effect act to change the consequences of it, how much worse must be the mission they were on! But that thought evoked another question. "Why not have Ashli find out where the Demon Earth is hidden?"

"Demons are something else," Breanna explained. "Way beyond the power of mortals to affect. The whole of the magic of Xanth is the mere leakage of magic from the body of the Demon Xanth, just as the whole of Earth's gravity is the leakage from the body of its Demon. We are like tiny ants in comparison. We can't even comprehend their natures, let alone control them in any way. That's why we have to have the Swell Foop to rescue the Demon Earth. Only with its mind-boggling power can we hope to accomplish anything."

"What does it do?"

"We don't even know. Just that each Ring of Xanth has such power as no mortal ever can wield alone, and it takes all six of them together to control the Swell Foop. It hurts my mind just to think about it too much."

"I'm getting scared."

"Join the throng," David said. "We might as well be fleas on an elephant."

She took his hand. "Hi, fellow flea!"

"Actually, more like germs on the flea on an elephant," Breanna said. "But it seems it's up to us. Once we get that sixth Ring."

The rest of the series of flights was uneventful. By the time they arrived in Florida, Jaylin knew both her companions pretty well, and was ready to do more than hold hands with David. She learned how he had sneaked a peek at lovely Chlorine's green panties at age twelve, and the forbidden sight had turned his eyes from brown to green and accelerated his maturation by a year. In the ensuing five years he had realized that there was more to a woman than underwear, but that original green image had never quite faded from his fancy. She made a mental note: When this business with the Swell Foop was all done, and she returned to Mundania, buy a set of green underwear. Even if she didn't care to show it, she wanted to have it.

"Actually, David's decent," Breanna remarked during one of their rest stops. "And his family is really nice. A girl could do a lot worse."

"You act as though I've already decided."

Breanna gave her another of those looks, and sure enough, Jaylin felt completely stupid. She would have to learn to mask her interests more effectively.

Mrs. Baldwin met them at the airport. "Hello, Jaylin!" she said, as if they had known each other for years. "Are you okay with this?"

Okay with what? Had the woman already marked her as a future daughter-in-law? No, it must be the dangerous mission. "I am nervous as bleep," Jaylin confessed. She was picking up some of Breanna's mannerisms. "But I'm ready to try my best."

"You will be suffering jet lag," Mary said. "It may be best to go immediately on into Xanth, where they can give you a magic potion to make you all right."

"I'll take them to the portal," David said.

He did. He drove them to No Name Key. Then, as they parted, he took Jaylin's hand and gently drew her into him. She yielded, coming to embrace him. They kissed. She floated.

Nothing more was said, but a promise had been made. There would be more to this, by and by. They separated, and she and Breanna entered the compound.

"Funny how things work out," Breanna remarked. "It was similar chance when I met Justin."

"Do things really happen by chance?" Jaylin asked, still flustered by the impact of the kiss.

"I wonder."

Breanna led them through a picture in a gallery, and suddenly they were on Centaur Isle with a black horse trotting up to greet them. "This is Putre," Breanna said. "He's the zombie dream colt."

"Hello, Putre," Jaylin said. "What a beautiful creature you are." Actually, any horse was beautiful, but she didn't feel the need to clarify that.

A little dark heart appeared above the horse.

"May I hug you?" Jaylin asked. She had a charge of love built up that had to be discharged.

The heart fractured into a cluster of smaller hearts, and these formed into the outline of a larger heart.

She took that as a yes. She went to hug his neck. The hearts fractured again, forming a cloud that enveloped the two of them.

"Now why do I think the two of you will get along okay?" Breanna asked rhetorically.

Jaylin was glad that hearts didn't show in Mundania; she would have embarrassed herself more than once. But it was time to get down to business. "I don't have much experience riding horses," she said.

"You can't fall off him if he doesn't want you to," Breanna said. "Look—it's really urgent that you get that Ring of Void as fast as you can. Why don't you go after it now, and I'll find my own way back to tell the others?"

"But I'd be lost here without you!" Jaylin protested, suddenly aware of the strangeness of the environment.

"Putre will take good care of you, and he knows where the Ring is, and where to find us once you have it. You can trust him."

Jaylin believed that. She just hadn't expected to be halfway on her own so suddenly. "Well—"

"Good enough. I hope you can figure it out quickly."

Jaylin climbed onto Putre's bare back, and it was surprisingly secure and comfortable. "You know where it is?" she asked uncertainly.

A speech balloon appeared above his head. "Only in a general way," it wrote. "It is in the Web."

"The Web?"

"Of the Internet."

"Oh, you mean like the Mundane Internet?"

"Like it, perhaps, but not part of it. This is the dream realm version. We must seek it in the gourd."

Jaylin didn't much like the sound of this, for all that there was no sound, just writing. "Must we?"

"It is where it is."

"But isn't that where all the bad dreams are? All the scary things?"

"Yes. But they will not hurt you. They will merely scare you."

"Oh, that's all right, then," Jaylin said weakly. She was trying for sarcasm, but was unable to rise to the occasion.

"I will take you there now," Putre wrote. And before she could think of a pretext to protest, he was off at a gallop, carrying her along.

She grabbed the curly mane at his neck to hang on, but really there was no need; she was staying securely on his back as if in a coasting easy chair. They moved along until he came to a green gourd lying on the ground. Then he dived—how that was possible for a horse she didn't know, but he did it—and they were on a collision course with the gourd. It seemed to swell up hugely, and they passed right through. She didn't even have time to let out a proper scream.

Then they were in a pleasant open forest, not at all frightening. "What happened?" she asked, looking around.

"This is one of the dream sets," Putre's speech balloon wrote. "Where the elements of dreams are made."

"But this isn't scary."

"It's just background material. Dreams don't become frightening until they have effective plot lines. Every element has to be fashioned just right for best effect."

"I suppose," Jaylin agreed, relaxing. "What now?"

"We must find the Web. We shall have to inquire."

"Does that mean we have to find a scary thing to ask?"

"This looks like leprechaun territory. They aren't very scary."

"That's a relief! Okay, let's find a leprechaun."

Putre's ears perked up. There was the sound of hammering. He walked toward it.

They came to a glade where several little bearded men were working on some kind of platform. They were intent on their construction and didn't see the visitors.

"Uh, hello," Jaylin said tentatively.

The nearest little man jumped, dropping his hammer. "Oh! Don't give a person such a fright!" he exclaimed. "You're like to turn a man's beard white."

"We apologize, handsome leprechaun," Putre's balloon wrote.

"Yes, we are very sorry," Jaylin agreed. "Your beard is such a nice shade of red."

The little man looked at Putre, frowning. Then he looked at Jaylin, and the frown melted. "Why, sure and it's a cute Mundane lass," he exclaimed. "What be the likes of you doing in a place like this?"

Putre made a small speech balloon angled her way. "He likes you. Maybe he'll help." That was the equivalent of a whisper.

She nodded. "I'm looking for the Web."

"Lass, you're in the wrong set! Gold we've got, but no web." He gestured around, and when Jaylin looked, she saw several crocks overflowing with bright gold coins.

"You really do have treasure!" she exclaimed, impressed. "I thought that was just a myth."

"It *is* a myth," the leprechaun said. "And we are it. Have you any idea how many people dream foolishly of gold they don't deserve? They never think of doing good honest work for it; no, they've got to try to steal it from us. Isn't that a shame?"

"It's terrible," she agreed.

The leprechaun angled his head. "Sure and I like the look of ye," he said. He turned to his fellow workers. "Anybody know the way to the Web?"

"Aye," one agreed. "I can point the way. But we have to test this set first."

"So we do. But maybe this sweet lass can help us."

"Me?" Jaylin asked. "I don't know the first thing about dream sets."

All of the leprechauns nodded. "She'll do," the other said.

"I don't understand."

"That's *why* ye'll do, lass," the first one said. "You aren't prejudiced. If it scares you, it must be good."

Jaylin realized that she had better cooperate, or they might not help her find the Web. "I'll try."

"It's like this. Pretend you're dreaming—of course you *are* dreaming, but you know what I mean—and you catch me and try to make me show you where my treasure is."

"Oh, I wouldn't do anything like that!"

"I said *pretend,* lass. Think of yourself as a big mean man who doesn't care how he gets rich."

"I'll try," she said again. She got down from Putre, and the leprechaun went back to work. This time, instead of greeting him, she pounced on him, grabbing him by an arm. "Ha, I've got you, leprechaun!" she cried. "Where's your gold?"

He looked cowed. "Please, mister bad man, let me go! That treasure will do ye no good, believe me."

"No! I want it now. Or else." She had no idea what else, but it was the only threat she could think of.

"All right! All right. Don't hurt me. I'll take ye there." Then, in a low voice: "Don't let go of me, or I'll vanish. The bad men have mostly caught on to that by now."

She had been about to let go of him. Instead she renewed her grip on his arm. "Take me to your treasure!"

The leprechaun led the way to the structure, which was now conveniently shrouded in mist. Only a few bright golden coins showed around the edges of the mist, evidently fallen from some huge crock of gold. Jaylin knew that this was all a dream, and the money wasn't real, and even if it was real, she wouldn't take it, but still she felt a tinge of greedy excitement.

"It is in here," the leprechaun said, showing an oval-shaped opening in the mist. "Take a look."

Jaylin put her face to the oval, but couldn't quite see inside. So she poked her head through.

Suddenly the mist cleared, and she saw that the structure was a gallows, and she was standing on the platform, and had just poked her head through the hangman's noose. "The wages of sin is death!" the leprechaun cried as he pulled a handle and a trapdoor opened beneath her feet. She was falling.

Jaylin screamed so piercingly that the entire scene shattered and collapsed in a heap of shards.

Then Putre was there, kicking the shards away, nudging her with his friendly nose. She grabbed his neck and cried into his mane. "That was horrible!"

"Then it will do," the leprechaun said, satisfied. "Put it in the can, boys."

Oh, yes: This was a mere demo. For a moment she had forgotten.

"Sorry we frightened you, lass," the leprechaun said. "But you know this *is* the realm of bad dreams. They have to be awful, or they're no good, so to speak. The Night Stallion has strict standards."

"I understand," she said weakly.

"Now we'll show ye the way to the Web."

They led the way through the forest, until it opened out onto a sheer drop-off. "This is a dream aspect of the Gap Chasm," the leprechaun said. "And there's the edge of the Internet." He gestured over the edge.

Putre walked forward, carrying Jaylin. They peered into the chasm—

and there, attached to it in several places, were strands of a monstrous net that stretched entirely across the gap. Each strand was crisscrossed by other strands, so that the pattern of it was clear.

"A literal net," Jaylin said faintly. "I should have known."

"It is our understanding that the Web is part of the Internet," the leprechaun said. "We regret that we can't be a wee bit more helpful, but it is all we know."

"Thank you. I hope your bad dream is a big success."

Then Putre set foot on the Internet, placing each hoof carefully at a junction of strands. Jaylin was quite nervous about this at first, but his footing seemed secure, and the net sagged only a little under his weight. They could cruise the net.

"But this net seems very big," she said. "It could take us a long time to search it all."

"And it's growing all the time," the speech balloon wrote. "Maybe you should orient."

"Orient?"

"The designated Ring Holders can sense the direction of their Rings."

"I didn't know that."

"Few do, because there has not been a call for the Rings of Xanth in several centuries."

"So how do I orient?" But Jaylin answered her own question. She thought of the Ring of Void, and became aware of a direction. "It's that way, I think," she said, pointing.

Putre dutifully followed the instruction. He was gaining speed as he got used to the Internet. She was not about to hurry him; she didn't want any foot to slip.

"How did you come to have such a—such a name?" she inquired.

The speech balloon appeared. "Each night mare associates with a sea of the moon. My dam was Mare Imbrium, and her hoofprint leaves a small map of the moon with her sea highlighted. That identifies the dreams she carries. I, being her foal, associate with a lesser region in her lee. In fact, it is a marsh or swamp, somewhat festering, named Palus Putredinus. Since I am now a zombie, it seems to be a fitting designation."

"You don't seem festering to me," she said.

"I was zombied very soon after dying, so there is hardly any rot."

"And do your hoofprints show that marsh?"

"Yes, of course, and the initials *PP*. You can see my marsh on the face of the moon, if you look carefully beside the Mare Imbrium. But no one cares about that, since I do not deliver dreams. Only the mares can do that."

"Well, I'm glad that freed you to help me."

The speech balloon did not reappear, but another little heart floated up.

Guided by her sense of direction, they came in due course to the Web. It differed from the Net in that instead of square intersections, it was a giant circle with many cables radiating from its center. It was plainly a very big spiderweb. That made Jaylin nervous.

Putre set hoof on the outermost strand. Immediately there was a vibration as something large came toward them. Putre tried to remove his hoof so he could back off, but it was stuck to the strand.

Belatedly Jaylin realized that this was of course the way it would work: Anything touching the Web would be stuck there until the proprietor came to gobble it up.

"Save yourself!" the speech balloon wrote. "Get off me. Don't touch the Web!"

Jaylin was tempted, but two things stopped her. First, she didn't want to desert the loyal horse. Second, she realized that the Web and spider had to be braved in order to get the Ring. So she remained mounted, and cudgeled her quailing brain for some bright idea what to do.

The spider charged toward them, its eight hairy legs touching the intersections of the Web without a miscue. When it came close, she saw that it had a human face. Amazed, she spoke without thinking, which was just as well, because otherwise she would have been tongue-tied. "What are you?"

The spider stopped at the edge of the Web, looming over them. "I am Arachid, a human/spider crossbreed, of course. Now if you are satisfied, I will just truss up and haul away this carcass for later consumption." It strung out some web and faced Putre.

"No!" Jaylin cried.

"No? Why not?"

"He—he's my horse. I need him to carry me away from here."

Arachid gazed down at her with eyes she realized were multifaceted.

"I think you need have no concern about that, since you will not be going anywhere."

"But—"

The spider flung a loop of silk that lassoed her neatly, tightening stickily around her arms and pinning them to her sides. "You appear to be a delectable morsel. It will be a real pleasure sucking out your juices."

Jaylin was too appalled even to scream.

A huge speech balloon appeared over Putre's head. **"YOU CAN'T DO THAT!"**

Arachid glanced at him, unimpressed. "You prefer me to suck out yours first?"

"She's the designated holder of the Ring of Void."

"Sure, and I'm the Night Stallion. Now if you are quite done entertaining me with fanciful stories—"

"LOOK AT HER!" the speech balloon wrote urgently.

"Oh, very well," Arachid said gruffly. It brought its face down close to Jaylin's, and she saw its vampirish sucking teeth. She quailed. "Cute face, nice dark hair, tender exposed neck. Ideal appetizer."

"Look into her eyes," the balloon wrote, though Jaylin wasn't sure how she could read it with the spider's horrible face in the way.

Then their eyes met. "Well, swat me for a buzzing bug and wrap me in flypaper," Arachid said. "It's true."

Jaylin managed to take a breath. "I—I have come for the Ring," she gasped.

Arachid sighed. "And I have to give it to you and let you go. What a waste of edible flesh!" It reached into its own mouth and drew a band from a fang. "Here it is."

She tried to reach for it, but the lasso prevented her. The spider jerked it with one leg, and it loosened and sailed off her body, freeing her. Then she took the Ring of Void and put it on her little left finger, where it fit perfectly.

"I guess that's it," she said shakily. "Uh, thank you, Arachid. You have been a great help."

The spider shook its head ruefully. "And she's polite. She must be excruciatingly sweet to the palate."

Jaylin felt almost—but not quite—sorry for it. "Maybe a nice fat fly will come along soon," she said.

"You speak as if you are unaware of the properties of the Ring."

"I guess I don't know much about it, just that it's needed for the Swell Foop."

"It controls the dream realm, and all that is within it. You can make the fattest of all flies come, if you wish, merely by invoking the Ring."

"I can?" She lifted her hand and looked at the Ring. "Fat fly, come here."

There was a sudden buzzing, and a plane, no a bird, no a fat fly the size of a pig came zooming in. It crashed into the Web and got stuck. "And that's only the beginning," Arachid said as it hurried over to secure the morsel. "You can rearrange the dream sets, summon all the night mares, or arrogate special powers to yourself. You can make of this entire realm a lucid dream."

"A what?"

"A controlled dream," Putre's speech balloon wrote. "The Ring governs everything, even the local rules of magic."

"Gee." She considered, then addressed the Ring again: "Give us the power of flight."

Then she floated from the Net, and so did Putre. His front hoof stuck for a moment, but the stickiness stretched and finally popped back to the Web, freeing him. Neither of them had wings, but they were flying.

"This way," the speech balloon wrote. The colt set off for the edge of the giant canyon they hovered over.

She flew after him. "Say, this is fun!"

His speech balloon formed and drifted back to her. "Dreams aren't bad when you control them."

"I'll say! Usually when I dream I'm flying, I have trouble getting off the ground and there's a pack of vicious dogs snapping at my feet."

"Yes, the night mares aren't in the business of bringing enjoyable dreams."

They soon came to the edge of the chasm and flew through the leprechauns' forest. They could have risen above the trees, but Jaylin wanted to say good-bye to the little men, so she flew at about twenty-foot elevation, dodging the branches.

And there they were. "Bye, leprechauns!" she called.

The little men looked up—and fell on the ground as if struck down by an unseen hand, staring upward.

Alarmed, Jaylin landed at the edge of the glade and walked back. "Are you all right?"

The leprechauns picked themselves up. "Aye, lass," the spokesman said, dusting himself off. "Sure and you caught us by surprise. You should give a wee bit of warning before you fly over like that."

"I'm sorry," she said contritely. "I guess it was a surprise. You see, I got the Ring of Void, and just learned how to fly. I didn't mean to startle you so badly."

"That too," he agreed.

"There's something else?"

He looked at her. "You don't know?"

"Know what?"

He took her aside. "Lass, here in the dream realm, and in Xanth proper too, a girl's underclothing has a special effect on men. Normally it doesn't show, but when you were above and we looked up—"

"You saw my panties!" she exclaimed. "It freaked you out!"

"Aye, lass."

"Oh, I'm sorry! I never thought—I'm from Mundania, and—I apologize."

"That's all right, lass. Truth be told, we don't much mind such a view. But maybe be more careful in future, aye?"

"I will! Thanks for telling me."

"And welcome."

She took off again, this time flying very low until clear of the glade. "I think I'm going to need a new outfit, if I want to do much flying."

The speech balloon appeared. "When we leave the dream realm, you will no longer be able to fly. But you will be able to conjure dream images."

"It's scary, how much power the Ring has. And it's just one of six!"

"Yes, that is why the Rings of Xanth are normally well hidden. Their power must not be abused."

"I'll try not to abuse mine. I just want to help the others do the job they have to do. But it sure makes me wonder what the Foop does!"

"I am not sure anyone knows, except the Simurgh."

"Well, I guess we'll find out."

Then they reached the portal that was the entry to the dream realm. They flew through it—and found themselves floating above the ground of ordinary Xanth, looking down at their two bodies lying beside the green gourd.

"I don't understand," Jaylin said, alarmed. "Are we dead?"

"No, merely still in the dream. Only our souls entered the gourd, while our bodies slept. See, we are both looking into the peephole. That is the way of it. We must break that connection to wake up."

"I wondered how we were able to fit through that tiny hole," Jaylin said. She looked around, and spied a large fallen leaf. "I'll use this." She landed, and reached down to pick it up. But her hand passed right through it. "Oops."

"Because we are dream images, we aren't fully real," the speech balloon wrote. "We shall have to use a dream barrier."

"All right." She concentrated, and conjured a small wooden board. She set this across the gourd's peephole.

Then she was on the ground, opening her eyes, and Putre was stirring beside her. She felt the full force of gravity, assuming it hadn't yet started to fade. Before her was the gourd, with the board across its peephole.

"How can a dream image be still there, once I'm awake?"

The speech balloon appeared. "You have the Ring."

"Oh. Right." There it was, on her physical finger. She got up and looked around. "I guess you had better take me to the others now."

She climbed onto his back, and he galloped off. This was quite an adventure—and it had barely started.

10
VOID

C he Centaur looked up. "There they come!" he called as Putre galloped into sight carrying Jaylin.

"Does she have the Ring?" Cynthia asked.

"She must, because she's smiling," Breanna said.

"And holding her hand high," Justin agreed.

"With the Ring thereon," Sim squawked. He had good avian eyesight.

Then zombie and maiden arrived. "We got it!" Jaylin said.

Justin went to help her dismount. "We know who you are," he said, "but perhaps we should introduce ourselves. I am Justin Tree. I have the Ring of Idea."

"I've heard so much about you," Jaylin said. "You were a tree for ever so long, until Breanna—"

"Well, I couldn't marry a *tree*," Breanna said. "And as you know, I have the Ring of Fire."

"And this is Sim Bird," Justin said, indicating him. "He does not speak in our language, but you can understand him when you know him. He has the Ring of Air."

"I am glad to meet you," Sim squawked. Sure enough, Jaylin looked blank.

"And these are Che and Cynthia Centaur," Justin said, indicating them. "They are another couple. They have the Rings of Earth and Water, respectively."

"I never thought I'd get to actually meet you," Jaylin said, evidently impressed. "In fact, I never thought I'd find myself in the Land of Xanth. But when Breanna came—"

"We did not know you would join us," Che said. "We had neglected to have a sixth member of our group, so one had to be designated. Breanna tells us that it was largely chance."

"Yes. I had a daydream where I misspoke fell swoop. I didn't think anything of it, until—"

"We understand. None of us anticipated this mission. It started when Cynthia went to ask the Good Magician a Question, and received a disproportionate mission."

"To save the Demon Earth," Cynthia said. "We had tended to think of him as an evil opponent, but now we understand that he is not evil, merely another part of the larger framework. Magic comes from the Demon Xanth, and gravity from the Demon Earth; we need both."

"What comes from the other Demons?" Jaylin asked.

"We aren't sure," Che said. "But I suspect that the strong nuclear force associates with the Demon Jupiter. The weak nuclear force may associate with the Demoness Venus, and the electromagnetic force with the Demon Mars."

"These sound like scientific concepts," Jaylin said. "What are they doing here in the magic realm?"

"All forces are needed to make the universe. A Demon's own force is more visible in his domain, but he does need at least some of the others. That is why we must rescue the Demon Earth; without the force of gravity, all the local Demons are in trouble."

"What about Saturn?"

"I think she associates with Dimension. That is not exactly a force, but it is essential to the well-being of the universe. Nothing can exist without some dimension of space and time."

"She? Saturn is female?"

Che shook his head. "No Demon is precisely male, female, or neuter; all can assume any guise at will. But the display is so pretty that I think of her as female. This really has no meaning beyond my private fancy."

"No, I like it. In my schoolbook Saturn is the ancient god of agriculture. Women did most of that, historically, tending crops while the men went out to hunt. Saturn probably was female, if we knew the truth.".

"Perhaps so," Che agreed, finding himself liking this girl. "And females tend to associate with practical things, so quantities and timing also fit."

"But now we need to get this mission the bleep out of the way, so I can marry Justin," Breanna said briskly. "Maybe tomorrow."

"Tomorrow," Justin echoed. They kissed.

"Yes, the mission," Che agreed. "We now have the Six Rings of Xanth, so can fetch the Swell Foop. But this may not be easy."

"Nothing ever is," Cynthia said. They also kissed.

"I don't think their minds are on it," Jaylin murmured to Sim. He squawked agreement.

"Yes they are," Che said. "We must now take the Six Rings and put them in line."

"What for?" Breanna asked.

"We can locate the Swell Foop only by sighting through the Rings."

"But we can't remove them until the mission is done," Justin protested.

"Yes we can," Breanna said. "At least, when it is mission-related."

"Oh. My error."

"Maybe the demon Type-O wandered by."

"I beg your pardon?"

"Type-O causes errors to appear."

Jaylin tittered. "Typo! He must visit Mundania, because I do that all the time."

"To be sure," Justin agreed. "I understand that Mundania also has the Post Orifice, where all the spare letters and articles go."

"Letters?" Cynthia asked, perplexed.

"*A, B, C,* and so on through the alphabet. There has to be a storage place for them when they are not in use."

Cynthia looked as if she had swallowed a bad prune. "And the articles?"

"*The, a, an.* They also must be stored."

"You must have been exposed to some really rabid puns recently," Breanna said severely.

"I was. Punny and Unpun. Nice enough folk, actually."

"You found the origin of puns!" Sim squawked, delighted.

"The origin of *some* puns," Justin said, qualifying it. "As well as the termination of a similar number. I doubt that this particular weed will ever be eradicated, however. Puns are fundamental to Xanth."

"Yes, they are the lowest level," Sim squawked.

"The basest bottom," Justin agreed.

A small black cloud was forming over Breanna's head. This time it extended to cover Cynthia's head as well. Che was having trouble keeping a straight face, and he saw that Sim's beak was trying to twist into a smirk.

"It's like a bad movie," Jaylin said, evidently not taking the matter as seriously as the other females were. "Every time you think it's bottomed out, another silly ass appears."

Putre looked indignant. "She didn't mean you," Che said quickly.

"She surely means the move-E," Justin said, his own face marvelously straight. "A thing that moves around to block your way. It can be destroyed only by a cri-tick, but that may have the perverse effect of making it seem larger."

"If you silly asses are quite done," Breanna said tightly, "let's get the bleep on with the mission. We need to remove our Rings so we can sight through them."

The others sobered, regretfully, agreeing that it was time. Each of them removed a Ring from a finger or toe. Che used thread to tie them together in the shape of a tube. Then he looked through it.

"What do you see?" Cynthia asked.

"Nothing, except a flying goblin child with rainbow-colored wings," he replied, swinging the tube around as he peered. Sure enough, in a moment the goblet passed close enough for the others to see.

"Hi!" she called. "I'm Megan. Can you tell me where the nearest rainbow is? I like to play on rainbows."

"You can do that?" Che asked, surprised.

"Oh, sure. Goblin/harpy crossbreeds have talents, you know. Mine is playing on rainbows."

"I think you will have to look for intermittent rain," Che said. "Rainbows seem to prefer that environment."

"Thank you." She flew on.

Che resumed his search through the Ring. Then he saw a vague brightness. "That direction."

"Nice going, hooves-for-brains," Breanna said. "You have just indicated the entire jungle to the north."

"Perhaps you will have better success," Che said, modestly nettled. He gave her the tube.

Breanna took it and swung it around. "All I see is a funny ogre."

"Ogre's aren't funny; they are stupid," Che said. "And justifiably proud of it."

"I know that, four-foots. But this one is different."

In a moment the ogre appeared. He did look odd. "Who are you, dimwit?" Breanna demanded.

"Me Stretch, no wretch," the ogre replied, pleased by her compliment.

"Stretch?"

For answer, the ogre stretched. As he did so, his body and arms and legs lengthened, and he became larger. But then he tottered; he had diluted his body and was weaker. So he compacted himself to half size, picked up a stone between two fingers, and squeezed it into a pebble. That was impressive; normally an ogre required a full ham-hand to do that. He had gained strength.

"That's pretty good," Breanna said. Satisfied, the ogre moved on.

She returned to her search and this time found it. "That way."

"That is half of the area Che indicated," Cynthia said.

"For sure," Breanna agreed, evidently feeling a nettle herself. She gave the tube to Cynthia.

Cynthia sighted through it. "All I see is a man touching plants. He is enlarging or minimizing living things."

"I suspect the Rings have spurious results if not closely guided," Che said. "They seem to be orienting on special people or talents."

She continued to look. "There is definitely a brightness in that direction."

"You have halved it again," Justin said. "I believe I perceive the semblance of a pattern here."

"Each new person narrows the focus," she agreed, handing him the tube. "After spying a bogus image."

Justin looked through it. "I see two girls, evidently sisters. They are staggering."

In a moment the girls came into the sight of the others. They were indeed walking in a very irregular manner.

"Hello," Justin said. "Are you in good health?"

"I'm Inebriated," one said.

"And I'm Intoxicated," the other said. "We're twins."

They staggered on past. "You had better not like that type," Breanna told him dangerously as his gaze followed the girls.

"Naturally not." Justin quickly resumed looking through the Rings tube. "I do observe light, in precisely that direction." He pointed.

"Half again," Jaylin said, smiling.

He gave her the tube, and she looked. "I see a nymph lode—I mean a lymph node." But her correction was too late. A piece of metal rose from the ground and flew away. "Oops, I guess I did it again."

"I believe that is metal that is attracted to nymphs," Che said. "It is traveling in the direction of the Faun and Nymph retreat."

Jaylin looked again. In a moment she had narrowed it down similarly. Then she held the tube for Sim as he looked. "There," he squawked.

They now had a definite line, bearing close to north. "If we saw no need for cooperation before, we have it now," Che said. "But I think we had better continue to verify, in case the direction is not constant."

"Now some of us can fly," Justin said. "Some of us can walk. I think we will make swifter progress if all of us fly."

"And how am I going to fly?" Breanna demanded archly.

"Summon the demoness."

"Oh! I forget my Ring." She looked around. "But then we'll have to take it out of the Foop tube."

"That is a problem," he agreed.

"I will carry you," Cynthia said.

"And I will carry you," Che said to Justin.

That left Jaylin. She looked perplexed, then Putre nudged her. The other zombies were gone, but he had remained. "And I'll ride you!" she exclaimed. "Maybe you can't fly, out here in real Xanth, but you can certainly keep up."

They set off. Che kept an eye on the zombie colt, but he did indeed keep up, running as fast as a dream.

They moved a reasonable distance, then stopped to verify. The direction remained north.

The third pause was at the southern brink of the Gap Chasm. The direction remained north.

"Can you cross that?" Che asked Putre.

A speech balloon appeared. "I can run down one side, across, and up the other."

"But I'll fall off!" Jaylin protested.

"No, you can't fall off a dream horse when you have the Ring of Dreams," Che said. "And Putre wouldn't let it happen anyway."

The girl still looked doubtful. Breanna interceded. "It's magic," she said. "You can't be blamed for not really believing in magic, despite seeing it all around; sometimes I wonder about it myself. If you come to mischief, it won't be because of the horse."

"We'll hover near, until you are sure," Cynthia said.

Jaylin did not look completely reassured, but she nodded. Cynthia took off, carrying Breanna over the brink of the chasm, and hovered there.

Putre trotted to the brink, turned the corner, and trotted straight down the cliff. The girl remained on his back, her eyes squeezed shut. After a moment she opened them, realized that they were not falling, and relaxed. It was just as if they were traveling horizontally, thanks to the magic.

After that, Che also took off, carrying Justin, and Sim did too. They circled over the Gap Chasm, watching the horse gallop on downward.

Then Che saw a stir in the depths of the chasm. "Is that what I think it is?" he asked Sim.

"The Gap Dragon," Sim squawked. "He couldn't catch a dream horse anyway, but I will go explain." He flew down toward the dragon.

"Perhaps that is just as well," Justin remarked. "The girl is nervous enough already; she would not care to encounter the Gap Dragon."

Che nodded. He was of course friends with Stanley Steamer, because they were both winged monsters, but it was the dragon's job to patrol the base of the chasm and steam and eat any intruders. Legitimate travelers usually crossed one of the bridges across the Gap, but their own party was in a hurry.

In due course the horse galloped across the chasm, and up the far cliff.

It was evident that Jaylin was now entirely relaxed; experiencing was believing. "And we saw the Gap Dragon!" she exclaimed as they crested the brink and returned to regular ground. "He puffed steam at us!"

Perhaps their concern about her reaction had been exaggerated.

They moved on north. Soon they reached the boundary marking the Region of Air. They were across it before they realized, but it could not be mistaken. Wind storms battered them, forcing the flyers to take to the ground, joining Putre and Jaylin. "This is where Cumulo Fracto Nimbus, the demon cloud, brought Hurricane Happy Bottom, saving the Land of Xanth from getting blown away," Che informed Jaylin as he landed beside her.

"We don't have to put up with this wind," Sim squawked as he landed beside them, his lovely feathers scuffled.

"But don't we have to get through this Region to reach the Void?" Jaylin asked as her hair blew across her face. Then she did a double-take. "Say—I understood you!"

"You must be getting to know me," he squawked. "Yes, we do have to pass though the several Regions, but we don't have to endure their rigors. We have the Rings."

"The Rings?" Then she caught on. "The Rings control their Regions!"

Che could have beat himself over the head with a wing. Why hadn't he thought of that? He was supposed to be Sim's tutor, but Sim was already beginning to out-think him.

"But we are unable to use the Rings individually while we orient on the Foop," Justin reminded them.

That neatly took Che off the hook. "Perhaps we should return the Rings to their individual users, and reassemble the tube at each boundary," he suggested.

The others nodded. It might be clumsy, but they needed to use the Rings in more than one way. They dismantled the tube and passed out the Rings. Breanna experimentally tried to put on Justin's Ring of Idea, but it wouldn't go on her finger; the Rings now accepted only their designated bearers.

Sim lifted his foot and squawked at his Ring of Air. Suddenly the storm wind died, and the air was still.

"Now that's more like it, Birdbrain," Breanna said affectionately. "Hi-yo, Cynthia, away!"

The centaur filly took off, darting a wry expression at the others. "Even that girl's annoyances become endearing," Justin murmured. Che had to agree as he took off.

They saw that Putre and Jaylin had no trouble keeping up, running below. Soon the party came to the boundary of the next Region. They paused before crossing it, wary of the sudden change they knew could occur.

"The Region of Earth is highly volcanic," Che said. "It can be difficult to find a safe place to stand, let alone walk, but the air is not much safer because of the ejecta."

"The what?" Jaylin asked.

Che started to explain, but she cut him off, laughing. "I was only teasing you, Che. I'm from Hawaii, where we have active volcanoes. I know what they belch into the air. Or in our case, what they spew across the land: molten rivers. Our whole chain of islands was formed from volcanic ejecta."

He nodded. "For a moment I thought of the Demoness Metria."

"Yes, with her confused words. Why is she like that?"

"She got trodden on by a sphinx, long ago. It split her personality into three aspects: a crazy adult, an innocent child, and the one with the problem of vocabulary. That's also the one with the insatiable curiosity about mortal affairs, so we see a fair amount of her."

Smoke formed. "Did someone say my name?" it asked.

"Oh, no," Breanna muttered. "Maybe I can use my Ring to banish her."

"Save it for the Region of Fire," Cynthia suggested.

"We were just talking about ejecta," Jaylin said brightly to the demoness.

"About what?"

"Matter, substance, material, stuff, rocks—"

"Flying hot out of a volcano?"

"Whatever," Jaylin said crossly. But she couldn't hold her frown more than an instant. Then they both laughed.

"Well, you'll see plenty of that next door," Metria said.

"No we won't," Che said. He poked his head through the veil and saw the ground beyond shaking, and heard a nearby volcano rumbling dangerously. He lifted the Ring of Earth. "Quiet," he said.

Immediately the ground settled down, and the volcano silenced. The Region of Earth spread out before him. A violent terrain, but no longer in motion, and its air was clean.

"The Rings of Xanth remain impressive," Justin remarked.

"Indeed," Cynthia agreed.

"That's almost like cheating," Metria said, disgusted. She faded out.

They took time to reassemble the tube and sight through it. There was no question: They had to enter the Region of Earth.

They crossed the Region, and soon came to the next.

"That will be the Region of Fire," Breanna said. "My turn." They verified the direction, then took apart the tube so that she could use her Ring. She poked her head and hand through the intangible curtain separating the Regions. In a moment she drew them back. "All clear, now."

The others crossed. Che saw a land of ashes and fading smoke. Gases jetted up from fumeroles that were normally on fire. The Region normally burned perpetually.

As he flew across, Che saw that already fresh grass and bushes were growing out of the ashes. There had to be a lot of flammable matter to feed the fires, which swept back and forth across the range. He wondered how this had ever gotten started; he would have to do some research to refresh his memory of those complicated past events, preparing for the time when Sim wanted to know.

Sim flew near. "How did this start?" he squawked.

Sigh. He would have to go on his present vague memory. "With an enchantment, of course. In the year of Xanth Three-seventy-eight the Seventh Wave settled around Lake Ogre-Chobee. The talents of its people were weak, so they set up a Talent Research Group headed by a man called Hydrogen, whose talent was to make dirty water become clean. They tried to develop better curses, so as to defend themselves from aggressive others. One of them named Loudspeaker learned how to amplify his voice and create Words of Power. Others continued their research. Soon they had eight Magicians. Unfortunately power corrupted them, and they became nasty and warlike. Loudspeaker led the forces of meanness, and Hydrogen led the forces of decency. Loudspeaker used terrible Words to enslave the air creatures north of the Gap Chasm, but Hydrogen hurled a curse that blew him away, leaving only the winds to form the Region of Air. Then Loudspeaker enslaved the creatures of the

Earth, and Hydrogen hurled another curse that blasted him out and made the Region of Earth. Similar battles made the Regions of Fire, Water, and Void, which was the last and most terrible curse. They have remained ever since, still powered by the continuing force of the curses that formed them."

"A most interesting history," Justin remarked. "Curses certainly should not be misused."

"Then what of the Rings?" Sim squawked.

This was the part Che hated, because he could not remember. In fact, he had not known of the Rings before this mission began. "I must conjecture that Magician Hydrogen or some other historical Magician formed them, just in case it was ever necessary to bring the Regions under control, and then hid them so that they could not be misused. There is much of Xanth that we do not yet properly comprehend."

"And the Swell Foop?"

"That is entirely beyond my knowledge," Che admitted, ashamed. The worst had happened: His student's need for knowledge had outstripped the ability of his tutor.

Sim stared at him. Worse, so did Cynthia and Breanna, and even Jaylin, riding Putre below, looked up, dismayed. How gross was his failure! How would he ever live this down? Centaurs were supposed to know everything.

"There appears to be a void in your information," Justin observed.

"Yes," Che agreed, ashamed.

"Obviously the Swell Foop embodies magic to make itself hidden, so that not even the most knowledgeable species, the centaurs, know of it. Otherwise it would not remain hidden long."

"For sure," Breanna agreed, and Cynthia nodded. Sim flew higher, satisfied.

Che discovered that he was getting to like Justin Tree. The man had a knack for putting a positive face on things. "Thank you," he murmured.

"I merely spoke the manifest truth," Justin said. But his hand patted Che's shoulder near the wing; he did understand. He must have supported Breanna of the Black Wave similarly, for she was a feisty girl prone to mischief. No wonder she wanted to marry him.

They came to the Region of Water. This needed no pacification, except for one thing: Cynthia invoked her Ring to cause the surface of the lake near Putre to tighten so that he could run across it without sinking in. Night mares could do that anyway, but he was a zombie colt.

At last they reached the margin of the Void. This time it was Jaylin who had the applicable Ring. "But how do I use it?" she asked.

That was all too good a question. "The Void is the most deadly Region of Xanth," Che said. "Nothing that enters it can escape it, with certain limited exceptions such as the night mares. I think we had better be very sure that our mission requires us to pass this point."

Once again they assembled the tube. It showed that the Swell Foop was straight ahead, inside the Void. They considered, and took the tube apart again, because they wanted the protection of the individual Rings.

"So how *does* she use her Ring?" Breanna asked. "We can't pave over the Void."

"Is it possible that the Ring of Void will enable us to enter the Void, and depart it?" Justin asked. "If so, we can enter it, recover the Foop, and safely emerge. All we need is to be in the company of the Ring."

"But can we be sure of that?" Che asked.

"The very thought of going into the Void turns me white," Breanna said.

"I've got an idea," Jaylin said. "I'll ask the Night Stallion. He ought to know."

"That lord of dreams is not much for answering questions," Justin said.

"For sure, you can't just conjure him up at a whim," Breanna said. "I was amazed when my Ring of Fire conjured the Demon Grossclout, but I think he wanted to appear."

But Jaylin was already rubbing the Ring. "Trojan, appear."

To Che's amazement, the Dark Horse appeared, huge and scintillating. "Justin Tree is correct," he said, and faded.

"That is some Ring," Cynthia said weakly. "I hope he doesn't punish us with terrible dreams."

"He doesn't need to," Sim squawked. "He has just deleted our excuse for not entering the Void."

The others nodded. Their worst fear now had to be braved.

"Well, let's go," Breanna said. She shot a dark glance at Justin. "But if we get caught forever in the Void, we're still getting married. You can't escape."

"I wouldn't think of it," Justin replied, pleased.

They marched across the line. Che saw that the region beyond the line was no black void, but a pleasant slope with flowers and trees. It seemed to be completely unthreatening.

Then Che saw two winged centaurs running by, a male and a female. "Look!" he cried. "Our kind!"

"Whose kind?" Breanna demanded. "Those are black human beings."

"Two iridescent birds!" Sim squawked.

Putre's speech balloon appeared. "Two zombie horses."

Che reconsidered. "My grandam Chem was in the Void with Smash Ogre and Tandy Nymph. They escaped by paying half their souls to the night mares to carry them out. She reported that each person saw his or her own kind, regardless what was really there."

"Ludicrous!" Breanna snapped. Then she gasped. "Che—you're full human!"

Che's eyes had been fixed on the two figures ahead. Now he looked in the direction of Breanna's voice. There was Cynthia, with another winged centaur on her back. He looked at Jaylin and Putre: two more winged centaurs.

"All of you are bright birds," the last winged centaur squawked.

"It seems your grandam was correct," Justin said. "We see only our own kind. That means we must inquire what kind are the two ahead."

Those two, having spied the new party, had stopped chasing and come toward them. "I am Branch Faun, and this is Lady Slipper Nymph," he said. "We were happily chasing, on our way to a celebration, when we slipped, collided, and fell into the Void. Have you come to rescue us?"

There was a brief pause as each person considered. "You know, if that Ring of Void really works," the Breanna centaur said, "we should be able to conduct them out of here. Why don't we try it?"

Che was as curious as she was about this particular aspect, because he was as doubtful as she as to its reality "By all means. Jaylin?"

The Jaylin centaur got off the back of the Putre centaur. "Please come this way," she said.

The two others followed her up the slope. Then all three disappeared. In a moment only the Jaylin centaur returned. "They're out," she reported.

"What did they do?" the Breanna centaur asked.

"They chased each other. Then they—I don't think I was supposed to see that." Jaylin blushed.

"Faun and nymph!" Che exclaimed. "Of course! They celebrated. That's what they do."

"They sure did," Jaylin said. "Then they got up and chased some more. They ran out of sight, so I came back here."

The Breanna centaur went over to her. "Fauns and nymphs don't have much ambition or memory," she explained. "They live for the moment."

"Some moment!"

"It's their nature. At least they weren't bored while they were caught here in the Void. This answers a couple of questions: It doesn't hurt or change folk to be here awhile, and the Ring can get folk out. I'm glad we verified that, because it has excellent implications for the rest of us."

"I don't want to chase around and—and celebrate!" Jaylin said.

"Of course not. You're not a nymph. But you do want to get out of here in good order."

"True," Jaylin agreed. Then, after a pause: "Actually, being from Mundania, I do know what—what they do. I've seen pictures. I just never—never saw it that—"

"That enthusiastically," Breanna said. "We understand. Now let's forget about that and go fetch the Foop."

"Yes," Jaylin agreed, evidently relieved.

They resumed their trek downslope. They saw other winged centaurs, but left them alone. They already knew what they needed to, and it was reassuring.

They came to a bucket. It seemed to be quite ordinary, and empty. On its side were printed the words KICK ME.

"If that's what it wants," Sim squawked. He advanced on the pail. He drew back one foot.

"Don't do it!" Jaylin cried, leaping to intercept him. They fell together in an apparent tangle of eight legs, four arms, and four wings.

"Squawk?" Sim asked as they untangled.

"It's another pun! An ugly one. To kick the bucket—"

Che caught on. "Is to die!"

"That's right," Breanna agreed. "You don't want to kick the bucket before your time. Especially not here."

Justin nodded. "We have ascertained that the Void is not necessarily death. But the bucket may be a shortcut to that state, for those who become tired of stasis. An ugly pun, indeed."

"Squawk," Sim agreed.

Che felt weak-kneed again. Sim had almost committed suicide while the others watched. "Thank you, Jaylin," he said. "You have no idea how much mischief you spared us." They had become accustomed to all living things being friendly to the Simurgh's precious chick, but the bucket did not share that oath.

"Well, it was just that there have been so many puns, I sort of expected one," Jaylin said.

"So nobody kicks that bucket," Breanna said firmly. "Let's move on."

The pleasant slope led down to a deeper funnel-shaped region, its sides steepening. They were reaching the awful center of the Void.

Jaylin stopped walking. "I don't want to make trouble, but could we—maybe try walking back some, just to be sure we can?"

"This makes eminent sense," Justin agreed, and she flashed him a smile. She was still a winged centaur, but her face was unchanged.

They turned back, and had no difficulty walking back up the slope. The Ring of Void was still working.

They paused, then resumed the downward trek.

Something came rolling down from behind them. They hastily made way, and it passed, accelerating as it did. It dropped into the central hole. There was no sound, and no sight of it. It was gone.

"For sure," Breanna muttered nervously.

But what choice did they have?

"I don't want to be—" Jaylin started.

"Go ahead and be," Breanna said. "I'm as pale around the gills as you are, right now."

"I was thinking—maybe if we all held hands—"

"For sure!"

Che agreed. They needed the reassurance of each other's proximity. They knew intellectually that the Ring of Void would protect them, but emotionally they remained in deep doubt. They formed a circle around the deadly pit and extended their arms. Sim would be extending his wings, and the night colt—

"Two of you take hold of Putre," Che said. They took hold, then let themselves slide forward into the black hole.

There was a feeling of enormous compression and simultaneous velocity. They dropped down, down, ever down into the depth. The universe seemed to whirl around them, dizzyingly stable.

Then they were at the bottom, or rather the center. Things were floating all around. "Are we all here?" Che inquired mentally, as he seemed to have no voice.

"I am here," Justin's reply came. It was a thought rather than a voice.

"Me too," Breanna's thought came, tinged with female.

"Present." That was Cynthia.

"Here." Jaylin.

"Squawk."

"Neigh."

They all laughed, though it was just a round of pleasant feeling.

"I suspect we are without our bodies at the moment," Che thought. "But we are functional. Now we must locate the Swell Foop."

"So let's assemble the Ring Tube," Breanna thought. "Here is my— oops."

"It is your Ring we want at the moment, not your private parts, however delectable they may be," Justin thought primly.

"Oh, shut up, lover! I mean I can't find my Ring."

"Just look on your little finger," Cynthia thought. "It should be, um— where *is* my finger?"

"Where is mine?" Jaylin thought, alarmed.

"And my claw?" Sim squawked/thought.

Soon it was clear, in a foggy way, that none of them could find their Rings, because they had no extremities on which to wear them. That was, it seemed, one of the unforeseen consequences of being bodiless.

"I believe we are in a quantum state," Che thought. "We are randomly mixed together, our material beings overlapping."

"Overlap your own female," Breanna snapped. "The only one I want overlapping me is Justin."

"He means that the rules of physics are different under extreme compression," Justin thought. "We are all occupying the same point. We are merged with each other, and our Rings."

"Then how the bleep can we line them up?"

"I am not sure. Perhaps we can align our bodies."

"Then who will be left to sight through the tube?" Cynthia thought.

"I don't want anybody sighting through *my* tubes." Breanna objected.

"I fear this is not feasible," Justin thought. "It seems the rules of engagement have changed in the quantum state."

"No they haven't!" Breanna flared. "We're still getting married the moment this is done!"

Someone sent a wash of humor.

"Perhaps we can operate without the tube," Che thought, "and perform a physical search."

"Of whom?" Breanna demanded. "Nobody's going to search my body but—"

"Or a mental search," Justin thought quickly. "Whatever way is feasible in this state."

"I'm not too eager to have anyone snooping through my mind, either," Breanna thought.

"I fear you are not *in* your right mind at the moment, dear girl."

"Is that so? Well, you can just take your—"

"She feels hysterical," Jaylin thought nervously.

"*Who* is hysterical?" Breanna's thought screamed.

"This calls for a firm measure," Cynthia decided. "Kiss her, Justin."

"Gladly." There followed a sensation of sheer ecstasy surrounded by overlapping quantum hearts.

"For sure," Breanna thought blissfully as she sank out of sight.

"You never kissed *me* like that," Cynthia thought to Che.

"Well, it's hard to caress your front side and your back side simultaneously."

"You could if you really tried."

There was a mental squawk and titter as Sim and Jaylin tried to visualize centaurs doing that.

"Neigh."

Putre was right: They had to stop fooling around and start searching. They agreed to spread out mentally and check all the objects their minds encountered. There should be some special quality to the Swell Foop that identified it.

They started the search. There turned out to be all manner of junk bobbling around them.

"I found a foop!" Breanna's thought came.

"So soon," Che thought. "Then we can depart."

"I found another," Sim's squawk-thought came.

"Two?"

"Here's another," Cynthia's thought came.

"How many can there be?" Che demanded. "There has been no indication that there is more than one."

"We need the Swell Foop," Justin's thought came. "It must be hidden among endless ordinary foops, which are probably worthless."

"You are surely correct," Che agreed. "The Swell Foop must have generated echoes of itself in the quantum state. We may simply have to bring all of them out, and sort them outside the Void."

But it soon was apparent that there were hundreds or thousands of foops. Apparently most of the soulless things that fell into the Void became foops. They would not be able to take all of them.

They paused for thought. This was an unexpected difficulty, though Che had not known what to expect. They could not search forever, because the Demon Earth needed to be rescued soon. But how could they find the right one?

"Dam!" Putre's thought exclaimed.

"That's 'damn' if you want to be technical," Breanna's thought muttered. "Not a fitting word for a colt your age."

"No," Che thought. "He means dam—a female parent."

"A mother horse," Cynthia agreed.

"Could it be—?" Justin thought.

"Mare Imbri!" Jaylin's thought came. "Wasn't she lost in the Void?"

"She did lose her body here," Che agreed. "Because she had half a soul, she survived as a day mare, and later became a tree nymph."

"Dam," Putre repeated. "I know you! Answer me."

"What you have found must be her body husk," Justin thought. "Without a soul, it evidently has no meaning here."

"A soul!" Jaylin thought. "Putre, she gave you part of her soul. Can you give part of your soul back?"

"I will try."

After what might have been a moment, in a less timeless realm, there came a new thought. "Oh, thank you! I have meaning again."

"Dam—don't you know me? I am your foal!"

"I had no foal."

"You lost your body before you had a foal," Che thought quickly. "Your half soul survived, and later had a foal with the Day Horse. This is he, after you entered the Void."

"I am amazed," Imbri's thought came. "But I recognize this soul fragment. It is indeed from Chem Centaur, who gave it to me."

"My grandam," Che thought proudly. "Her soul regenerated, and my dam Chex had a full soul, and my soul is full too."

"I have so much to catch up on," Imbri thought. "Not that it matters."

"It does matter!" Che thought. "You deserve to know."

"We can never leave the Void, so it doesn't matter."

"But we *can* leave! As soon as we find the Swell Foop."

"I know where that is. It is the only foop of any value."

"Find it for us, and we will take you out of here," Che thought, and felt the emphatic agreement of the others. Especially Putre.

"Why, it is right here. Do any of you have hands?"

"Yes, two of us are centaurs, and three are human."

"Here." Something came into his mental space. He knew immediately that it was the Swell Foop, for it had an aura of grandeur.

"Then we must leave," Che thought, exhilarated. "Take hold, folks, and make sure to include both horses."

They took hold, and when the new circle was complete, Jaylin willed the Ring of Void to lift them out. They moved outward from the ball of the center, gaining velocity, and shot upward. They found themselves standing in a ring around the Void-hole, holding hands or grasping fur.

"Continue on up and out," Che said, quickly letting go to catch the thing that threatened to drop back into the hole. He mustn't lose that!

They climbed without difficulty, eight creatures. The fair flowered slope beckoned enticingly, but they did not relent. The vague border curtain was near.

Then suddenly they were out of it and back at the verge of the region of water. Their natural shapes were back: two centaurs, three human beings, one bird, and two black horses. They had made it—with the Swell Foop. And Mare Imbri!

11
LIAISON

J ustin gazed at the object Che Centaur held. Now that they were safely out of the Void, it looked exactly like a warty rock.

"This is it?" Jaylin asked, sounding disappointed.

"It surely is," Che answered. He set it on the ground next to the lake. "Touch it."

Jaylin touched it. "Ooo, it's swell!"

"Precisely. But I'm at a slight loss as to how to use it."

The others touched the rock, and agreed that it was definitely the Foop. But no one had any idea how to use it.

"The Six Rings of Xanth are supposed to control it," Cynthia reminded them.

"Perhaps we should depart the Region of Water and find a more secure place to consider," Justin suggested.

"For sure," Breanna agreed for all of them.

Jaylin mounted Putre, and the party moved rapidly out of the Regions and south across the Gap Chasm, and on to Castle Zombie. There they hesitated.

"Mare Imbrium," Justin said. "We are very glad to have you back with us. But there is a complication."

A dreamlet cloud appeared over her head. In it was the head of a black-haired human woman. "I know," that woman said. "Putre has caught me up with what happened after I fell into the Void. Not only do I have a foal, I have become a tree nymph."

"I think this will make it difficult for you to return to your prior situation," Justin said gently.

"That's right!" Breanna agreed. "How can there be two of you?"

"They should get together and talk it over," Sim squawked. "They can decide what is best."

The others circled a glance around, nodding. Sim was indeed a very bright bird.

"What of Putre?" Jaylin asked.

"He should go with his dam," Justin said. "He found her. There is no further need of him to locate the Ring of Void, or to convey you there."

"I guess that's right," Jaylin agreed. She went to hug the colt. "I'll miss you, horseface. You really helped me."

A little heart floated up. Then the two horses departed, and Jaylin wiped away a tear.

"You can see him again, after we're through with the Foop," Justin said.

"In Mundania?"

He had no answer for that. He wished he had not spoken.

"We'd better go inside and catch up Jonathan and Millie," Breanna said. "And figure out the Foop."

Soon they were in the throes of it. "Six Rings and a rock," Breanna said. "Who would have thought they'd be so hard to put together?"

"Perhaps if we knew what the Foop does, we would know how to invoke it," Cynthia said.

"Considering the power of the Six Rings," Che said, "the Foop must be of a greater magnitude. It is hard to conceive of anything in Xanth that would require more than the control of all the Regions and the creatures and things within them."

"Well, our mission is to rescue the Demon Earth, so it must have power beyond Xanth," Justin said. "In fact, if only another Demon can have abducted D. Earth, it must have power of the Demons themselves."

"That makes a conceivable need," Che agreed. "Each of the major Demons has equivalent power, and we have seen how all the magic of the Land of Xanth is mere trace leakage from the Demon Xanth. This thing must be potentially stronger than the Demon Xanth himself."

"So maybe we should ask him," Jaylin said.

There was a silence. Then Justin broke it. "We could do that, but he might not like the idea of our using the Foop."

"A rival power," Che agreed. "It does seem better that we discover this on our own."

They studied the stone. "What are those warts?" Breanna asked.

"Stones are seldom regular," Che said. "They are fragments of larger processes. I assume the projections are random."

"Random can be dangerous," Sim squawked. "We had to deal with the Random Factor."

"Why would anything about an object of this potential power be random?" Breanna asked.

They considered again. Then Sim put it together: "I note six projections," he squawked. "We have six Rings. They must have to be touching the Foop to control it."

"One Ring per wart," Breanna said. "It works for me."

They took off their Rings and tried placing them on the projections. Each one fit perfectly. Obviously that was where they were supposed to go.

"Now what?" Cynthia asked.

"Maybe we have to invoke it, the way we do the individual Rings," Jaylin said. "Maybe just thinking what we want."

Breanna held her spread hands over the rock. "Rise, Foop," she intoned dramatically.

Nothing happened.

"Is it possible," Justin asked, "that there needs to be a particular order? That is, each Ring must be on a designated knob?"

"It sure as bleep is," Jaylin said. Then, seeing the other glance reprovingly at her, she apologized. "Sorry about the bad word. It just slipped out. What I mean is, that with a computer in Mundania you have to have everything just exactly right. You can't change the order to suit you. This must be like that. Maybe it's like a code, to be sure nobody gets it activated by accident."

"But if there's a set order," Che asked, "why do the knobs accept the wrong Rings? We can't put the Rings on the wrong people."

"That must be part of the protection," Jaylin said. "It's like a secret code, and you have to know it to get it right."

"But we *don't* know it."

"So I guess we have to crack the code. Then we'll know it for next time."

The others nodded. They started changing the positions of the Rings. It was surprising how many patterns there could be for six Rings with six knobs.

A swirl of smoke formed. "We're getting something!" Breanna said.

Then it formed into the Demoness Metria. "What's up, doctors?" she inquired, her outfit becoming almost but not quite translucent, so as to compel the eyes of the males in the party without quite cauterizing them. It was evidently a fine art; Justin appreciated the precision of it without quite being able to remove his own eyes from the sight.

Breanna looked as if she were stifling a bleep-loaded outburst. Justin knew why: Metria was normally mischief, and this was a very important project. If they told her to go away, she would remain to pester them. But if they didn't, she might remain anyway. The question was how to get her to depart without alerting her to the fact that something extremely interesting was occurring.

"We are merely contemplating this dull rock," Justin said. That was technically accurate.

The demoness turned, showing more silhouette than a normal woman could manage in a lifetime. "Say, that looks just like a foop."

"A smelly what?" Breanna asked.

"A piece of filth, dirt, dung, muck, feces—"

"Poop?"

"Whatever," the demoness agreed crossly. "A smell poop." She started to fade out. But then she reversed. "Hey, wait—that wasn't the word! I said foop, not poop. What are you doing with a foop?"

"Bleep!" Breanna swore. "It almost worked."

Metria looked at her. "Are you trying to get rid of me, or only pretending to try to get rid of me?"

"Does it matter?"

"No. Obviously you folk are into something interesting here. You might as well tell me, on the off chance that I'll find it boring and fade out."

Breanna shot a desperate glance at Justin. He was able to receive it because he had managed to avert his eyes from the demoness when she faded and was keeping them clear now. It was a struggle, because his eyeballs were straining to return to the barely showing cake and buns.

"It is indeed a foop," he said. "We are trying to determine what it may be good for."

"That's easy. It controls demons. Since nobody in his right mind wants to do that, I'll just remove it and throw it away, saving you the trouble." She reached down toward the stone, her décolletage flexing dangerously.

"No!" Justin and Breanna cried together.

The demoness paused. "Do you care to come clean now? I called your fake."

"Our what?" Justin asked.

"Pretense, dupe, counterfeit, dare, challenge—"

"Bluff?"

"Whatever. Tell me all about it, or I'll steal the Foop and throw it away."

"This is—this is—" Justin sputtered, unable to get the word out.

"Blackmail?" the demoness inquired sweetly, her short skirt becoming scantier.

"Whatever!"

"I guess we'd better tell her," Breanna said reluctantly.

"Very well," Justin agreed, though he would have preferred to utter a brush-scorching expletive. "This is not just any foop—it is the Swell Foop."

For once they saw the demoness aghast. Her clothing became entirely opaque. "The Swell Foop! You actually got it? I thought that was an untamed quack pursuit."

"A what?"

"A feral ugly-duck hunt. One quarter of an inch off-center."

"A wild goose?"

"Whatever! Have you any idea how dangerous that thing is?"

"No. Do you?"

"No. But it hasn't been used in centuries."

"So what were you saying about a foop controlling demons? Does the Swell Foop do that?"

"Of course. It controls Demons. You know, the major ones, big *D*'s, like the Demon Xanth." She frowned. "If I may get serious a moment, you don't want to mess with that one."

"It is not our choice," Justin said.

"I suppose it isn't. But you are entering treacherous waters."

"It's weird seeing you serious," Breanna said.

"It's weird being near the Swell Foop."

"So how does it work?"

"I don't know."

"You don't know!" Justin exploded. "You said—"

"I said it was dangerous. I did not say I knew how to operate it. No demon does, of course. Otherwise we'd turn it permanently off."

"Really?"

"No. No demon can touch it."

"But you threatened to steal it and throw it away."

"That was a bluff, even for a regular foop. They are immune from demon molestation." Then she reconsidered. "However, I might stop you from using it, if I freaked you out." Her clothing began to turn glassy.

"Metria, this is serious business," Justin told her sternly. "If you don't want to help, then kindly fade out."

"Spoilsport." Her clothing opaqued again. "A demon girl just wants to have fun."

They returned their attention to the Foop. "How will we know when we have the right combination?" Jaylin asked.

"We shall have to give it a command each time we change the Rings," Justin said. "When it responds, then we'll know."

They tried a combination. "Swell Foop, rise," Justin said. To no avail.

"It occurs to me that we may be trying the wrong testing procedure," Che said. "The Foop may not do things to itself, but rather it must affect demons."

The others nodded. "Then Metria can indeed be of assistance," Justin said. "If the Foop makes her do something not of her own choosing—"

"How can we tell?" Breanna asked. "She may choose to humor us."

"It is a risk we shall have to take."

"I'll cooperate," Metria said. "Because this is interesting."

"Hold on," Cynthia said. "If we try things on her, and they work, it may simply be because she is cooperating, not because of the Foop."

"Excellent point," Justin said. "Metria, you must help us by being completely perverse. Don't do anything we ask you to, unless you are compelled."

The demoness smiled. "This may be fun."

Justin tried, with the Foop Rings the same as they were. "Demoness, turn around."

"No way," Metria said.

They tried another combination. "Turn."

"No."

They tried another. "Turn."

"Go jump."

Justin, uncertain whether she was teasing them, was becoming quietly pained. They had thought they had success when they got the Foop; now failure was looming. He tried another combination. "Turn."

"Ouch!"

All of them were startled. "What's the matter?" Justin asked.

"I got a sudden pain in my posterior. But I'm not turning."

She was starting to be truly uncooperative. He hoped they found the right combination soon.

Breanna touched the Foop. "I'm disgusted. We're not getting anywhere."

"You and me both," Metria said, turning mottled gray. "We're all wasting our time."

"I came all the way here to Xanth, and braved the Void, for nothing?" Jaylin asked sorrowfully. She touched the Foop. "For this dull stone?"

"The thought makes me cry," Metria said, and bright tears flowed down her face.

Justin suspected that they were being mocked. He tried a new combination. "Turn."

"No, it's your turn."

Several combinations later, they still had no results.

Then Sim thought of something. "For a moment there, we had emotions," he squawked. "And the demoness shared those emotions."

A glance of sheer amazed surmise circled them. "Emotions!" Che exclaimed. "It generates Demon emotions!"

"And little *d* demon emotions," Metria agreed, surprised. "I'm excited."

"And you're faking it," Breanna said. "This isn't that setting."

"Curses! Foiled again."

"But is that the same as controlling demons?" Justin asked.

"I believe it is," Che said. "Human beings are ruled by their emotions, and even centaurs have been known to be strongly influenced."

"But merely feeling pained or disgusted or sad does not necessarily govern what a person does."

"Why are you marrying Breanna?" Cynthia asked.

"Because I love her. But that doesn't mean—" He paused. "Love is an emotion! I am indeed governed by it. Still, I also feel a certain, um, attraction when Metria displays her, shall we say, infernal charms, but I don't act on that."

"Really?" the demoness asked. "I have been holding back, out of deference for the defects of mortals, but—"

"For the whats?" Breanna asked, frowning.

"Imperfections, weaknesses, faults, failings, flaws—"

"Foibles?"

"Whatever. But if I chose to be seriously seductive—"

"Don't bother!" Breanna snapped.

But she was too late. The demoness had already faded her outfit to bra and panties, and Justin's eyeballs had locked into place. Those tiny bits of cloth barely constrained incredibly luscious quivering masses of healthy sculptured flesh. He reached for that divine form, unable to help himself.

Then the vision was cut off by Breanna's body. "Point made, demoness," she said as Justin's eyeballs broke free of their ruts and resumed mobility. "Men are ruled by their emotions. But we women aren't."

"Then why did you intervene?" Metria asked evenly.

"Because it griped me all to bleep to think of my man making out with a vamp like you."

"You were governed by jealousy. That's an emotion."

Breanna stared at her for a moment and a half. "Bleep!"

"Point made," Che said, having the wit not to smile. "Humans are emotional creatures."

"Oh, I could arouse a centaur too, if—"

"Point made!" Cynthia cried, covering Che's eyes before he could see the centaur filly shape that was forming.

"However, the fact that human beings are governed by their emotions does not mean that demons are," Justin said. "Demons really don't have emotions."

"That's what's weird," Metria said. "Suddenly I did have emotions, and if they had been stronger, I think I would have done whatever they wanted."

"That's it!" Sim squawked. "Demons have no experience with emotions, so no experience controlling them. Even a slight emotion might rule a demon."

"Or a Demon," Justin agreed. "I believe we have indeed discovered the key. The Swell Foop generates emotions in demons, and surely has the power to do the same with Demons, thereby governing them."

"That may be the only way a Demon can be controlled," Cynthia said. "They are immaterial beings with such enormous power that no physical constraint could be effective."

"Maybe we'd better wind the Foop back to that setting," Jaylin suggested.

"For sure!" Breanna agreed. "Change it back, Justin."

Justin felt dread. "I don't remember the precise positioning of the Rings," he confessed. "I was changing them randomly."

"For ship's sake!" she exclaimed.

"For what's sake?" Metria inquired.

"Cargo, load, freight—stop that! We've got to get that setting back!"

"We were all participating," Che said. "Surely someone must have tracked the changes."

"I did," Sim squawked.

"Then tell me where the Rings were when Metria had emotions," Justin said.

Sim did, and Justin reset the Rings. "Now we must verify it."

"Just like that?" Jaylin said, surprised as she touched the Foop.

"That's amazing!" Metria exclaimed. "I'm astonished. Astounded. Stupefied!"

"She's surprised," Breanna said. "Maybe for real, this time."

They verified it with several other emotions. Whatever emotion they thought of when touching the Foop, the demoness reflected. They had the setting correct.

"So are you through vivisecting me?" Metria asked. "I have a husband I have to send back into nonsensical bliss, and a son I need to collect."

"You're a family demoness!" Jaylin exclaimed. "Actually, I knew that, but it seems so—so—"

"Incredible?"

"Whatever," Jaylin agreed, forcing a frown. "But I remember now. You have half a soul, so you have to act halfway decent, for a demon."

"It's a pain," Metria agreed. "I got married to satisfy my curiosity, and Demon Professor Grossclout said I was going to get what was coming to me. I thought it was just an empty threat. But when I got half my mortal husband's soul, I became smart too late. Well, I'm off." She popped out.

"But what do we do now?" Cynthia asked.

"We had better ask her," Justin said. "If we can recall her."

"Does the Foop have a distance limit?" Che asked.

"We shall find out," Justin said. He touched the Foop. "Overwhelming need to return," he murmured, focusing on Metria. "Come back to me."

The demoness reappeared. In fact, she was suddenly plastered against him. "We've got to stop meeting this way," she said, kissing him. "I'm overwhelmed." Justin was too startled to protest.

"Wrong motive," Breanna said, annoyed. "Get into your own space."

"But I thought he really needed me."

"Like a cockatrice on his nose, he needs you."

The demoness pried her torso away from Justin's front with a faint sucking sound. "I just couldn't leave you folk like that," she said. "That half soul is really a drag."

"It wasn't your conscience," Justin said, recovering a portion of his equilibrium. The demoness did know how to kiss! "We drew you back with the Foop, because we have another question."

"Oh. I thought you *needed* me."

"I'll bet!" Breanna said ferociously.

"It seems she was required to answer the call," Che said, "but allowed some interpretation in the manner of it. That is generally mischief."

Metria nodded knowingly. "So what's the question?"

"The question," Cynthia repeated, "is what do we do now?"

The demoness looked flattered. It was of course pretense, but an apt emulation. "You mean you actually want my opinion?"

"Strong desire to help," Justin murmured, touching the Foop.

Metria considered. "Now that you have it working, I think you need to go to a higher power. This is capital *D* Demon business. Talk with Demon Xanth." She faded, except for her mouth, which floated across and caught Justin's mouth with another passionate kiss.

"Bleep!" Breanna swore, firing off the blackest of looks. But the mouth was laughing as it dissipated into mist.

Cynthia was nodding. "That does seem good."

"It's *no* good! I'll kiss him better than that."

Justin wasn't sure of that, but knew better than to say so. He loved Breanna, but it was evidently hard for an eighteen-year-long life to compete with the experience of centuries.

"Cynthia means the advice," Che said, his face struggling with an expression.

"I knew that! And that better not be a smile pushing out your muzzle, horseface!"

"It's an expression of disgust at the demoness's crude manners," Cynthia said. But a similar expression was lurking near her own muzzle.

"At least we established that the Foop operates at a distance," Che said.

"How do we talk with the Demon Xanth?" Jaylin asked.

"Invoke him," Sim squawked.

Justin nodded. "Desire to help us," he said, thinking of the Demon Xanth as he touched the Foop.

There was a weird swirl as the scenery shifted. Then the six of them were standing in an elaborate castle courtyard. A lovely young woman with greenish-yellow hair stood before them.

"Do come in," she said. "I am Chlorine. My talent is poisoning water, but I use it only for beneficial purpose. I will speak for Nimby." She turned and led the way into the castle. Justin couldn't help noticing that she had a very interesting walk.

"You notice too much," Breanna muttered darkly. She knew his thoughts just from seeing what he was seeing.

They followed Chlorine, bemused. "Where are we?" Jaylin whispered.

"This is the Nameless Castle," Sim squawked. "Where I was hatched, six years ago. I know it well."

"The Nameless Castle!" Jaylin exclaimed, thrilled. "The one that floats on a cloud?"

"It does indeed," Justin agreed. "Attendance here is by very special invitation only."

They entered a grand chamber. There stood a dragon with diagonal stripes of pastel pink and bilious green, and the head of a donkey: a dragon ass, the silliest of creatures. "This is Nimby, my beloved," Chlorine said. "He prefers to leave the talking to me." She cracked half a smile. "We get along well."

Jaylin was standing next to Justin. "How do we know it's really him, then?"

The donkey head twitched an ear, attracting their attention. Then his eye caught theirs, and seemed to expand enormously. Suddenly the chamber seemed to scintillate with rainbow colors, and the walls of the room faded away, leaving them standing on a medium-sized white cloud. The panoply of the Land of Xanth was passing slowly below them in all its mottled grandeur.

"I believe it," Jaylin breathed, awed. So did Justin.

"You have obtained and activated the Swell Foop," Chlorine said, as the outdoor scene slowly reverted to the original chamber. "You wish to rescue the Demon Earth and preserve gravity in our region of the universe. You need advice on how to proceed." She paused.

"Agreed," Justin said. "It is Cynthia Centaur's mission, and we are assisting her."

Chlorine glanced at Nimby, who twitched an ear. "This is complicated," she said. "We do not know where the Demon Earth is, only that nothing short of an attack by another Demon could have done it. We do not believe that any of the local Demons are responsible. We fear it is a foreign Demon. Therefore this is not a matter that can be settled by local negotiation; it is a system problem." She paused again.

"We have no idea how to proceed," Che said.

"You will have to enlist the support of six of the local Demons,"

Chlorine said. "Nimby will arrange a conference, but you will have to make the liaison."

"Won't Nimby be with us?" Cynthia asked, clearly daunted.

Chlorine looked at the dragon again, and received another ear twitch. "The Swell Foop is a Xanthly device. Each Demon has such a unit, but this is the one that was activated. Because it is Xanthly, it does not affect Nimby himself, and his participation will therefore not be trusted by other Demons whose participation is essential."

"But we have no idea how to approach Demons," Justin protested. "Especially when we have so little idea what we are doing."

"What you need to understand is that Demons exist solely for status," Chlorine said. "They achieve this by a series of contests with each other, whose rules are agreed in each case and may not be changed or abridged." She smiled. "I came to associate with Nimby as a result of one such contest. He came to me in his present form, spoke to me one time only, and thereafter merely responded to my wishes. I wished for beauty, health, intelligence, and the like. I did not know that in order to win, he had to receive one tear of grief or love for him. In time, thinking him dying, I did shed that tear, and thereafter our reality changed significantly. You must negotiate the terms of some similar contest with the other Demons, in order to enlist their cooperation in your mission. You will not be able to accomplish it without them, and it is doubtful whether you can do so even with them."

Justin's mouth dropped open. "Six Demons—with all their phenomenal powers—might not prevail?"

"That is correct, because we do not know the complete nature of the opposition. It may be that Demon Earth is captive and can be recovered. But it may be that he has already been more severely compromised, in which case the game is lost."

"This is no game!" Justin said, and immediately regretted it. Obviously Nimby and Chlorine knew that; it was merely a figure of speech.

"It is a game to the Demons," Chlorine said evenly. "With the exception of Nimby, none of them care about the fate of life in the universe. Life is an incidental by-product of the gaming process, useful on occasion because of its erratic and seemingly random nature. It is never certain what a living creature will do; therefore wagers can be made on certain outcomes, as was the case when I participated." She smiled. "One completely unanticipated aspect was that Nimby, in his effort to understand me and the human condition better, came to appreciate some of the quirks of it, and to like me personally, for all that I am greatly enhanced over my original state. Hence our subsequent relationship, which is entirely at his convenience. However—"

She was interrupted by the sound of a baby crying. "Oops, Nimmy's awake. I'll be right back." She hurried from the room.

"The stork!" Breanna exclaimed. "The stork delivered! I remember when she learned of that, two years ago. Sure surprised her!"

"That's right," Justin agreed. "That must be a remarkable baby, considering its parentage." For the Demon Xanth had all power in the Land of Xanth, when he chose to exercise it, and could cause the storks to deliver any kind of baby with any magic talent, to any woman. Chlorine had clued him in on appropriate gifts of this nature, and Breanna herself was slated for something special when the time came. That was one reason she was so eager to get married.

Chlorine returned, carrying a glowing bundle. "Folks, meet Nimbus," she said. "His talent will be mixing metaphors, when he learns to speak."

Justin was perplexed. This was a rather ordinary talent, and the baby looked completely unremarkable. How had this happened?

"Isn't that like closing the barn door after the milk's been spilt?" Breanna asked, then did her best to blush. Evidently the baby's proximity had caused her to reflect his talent. "I mean, why not make him a Magician?"

Chlorine smiled. "We decided we wanted the experience of an ordinary child," she said. "I was ordinary at best, and Nimby lacks experience, so this made sense, don't you think?"

"For sure!" Breanna agreed, and the others nodded.

But Justin became aware of something else. The chamber had subtly changed around them, and now resembled the interior of a barn, with a puddle of milk on the floor. He glanced again at Baby Nimbus, and saw that his glow had intensified, fairly lighting the barn.

The others were looking around in wonder, evidently seeing the same thing. "The glow," Cynthia said. "Is it—?"

"Glow?" Chlorine asked. "His name is Nimbus, not Glow."

"And the barn," Che said. "That's—"

"Barn?" Chlorine asked, her fair brow furrowing.

Justin looked at the dragon, but the dragon averted his gaze with studied innocence. Then Justin caught on: Chlorine had asked for an ordinary baby, but Nimby had arranged for the delivery of an extraordinary one. Nimbus had a glow of almost angelic proportion, befitting his name—but Chlorine could not see it. And Nimbus's talent was not only affecting others, it made the mixed metaphors literal, or at least apparent as illusions. But Chlorine was not aware of that, either. The time would come when she would be surprised, possibly pleased or dismayed, but it was not their business to inform her.

"Our confusion," Justin said. "We have been faced with perplexing things, and have not quite recovered. We shall surely soon untangle this knot and sail across smoother mountains." As he spoke, the baby's glow intensified again, and the barn became a mountainous landscape with a giant rope knot coursing through it, making ripples in the terrain as it slowly unraveled. "Of course his name is Nimbus, and it is a nice name," he continued hurriedly, focusing hard to avoid further influence by the talent. "His talent should be interesting, once it manifests." He sent a glance around, trying to warn the others.

"Of course," Sim squawked, catching on quickly. In half a moment so did Che, followed in three-quarters of a moment by the others.

"I must return to business," Chlorine said. "Nimby, dear, you will have to change form for a while." She held the baby out to him, together with a fresh milkweed pod.

The dragon disappeared. In its place was a completely handsome man of princely aspect. He took the baby and pod, and settled into a chair, helping Nimbus to drink. The knotty mountain scene faded.

"She's really got him broken in," Breanna murmured appreciatively. "Observe and learn, Justin."

"As I was saying," Chlorine said. "My relationship with Nimby is entirely at his convenience, but it appears that convenience will last a few more decades. He likes learning about the microcosm. Similarly, there could be ongoing complications of this next Demon game. So consider carefully as you negotiate; you do not wish to conclude with unexpected awkwardness. The Demons not only have mind-boggling powers, they are quite literal-minded."

"We have to negotiate?" Justin asked. "With other Demons? When we have no idea what we're doing?"

"You will be helping the Demons to rescue D. Earth. The Swell Foop can affect them regardless, but it would be better to obtain their voluntary cooperation."

"But if we don't know how to do it, and they don't know, either, how can we accomplish anything?"

Chlorine glanced again at Nimby. One ear wiggled. That startled Justin, but of course the Demon could make a human ear move if he wanted to.

Chlorine nodded. "Since it must be a Demon who has abducted D. Earth, and Demons exist to challenge for status, you will have to locate D. Earth's captor and challenge him to a game of status. The Foop will locate D. Earth, and therefore his captor."

"Challenge an unknown Demon!" Justin exclaimed. "This is preposterous."

"Therefore you must prepare your case carefully, to make it seem reasonable to the other Demons."

"Reasonable! We don't even know how to get in touch with—"

"The conference of Demons is scheduled half an hour hence, at this site. I suggest you use that time to confer with each other and prepare your case."

"Half an hour!" Justin cried, appalled anew.

"For your convenience, we have set the clock," Chlorine said. She gestured, and a large framed picture appeared on the wall, showing a timer set at 30 minutes. As they watched, it clicked to 29. "One other thing to remember: The Demons are enormous, quite beyond mortal comprehension. For your convenience they will limit themselves in the manner Nimby does for me, so that no more than one percent of their attention focuses on you. They will still be rather beyond your scope, but at least you will be able to have a dialogue. They will emulate mortal limitations, so as to seem, well, remotely human. That should help."

"But—" Justin said. And stopped, for they were alone in the chamber. Their three hosts had faded out.

"At least they left us a nice snack," Breanna said, going to a table piled with appealing delicacies.

"Dear girl, food is the least of our concerns!"

"No, I think we have enough to go on," Sim squawked.

"Yes," Che agreed. "Let's eat well, preparing for the encounter, and set up our presentation. I think Justin is the fairest spoken among us, so he should be our spokesman."

"Me! But I have no idea how—"

Breanna stuffed a spinach cookie into his mouth. "Shut up and listen," she said.

Justin shut up and listened, and what Sim squawked and Che said slowly came to make sense. He could after all make the case, for whatever it was worth.

They finished their snack and made themselves comfortable around the edges of the chamber. The timer reached *zero* and bonged, then winked out of existence.

Nine figures were in the chamber. They appeared to be human in body, wearing voluminous robes, but their heads were rotating spheres. They stood in place, neither moving nor speaking. They were evidently emulating mortal status.

Justin realized that they were waiting to hear his presentation. He plunged in. "Salutations, Demons," he said formally. "We are six mortal creatures from the lands of Xanth and Mundania who wish to enlist your help on a mission to rescue the Demon Earth from captivity. We have obtained the Rings of Xanth and the Swell Foop, and learned how to operate it." He lifted the stone with its six Rings.

Now there was a stir among the visitors. One with a small hot head glided forward, reached out to touch the Foop, and did not. "True." Then, as Justin wondered who that one was, print appeared on the robe: MERCURY.

Simultaneously, names appeared on all the others. The Demons were all named after the planets, or were the planets; Justin had never been quite sure about that. EARTH was missing, and there was one he didn't recognize: NEMESIS. Odd that he hadn't heard of that planet, or seen it in the night sky during his decades as a tree. But obviously it existed, or its associated Demon would not be here.

Well, on with it, before they lost patience. "We know that the Swell Foop will generate emotions in you, and thereby control your actions. But we don't wish to aggravate you. Rather we want to enlist your cooperation in our effort to save the Demon Earth from captivity. We believe that it is to your interest to save him, because his force is gravity, and we all need at least some of that on occasion."

He paused. There was no reaction. That, he hoped, was good news. So he continued. "We doubt that even with the Foop we'll be able to rescue Demon Earth ourselves. We need the formidable power and expertise of Demons. That way we may be able to arrange a challenge for status with the captor Demon, proffering terms he will not care to decline. If we win, we will restore the Demon Earth to his accustomed place, and gravity will not be lost." He did not speak of losing; that was not expedient at this point.

Still no response. "Because Demons are not accustomed to emotions, we believe that a liaison between Demons and mortals will be expedient. In that manner the formidable emotions generated by the Foop will be filtered and modified by creatures who are accustomed to them, giving our team an advantage."

They just stood there. Was he making sense to them, or washing out? Now he would find out. "To have a fair game, one that the captor Demon will wish to participate in, the stakes must be conducive. We must be able to offer something the captor Demon desires. I am unable to say what that might be. Here I need your input."

"A second Demon," the Demon Nemesis said. His head was the largest of all of them, a dense brown sphere.

"Will that be sufficient to induce him to play?" Justin asked.

"Two Demons," the Demon Neptune said.

There was a pause. "The two of you are volunteering?" Justin asked.

They nodded. "I am the least apparent yet most influential of our number," Nemesis said. "My associated planet is beyond the sight of the others, but is more massive than all of them combined. The captor will desire my ambiance of Dark Matter."

"I am not the largest or prettiest member of our group," Neptune said. "But my Higgs boson particle field generates mass itself, without which none of the others could exist, and my aspect of energy moves all things. The captor will desire that too."

Justin was amazed at the significance of these two obscure Demons. Indeed, Dark Matter was invisible yet most pervasive, a phenomenal mystery, and mass/energy was the fundamental building block (as it were) of existence. "And this would bring the other Demon in?" he inquired, to be absolutely sure, for there was no certain predicting what motivated Demons. Now the others nodded.

"Then if you will choose from our number to align with, we can institute the challenge," Justin said, privately amazed that this was falling into place so neatly. They had thought it should, but knew that with Demons nothing was sure. Demon Xanth had communicated with them on a Demonly level, so they readily understood the situation, but was that enough?

This time there was a long pause. Justin felt quite nervous. Which Demon would choose him? What would such an association feel like? What would the contest itself be like? None of them had ever been involved in anything like this before.

Demon Mars, with a small red head, floated toward Sim, then veered and went to Che. The Demon walked right into the centaur and disappeared. He had Chosen.

Demon Jupiter floated toward Sim—and faded into the big bird. He too had Chosen.

Demoness Venus floated to Breanna.

Demoness Saturn floated to Cynthia.

Only Justin and Jaylin remained. They waited, but no other Demons came. Instead, they faded out. This, it seemed, was it: Four Demons were playing, two were stakes, and three were not participating. "But what about us?" Justin asked somewhat plaintively.

Chlorine reappeared. "You have not been neglected," she said. "One of you is needed to animate the Demon Earth, and the other to animate the enemy Demon."

"The enemy Demon! But we oppose it!"

"It must be given the same situation as the rest," she explained. "A mortal body. If it plays, it will choose one of you. The other will go to the Demon Earth."

Oh. That did make sense, he supposed. "But how could it choose me, when I oppose it?"

"The game will not be that straightforward."

Somehow that did not reassure him. "Well, what is the next step?"

"Use the Foop to locate the Demon Earth."

Oh. Yes. "I will now, with the acquiescence of those participating, use the Swell Foop to orient on the Demon Earth."

There were no demurrals. This business of nonresponse was eerie.

Justin picked up the Foop. "Demon Earth," he said, concentrating on the identity.

He felt nothing. But that might simply mean he wasn't facing the right way. He turned, slowly, holding the stone.

As he completed his circle, he felt a slight warmth in the stone. He focused on that, turning back and forth, but there was no further heating.

Then he tried lifting it—and felt more warmth. The direction was up, not around! He set it on his shoulder and turned again, verifying the orientation. "That way!" he cried, pointing.

"Where is it?" Jaylin asked.

Che tilted his head, calculating azimuth, elevation, and chronology. "Fornax," he said.

Justin's jaw dropped. "But that's no planet! That's a foreign galaxy!"

"Fornax," Che/Mars repeated angrily. "This is worse than any of us anticipated."

"Worse?" Justin asked, dreading the answer.

"That is the region of contra-terrene matter," Neptune explained grimly. "That has the potential to destroy all of us."

"Contra-terrene matter!" Justin exclaimed, appalled. "But mere contact with that is lethal!"

"Not in the presence of the Swell Foop," Breanna/Venus said. "Its magic protects us. So that is where we must go to engage the foreign Demon."

"And if we lose that encounter?" Justin asked.

There was no answer. That was more than enough answer.

12
FORNAX

Cynthia saw the Demoness Saturn approach her. She feared this aspect, yet knew it had to be. She stood her ground, and the daunting entity floated right into her.

Then it was like a soft explosion of change. Broad flat rings seemed to surround her, and a series of moons of varying sizes. Her body seemed suddenly possessed of enormous size, but also much vapor. A dread awareness permeated her every nook and most of her crannies. The perspective of the Demon was at once vast beyond any possible understanding, and limited, for it had no feeling, only consciousness. And Cynthia knew that only one percent or less of that consciousness was tuning into this situation. Even so, the power of that mind was awesome.

"Saturn?" she asked absurdly. She did not speak aloud, but phrased it as a question in her limited mind.

"This is mortality." It was not quite a question, not quite an observation, just a phrased thought.

"This is mortal existence," Cynthia agreed. "We live and die in the course of a variable span of time, and accomplish whatever we are going to in that limited span."

"Curious."

There was no further response, so Cynthia returned her attention to the scene before her. She saw Che, Sim, and Breanna standing somewhat slack-jawed, and knew they were making similar adjustments. Only Justin and Jaylin remained normal. Justin was holding the stone that was the Swell Foop and turning slowly around in a circle. The girl was just watching; all this was obviously a bit much for her. Small wonder; it was a bit much for Cynthia too.

"Fornax," Justin said. "That is where we must go to engage the foreign Demon."

"Fornax!" Cynthia repeated. "But isn't that a constellation?"

"A small foreign galaxy," Che clarified. "Now it is clear why we require the cooperation of other Demons. Only they can travel the immensity of nonmagical space."

"True," Sim squawked. "The Demons are beyond time and space. Our realms are but specks on their horizons."

"How do we get to Fornax?" Jaylin asked. "Is there even any air there for us to breathe?"

"I hope so," Justin said. He looked around. "I think we are ready to depart."

The universe swirled. Stars whizzed past, starting small, growing huge and hot, and retreating back into dots of light. Huge clouds of dust loomed, squeezing together to produce new stars, then compressing into dense dark holes that sucked spirals of living stars in after them. The spirals formed patterns of rotation that shaped into lighted galaxies. But they were only a tiny part of the much larger scope of the cosmos. Cynthia gazed at the mind-bending extent of that universe and was mesmerized. She had never imagined such material or structure or pattern. It was beyond awe-inspiring.

Then she was gazing glassily into another castle chamber. They had arrived somewhere. There did seem to be air to breathe; either it was natural, or the Demons had conjured it for this setting. No sense wasting their mortal hosts before the game started. Was that her thought, or Saturn's? Did it matter?

In the center of the chamber was a scintillating alien presence. Cynthia knew it could only be another Demon.

Justin stepped shakily forward. "Demon Fornax, I presume?"

There was no response.

"May—maybe if you assumed human form, or something," Jaylin said hesitantly. "So we could—could relate to you."

The scintillation became a robed human figure, too well covered to suggest age or gender.

"Thank you," Justin said. "We have come to rescue the Demon Earth. Will you play a—a game?"

"No."

"We have the Swell Foop," Jaylin said. Justin held up the stone. "We can employ it to give you emotions. This could complicate your situation in adverse ways."

Cynthia marveled that they dared to threaten a Demon. But Saturn's thought reassured her that Demons, having no genuine emotions, saw threats as mere aspects of bargaining. The position of the visiting group was stronger than Demon Fornax had judged.

"Terms," the figure said. It wasn't exactly a voice, but more of a projected thought. Fornax had decided to play after all, feeling no shame in the reversal. The Foop was showing its usefulness.

"Yes, of course," Justin said. "We offer two Demons to join your cause, against the single Demon you have acquired. Is this a satisfactory stake?"

"Affirmative." Evidently Demons both domestic and foreign understood such things, and needed no explanations or amplifications. Cynthia caught the edge of a passing Saturn thought and realized that the verbal interchange was only the audible portion of a larger dialogue; like the universe, most of it was not apparent to human senses. Probably some of the other 99 percent of the Demons' attention was being used in that hidden interchange.

"Then we must agree on the rules of play. We suggest that our company of mortals engage in a contest, limited to mortal perceptions and abilities."

This too was standard; Demons often wagered on the outcome of seemingly random mortal interactions.

"Dull." Demon Fornax preferred an interesting game.

"With this novel aspect," Justin continued. "Each mortal associates with a Demon who may proffer advice but not make decisions, prime players excepted, the advice based on no more than the mortal's perceptions. No omniscience or omnipotence. This reduces the Demons to mortal limitations."

"Curious." That was what Saturn had thought of mortal existence.

Demons evidently were intrigued by curious things. But that reaction fell short of complete commitment. It was interesting watching the bargaining; evidently Demons were quite careful about the rules of engagement.

"And the Swell Foop will apply a mortal emotion to each Demon, for the duration of the game or beyond."

The Fornax figure scintillated for a moment before settling back into dull format. Its interest had been evoked. "Details."

Justin spread his hands. He had reached the limit of his information.

There was a flash of information in Cynthia's mind. Suddenly she understood. "Each mortal figure will touch the Swell Foop, and it will apply an emotion to the Demon associating with that mortal. Emotions will not repeat; each Demon will have a different one. Because actions and expressions will be governed by the associating mortal, the emotions will not overwhelm the Demons. But the mortals will be affected by them to a limited degree, and so will any other mortal and Demon that is physically touched by those mortals. In this manner, mortals and Demons will be able to share their emotions, to an extent. This can complicate the interactions and render the outcome of any specific encounter doubtful, and therefore complicate the outcome of the game similarly."

The Fornax figure scintillated again. There was definite interest here. "Choice of mortals."

Saturn flashed again, and Cynthia spoke her thought. "Four mortals are committed. Two remain. Choose one, and the other will be assigned to captive Demon Earth." She faced the two. "Justin. Jaylin. Present yourselves."

The two exchanged a nervous glance. Then Justin spoke. "I am Justin Tree, so called because I was for many years in the form of a tree. Now I am in human form again, and about to be married to Breanna of the Black Wave. Assuming we recover the Demon Earth."

It was Jaylin's turn. "I am Jaylin of Mundania—the region Demon Earth normally associates with. I'm—I'm an ordinary fifteen-year-old girl who got into this by sheer accident. I don't know much of anything about anything."

Fornax scintillated again. "Setting?"

"We suggest a medieval castle similar to the kind that existed a while ago in Demon Earth's terrain: fashioned of stone, with many chambers, high turrets, dungeons, passages, features of opulence, and armed guards."

"Challenge?"

"The rescue mission will start outside the castle, and will have to enter, steal a set of door keys, locate the prisoner, and conduct him outside within a day and night. Ten guards to defend against such accomplishment."

"Mechanism?"

More information flooded Cynthia's mind. "Players and guards will be deactivated by a touch on the torso. Touches accomplished by the tips of extremities: hands or feet. Remainder of limbs used to defend against touches. Deactivated players to remain in place, inert until the game is finished. Prime players Earth and Fornax may not be deactivated, only partially nulled. If either is deactivated before the completion of the game, the game is null and must be replayed. Only the escape of Earth determines the outcome."

"Nuances?"

Once more Cynthia received a flash, and spoke. "These will be facilitated by the assigned emotions, which may cause players to do illogical things."

"Which?"

"Emotions to be randomly selected, and announced as assigned, so that all know the guiding drives of each."

Now Fornax demurred. "Assigned by hidden compatibility, anonymously."

A flash of something like pleasure passed though Demoness Saturn: the joy of negotiating for advantage. This was close to the essence of every Demon. Fornax was bargaining. Cynthia looked around, and the others met her gaze briefly, and meaning was transmitted between their occupying Demons. "Agreed."

Fornax scintillated again. "Done. Begin." The figure moved across the chamber and abruptly merged with Jaylin. The girl looked startled, then understanding.

Justin, still holding the Swell Foop, looked around. "I have no Demon associate. I am unclear what I am supposed to do at this point."

"Hold the stone out," Fornax said. "Each of us will touch it.

Thereafter you will follow the guard to the cell where Demon Earth is confined. He will merge with you and touch the stone. At that point the game will commence."

Justin held out the Swell Foop. The Demon Mars, as Che Centaur, approached, laid a hand on it briefly, and walked on. After that Breanna touched it, and Sim, and Cynthia herself. She received a phenomenal infusion of the same emotion she had just almost had: joy. This was so strong she felt like leaping into the air and clicking all four hooves together. But she controlled the urge, masking her emotion so as not to give it away to Jaylin/Fornax, who was watching closely. No sense in yielding any possible advantage to the opposition. She walked on and turned back to watch Jaylin.

Jaylin touched the stone. An odd expression crossed her face, then was quickly smoothed into neutral. Fornax had been jolted—but by what?

A guard stepped forward and paused near a doorway. Justin nodded, and went to join him, carrying the Foop. "Until we meet again," he said, perhaps a bit nervously. They departed the scene.

Then Cynthia and the others were outside the castle. It was a huge edifice, constructed on an outcrop of rock hanging over a violently heaving sea. The only land entrance was a single winding road that followed a ridge up to the castle gate. The few windows were small and barred. It looked forbidding indeed.

"We have twenty-four hours," Che Centaur said. "Fortunately we aren't limited to the ground."

Cynthia held down her burgeoning joy, for there was still necessary business to accomplish. "Before we plan our strategy of attack, are we allowed to inform each other of our emotions, so that we can better coordinate?"

She felt the answer from Saturn as she phrased the question: affirmative.

"However," Sim squawked, "we should not voice them, for a guard may be snooping, and what any guard sees or hears will be relayed immediately to Fornax."

Cynthia realized not only that his point was valid, but that his Demon was allowing him to say it aloud so that all the mortals would understand. They would have to plan their strategy in silence too, and without obvious gestures, lest they be correctly interpreted by the enemy forces. The extra powers of the Demons were now limited, by the rules of the game, so they could not communicate with each other telepathically.

Sim extended his wings. Che touched one wing, and Breanna touched the other, each of them reaching out in turn with their free hands. Cynthia took both of them with hers, completing the circle of four. Information and emotion flowed.

Suddenly she knew that Sim/Jupiter was afraid; his assigned emotion was fear, inspired by his concern that they would lose this game and put all of the local System in jeopardy of takeover. For if they lost, both Nemesis and Neptune would join the enemy, giving Fornax a substantial portion of the system, together with their formidable attributes of Dark Matter and Mass. Dark Matter was the major substance of the universe, for all that it was invisible, like Nemesis himself. And none of the rest of them would have any substance at all without Mass. Che/Mars was angry about the same prospect. Breanna, in contrast, was in love, not only with Justin, but carrying Demoness Venus along with her into love of Demon Earth. And of course now the others knew that Saturn was suffused with joy. Fear, anger, love, and joy—these were the emotions that complicated their organization as a rescue party or an attacking force.

But what emotions did Fornax and Earth have? These were critical to the rescue, but there seemed to be no way to know them in advance. However, they knew that each Demon had been given a different emotion, so the four emotions here could be excluded from that consideration.

Meanwhile their plan of attack: The demons were unfamiliar with mortal castles, so left it to the mortals. The keys would be in the highest turret, the only one that wasn't locked closed, because it had been assumed by the castle builders that no attack would come by air. So they would have to fly to it, starting their penetration of the castle there. This was part of the detail of the game agreement somehow worked out in the course of the negotiations. Cynthia wasn't sure how it had been accomplished, but of course she wasn't an omniscient omnipotent Demon.

But the guards would surely be lurking in that vicinity, to catch and nullify the attackers when they came. How could that be handled?

The joyful, loving girls would go first, to provide a distraction, while the fearful, angry men got the keys. Could the guards be distracted? They were in male human form: obviously they could.

The four separated, their conference done. Breanna mounted Cynthia. Cynthia flicked them both, glad (overjoyed) to verify that she still had her magic, spread her wings, and launched into the air. Oh it was good to fly again, in fact, it was wonderful; she felt such joy of the occasion. And realized that it was her emotion coloring everything; she had to keep that bottled lest it interfere with their mission.

"Distraction?" It was the thought of Saturn, who was not properly familiar with mortal ways.

"Male humans exist to stare at the bodies of mortal females," Cynthia replied, simplifying somewhat. "The sight of bare breasts, for example, can cause them to pause in whatever else they are doing, and the sight of partly exposed human buttocks can distract them entirely."

"Curious." Obviously such things did not distract Demons.

They reached the highest parapet below the turret. Two guards were on it. They carried no weapons, for that was not the way of this contest. Their eyes and hands were sufficient.

"Now for the distraction," Cynthia said. She hovered just beyond the reach of the guards, pumping her wings vigorously but with deliberate inefficiency, causing her breasts to bounce. This was one of those rare times when she wanted men to stare at her body.

The mouths of the guards went slack as their eyes went round. They were drinking it in.

Cynthia slid slowly sideways until she touched the rampart. Breanna jumped off. Then Cynthia hovered longer as the girl scrambled over the parapet and circled around behind the guards. They could have seen her had they glanced around, but they were too busy staring at bounces. Breanna slapped her hand on the back of one, then jumped to do the same to the other. Both men sagged; they had been nulled.

Cynthia flew over the parapet and landed on the rampart. There was just room for her equine body. "We took them out!" she exclaimed joyfully.

"For sure!"

Then they heard something. Cynthia turned. One more guard was charging along the rampart. She couldn't turn; the section was too narrow. She spread her wings and flicked herself, so as to take off and get clear. But he was already too close. He slapped her on the rump, and she lost volition. She had been nulled.

She sagged silently to the floor. She still saw and heard and felt, but she could no longer move or speak. The guard scrambled over her body, going for Breanna. The girl might maneuver to take him out, but it was less than an even bet. Then two of the four rescuers would be down, with only two guards out. Disaster.

In the time it took the guard to scramble over Cynthia's body, Breanna turned around, as if to flee. But it was unlikely she could outrun the guard; she would merely be presenting her backside to him for easy nullification. Also, there might be another guard farther down the rampart, so that escape afoot was by no means certain anyway. She could not fly away; the guards had had the wit to take out the flying person first. Better to face him and fight, hoping for a lucky score.

The guard landed on the floor. He advanced on the girl, who seemed so small and helpless before him. She wasn't even trying to flee; she just faced away from him. The guard reached out.

Breanna hoisted her skirt, revealing her black panties. The guard froze in place, freaked out. The girl reached carefully back with one foot and touched him on the belly. He sagged to the floor, nulled. Only then did she let her skirt fall back into place.

She turned to face Cynthia. "I'm sorry, horseface," she said sadly. "But at least we took three of them out for one of us. I guess I have to leave you here, until the game is done. You did well." She made a salute, and ran off along the rampart, soon disappearing.

Cynthia was left to her own devices. This promised to be a really dull wait until the end of the game. But then Saturn spoke in her mind. "I find your tiny mortal culture interesting. If the mere appearance of your front or a girl's rear causes males to become inanimate, how do you ever manage to have social interaction?"

"Well, you have to understand that there are cultural distinctions," Cynthia replied. "Centaur males don't react the same way, and the rears of girls are normally covered."

Their dialogue continued, and in due course moved into Saturn's special Demon power of Dimension, the measurement of the universe. Without dimension of space or time, nothing could exist. The other

Demons mostly represented forces, but only Dimension could quantify or clarify those forces. Therefore Saturn's power of measurement was probably the essential key to existence itself. "Did you know that the universe's dimensions are constantly changing?" Saturn inquired. "It is expanding enormously." Cynthia had not known that, and was fascinated. They had nothing to do but educate each other, and Cynthia found herself learning more about the ways of Dimension than she had ever dreamed existed. It was a fact that Saturn had the most appealing dimensions in the System. Apparently Saturn was similarly satisfied with what she learned of the tiny odd nuances of mortal males and females. The time passed surprisingly rapidly and interestingly; time was, after all, a dimension. In fact, it was a joyful occasion.

Sim Bird watched the girls fly up to the high castle rampart. "They will be ambushed," Jupiter said fearfully.

"They can handle themselves," Sim silently squawked in response. "They have formidable powers of distraction." He was privately amazed that a Demon as clearly mighty as Jupiter should be so timid.

"It is not my normal state," Jupiter replied. "My power is the Strong Force, which binds atoms together. Without it, matter could not exist. I fear nothing; I am the binding force that prevents the universe from dissolving into pure radiation. But the Swell Foop drew on my concern for the outcome of this game and gave me Fear. It is not a pleasant experience."

"Of course it isn't," Sim squawked quickly. "It is a crippling liability which we must conceal from the enemy. Meanwhile, please tell me more about the Strong Force." He did this partly to distract the Demon from his assigned fear, but he was also most interested in the subject.

Jupiter was glad to oblige. And while he was distracted by his own comprehensive discussion, Sim nodded to Che Centaur and quietly took off, flying close to the castle wall so that he could not been seen by the guards above. Che, in contrast, flew well clear of the castle, where he could see and be seen.

Sim flew back and forth, climbing up against the wall. When he was near the top, Che waved, signaling that the way was clear. The girls had taken out the guards.

He stroked more strongly, lifting rapidly over the parapet. There were

Cynthia and three guards, fallen in place, evidently nulled. That meant that only seven guards remained, as the enemy could not afford to have them all concentrated at the top. But their group had suffered its first casualty. Poor Cynthia!

He landed on the rampart, then hunched down and ran by foot along it toward the high turret. He encountered stairs and scrambled up them, still keeping his head low. Landbound creatures tended to think that birds always flew, and were clumsy on their feet; this was not the case. The air was just normally a superior route.

He entered the turret. There was no guard; the girls had evidently lured him out and nulled him. There were the keys: five of them on a ring. One for each player. He picked up the ring with his beak and left the turret.

Back on the rampart, he lifted a wing to signal Che: It was clear to come in. Che flew toward him, but also kept looking around the castle to be sure no more guards were lurking in ambush. He landed, his body taking up the width of the rampart. Sim lifted the ring of keys, and Che took it, detached one, and gave the ring back.

They moved on along the rampart, looking for Breanna. In a moment she appeared, silently signaling them. She had been hiding in a crevice. She came to take a key and touch hands and wings. In that manner she and Venus acquainted them with the result of their survey: no other guards atop the castle.

Now came the next stage of the challenge: to go down into the depths of the castle, avoiding guards, locate Justin/Earth, and lead him out. This would not be easy.

The three unlocked the door to the main castle. They knew the seven guards remaining could be anywhere, so they had to go carefully. They touched wings and hands briefly: Should they go together, or split, so as to search more rapidly? They decided to split, but to meet again in an hour in the castle's main room, if feasible. They would avoid guards, because any guards they nulled would be an indication of their recent presence. Only if they had no choice would they null a guard.

They came to a divide, and split. Breanna touched his wing a moment: "Don't get lost, Birdbrain!" she thought affectionately.

"Don't flash your black bottom at anyone," he thought/squawked in response.

He followed his section of the passage to its end, keeping his sharp avian senses alert. He did not have to be much concerned about getting ambushed, because he could hear or smell a foreign presence from a reasonable distance. Since the passage was lit by flaring torches every few feet, he could see well enough too.

What he couldn't do was fly. There was not enough room. That bothered him. But his feet would suffice for this.

"You are bold," Jupiter said in his mind. "So am I, when not under the spell of a magic emotion."

"It is unfortunate," Sim agreed noncommittally. He had been almost awed at the notion of associating with a Demon, but that was fading into complacency with experience.

"I was contemptuous of associating with a mere mortal," Jupiter said. "But that too is fading with experience. You folk are indeed able to function on your restricted level. There is also considerable novelty in experiencing emotion, even this negative one. I am able to feel some of your other emotions too, when they arise."

On either side of the passage were doors. Sim considered using his key to unlock and open them, but feared that any such action could alert a guard or the mistress of the castle. So he listened, and peeked through each keyhole, and concluded that the chambers were empty. Had Justin Tree been in any, Sim should have been able to hear his breathing. And why would a guard be locked in an otherwise empty chamber?

The passage terminated in a stairway going down. There was a wire mesh door across it, and that door was locked. So he would have to use his key after all.

He hooked the key on the claw of a toe, lifted his foot, and put the key in the lock. He turned, and the door opened. He passed into the stairway, then turned and locked the door behind him. As far as he knew, there was no magic here to ascertain the passage of a person, so any guard that came would assume that no one had passed.

"You are cunning," Jupiter said with a tinge of admiration.

Sim was getting to like this Demon, or at least the one percent he knew of him. "I hope it suffices."

The stair wound down to another story. Sim considered unlocking its screen door and checking its chambers, but it occurred to him that Che or Breanna would be doing that from another direction. The prisoner was more likely to be hidden in the very deepest dungeon, the hardest place to locate and rescue him. Better to find him quickly, then coordinate with the others to get him out. For it surely would not be as simple as merely leading him back the way Sim had come. The absence of further guards was becoming suspicious.

"I agree," Jupiter said. "There must be a trap."

"If there is, the prisoner is surely the bait."

He continued on down the stairway. It passed floor after floor. The castle was huge!

At last it ended on a dank floor. Mold grew on the stones here, and the torches guttered as if not getting quite enough air. This had to be the bottom level.

He unlocked the gate and walked onto the floor. There was still no sound from any of the chambers along it. "So many empty rooms," Jupiter said. "What is the use of them?"

That was a good question. Sim unlocked a door and opened it. He peered inside. It was completely dark, so he fetched a torch, hopping on one foot while carrying it with the other. He lighted the chamber.

It contained a human skeleton in shackles. "Fornax would not kill him," Jupiter said. "That would abort the game."

"True. It is a prop in a setting, to make the castle seem authentic."

Sim retreated from the chamber, returned the torch to its holder, locked the chamber door, and went on.

At the end of the passage he found another locked door. He opened it and discovered a large empty dungeon. But there was the barest trace of something. A faint scent. As of—shoes.

It was too dark for his eyes to be useful. He fetched a torch and found a holder for it within the dungeon. Now he saw the extent of the chamber; it was large enough to hold a number of prisoners in comfort, if that was not an oxymoron. But it was bereft of any captives, even bones.

Except for a pair of shoes near the center. Justin's shoes. Sim recognized them by sight and smell.

But where was Justin himself? The dungeon had no exit except the single locked door. How could Justin have escaped it, without a key, leaving his shoes behind?

"I fear treachery," Jupiter said. "This has the aspect of a trap."

The Demon was paranoid, because of his assigned emotion, but he might be correct. There was definitely something weird about this. "How so?" he asked.

"Maybe Fornax made him leave his shoes as a decoy, and took him to another cell. You will be locked in here, unable to pursue your rescue mission."

"But I can't be locked in as long as I have the key."

"True. But then why leave the shoes?"

"Maybe Justin found another way out, but could not take his shoes."

Sim went to the shoes—and discovered a round hole just beyond them. Beyond it was a large stone cover for the hole, that evidently would fit perfectly to make the floor level. The hole was deep; in fact, it seemed to open into another chamber below.

"An oubliette!" Sim squawked. "They put him down the hole without his shoes! The rats will be gnawing at his toes." He stuck his head down the hole, but could see nothing. There was only dank silence down there.

He fetched another torch and tossed it into the hole. It dropped into a deep pit and guttered in a chamber whose sides were not visible from above. There was no help for it but to climb down and take a direct look.

"I don't trust this," Jupiter said fearfully.

"He could be bound and gagged, so that he can't call out to us," Sim pointed out. "I can climb reasonably well. It won't take long to check."

He stepped into the hole, and used feet, wings, and beak to brace himself against the rough stones forming the sides. He wedged down until he reached the point where it widened into a cavelike chamber, with water dripping slowly from the ceiling. Indeed it seemed to be a cave, with extensions crawling out to the sides. He dropped to the floor and followed one tunnel until it ended in nothing, then followed another. Before long he had explored them all, and found neither exit nor prisoner. It had, after all, been an untamed gander chase.

The torch was guttering out. Quickly he returned to the entrance hole—and found that it was blocked. Someone had replaced the heavy floor tile, sealing off the oubliette. It would not be possible to dislodge it from below; there was insufficient purchase. He was trapped, just as Jupiter had feared.

"I fell for it," he squawked in abysmal dismay. "How could I have been so stupid!" For he was supposed to be the very smartest of birds. That ignominy was worse than the fact that he had been made another prisoner. "The lack of guards, the prop-bones, the shoes—all designed to trick me into trapping myself, and I did exactly that. I am a prime idiot!"

"Yes, of course," Jupiter agreed sympathetically. "But mortals are expected to have such limits. We shall have to wait for the game to end."

"How can you be so philosophical about it?"

"I am a Demon. Time has little relevance to our interests. Perhaps if more than one percent of my attention were here, I would be more concerned. As it is, my inculcated fear is eased, because my aspect of this game is abated. Let me tell you all about the strong nuclear force."

Actually, Sim was interested. Resigning himself to his captivity, he settled down to listen to the Demon's information. But meanwhile he wondered: Exactly where had Justin and the Demon Earth been so cunningly hidden?

Jaylin stood in near shock as the Fornax figure came toward her and abruptly moved into her. She was being possessed! But then the Demon's awareness spread out through her body and into her mind, and it was all right. "I am Fornax, mistress of contra-terrene matter."

"But that's explosive! I mean, the moment it touches real matter, they both dissolve into pure radiation."

"Your well soup prevents that from happening, so we can associate physically while playing the game."

"Well soup?" She giggled mentally. "Oh you mean Swell Foop! Yes, it's magical. But I never expected to associate with—with—"

"The enemy. I am aware of that. It is for your innocence I selected you."

"I'm not innocent! I'll have you know I kissed a boy behind the kitchen once, and—" She stopped, realizing that not only was the example meaningless to this alien entity, it was hardly a solid example of un-innocence. These Demons, as she vaguely understood it, were not exactly male or female; they were hemale and shemale and all points between. Fornax merely seemed female as a convenience. Innocence hardly applied. It could be worse, if Fornax decided to be male without leaving Jaylin's body. "Okay, I'm innocent. I don't know anything that might help you, and I don't want to help you anyway."

"But you shall help me, for that is the nature of the game. What is this about kissing a boy?"

"Nothing that would interest you."

"I will decide that."

Jaylin tried to resist, but discovered that she did indeed have to co-operate. For the others, the mortal creatures' decision might be the one that counted, but in her case it was the Demon's will that governed. That was probably inherent in the bylaws for using a creature provided by the enemy. She reviewed in her mind the scene in which she had kissed the boy. Of course there was also David, but she had done that openly, so it didn't count.

Meanwhile, Fornax was using her voice to address the others. "Hold the stone out."

The others paraded by, each touching the Swell Foop. Then Fornax made Jaylin touch it. A flood of emotion came, causing her to reel.

"What is it?" Fornax demanded, reeling with her. For the moment the alien Demon was helpless.

Jaylin sorted rapidly through her experiences of emotions. She was feeling an overwhelming surge of urgency, but of what nature? She desperately wanted something, but what? She felt as if she would expire if she didn't get—what?

Then she had it. "Desire! The emotion of desire!"

Fornax, highly disciplined, already had her reaction under control. "This must be explored."

Jaylin looked around. The others were gone, including Justin. "It's started?"

"True. They have one full day and night as you measure it to bring Demon Earth and his attached mortal body out of this stronghold. They may be able to accomplish this, if we do not interfere; I doubt the guards can withstand them, as those are merely programmed humanistic golems. We shall have to see to it ourselves."

"*You* have to," Jaylin said. "Not me."

"When you go against my will, you will experience this," Fornax said. Then something distressing developed, not exactly pain, but faintly infinite regret that soon became other than faint. Jaylin *couldn't* balk the Demon's will; she would kill herself first.

"Got it," she said, and the feeling eased.

"My will is your will."

And that turned out to be the case. Jaylin had free will only where it did not conflict with Fornax's purpose. "How can I serve?"

"In this manner." Fornax spread out a thought.

"I can't do that! I never—" But that regret returned, draining her. "I can do that," she said, ashamed. She realized that she was like a horse who had discovered the futility of fighting against the bit; it was easier to let the rider's will translate immediately to action, so that there was no mental or physical discomfort.

She walked to the doorway that Justin had used as he departed. Justin stood there with the accompanying guard. "Who are you?" she asked for Fornax.

"I am—Demon Earth," he said.

"Give me the stone."

He handed the Swell Foop to her. She held it in place. "Touch it."

He touched it. His face lighted. "Hope!" he exclaimed. "Now I have hope!"

"What is hope?" Fornax asked Jaylin.

"It—it is akin to desire. It is the belief that—that something good will happen. The wish for it to happen."

"Then we are compatible. That is fortunate."

"Compatible?"

"Hope and desire. He hopes to escape. I desire to prevent it. I will transform his emotion into a hope for a better situation with me."

"I don't see how." Jaylin could question the Demoness; that was not the same as opposing her.

"I do not know, but you will help me to discover the mechanism."

"I will not!" But then the regret, and she had to back off. "I will."

All this was internal. Now Jaylin faced Justin. "Take off your shoes. Give them to the guard."

He looked perplexed, but did as directed. Then Jaylin addressed the guard. "Set the shoes at the brink of the open oubliette. Lock the main chamber entrance and hide in a neighboring cell. If any person enters the oubliette, quietly replace its entrance stone. Then return to normal guard duty."

The guard departed with the shoes. "Follow me," Jaylin said. She led the way back into the main chamber, and thence to a smaller chamber adjoining it.

When they were in the smaller one, Jaylin closed the door. Then she looked around the room. It was richly appointed, with elegant decorative carpets on the walls, a shining gemstone floor, padded couch, large clear mirrors, and a table with a full meal laid out.

"What is your will?" Jaylin asked him.

"To return to my familiar planet and be as I was," he replied. This was clearly the Demon Earth speaking.

"You can do that soon, if you join me."

"I will not join you." But he seemed distracted, and Jaylin knew why: He had only very recently been merged with a mortal human body, and then been given a strong emotion, when he had never had emotion before.

"This is a mortal human male," Fornax said internally to Jaylin. "You are a mortal human female. This is a suitable kiss occasion."

"No it isn't!" But again that regret. Still, she tried to fight it. "He— Justin is about to marry Breanna. He doesn't want to kiss me."

"*Make* him want to kiss you."

"I can't do that!" But her protests were becoming faint. She had to do what Fornax desired—and because of the Swell Foop, that desire was excruciatingly strong. "I will need—a better outfit."

Fornax explored her mind, and in a moment that outfit formed around her. Jaylin wasn't sure whether this was magic or science or something else, but it worked. Now she was garbed in a rather-too-sexy evening gown that included a strapless push-up bra, and her hair and wrists sparkled with rubies and diamonds. Her feet looked twice as dainty as was possible, in Cinderella glass slippers, with too much leg showing. She knew that her face was made up exotically.

She gave Justin a steady yet smoldering gaze. "Earth, I am Fornax," she murmured. "Your best hope of freedom lies with me. I desire you. I will kiss you."

He stared at her, neither man nor Demon quite grasping her intent. "Let me go."

She glided up to him, took him by the shoulders, and kissed him on the mouth. "Take me," she whispered huskily. The dialogue, like the outfit, was borrowed from Jaylin's memory of any number of romantic movies.

"I don't understand."

"He is not responding," Fornax said internally to Jaylin.

And Jaylin had to explain, though she hated to. "Demon Earth has no romantic experience, and mortal Justin has no interest in any girl other than Breanna. It is not right for me to kiss either of them. In our culture, that's not the way it is done. He—he has to *choose* to—to kiss me."

"Make him choose."

"I can't!" But neither could she refuse. She retreated, and thought of all the other romantic and/or sexy movies she had seen, and tried to emulate their more provocative leading ladies. "My feet are wrong, I think. They are innocent-girl-at-ball. I need smooth stockings and high heels."

And she had them. She had never worn any such things before, but this was an emergency. "Demon Earth," she said, speaking for Fornax. For herself too, really, because she wanted to make it halfway clear that she wasn't trying to mess up Justin and Breanna. "What does it take to get your attention?" She let her robe fall somewhat open at the top as she took a deep breath, and performed a slinky step back toward him. She hated trying to be a fascinating bitch, yet there was also a certain illicit satisfaction. If only it weren't Justin she was trying to vamp!

Her trailing robe caught on her stiletto heel. She tried to catch her balance, but the robe entangled her legs, and she crashed ignominiously to the floor. She saw stars and a moon or two as her face struck. What a washout!

Then the pain started, and the physical side was only part of it.

13
LOVE

Justin saw Jaylin fall, and was appalled. He jumped forward, trying to catch her, but could not react in time. She
crashed to the floor, striking her face. Ouch!

He kneeled beside her. She seemed to be unconscious. He put his
hands on her shoulders, trying ineffectively to turn her over so he could
assess the damage. Whatever had possessed her to—well, actually, he
knew the answer to that. She was possessed by the Demoness Fornax,
who was trying to use her human body to bemuse his own human body.
On the theory that what happened to the humans would be echoed by
the Demons. That Earth's hope would merge with Fornax's appeal, cor-
rupting him.

"You resisted her blandishment," the Demon Earth said. "Why are
you now going to her?"

"She's hurt," Justin explained internally. "She's just an innocent girl,
forced to play a role she did not seek. I bear her no ill will." He tried
again to turn her over. Her body turned, but her robe turned more, uncovering some flesh. He hastily pulled it back.

"Why do you re-cover her?" Earth inquired. "That is interesting flesh,
according to your eyes."

"I do not wish to embarrass her unnecessarily. It is her face that is
bruised." Indeed, the bruise was starting to show, and blood was flowing

from a split lip. He fished for a clean handkerchief in his pocket, but found none, for the guard had taken it and some buttons, so he reached up to the table and found a cloth napkin. He used it to mop her face.

She groaned. "Jaylin," he said. "You are in safe hands. You fell. Your face is cut and bruised. Do you hurt elsewhere?"

She sat up as he steadied her. "I don't think so. Oh, this is embarrassing."

"I understand. We are caught up in a game of Demons. We do not have complete volition."

She smiled. "Thanks for understanding. I wouldn't really—I mean, Breanna is my friend—"

"Say no more. Maybe you can get the Demoness to allow you more sensible clothes, however."

"Yeah." She leaned forward, still sitting on the floor, to reach her feet. She flipped the split skirt of the robe aside and raised one knee so she could pull off the ridiculously elevated shoe. She lifted the other knee, letting more skirt fall away as she got the second shoe off. Her knees drifted apart.

Suddenly Justin caught on. He turned his face away just before her panties showed. "Female canine!" he muttered.

"Bleep!" she swore. "Now I can't verify whether it works." She got to her feet.

Justin turned cautiously back to face her. Her robe was now in decorous place, showing nothing below the too-low décolletage. "When did you return, Fornax?" he asked.

"I never left. But I let the mortal handle it, as long as she was making good progress. But she tried to balk after getting the shoes off, so I had to act." Her face had healed, the injuries abolished.

"So I can't trust her, because she can become you at any time."

"Oh, come on now, Earth. Look at it through mortal eyes. Is there nothing you would like to experience?" She put one hand to the upper hem of the robe.

Justin tried to turn away, but Earth prevented him. "That mortal flesh is interesting, now that I am in a mortal host. I would like to see more of it."

"She is trying to trick you into not getting rescued," Justin retorted hotly.

"Surely there is no harm in just looking."

"There can be phenomenal harm!"

"I doubt it."

Fornax was watching him through Jaylin's eyes. Slowly she drew the robe to the side, so that more of the flesh of her upper torso was exposed. Earth watched, his interest increasing.

"I came here to rescue you," Justin said. "Do not allow her to deceive you!"

"What deception is there? She is merely uncovering the natural body, abolishing the deception of clothing. I hope to see it all."

"That hope will be your undoing! Would you have any interest at all if you were not with a mortal body?"

"Naturally not. The moment I leave this body, I will lose interest. That is why I wish to appreciate it now, while I am able to."

"But don't you see—if she manages to distract you long enough to prevent your rescue, then the mortal bodies will all be abolished, and you will be forever her prisoner. For the sake of a moment of mortal experience, you will sacrifice your immortal freedom."

Earth hesitated. "What you say is true. It is not worth it to allow one percent of my attention to spoil the situation of the remaining ninety-nine percent."

Justin was amazed. One percent had been set as the upper limit of Demon attention for this game, but apparently that was not based on the conventional standard. The Demons were even more unimaginably beyond mortal comprehension than he had thought.

"True." Earth started to turn away.

Fornax snatched the robe the rest of the way clear, together with the supportive undergarment, showing a full half of upper torso. Justin's eyes were caught. The Demoness had acted the moment she saw the decision go against her.

"We can still turn away," Justin said, staring. "Such a view is not completely compelling. Just make our body turn, carrying the eyes along."

"Agreed." Their body began to turn.

Fornax stepped quickly forward to embrace them. But her bare feet snagged on the dangling fringe of the robe, and she tripped again, falling into him. He caught her, but the view of her torso had been interrupted, and his eyes were free.

She tried to draw away, ripping off the rest of the robe. But he held her close, preventing it. She tried to catch his head for another kiss, but he averted his face and she caught him on the ear. His ear tingled with the passionate force of it, but he was not close to freaking out.

"Bleep!" she swore again. "So you will not have it yet? Then remain confined in your room!"

And he had to obey, for he was her captive. He watched her whirl and flounce out, shutting the door behind her.

Justin sat down on the bed. He wasn't sure how Demon Earth had been held before, but now that Justin was here, it was physical confinement.

"I was locked in stasis," Earth clarified. "I could not move at all, or extend my powers beyond this chamber. Now I share your mortal body, but my powers remain severely limited. I have no omniscience. That is uncomfortable."

"How did Fornax capture you? I thought each Demon was all-powerful in his own region."

"That is correct. I was tricked."

"Tricked?"

"I received news that there had been a grueling contest of status among the foreign Demons, with Andromeda raiding Fornax and forcing its Demon to flee. Thus Fornax was undefended, and might be appropriated without opposition. So I made a quick raid of my own, to incorporate it, adding the power of antimatter to my arsenal—and it was a ruse. Fornax captured me away from my base, and I was helpless. It was a most humiliating defeat."

"But perhaps the emotion of hope ameliorates it," Justin suggested.

"It does. I never experienced positive emotion before. It is a wondrous thing. For the first time in my existence, I care what happens to me personally."

"You did not care before? What about when Demon Xanth invaded your domain, and you tried to trap him there?"

"That was a matter of status. Had I succeeded in trapping him, I would have gained. As it was, he gained. He has been remarkably fortunate in recent games."

"That may be because he has associated with the mortals of his realm, gaining insights and a different perspective. He has been learning emotion, and dreaming, and it has been changing him. That appears to give him an advantage, because he has become less predictable, in the mortal manner."

"So we gather. I understand he has even associated himself on an even basis with a mortal creature, and devoted much attention to her."

"Yes. That would be Chlorine, who was a bad-tempered wench with the talent of poisoning water. He transformed her to a lovely woman— physically, mentally, and emotionally—and I believe married her. At any rate, they now have a child."

"What do you mean by lovely?"

"She is pretty, beautiful, esthetic, appealing to the eye and touch. A suitable love object."

"Love—what is that?"

Justin laughed. "Perhaps we shall never completely understand it. I love Breanna of the Black Wave."

"She is lovely?"

"Yes. But it is more than that. She is imperious, forthright, aggressive, and quick to take offense."

"These resemble Demon traits. That is why she compels your love?"

Justin shook his head ruefully. "No, they might be considered faults in a woman. But they only make me love her more."

"You like faults?"

"I don't know how to explain it, because the whole business is rather new to me, for all that I have loved her three years. I—I simply want to be with her, in every way. Without her I am incomplete."

"Does Demon Xanth love Chlorine?"

"Yes, I believe he does."

"And that emotion contributes to his success in Demon contests?"

"It may. I really am not party to Demon ways."

"I am. Xanth has changed, and thereby benefited at the expense of other Demons. I want to learn his secret. Teach me love."

"Demon Earth, this is impossible! Love cannot be taught, only experienced."

"Xanth learned it. I can learn it. Teach me."

Justin cast about for some way to clarify it for an entity that had no emotion other than the one implanted by the Swell Foop. "My own understanding is imperfect. I cannot describe it. But perhaps if I give an example of our interaction, that will suggest its nature to you. You might picture it as something you are doing, and try to gain the feeling thereof. Then, possibly, you will understand."

"An interaction of love?"

"Yes. Of the way Breanna and I relate. I think you have not seen her. She is a young female human being with—"

"I have seen the human body Fornax is using. Is that similar?"

"That would be Jaylin. Yes, in the broad essentials, though they are quite different people. For one thing, Breanna is of the—"

"Jaylin will do. I can picture her in your scene."

That suited Justin. He wasn't at all sure he wanted the Demon Earth picturing Breanna as his own love object. That might be foolish jealousy on his part, but at least Jaylin was neutral. "Very well. Since you can experience the emotion of hope, think of love as an intense variant of that, with a person as the object."

"Present your example."

"Well, it happened soon after Breanna insisted that I convert from tree to human form. I was as yet a bit unsteady on my feet, after about seventy-six years with a trunk instead of legs. She said she didn't mind—" As he spoke, he visualized the scene, and the Demon Earth watched that picture.

Justin tripped and almost fell, but Breanna caught him, hugging him to her. She brought her face to his and kissed him. This was the first time, and it made him dizzy, so that he might have lost his balance again, but for her firm clasp.

"I apologize for my infirmity," he said. "It is merely that—"

"If you don't get steady, I'll kiss you again," she said as she let him go.

He essayed another step. "If you intend that as punishment, it is misdirected. I—" He started to fall.

She caught him again, and hugged him, and kissed him. "It is not intended as punishment," she said. "But as encouragement. I figure a few hundred kisses should do it."

"A few hundred!"

She made a cute frown. "I'm willing to go a thousand, if necessary. But you had better make some progress."

"A thousand!"

She glanced quizzically at him. "You don't get it, do you?"

"Get what?" he asked, perplexed.

"I'm teasing you."

"Teasing me? I thought you were helping me to walk."

"That too. What I mean is, I'm pretending that you don't like to be kissed, so you will hurry to walk well."

"Oh, Breanna, I don't regard—"

"Or that you are a very slow learner."

"I apologize for that."

"It's a bleeping pretext to kiss you!" she snapped.

Justin was momentarily stunned by the bad word from her dear lips. Then she kissed him again, and he began to understand. "Tease me some more," he said blissfully.

"That's more like it." Then she saw something ahead. "What's that?" Her moods were mercurial, shifting from romance to practicality in a fraction of an instant. He liked that about her. But of course he liked everything about her.

He looked where she was looking. "That is a suit tree," he said, for he knew trees well. "It grows flight suits."

"Flight suits! You mean they fly?"

"They enable those who wear them to fly. Would you care for a demonstration?"

"Sure. Maybe flying'll be easier than trying to walk with you." Then, before he could misunderstand again, she kissed him once more.

They donned flight suits and flew up over the forest. The flight suits made it easy; all they had to do was think high, and they lifted, and think forward, and they moved that way. But then they began to lose altitude.

"I fear the magic energy of the suits is being expended," Justin said regretfully. "They are not intended for long flights. Just far enough to get their seeds spread a reasonable distance."

"That's okay." She flew into him, grabbed him, and kissed him as they descended.

And their descent stopped. But when the kiss ended, they dropped down again. "Your kiss made me light-headed," he explained. "So the suit was able to sustain me."

She laughed. "You know, every so often I still forget how literal Xanth can be."

They landed beside a tangle tree, and kissed again, as Justin was still a trifle unsteady. A tentacle reached out to wrap around Breanna's leg. "Oh yeah?" she demanded, drawing her sharp knife.

"Stop!" It was a wood nymph with tangled green hair. "Don't you dare hurt my tree!"

"Who are you?" Breanna demanded.

"I am the nymph of this tree."

"Tangle trees have nymphs?"

"Indeed some do," Justin said. "Note her matching hair."

"Then tell it to un-tentacle me," Breanna said.

The nymph touched the tentacle, and it unwound. "That's good," the nymph said, speaking to the tree. "We mustn't eat people who are in love." She patted the tentacle, and it formed into a heart shape.

"Everybody loves a lover," Justin said, as the memory scene concluded.

The Demon Earth was not quite convinced. "All you did was kiss."

"Yes. That was all we wanted to do. That is the way of love."

"I shall have to try it."

"There is nothing like a loving kiss," Justin said. "Fornax kissed you, but that was calculation rather than love, so it lacked full impact."

"Then what of the sights of the body? You did not wish me to see those."

"That is different. A woman uses those to bemuse a man, or even freak him out. It's a weapon. Fornax was trying to dazzle you with a female bosom, and then with panties. You would have been helpless."

"Doesn't love make you helpless?"

Justin paused. "You have a point. But there is a distinction between sex appeal and love. Fornax does not love you; she merely wishes to dazzle you long enough to win the game."

"Kisses are love. Body sights are dazzle."

This remained difficult. "Not necessarily. Fornax's kisses aren't love. They are a deceit. But if she can make you love her, then she can win."

"But she can show me the body at any time. Why did she not do so?"

"Well, she did, at the end. But we managed to prevent her from stripping all the way down. Otherwise—" Then Justin suffered a realization. "Panty magic! It shouldn't exist here!"

"Magic does not exist beyond the Demon Xanth's domain," Earth agreed. "Except in very limited degree. Each Demon has its own special force, substance, or quality."

"So Jaylin's panties would not have freaked us out," Justin said. "Fornax must know that. So she pretended, but stopped short of full revelation. She can't completely dazzle you; she has to make you desire her."

"I did desire her, when I touched her."

"Yes, I felt it too." Then Justin suffered another realization. In Xanth, a bulb would have flashed, but here it was just a bright thought. "Desire! That's her emotion. When we touched, she felt some of your hope, and thought she might win you, and you felt some of her desire."

"That is a viable emotion?"

"Yes, desire is an emotion. Now we know her weakness. She desires! She is no longer just trying to gain status; she wants the thrill of victory."

"In what manner does this knowledge improve our situation?"

"We now know more than she thinks we do. When she tries another bluff, threatening to show panties, we can call it, or we can pretend to be freaked out, so that she will think she is winning, when she is not."

"Suppose she kisses me again, and shares her desire? Will I not then be in her power?"

"Not if you only pretend to be overcome by that desire. I think she wants to subvert you, so that when a member of our rescue party comes to lead you out, you will decline to go. Make her believe that you have been successfully subverted, and then go when the rescue comes. That will turn her ploy against her and give us victory."

"You reason like a Demon," Earth said approvingly. "But the contact with her mortal body was pleasant, and now that I have seen how love is made up mostly of kisses, I will enjoy more of those with her."

"Just make sure that it doesn't become real," Justin said. "You must seem to love or desire her, even to freak out, without actually doing so. On that hinges victory—or defeat."

"Victory," Demon Earth agreed, feeling strong hope.

But Justin had a private, nagging doubt. Desire could be treacherous, as could any emotion. Fornax's next approach, as she learned to handle emotion, might be considerably more formidable.

Breanna led the way down the passage, with Che closely following. "I'm afraid there will be some trick," she said internally to Demoness Venus. "This has been too easy so far."

"I never knew what love was, before," Venus said dreamily.

They came to a well-lighted cross-hall. "We will check this way," Che said.

"Watch your tail, horsehead," she told him as she took the darker passage. "There are still seven guards out there somewhere."

"We'll pulverize them," he said gruffly. That was angry Demon Mars talking. She hoped Mars was as tough as he talked.

"He is," Venus said. "He controls the electromagnetic force."

"That's right—each of you associate with a force, don't you. Sort of the way we mortals each have a magic talent. What's yours?"

"The weak nuclear force. It's not really weak; that's just in comparison to the strong force. It operates between elementary particles. I don't use it much."

"I never knew that Demons had forces," Breanna said. "I mean, before this mission."

"We Demons operate the universe," Venus said. "We are everywhere, taking local form where convenient. Without us, nothing would exist." She paused. "In fact, nothing *does* exist."

"No, hold on there half a moment! How can we be here talking about it, if nothing exists?"

"It is in how you look at it. The universe is without form and void, but we have made an imperfection that stirs up an equation of particles and anti-particles balancing each other, and energy and anti-energy. All together it amounts to nothing, but as long as the elements are apart, the universe seems to exist. We Demons are the aspects of the equation."

Breanna struggled with that. "My head feels like solid wood at the moment. An unsolved equation makes the universe exist?"

"Consider the equation $6 + 5 = 12 - 1$. What happens when you solve it?"

"That's $11 = 11$. If you put both numbers on the same side, you get $11 - 11 = 0$, or $0 = 0$. Nothing."

"Precisely. When you solve it you are left with nothing. But if you don't solve it, you have several real numbers. We Demons are those numbers."

Breanna concentrated, and almost saw it. "You know, my talent is seeing in darkness, but this is something else. I guess I need a little more. What are those numbers in practical terms?"

"If you take a person made of matter, and put him together with his antimatter opposite, they will neutralize each other and be nothing."

"I thought it would be total conversion to energy."

"No. Total conversion to nothing, as with the solved equation. Implosion, leaving no trace. That is why we can't afford to let Fornax join us. She is on the other side. It will be the end of us. The universe as we know it exists only as long as these elements are kept apart."

"But wouldn't that destroy Fornax too?"

"Yes."

"Then why is she so eager to take over?"

"It would be very high status to destroy the universe."

And Demons cared only about status. "For sure."

The passage came to a closed-off stairway, completely dark. Breanna used her key to open it, and stepped cautiously down. She had no trouble seeing her way, but was wary of it for other reasons. She moved as quietly as she could, alert for guards, but there did not seem to be any in this area. Where were they?

The next floor down turned out to be a high balcony of a giant ballroom. There was music wafting up from an orchestra, and couples were dancing below.

Couples? She had somehow thought this castle was empty, aside from Fornax and Earth, except for the raiders and the guards. So what was going on here?

"I love it!" Venus said. "We must join them."

"And give ourselves away?" But Breanna felt the love too. Dancing was one of the things lovers did. She had never really danced with Justin. Unless she counted the time near the beginning when he had been unsteady on his feet, and she had played a game of hugging and kissing him every time he stumbled. That had been fun. He had been nearly a century old, but childlike in his inexperience with love.

"Love!" Venus thought avidly. "You love!"

And Venus had been primed with that emotion. "For sure. We're about to be married."

"I want to get married!"

"I don't think Demons do that."

"What of Xanth?"

"He fell in love. I guess you're right; Demons can do it, if they have a mind to. But your emotion will fade when this game is done and the Swell Foop goes out of play."

"I don't want to lose it. I must keep it."

Breanna pondered. "I suppose if Xanth could learn it, so could you. Try to remember exactly what this feeling of love is like, so you don't lose it."

"Tell me of your scenes of love with Justin Tree."

"Well, we haven't consummated it yet. That comes half an instant after the wedding. We have done some necking and petting, but that's not the same thing as love. Really, it's just being together when you're in love."

"How was it?"

Breanna thought back to that early sequence, reliving it. They had found flying suits, then almost run afoul of a tangle tree with a nymph with tangled hair. She got back into the scene, enjoying the memory.

Farther along in the forest was a handsome yellow stallion. They paused in their chronic kissing to admire him. "You don't see many straight horses here," Justin remarked.

"I don't see many kissing couples here, either," the horse replied.

Both looked at him more closely, startled. "Did you talk?" Breanna asked.

"Of course I talked. But you started it. I don't suppose you have a nice filly for me to kiss?"

"I'll kiss you," Breanna said. "If you tell me who you are and how you came here."

"I belonged originally to Achilles, but he had a foot problem and died. He was Greek, incidentally. Since then I have wandered a bit. This seemed like a nice land, so I am grazing it for a while."

"Achilles' talking horse!" Justin exclaimed. "You are famous."

"I wouldn't know about that. I don't normally talk to strangers, but you provoked me."

"We didn't mean to," Breanna said. "We apologize, gourd style." She reached up to hug his head and plant a kiss on his nose. Horses of any kind liked girls' kisses.

"Where is this gourd you speak of?"

Breanna looked around. "It's an entry to the realm of dreams. They do have dream horses there. You might want to investigate." She spotted a gourd. "There's one! But one thing about them: You don't want to stay at the peephole too long, because—"

She stopped, because Xanthus had walked to the gourd, put his eye down, and disappeared into it.

"Then again, maybe you are a dream horse," she concluded. Then she turned to Justin. "Where were we?"

"I think we were about to kiss."

"That's it! Thanks for reminding me." She kissed him.

A harpy landed on a nearby branch. "Disgusting!" she screeched. "Haven't you idiots anything better to do than smooch all day?"

"No," Justin said dreamily.

"No? How would like some poop on your head, bleep-brain?"

"If you can't say anything positive, I'll smooch *you*," Breanna said evenly.

The harpy almost fell off her perch. "No thanks! I'm not of that persuasion. I'll take a goblin any day."

"A goblin?"

"Don't you know, pantywaist?" the harpy screeched. "There are so precious few males of our kind, we go after goblins now. They have the other halves of our magic talents. They provide the definition, we provide the strength. Together we can do anything."

"No you can't," Breanna said hotly. "You can't have any talents that have been had before."

"That's all you know, soot-face. Talents can occur up to once per species, per generation. We researched it. We have a lot of talents to go."

"How about the talent of getting lost?"

"We can have that too, smooch-for-brains. I'll show you." The harpy spread her dirty wings and took off.

"That was clever," Justin murmured.

"Well, I'm not nearly as dull as I seem." She kissed him again.

They continued in similar manner until they got where they were going. They celebrated that event by kissing again, and went on with their lives.

"So you see, without love, it's pretty pointless," Breanna concluded. "But with love, it's completely fulfilling."

"I must go kiss someone!"

"I don't think that's wise." But Breanna was swept along by the Demoness's eager new emotion. They made their way down the stairs that circled the ballroom. Could any of the dancers be guards? But there were only seven guards remaining, and there were dozens of dancers.

Then at the foot of the steps she spied a handkerchief. "That looks like Justin's!" She picked it up and sniffed it. "It *is* Justin's. He's here!"

"Where?"

They looked carefully, but none of the dancers looked like Justin. In fact, they all looked the same: The men were identical, and the women were too.

"These are robots or illusions," Breanna said.

"I must kiss someone," Venus repeated longingly.

"I wonder if Justin could be hidden among them, made up to look like one of them, so we would pass him by?" Breanna asked. "How would we know?"

"Kiss them!"

"You know, maybe that would work. I'd know Justin anywhere by his kiss. He is so delightfully amateurish."

They decided on the bold approach. They took one more look for guards, then took away all the torches so as to darken the ballroom. The dancers continued without seeming to notice. They cut in on the nearest couple, taking the dancing man away from the dancing woman. He did not seem to notice the difference. They danced a few steps with him, then kissed him. He was definitely solid, no ghost, but completely unresponsive.

"A life-sized golem," Breanna said distastefully. "Or the equivalent. A robot. No soul, just a mocked-up body on a set program."

They turned the man loose. He continued dancing, now without his partner, who was dancing by herself. They cut in on another man, and kissed him, with no better result.

"This is fun," Venus said. "But it would be better if the men were real."

"For sure. If we find Justin, he'll be real."

But it became apparent, as they broke up more and more couples, that Justin was not among them. His handkerchief was here, but he was elsewhere.

They did the last man, and turned away, disappointed. And there was a guard, reaching for them, about to tag them.

Breanna had no time to think. She surprised the guard by stepping into him, grabbing both his hands, and kissing him.

He stood there for a moment like a golem. Then he crashed to the floor, stunned.

"I guess that counted as a tag," Breanna said. "One more down; six to go."

"Let's kiss them too!"

"We're better off avoiding them. We're looking for Justin, not guards."

"But where is he?"

"That's the sixty-four-dollar question."

"The what?"

"It's something I picked up from Justin. He's just full of ancient archaic lore. He says that once upon a time in Mundania there was a quiz show that started with one dollar for the first question, then doubled it, and kept doubling until the last one was worth sixty-four dollars. It means a make-or-break question. Why anyone would want any dollars in Xanth I don't know. But—hey, look at that!"

"All I see is a button."

"That's one of Justin's buttons! I'd know it anywhere. He's been here!" She ran to pick it up. "Yes—he likes these old-fashioned shirts with buttons that catch on things and rip off. He's twenty-one, physically, but mentally he's still pretty old. I love him for that too; he treats me like an old-fashioned lady."

The button was at the portal to another large chamber. Here there were ancient paintings on the walls and statues from extinct cultures. "Definitely Justin's type," Breanna said, ignoring them.

But there were no people here, and certainly not Justin. At the far end was another chamber, containing potted flowers. "I love these!" Venus said, sniffing a red red rose.

"You love everything. But they are nice. I wonder why Fornax bothered with things like art and flowers?"

"To corrupt Justin, and thereby Demon Earth."

Breanna would have looked at her, but of course couldn't. "Cultural things would do it, if anything could. Justin's big on culture. But not if joining Fornax leads to the destruction of the universe. Justin's not *that* dedicated."

"But he might forget, if also blinded by love."

"He loves me, but he's not blind."

"Fornax will try to seduce him."

Breanna froze. "You're sure of that?"

"Why else did she assume a female mortal form? It is the way we Demons operate."

"But Jaylin's just a girl, and Mundane at that. She wouldn't—"

"Two things," Venus said seriously. "Fornax is not a girl, she's a Demon, and she governs, unlike the way it is with the rest of us in this game. That was part of the negotiation, so that she would accept one of our mortals. Jaylin will not have a choice about the use of her body. And the fact that she is Mundane will appeal to the Demon of Mundania. She is of his realm."

"Great fishes and little gods! This is devilish!"

"Demonic."

"For sure! We've got to find Justin!"

"And kiss him."

"That too." Breanna hurried on, ignoring the lovely flowers. They had become symbols of corruption.

At the end of the art gallery was another portal, and on its floor was another button. Breanna swept it up and charged through to the next chamber.

It was a balcony overlooking the castle wall. There was a sheer drop to the darkly heaving sea far below. A chill wind blew. There was no sign of Justin.

"Why do I suddenly think this is a wild-goose chase?" Breanna demanded rhetorically. "That we've been led along a nowhere trail?"

Then the door slammed closed behind them. Breanna turned to it, bringing out her key. But the keyhole was blocked with another key from the other side, left in place.

They were trapped on the balcony, with no exit save the deep dark sea. Even if they could survive a plunge, how could they ever get back into the castle in time to do any good?

Che followed the passage to the end, where it terminated in a locked descending stairway. He unlocked the door, took a torch, and stepped cautiously down. The stairs, like the passages, were broad enough to accommodate his body; that was one of the terms of the game. He would have preferred to fly, but of course there was no room inside the castle.

The next story was evidently dedicated to castle business. There were chambers filled with bedding, uniforms, chamber pots, and similar servant supplies. But no servants; they had been removed, if they had ever truly existed.

"This is a waste of time," Demon Mars said angrily. "There's nothing here."

Che was inclined to agree. He moved down another story. This one contained storerooms with bags of grain, bins of turnips, wine kegs, and hanging carcasses. Kitchen supplies.

He came to a dining room. Food was laid out on a large table. The look and smell of it was very appealing. He reached for a toasted roll.

"If I were Fornax, I'd bait my trap with poisoned food," Mars said.

Che's hand paused, then reversed. "Good point. We need to beware of everything, not merely guards."

They moved on, discovering many things, but no Justin/Earth. Also no guards. "I distrust this," Mars said. "There are no guards here because it is irrelevant. Fornax doesn't mind how much time we waste searching where our quarry isn't. In time we will blunder into a trap and be done for."

Che considered. It made more sense than he liked. "Then let's do the unexpected. Rejoin the others of our party, and seek Fornax herself."

But here the angry Demon had some caution. "Fornax is a Demon. Mortal bodies can't touch her."

"They can touch her mortal body, though. What would happen if we abducted Jaylin and took her out of the castle?"

"I doubt we could succeed. This is her bailiwick."

Che pondered. "What are the chances that Justin and Earth are near her?"

"Very good! That way she can be sure her prey is not escaping. It is Demon logic."

"Let's get the others." But then Che hesitated. "Which one first? Sim is very smart, but Breanna can see in darkness."

"Breanna," Mars said.

"Breanna," Che agreed. It was not that he valued one over the other, but that the girl's talent could indeed be most useful. They might accomplish more in darkness than in light, especially if the guards needed light to function.

They returned to the upper passage where they had separated from Breanna of the Black Wave. They walked down that passage, tracking the faint scuff marks on the floor and the fainter lingering smell of her black lotus perfume. She went down a stairway to a darkened ballroom, where human beings were dancing, by the sounds.

"Odd that it is in darkness," Che remarked.

"She eliminated the torches," Mars said.

The Demon was right. The girl had rendered the chamber dark, because she was at no disadvantage, while the guards might be. But it seemed she had not located Justin here.

Che circled the dark room, guided as much by sound as sight, for there was almost no illumination. Beyond was another chamber, where the torches had not been disturbed. It contained statuary and paintings of archaic style. Breanna had moved right on through it to a room containing flowering plants. Beyond that was a locked door with a key still in it.

"Beware!" Mars said. "They would not leave their key."

Indeed they would not. Something was wrong. Breanna's traces led up to that door, and not away from it.

"Where would that door lead?" Mars asked.

Che checked his mental coordinates. "Outside the castle. We are at the outer wall."

"Then they have been locked out."

Che looked around carefully. "A guard must have done it. Sneaked in and closed it behind."

"That means there is a hidden guard here."

Che checked more carefully. Then he saw it: a panel that did not quite match. He tapped it, and it make a hollow sound. He found a crevice, got his fingers in it, and slowly swung the panel open, like a door. There was a space behind it large enough to hold a guard. It was empty.

Now they knew how it was done. Che went to the door, turned the key, and opened it. But he did not step through. "Black Wave," he murmured.

"Horsetail!" Breanna cried, appearing. She had obviously been ready to tag him out as he came through the doorway. She stepped into him and hugged him. "We got tricked. I sure am glad to see you."

"Yes. The guard hid in a panel until you passed by. We concluded that Justin and Demon Earth must be near Fornax, and that searching the rest of the castle may be a waste of time. So we thought we should merge our forces and broach the Demoness."

Breanna nodded. "Let's get Birdbrain and do it." But she paused. "First—show me that panel."

He showed her. She put her finger to her lips, and pointed to the other side of the door.

Of course! There could be another panel—and the guard could be there. He nodded.

Breanna tapped the nearer panel. "That's really something, Che," she said aloud. "I wonder whether I could fit into it?"

Meanwhile Che was moving as silently as possible toward the other side. He found a similar panel.

"Don't close it on me, Che!" Breanna exclaimed. She tapped the floor with her foot, as though a hoof were landing there.

The panel Che was watching cracked open. He caught it and yanked it the rest of the way. A guard fell out. Che tagged the guard on the shoulder. Another down.

"We're getting smarter," Breanna remarked, with satisfaction. "We thought the guards would all be walking fixed routes. They're more canny."

"It occurs to me that perhaps we have been going about this wrong," Che said. "We have searched for Justin, and the guards lurk in ambush. We should search for the guards instead."

"And take them out!" she agreed. "Then we can search for Justin without always looking over our shoulders."

"But first let's check on Sim. I'm concerned."

"For sure."

They returned to the top passage, and tracked Sim. He had gone on down to the base of the castle, where there was a dungeon. Sim had passed though it to another locked chamber. But that chamber was empty—except for a pair of shoes.

"Justin's shoes," Breanna said. "Decoys—same as his handkerchief and button."

"But where is Sim?"

Sim was nowhere. His traces went up to the boots, and stopped.

Then Che spied another crevice. He pointed to it. Breanna nodded. She stood guard while Che worked on what turned out to be a stone set flush with the floor, the cover to a deep hole. "Sim," Che called down that hole.

There was a squawk. "Here!"

Sim scrambled up, and they helped him out. He was all right. He had been tricked and trapped just as Breanna had. They felt the continuing fear of the Demon Jupiter, but helped moderate it with their love and anger.

"So where is the guard that did it?" Breanna asked.

Che focused on that, and soon found the traces. The guard was hiding under another flush stone in the floor. They hauled up the stone and tagged him before he could get out. Another enemy down.

They quickly explained their new strategy to Sim: to eliminate the guards, then go after Fornax, expecting to find Justin/Earth in her vicinity. To take control of the situation, rather than reacting to false trails.

But as they made their way back through the dungeons, the enemy surprised them. Supposedly locked and empty cells burst open and five guards charged out, converging. "It's the blitz!" Breanna cried. "Watch your tails!"

Che tried to, but three guards were coming at him. He tagged one, and blocked the hand of another, but the third one caught him on the flank. He lost volition. He could still see and hear and think, but could not act; he had been nulled. Beside him, Sim tagged a guard, but fell to a second. Behind him Breanna managed to tag the third guard with her foot. But now the two remaining guards were advancing on her. She might get one, but the other would get her. Then all of them would have been nulled, with no one to rescue Earth.

Breanna realized as much herself. "I gotta get out of here!" she cried, fleeing. "Sorry, fellows!"

The guards pursued her. Che could not turn his head to look, but knew she was agile on her feet. Then the torches started getting doused. She was making the dungeon dark, so she would have the advantage. She could see the guards, but they could not see her.

Sure enough, she soon nulled them both. Then she returned to Che and Sim. "I guess I'm it," she said. "Just the luck of the draw I didn't get tagged." She hugged Sim where he stood. "Don't get into any trouble, Birdbrain." Then she hugged Che again. "Same to you, hoofer. I'll be ba-a-ack." And she was gone.

"Luck of the draw," Mars repeated angrily. "*We* should have been the ones to survive."

"I know she'll do her best," Che replied. "She has a fighting spirit."

"Venus is a cunning thing."

"But she's in love with love."

Overall, the prospects seemed chancy at best.

14
Desire

ornax paced with Jaylin's body. "Where is that courier guard? It's time for his hourly report."

Jaylin tried to conceal her private glee, but of course that was impossible. Fornax's mind was right with hers, and knew her thoughts. So she had to speak. "You know you lost five guards. The rest must have gotten nulled too."

"Charging three enemies together? That is unlikely." But the Demoness's desire was strongly tinged by doubt. The Swell Foop had given her one emotion, but she was picking up others from Jaylin. The mortal filter not only softened the prime emotion, it relayed a minor symphony of lesser emotions.

Again Jaylin tried to hide her thought, but could not. "Breanna of the Black Wave can see in darkness. That gives her an advantage in the dungeon."

Fornax made a mental picture of two huge black holes colliding and transforming into a single super-quasar that blew out a quarter of the universe in a shower of ferocious implosions. Jaylin wondered what the image would have been had her Fooped emotion been rage instead of desire.

"Then we shall have to act," Fornax said. She got Jaylin's body up and marched into Justin's cell.

This did not look good.

"Earth, do you not find me interesting?" Fornax demanded as Justin stood before her.

"I hope you have decided to release me," he said. That would be Demon Earth, rather than mortal Justin.

"I desire to keep you with me. We can do much together."

"I hope only to go home."

Fornax opened her robe enough to show a bit of unharnessed breast. "Perhaps, after this."

He averted his eyes. "That is not your body."

"It will do." Fornax stepped toward him. "Look."

"Unhand that man!"

Both Fornax and Jaylin were startled. They turned. There was Breanna of the Black Wave, or maybe Demoness Venus. She had won through!

"Breanna!" Justin cried gladly.

"Justin—Demon Earth—come with me. We're leaving this castle." Breanna stepped toward him.

Fornax moved to intercept her. "No. He remains with me."

"Don't let her tag you!" Justin cried.

"Be quiet, or I'll freak you," Fornax snapped, flipping her hem up partway.

"That's right," Breanna said. "You can tag me, but I can't tag you, because you're a king."

"A king?" Fornax asked, perplexed.

"The lead piece in a chess game," Jaylin explained. She spoke aloud, because in the distraction of blocking off Breanna, Fornax had left the voice connected. "The pieces can be taken and removed from play, but the king can't. He must be checked—threatened—and warned. Only when he is cornered and unable to escape check does the game end."

"Then what is Earth?"

"He is the other king. Kings can't tag each other."

"But I will prevent his escape, and win the game," Fornax said. "Then I will be able to use him in the manner I desire." She flipped the hem again. She was really intrigued. She had some embarrassing ideas about what to do with their mortal bodies, before proceeding with the next stage of her nullification of the universe. Jaylin would have blushed, had she had sufficient control of her body.

"The bleep you will!" Breanna said. "I'm taking him out of here, and you can go soak your steaming butt in a watery nebula."

"Not if I tag you first." Fornax lifted Jaylin's hand. It was an uneven contest, because Breanna could not tag back; all she could do was block.

Breanna tried to get around her, but Fornax maneuvered to stay between her and Justin. "Have it your way, then, canine," Breanna said, and grabbed Jaylin's hands, preventing a tag. She tried to heave her to the side, but Fornax countered, trying to throw Breanna to the side instead.

They struggled, each shoving the other forth and back. Their bodies came together, hands still locked. They were in a kind of dance, but it wasn't friendly.

Then it changed. Demoness Venus was with Breanna, and she was suffused with love. That love transferred, making Fornax feel it too. She loved Venus.

"Feel that desire!" Venus breathed. She kissed Fornax on Jaylin's mouth.

Fornax kissed back. "I love you," she whispered.

Then Breanna pushed her violently away. "The bleep you do!" She retreated, breathing hard.

Jaylin remembered that the mortals controlled the bodies of the lesser pieces. Breanna had asserted herself and broken up the clinch. "Thanks," Jaylin said.

Breanna's lips quirked. "It's Justin I want to do that to, no offense."

Fornax, having tasted the interaction of their emotions, was now reconsidering. "Yes, it is Demon Earth I desire, not another female."

"Go desire some other man," Breanna snapped. "This one's mine!"

"Not while the game continues." Without warning, Fornax spun about and threw herself on Justin. She wrapped Jaylin's arms around him, bearing him back against the wall, pressed Jaylin's front to his, and kissed him fiercely. Unable to retreat, Justin sank to the floor, but she stayed with him, wrapping Jaylin's legs around his and tearing at his buttonless shirt.

Breanna made a sound like that of a tiger whose tail had been trodden on. She pounced on the pair, taking handfuls of whatever was there. That happened to be Fornax's robe, which was coming apart. She brought her face down, baring her teeth for a vicious bite of whatever else.

Again, the Demon emotions took hold. Now there was a melding of extreme desire, love, and hope. It was clear by the Demon thoughts that all of them felt all three. Instead of biting off someone's nose, Breanna kissed someone's mouth. It wasn't clear whose. Instead of trying to push away a torso, Justin's hand stroked an anonymous breast. Meanwhile clothing was getting shredded.

And again, Breanna fought back. "Break it up!" she cried, shoving away someone's face and someone else's chest. "This isn't what any of us want!" She got a knee in between several legs and wedged them apart.

Fornax rolled on the floor, ejected from the cluster. She jumped up. Breanna and Justin climbed back to their feet, panting. The three of them stared at each other at close range, then backed away, giving themselves more room. Justin's shirt was half off, Breanna's skirt was rolled up around her waist so that her black panties were exposed, and Jaylin's robe was open to the floor.

Justin shrugged. "You ladies are showing more than you ought," he said, as he tucked his shirt back into his waistband.

Breanna started to untangle her skirt, but paused. "Justin, why aren't you freaked out?"

He smiled. "This is not Xanth. The magic is limited. I think what you are both showing is most interesting indeed, but hardly sufficient to make me forfeit my consciousness." That realization had evidently made him largely immune to the effect that had mesmerized him before.

Jaylin and Breanna exchanged a glance, then completed their reassembly. A significant weapon had been nullified. "So we have a stand-off," Breanna said. "Nobody can score."

"I think not," Fornax said. "The object for me is to prevent Demon Earth from departing this castle today. I can do that by clasping him—"

"If you do, I'll clasp *you*," Breanna said. "The way I just did, making it a threesome."

"And suffer the consequences of unfettered desire, love, and hope?"

"If that's the way it's gotta be, to stop you from molesting him."

"I think you have not thought this through," Fornax said smugly.

"Yeah? How not?"

"First, your contact will not prevent what you quaintly call molestation, but augment it as you yourself participate in it. The assigned emotions will merge and govern."

"Bleep," Breanna swore, conceding the point.

"Second, if we indulge in reckless passions indefinitely, as seems likely given the power of the emotions and the Demons involved, the time will expire without Earth's escape, and the victory in the game will be mine."

"Double bleep!"

"So why don't you save yourselves embarrassment and concede the game? Then, Venus, you may join in, if you wish, indulging your love without distraction. And you, Breanna, may in due course take Justin back to your homeland, because he is merely the carrier, not the object of the game. I have no designs on him personally. There is no need for us to quarrel further."

Breanna hesitated.

"Don't do it," Justin said. "Fornax represents contra-terrene matter. If she assumes power in our realm, all of it will be destroyed. There will be no love for us, no marriage, because we will cease to exist."

"Triple bleep! That's worse yet. We can't let her win."

"I will not let him go," Fornax said. "If you attempt to join him, I will join you, and we will have the threesome, which will be my eventual victory. I think you would prefer not to indulge in that scenario."

Breanna paused, evidently consulting with Venus. Jaylin quailed; she saw no way to balk Fornax's victory. Certainly she didn't want to be part of any group passion scene.

Then Breanna nodded. "There is another option. Justin can just walk out the front gate." She faced him. "Here's the key. Go." She tossed it, and he caught it.

"I will not allow that, either," Fornax said evenly. "I will clasp him the moment he moves toward that exit, and thoroughly seduce him. He will not be able to leave, even if he should want to."

"We've been through that already," Breanna said. "I won't just stand by and let you mess with him."

Fornax shrugged. "A twosome or a threesome; both are intriguing, and both will bring me victory. We shall have to play it out." She took a step toward Justin.

Breanna leaped, tackling her before she got there. The two of them crashed to the floor in a tangle of limbs and flying hair. "Get out of here, Justin!" she cried as she wrestled with Jaylin's body.

But Fornax refused to yield. "Remain with me, Earth! We shall satisfy both hope and desire together."

Justin, evidently prompted by Demon Earth, hesitated. Jaylin wasn't sure which one governed that body. If it was Earth, Fornax might influence him. If it was Justin, Fornax's control of Jaylin's body might influence him. What would he do?

"Leave the castle!" Breanna screamed as she captured Jaylin's hands and held them tightly, preventing any tag. "The moment you're out, we win. Then we can go home and get married, and I'll give you everything you ever thought about dreaming of, and some you wouldn't even have the nerve to imagine. And the Demon Earth can watch, for all I care. I came from Mundania, after all. Just start walking!"

Justin nodded, and started walking.

"Stay!" Fornax called. "Then you can enjoy everything she has *now,* and everything I have too, all together." She managed to shift about so that the robe was open again, and Jaylin's panties were showing. "Everything! In one swell foop, as it were."

Justin paused. That was one potent offer, unfortunately. And Fornax wasn't bluffing. She wanted to keep Justin/Earth thoroughly occupied for the rest of the day and night. Jaylin quailed.

"It's the Swell Foop that got us into this," Breanna cried. "It's time to wrap this up and retire it. Walk!"

Justin hesitated, then resumed walking.

Fornax could not free her hands, but she was able to stretch Breanna and herself into a rather naughty position, in the manner of female wrestlers. "Look at this!" she cried. "You will never have another chance! In duplicate, yet. You will love it, I guarantee. Stay and be wickedly delighted."

Justin paused, looking. He was, after all, a man. He couldn't help it. He seemed to be on the verge of freaking out despite the lack of freakout magic.

"If you love me, leave me!" Breanna cried, struggling to get something halfway out of sight.

And that did it. Justin wrenched his gaze away and walked on out of the room. They heard his footsteps moving toward the front gate.

"Don't goooo!" Fornax wailed despairingly.

The footsteps stopped. "Justin was always a sucker for a maiden in distress," Breanna muttered ferociously.

"Don't gooomph!" Fornax cried, as Breanna stifled her piteous wail with a comprehensive kiss. Woman to woman it might be, but love and desire set Fornax back; she wasn't used to this.

After a moment the footsteps resumed. Justin continued on out of the castle. Every time Fornax tried to wail after him, Breanna stuffed her mouth with another kiss. Fornax tried to fight it, but the powerful emotions vitiated her effort. She didn't know how to handle them. Neither did Jaylin.

"You can quit now, girls," Che said. "It's done."

They paused in their struggle. "Done?" Fornax asked.

"He's out," Sim squawked. "We won the game. Our folk are no longer nulled."

"Bleep!" Fornax said. "I almost had him."

"There's no call for language like that," Cynthia said. "There will be other games."

They disengaged and stood up, wild-haired and ragged. "There will be other games," Fornax agreed.

"We shall be returning to our own galaxy now," Che said. "Do you wish to come along?"

"What are you talking about?" Breanna demanded as she tried to repair what was left of her skirt. "This bleep of a bleep tried to destroy our whole universe! You're inviting her along?"

"There was nothing personal in it," Sim squawked. "Demons vie for status."

"Yes, I am curious to see your environment," Fornax said as the castle disappeared, leaving them standing with Justin. "Perhaps Earth will show me some more mortals." She flounced her robe, in the guise of adjusting it. Jaylin would have tried to blush again at the way her flesh was being flaunted, had she been able. Why hadn't Fornax left her body?

"Because I will be conveying it to your galaxy," the Demoness replied internally.

"There is no need," Earth said through Justin's mouth.

"What, did I not tempt you a little?" Another flounce, this time making sure he saw. He did; Justin's eyes began to glaze. She was getting better at it, or maybe he was no longer fighting it.

"Cut that out!" Breanna said.

"You admixed your love with my desire," Fornax retorted. "If you don't want to kiss me more, then allow me to explore other options."

"Not with my man!"

"He is merely the shell hosting the Demon Earth at the moment."

"True." This time it was the Demoness Venus speaking.

Justin picked up the Swell Foop. Then they were zooming through the universe, seeing stars and clouds of dust zip by. They landed in the main chamber of the Nameless Castle.

"The mission is done," Cynthia reported. "Demon Earth is with us."

"True," Earth said with Justin's mouth.

Chlorine nodded. "Then we can relinquish the Swell Foop and the Rings of Xanth."

Justin gave her the Foop. She took it—and it vanished.

"What happened?" Jaylin asked, startled.

"It hides itself," Chlorine explained. "It will be just as challenging to find next time. Now you must return the Rings to the Zombie Master."

"But the Rings were on the Foop," Jaylin protested. Then, startled, she looked at her own hand. The Ring of Void was there. She saw the other Rings on the other hands. They had returned to their holders when the Swell Foop departed.

"Will do," Breanna said.

The Demons remained with them, apparently interested in the proceedings. But that rang false to Jaylin. "Why should Demons have any concern at all about anything mortals do?"

"Normally we do not," Fornax replied. "Mortals are useful only in the introduction of random elements for games. But this game introduced emotions. Until they fade, it is not safe for us to leave our hosts."

"Not safe? But mortals can't do anything to Demons."

"Emotions can have destructive effect when not filtered through mortal beings. The game is done, but we are not yet free of the effects of the Swell Foop."

Jaylin decided not to argue the case. She just wanted to get on with things so she could return home. She realized that this was probably an aspect of the Foop-sponsored desire, so Fornax was right: It had not yet faded.

They moved the party to Castle Zombie. Fornax was using her omniscience to look about, learning details at an incredible (for a mortal) rate.

"But I thought no Demon had power outside its own bailiwick," Jaylin thought.

"We do if there is not a game rule prohibiting it," Fornax explained. "At the moment we are between games."

"You seem remarkably sanguine about losing your game."

"Demons are. Had the Swell Foop given me the emotion of anger or grief, I would not be as accepting. As it is, I merely wish to explore the further ramifications of desire, before entering the next game."

They met with the Zombie Master and turned the Rings over to him. "New zombies will hide them," he said, satisfied. "For their next time of need, in a few centuries."

Jaylin saw Roxanne Roc sitting in sight of Castle Zombie, ready to resume her duties. The big bird had had more of a respite than she might have expected, but she was obviously prepared to return to work.

"All of you are invited to the wedding," Breanna announced. "Coming right up, or else."

The assorted guests made their ways to the glade where the wedding was scheduled. "How did everyone get here so fast?" Jaylin asked, perplexed. "How could it be organized, when Breanna just announced it?"

"I helped," a nearby man said. "I am a talent agent. My talent is finding talented people. I found people who knew when the wedding would be, and what to do to prepare for it." He looked around, fixing on another man who was straightening some chairs. "Like this one, whose talent is to bring something forward or back in time. He got the chairs from the future, and the wedding ring from the past, which the groom had forgotten about."

Jaylin shook her head. "It's good to be back in Xanth, where puns and talents abound, and folk are so helpful."

"It does have a certain naïve appeal," Fornax agreed.

A soft nose nudged Jaylin. "Putre!" she cried gladly, turning to hug the zombie horse.

But he had bad news. "The Night Stallion will not allow me to remain in Xanth," his speech balloon wrote. "Now that my mission is done, I must be abolished. I came to bid you parting. It was a pleasure to associate with you."

"No!" Jaylin cried. "He can't do that!"

"I am originally a dream horse," the balloon wrote. "My fate was postponed while I served duty as the knower for the Ring of Void. A new zombie will take the Ring. I am now expendable. You were kind to me, and I thank you for that."

"No! It can't be!" Jaylin protested tearfully. "You're a good horse."

"I am allowed to attend the wedding, as it is a zombie function. Thereafter I will cease to exist."

She hugged him. "I'll do something," she promised. But she had no idea what. She herself had no magic, and was not going to be in Xanth beyond the wedding, either. She felt tearfully helpless.

"Fascinating mortal foolishness," Fornax remarked.

"Oh, shut up! You're no help at all."

"Perhaps. Would you like to play a game?"

"What?"

"A Demon game, whose rules are set and whose outcome is unknown."

"I'm not a Demon! I'm not even a little *d* demon. I'm just an ordinary Mundane girl. How can I play any such thing? Anyway, I don't like what you did with my body."

"Then you will not like this game. I want to borrow your body again."

"Borrow my body! You tried to use it to seduce Justin Tree!"

"To corrupt the Demon Earth, to win the game. I will accept reasonable limitations in this instance. This is not really a game so much as a supplementary adjunct to a potential full Demon game, somewhat as was your case in the prior one."

Despite her horror, Jaylin was curious. "Why in the universe would you want to borrow my body again?"

"To have a base to visit Demon Earth."

"He doesn't want anything to do with you."

"That is an exaggeration. I succeeded in intriguing him. Perhaps I can complete the seduction."

"With my body? No way!"

"I will agree to leave your body unseduced."

"I don't understand."

"The emotions engendered by the Swell Foop are fading. They could have been devastating, had they not been filtered through mortal bodies. Even so, they were moving. It was the dire threat of such emotions that caused me to agree to the game that cost me my captive; the Foop could have ruined me."

"Ruined you? Those emotions just seemed to be frosting on the cake; you could have played your game without them."

"But I would not have. The Demon Earth was in my power, and would have had to join me. I had no intention of risking that advantage on a wild gamble."

"But you played the game!"

"Precisely. The Swell Foop was like a—" Fornax paused to fish a suitable analogy from Jaylin's mind. "A cannon pointed at my head. It could have given me the unfettered emotion of grief, so that I wished to expire, or of love, so that I would have done anything for those who controlled it. The Foop's active presence doomed me."

"Then why didn't the other Demons just use it on you, to win without having to risk two more of their own number?"

"Because if they destroyed me, they would also have destroyed Demon Earth, who was in my power. They needed his gravity."

It was slowly coming clear. "So they offered you good stakes in a fair game, and you accepted."

"I accepted," the Demoness agreed. "And lost. But not as much as I would have lost otherwise. As it is, I have now directly felt the power of emotion, and have become interested in mortal affairs. But I cannot intrude on another Demon's terrain hereafter without a normal-matter landing site. I want you to be that site."

"So you can yank me out of my Mundane life and drag me off to your galaxy?"

"I will undertake to leave you in your familiar setting. In any event, I may not utilize your site in this century."

"This century!"

"Or I may. Time is largely meaningless to Demons. I want the right to use it."

"No!"

"You have not heard what I offer in return."

"What?" Jaylin demanded rebelliously.

"The life of your zombie horse."

Jaylin froze. "You can save Putre?"

"I can arrange it, with the cooperation of other Demons."

"Why the bleep should they cooperate with you?"

"They will if I face them with a worse alternative, as they did with me before."

Jaylin suffered a complete and surely foolish reversal. "You do that, and I'll make your deal. You can visit my body, provided you don't misuse it. I'll want another Demon to forge the agreement—the rules of the game. So I don't get scr—cheated."

"Agreed." Fornax sent out a mental signal, and Sim Bird joined them. "Squawk?"

"Jupiter, as an experienced game player, and to facilitate a conclusion to the present situation, forge a fair objective agreement between me and this mortal girl."

A monstrous mind-bending mass of information flowed between them. "Squawk."

It was done. Jaylin didn't have to ask; she had felt the exchange, and knew beyond any doubt that a tight Demonly agreement had been forged and would be honored. They had used at least another one percent of their joint attention; there were surely clauses that were well beyond her potential comprehension, protecting her. Demons did not bend the rules of any game in any trifling respect; they were absolute. She was quite safe.

After that, things went rapidly. All of the Demons remained at Castle Zombie to watch Breanna marry Justin. Jaylin now understood that this was not because they truly cared, but because they were waiting for their emotions to fade so that they could safely desert the mortal filters. "She is a good girl," Fornax remarked. "She deserves him."

"But you were trying to take him from her!"

"Only for the game. He is, after all, a mortal."

"But he managed to resist your blandishments."

"I was barred from using my Demonly powers. I was confined to yours. I could have made him love me."

Jaylin realized that the Demoness was neither bragging nor bluffing. She was speaking literally. That made Jaylin curious. "Why didn't you cheat?"

"Cheat?"

Jaylin explained the concept.

"Fascinating! We must have a game with cheating!"

What mischief had Jaylin sown? "No need."

"It wouldn't work against another Demon, of course, but a mortal would be easy."

But it was time to pay attention, for the wedding was in progress. Justin was handsome in a formal black suit, and Breanna was lovely in a full black gown. Even the zombie attendants were formally garbed. King Xeth seemed to be best man, and Zyzzyva Zombie was matron of honor.

"But brides are supposed to wear white," Jaylin said.

"Why?" Fornax asked.

"To show they're virginal, or something."

"She is virginal, but prefers black."

"How do you know that?"

"We are beyond the game. I can be omniscient as usual."

Jaylin decided not to ask why she had had to ask about white, if she was omniscient. She might get more of an answer than she liked.

"We do miss trifling details on occasion," Fornax agreed. "It can be easier to seek mortal interpretation."

The Demon Grossclout had appeared to conduct the service. Even he seemed slightly awed by some of the members of the audience. "If there is anyone here who has reason for this union not to be made, let him speak now." He paused ever so briefly. "There being no objection—"

Fornax jumped up. "I have an objection," she said with Jaylin's voice.

Oh, no! What mischief was this?

Grossclout frowned. Naturally he wasn't fooled by appearances. "What is your objection, Demoness Fornax?"

"One of the zombies the bride values is to be destroyed after the ceremony. The bride objects."

Breanna had opened her mouth, surely to protest interference by this particular Demoness. But she paused. "Which zombie?"

"Palus Putredinus, the zombie dream horse. Mare Imbrium's foal."

There was an intake of breath across the gathering. Everyone knew Mare Imbri.

"He's to be destroyed?" A small black cloud formed over Breanna's head.

"The Night Stallion will no longer tolerate his existence," Fornax said.

"Bleep!" The whole assemblage winced at such a crude imprecation from such a lovely bride. "For sure, I don't want my wedding spoiled by that. Putre really helped us find the Foop. We owe him. Besides, he's a nice horse, and Mare Imbri has had more than enough grief without losing him."

"He can be saved, if the attending Demons agree," Fornax said.

"How?" Breanna demanded.

"He can be converted to a mortal horse and banished to Mundania."

"But that's cruel! No immortal wants to be mortal, and no Xanthian wants to be sent there."

"He will be glad to go, if—"

"If what, C-T canine?"

"If the Demon Earth accepts him, and he can find a home in Mundania."

Then at last Jaylin caught on. "I'll take him!" she cried.

Breanna turned to Justin. That was when Jaylin realized that the Demoness Venus and Demon Earth were not only attending the wedding, they remained with their former hosts. Their emotions had not yet faded, either.

Justin nodded. Evidently the Demon Earth wanted to get this wedding done with so he could return home. Accepting one horse was a small price for avoiding the mischief Breanna would otherwise make. It was perhaps not remarkable that even a Demon was wary of her ire.

Breanna smiled, and the cloud over her head dissipated. "For sure. Let's get on with the nuptials."

That was all. But Putre disappeared from beside Jaylin. "He is there, invisible until you claim him," Fornax said.

"Thank you," Jaylin breathed. For the first time, she really appreciated Fornax's presence. The Demoness had delivered.

Now the wedding continued. It was beautiful. Breanna of the Black Wave, having finally grounded her man, was all chocolate sweetness and black light. The couple kissed, and all the women in the audience cried. That included Jaylin.

"Pointless sentimentality," Fornax sniffed.

"You're crying too!" Jaylin retorted.

"Not by choice." But after a pause, she added, "I wish I could marry."

So her emotion of desire had not yet faded enough. "Do Demons marry?"

"Not hitherto. But we never had emotions before. At last I understand why Demon Xanth acted as he did. He caught a case of emotion."

"I guess he did. He and Chlorine have a baby now."

"A baby. Fascinating."

"Do Demons have babies?"

"Not hitherto."

Jaylin shook her head as the ceremony concluded and folk mixed and chatted and went for refreshments. "I want more of these," Fornax said as she used Jaylin's mouth to eat a wincing misfortune cookie.

"That emotion of desire is really tearing you up, isn't it!"

"Yes. Perhaps Demon Earth's emotion of hope will linger long enough for me to share my desire and make a game of marriage and family."

A genuine lightbulb flashed over Jaylin's head. "That's why you want to borrow my body again! To approach Demon Earth in his own domain. Because you like him."

"Desire him. There is a distinction."

"Because of that lingering emotion. The Foop really got to you. So you want to follow up."

"Without being caught loose outside my own domain, and trapped," she agreed. "Your terrene body will protect me against that, and I will be able to have a safe dialogue with him. This is not a physical thing, but a site for an intellectual encounter, to negotiate terms of a special game whose actual arena of play will be elsewhere. It will not interfere with your routine at all; you need not even be conscious of my presence."

Jaylin considered. "I think I'd rather be aware, if it's all the same to you."

"It is all the same. Demons are normally indifferent to the concerns of mortals."

"But I don't think the Demon Earth has any romantic interest in you. He just wants to go home."

Fornax paused, considering. That was unusual, because the Demon minds could process worlds of information in microseconds. "He has an interest in a female, but she does not return it. This allows me a prospect."

"Well, I guess it's your business. It should be interesting."

"Interesting," the Demoness agreed with an obscure slant of mood.

Che and Cynthia Centaur approached. "Isn't this a joyful occasion!" Demoness Saturn exclaimed with Cynthia's voice. Jaylin could recognize them all, because of the effect of radiating Demon omniscience.

"A tedious pain," Demon Mars said angrily with Che's voice.

"Who would have thought it would be such an adventure?" Cynthia asked. "How little did I imagine that my simple query to the Good Magician would take me out of this galaxy."

"It was still a pain," Mars said.

"A bit of anger management," Cynthia murmured. Then she turned into Che and pressed close, giving him a double-breasted kiss. Saturn's lingering joy overwhelmed Mars's lingering anger, silencing him.

"I wonder whether *we* could do that, Saturn," Mars said musingly.

"Not in these bodies!" Cynthia said, jerking her bare front away from Che's.

Che and Saturn both laughed. They were rapidly catching on to the remaining mortal emotions.

"I desire that!" Fornax breathed longingly.

"I fear you can't have it," Jupiter squawked.

Fornax whirled and kissed him on the beak, silencing him too. She was making Jaylin's body do things, but at this point Jaylin didn't mind; she was too busy giggling.

The wedding celebration was winding down. The Bride and Groom disappeared, surely eager to celebrate love and hope in their fashion. In fact, they were in Castle Zombie, perhaps doing things zombies did not imagine. Jaylin bid farewell to the friends she had made, and turned inwardly to Fornax. "I'm ready to go home, before your emotion fades the rest of the way, and you depart and leave me stranded here."

"Curses! She caught on." The Demoness was still picking trace odds and ends from Jaylin's mind.

It seemed but another moment when Jaylin appeared in the Baldwins' house. Fornax was proving useful for traveling purposes, as she had the ability simply to appear at the destination.

There was David. "He's cute," Fornax remarked silently.

"Jaylin!" David cried. "You're back!"

"You noticed," Fornax said, inhaling. Jaylin was back in whole conventional clothing, but the Demoness had been quite quick to catch on how to use it to best advantage. "But this is not my back; it's my front." She angled it for best advantage, reaching a hand back to draw the shirt tight from behind.

This was becoming embarrassing. "Will you let go of me?" Jaylin demanded silently.

"Not yet. I have to deliver you all the way home." She turned slightly, shifting her knees to accentuate the profile of a hip.

"You've changed!" David said, his eyes attempting to lock onto her chest and hip simultaneously.

"Be quiet and kiss me, wonder boy."

"Please, Fornax—I'd rather kiss him myself!" But the Demoness was still busy exploring the nuances of desire.

David took her in his arms. Fornax nudged closer and gave him a deep kiss as she squeezed his thigh.

"Really changed," he said, amazed.

"That's only the beginning," Fornax said. "Now I must go home. Call me."

And they were standing at Jaylin's door in Hawaii. "Now I will leave you," Fornax said. "I have used up the last of the desire. It was fun. When David calls, tell him that he and his sister have been granted passes to Xanth, and their parents too."

"They have? How do you know?"

"My omniscience, of course. I will come to you at my convenience and inclination. Should you ever wish to host me again on your own initiative, stroke the ring and think of me. I may oblige."

"Don't hold your breath," Jaylin said. But she wasn't entirely sincere. The Demoness had shown her things that might be worth remembering. "Ring?"

She was suddenly alone, except for the ring, on the same finger the Ring of Void had been. It looked entirely ordinary, even dull, but she knew it wasn't. Not by a lo—oo—ong shot!

Nikko was barking. The door opened, and there was her mother. "Jaylin!" she cried gladly.

"Mother!" Jaylin cried, hugging her.

"I'm so glad you're back early! I was concerned."

"Early?"

"Florida is a long way away. You can't have had more than a few hours there. Did something go wrong?"

Jaylin did some quick mental addition and realized that the trip to Florida, and thence to Xanth and Fornax, had taken less than a day. The trip back to Xanth had been instant, and from Xanth to Hawaii almost instant. Add in the time spent in the castle, and at the wedding—it was about two days.

"No, nothing; it was just a bit faster than it might have been."

"How was it? Did you have a nice visit?"

How could she tell her mother all of what had happened? That she had gone to another galaxy, and tried to seduce her friend's fiancé, and agreed to host an impossibly powerful foreign Demoness. Mother would never understand. "It was great, mother. I had all kinds of adventures. And—" She hesitated. Was Putre really here? "Excuse me. I have to—" She hurried on through the house.

"Of course, dear."

But it wasn't the bathroom she was going to. She went on out the back. There was nothing there. Had she been deceived? "Oh, Putre," she murmured sadly.

Something nuzzled her elbow. There was the black horse. She had invoked him by speaking his name. "Oh, Putre!" she cried, clasping his neck tearfully.

Then she stood back a bit. "Can you still talk?"

Putre shook his head. No speech balloon appeared. He had become Mundane.

"I love you anyway!" she said, hugging him again. For an instant she thought she saw a little heart float over his head, but that was surely imagination.

Then she turned back toward the house. How was she going to explain this to her folks? The truth would never do.

She heard the phone ringing. That would be David, calling from Florida; she just knew it. She had things to tell him, especially now that Demoness Fornax was gone. She hurried inside.

Epilogue

Jaylin's mother shook her head. How the girl had come by a horse and brought him here she could not imagine. But that was only part of it. How had she gotten home from the airport? All the girl would say was that a friend had brought her, and that she had found the horse. It was obvious that the horse was nice enough, remarkably well trained, and devoted to her, adding to the mystery. She must have found him in Florida. Yet how could he have been shipped here so rapidly?

And that weird phone call from her pen pal, David. Jaylin's mother did not believe in snooping, but she had been unable to avoid overhearing bits about some kind of demon and desire. That was probably one of those violent computer games, with fantastic creatures galore. They must have played it in Florida. The story line seemed to involve something about the distant galaxy Fornax, and rescuing a demon called, of all things, Earth, and how some demoness was interested in him but he wasn't interested in her. Neither David nor Jaylin could figure out why he wasn't, for she was an incredibly sexy creature, with powers akin to his own. Could he be interested in someone else? But the only other person he had really gotten to know was Jaylin herself, who had helped rescue him, though not in any ordinary way. Why would he care about *her*? Both of them had laughed uproariously at that notion. Then at the end, Jaylin had made a kissing gesture at the phone, and hung up. It was probably just as well that her romantic pen pal was several thousand miles away. She was, after all, only fifteen. What did she know of the pitfalls of young romance?

Jaylin's mother had a bad dream in the night. Something about an impossibly powerful earth spirit taking an interest in her daughter, because she had inadvertently helped him and stirred his emotion. So he was watching her, and watching over her, experiencing the odd feeling of hope. Hope for what? That wasn't clear, but Jaylin's mother woke in horror.

The day was all right. Jaylin seemed to be normal, as she tackled the problem of getting feed and shelter for the new horse. That was going to be expensive, and the girl's allowance couldn't possibly cover it. But he *was* a nice horse, and Jaylin's mother couldn't help liking him, despite Jaylin's insistence on calling him an ugly name. She had checked on him at night, after Jaylin was asleep, and found him staring up at the moon. What could he possibly see there? She had patted him, and he had nuzzled her, and for a moment the stars over his head had seemed to form a heart-shaped pattern. A trick of night mist, surely. They would make do somehow, though caring for a horse had not been in their plans.

Now it was day, and Jaylin was out riding the horse, bareback. That seemed unsteady, but they were having no trouble at all; the horse was perfectly docile, and seemed to answer to voice commands. He didn't stray, either, when alone, despite the lack of a suitable fence; he remained right where Jaylin asked him to. He seemed to understand every word she spoke. It was uncanny.

It was a cloudy day, and rain was starting. But Jaylin wasn't coming in. What was the matter with that girl? Her mother was about to call to her, but paused in midbreath. Something really weird was happening.

It was raining everywhere, except on the girl and horse. There was a patch of sunlight on them—and it followed them like a spotlight as they moved. It illuminated Jaylin especially, making her hair shine, flattering her features, making her as pretty as an angel. It was as though the land and sky loved her. She seemed quite unaware of it.

Jaylin's mother stared, and suffered a memory of her bad dream. Could it be true? An earth spirit, watching over her, and hoping for something?

Hoping for *what*?

Author's Note

This is the twenty-fifth Xanth novel. You might think I'd be tired of them by now. No, I enjoy each one, and despite the verdict of cri-ticks each one is different and original in its own fashion. They all have common elements, of course, such as puns, romance, adventure, magic, and continuing characters and setting. There's usually a struggle to get into the Good Magician's castle, and a bit of naughtiness, but also some genuine human discovery and muted social comment. Xanth parodies Mundania, which we know as the dull real world, and pokes fun at anything within range, but there are underlying values of integrity and decency. It is what I consider wholesome entertainment.

Swell Foop was more of a challenge than most, because of the necessary structuring. I had to align six Rings with six ordinary characters and six zombies and hiding places, as well as nine Demons, six emotions, and nine fundamental aspects of the universe. All without slowing down the adventure and wonder, or violating the Adult Conspiracy too badly. Each time I thought I had it all worked out, there'd be another wrinkle and I'd have to reorganize. Even the computer speller fought me; when I used the word "fumeroles" it wanted to correct it to "females." Did it know something I didn't? I had to review game theory to work out the Demon game climax, figuring out who would win in what circumstance.

How much simpler it would have been to have handsome Bat Durston stumble into Xanth, find a magic sword, and rescue a lovely princess from an evil wizard. But I leave that to other writers; Xanth has never been exactly that kind of fantasy.

Some may wonder about the Demon Nemesis. That's a take on speculative astronomy. There are indications that our Solar System is not limited to eight and a half planets (Pluto being the half). There may be a massive additional body way out there, perhaps a brown dwarf, that we know of only by its slight gravitational effect on the rest of the system. This is Nemesis, and it is possible that in the next few years astronomers will finally verify its presence. Similarly, they may nail Dark Matter. There is a lot more to the universe than we can see at present, but we know it is there by its gravitational effect on what we can see. What makes it more interesting is that it isn't necessarily far away; it seems to be everywhere, far and near, even between your eye and the page of this book, but tantalizingly ghostly in its obscurity. It may be so tenuous as to be invisible, yet it comprises more than 90 percent of the substance of the universe. Such a fantastic thing surely deserves a place in fantasy fiction.

There was also the challenge of using the reader suggestions. Some wonder why I bother; the answer is that I feel the material will be fresher if there is some outside input, and I do like to please my readers when I can. More than a hundred were used this time, and I did catch up, except for several that simply would not fit in this novel and will be used in the next one. Often I can't do justice to particular notions, and I regret that, but the needs of the story do come first. Sometimes a perfectly valid reader comment or question doesn't relate. Here's an example: A reader, James <jamesbro@erols.com>, asked about the Demon Litho. Who? I asked. So he documented his case: Litho is the one who made the wiggles, mentioned in *Vale of the Vole*. So who is he? Darned if I know. I conjecture that he may be an aspect of Demon Earth, maybe an alternate name. But since when did Earth mess in with the magical creatures of Xanth?

But on occasion a reader suggestion becomes an important element of a novel, and that happened here too. Such as the Six Rings of Xanth. The suggestion was for Five Rings, but I modified it to add the Ring of

Idea. Much of the novel is structured around the quest for those phenomenal Rings.

And sometimes something weird happens. You see, most suggestions I use, and credit in the Author's Note, and that's it. But sometimes I need a name for a suggested character, and then I may simply borrow the name of the one who suggested it. I do this irregularly and somewhat whimsically, so that I don't get flooded with requests to put every reader's name in; a reader can be surprised to discover his/her name in the main story. Usually it is merely a passing reference, of no real consequence. But sometimes it gets complicated. There is a huge example in this novel. As I finished the prior novel, *The Dastard,* a notion came in that just missed that one; it was too late to include it. So it became the first reader suggestion for the following novel, which is this one. It was that there should be a quest to seek a Mundane person who would be the only one who could get something important in Xanth. Well, I was working out the story of the Swell Foop, and this fit right in: a Mundane could be the one to find it. So I took the name of the one who suggested it, Jaylin. But as the story line filled out, that character became more important; in fact, she became one of the six viewpoint characters of the novel. She also had a more challenging role than anticipated. One that might not be considered appropriate for a real person.

I pondered, then wrote to Jaylin's mother. As it happens, I know her; she's three days older than my elder daughter, and sends me eye-catching Hawaiian calendars. So I explained the situation, and offered to change the name of the character. That is, Jaylin would still get credit for the notion, but would not be named as the character. But she decided that it was all right to leave the name, and so her daughter became a character in the novel. All because Jaylin sent in a notion just too late for the prior novel, and I stuck her name on it.

As it happened, I wrote this novel in two parts. Back in Mayhem 1999 I had finished writing *DoOon Mode* and was set to proofread the five novels of the Bio of a Space Tyrant series I was putting back into print via Xlibris, a self-publishing service. But the new scanner we had gotten wasn't working, and while we struggled with that delay, I went ahead and wrote the first two chapters of *Foop.* I don't like to waste time. Then we finally got the scanner working; it turned out to be a conflict between it and the modem, and my wife scanned the novels into the computer and I proofread them and made notes for the sixth novel in that series, *The Iron Maiden*. But before I finished that the *Princess Rose* movie project came up, with a short deadline, and then I had to return to *Foop* because my spare time was gone. Before I finished, I had to pause to proofread the galleys for the republished edition of the tenth Xanth novel, *Vale of the Vole*. So it was a busy and somewhat fragmented summer. Maybe there are writers who can start a novel and finish it without interruption; I don't seem to be one of them.

In fact, those were only the literary interruptions. There were also mundane ones. Once I got a modem and learned how to do email and go on the Internet, life became faster. The Internet moves much more rapidly than real life does. My regular correspondence slowed to about a hundred letters a month, but three hundred emails a month to hipiers@mindspring.com made up the difference. I read them all, but let www.hipiers.com send routine answers to most. Reader suggestions started coming in by email, complicating my credits when all I had was the online name. Sometimes I didn't catch the name at all, so the present list is imperfect.

It got worse. Internet publishing was growing, where books are done electronically and downloaded to the computers of those who buy them, to be read onscreen. New publishers were appearing, and I wanted to know more about them, because I receive many queries from readers who are hopeful writers: How and where can they get published? The answer is that perhaps only one in a hundred will be published conventionally, but many more could achieve it electronically. But I knew little about it. So I started my own ongoing survey of Internet Publishers, and ran it on HiPiers, updating it every two months. This was of course just my observation and opinion, not worth more or less than any other person's, but it represented my answer to my readers. Now they knew what I knew about it, and could be guided accordingly. I got feedback from both publishers and writers, some with quite useful information, positive and negative. I am known in some circles as The Ogre; that began with a false accusation decades ago, but I like it because I really am pretty ornery when it comes to telling the truth or standing my ground when I believe I am right. I got into trouble for that in college, and in the U.S. Army, and as a writer. I think a lie is an abomination, and I have on occasion gone to law when deceived or cheated, making my case the hard way. Ogres are hard to silence, being justifiably proud of their stupidity. There was a stir when I blew the whistle on an Internet publisher who wasn't paying royalties, but generally response has been positive. Most of the publishers seem to be good, and I support Internet publishing on general principle, because I think it is good for writers. I had a conflict of interest, because I had invested in two publishers. So I identified those publishers, so others would know where I might be biased. I didn't invest to make money, but to do my bit to give every hopeful writer a fair chance to realize his/her dream. Venture capital investing is a scary business, resembling high-stakes gambling, not something a duffer should get into, but I have already mentioned the ogre mentality. At such time as I kick that bucket in the Void, I hope to be remembered for two things: writing some good books, and helping change Parnassus (the publishing system) for the better.

Because of that investment, I was on the board of directors of Xlibris, the one where I was republishing my old novels. They had a board meeting in Philadelphia, but when I tried to attend it, my usual problems with traveling manifested, in this case bad weather. Hurricane Floyd swiped at Florida, disrupting air travel, and moved on to Philadelphia, severely wetting North Carolina on the way. In fact, there were pigs on the roofs of barns because of the flooding. So the board meeting was postponed a week, and I hope the folk who got wet didn't catch on why that storm came at that time.

And if that wasn't bad enough, I became senile. Um, let me rephrase: I became a senior citizen. I turned sixty-five and went on Medicare. Maybe that's why I lacked the wit to figure out the rule for zombies and magic talents: Do they keep them or lose them? I had it happening both ways. I think I'll have to leave it to my smart readers to figure out a consistent rule. But no, I don't have the wit to quit writing; I have no plan to retire. I simply like writing too much to stop. So I continue with my exercise program, jogging, cycling, archery, and so on, all at the duffer level, staying physically fit.

Meanwhile family life is fine; my wife and I had our forty-third anniversary quietly at home. Our daughters are grown and on their own. Penny is a doula and midwife assistant in Oregon; you may not find "doula" in your dictionary, as the term is new, so I'll clarify it here. It is a person who helps an expectant mother through the process. If you plan to have a baby, and are daunted by the prospect of advancing pregnancy and giving birth, hire a doula. She will put you at ease, whether this means helpful advice or holding your hand or getting help when things go wrong. She will if you wish go with you to the doctor or hospital or do other things related to healthy childbearing, such as find authorities on breast feeding, as she will know how to make such contacts. In short, she will be your friend when you most need one. Cheryl works in the editorial department of a small-town newspaper. That doesn't mean she writes editorials; she does copyediting, spot revision, spot graphics, page layout, computer database maintenance, phone liaison, and the other invisible things that make a newspaper work. Once there was a problem with the long distance phone connection, so Cheryl called her mother locally, and my wife called the phone company long distance, and they got on it and fixed the problem. The man said it was the first time he'd been called by a client's mother. And of course there's our big dog, Obsidian, the one who believes that anything in the universe can be improved by the addition of a cold wet nose. I put her in my online novel *Realty Check,* where all the other characters are fictional.

We live on our small tree farm, and in this period we had the trees thinned. The slash pines were planted in tight rows, but they have been growing for twenty years, and need to be better spaced out to achieve full growth. So every third row was taken out and sold for pulp. I was sorry that some trees had to die, but it *is* a farm and has to be managed properly. Meanwhile the grass and shrubbery will grow in those vacated rows, providing browsing for deer and gopher tortoises and the rest. We regard it as an unofficial wildlife refuge; the only thing we allow to be hunted is the feral pigs, because they tear up the ground and ruin it for all the rest. These days when I walk through the forest I carry a boar spear, not to hunt boar, but to make sure they don't hunt me.

Readers continue to ask about Jenny, who was struck by a drunk driver and paralyzed at age twelve. At this writing she is eleven years older, still paralyzed, but preparing to go to college. It is a long, slow haul, when her mobility is so limited, but she's trying. Her character Jenny Elf is married now, and I shall have to figure out what the stork is bringing her. Fortunately I have another year to ponder that.

Now the credits, given in the general order of use in the novel, grouped when one person had more than one. I regret the names which are incomplete or absent, and will try to be more careful in future. This catches up roughly through NoRemember 1999.

The Demon Earth is not evil—Ariel Victoroff; amateur crastination, fowl ball, Vita men, intuition as a talent—Clay Gilmore; talent of causing random headaches—Jason Combs; talent of using music to heal wounds—Robert; insight: talent of seeing inside a person and telling what is wrong—J. Hoffman; Metros, Chronos—Cindy Rempel; the inconsistencies of Humfrey's use of youth elixir—Alan Chick; Where do puns come from?—Heather Oglevie; strawberries with straws, chick peas and navy beans, fur tree—Aaron "dzeghers"; the Five (Six) Rings of Xanth—Mike Henderson; Anna Gram—Brian Stewart; twin girls with random springs talents—Molly Suver; mere makes folk feel insignificant, metallergy makes folks sneeze—Rob and Rene; talent of seeing the future of an object—Daniel@Genius; Vanna Jane Morrow Shelton—R. Morrow Shelton; Rusty—Amber Middleton; Demons Molish, Lete, Flower—Juno Farnsworth; females sending smoke signals, *Charades* with puns—Nuwisha Man; talent of making animals sing—Tham Shu Fen; talent of forming living things into useful shapes—Eric Miller; male underwear freaking out females—Lenora Kenwolf; M-path, iron E's—Roger and Rosa Motti, Laura Cavallo; things go right, not left—Rafi; Ersup, who looks in purse to find something personal about whomever she concentrates on; Candi with the sweet tooth—Erin Price; magic infuses new adults too slowly to see—Ian Kurz; cross winds, sun glare—Meredith Holla; other types of centaurs with bodies of felines, deer, zebras, oryx—Lane Law; opti and pessi mist—bsukert; Com Ponent—Brian Ott; illusion of touch—Brandon Roberts; roc's flight feathers to make a flying machine, poke weed, wormhole leads to random time—Anonymous Peasant; tempera paint—Brianne "Brie" Smith; begonia, bring back Smash and Tandy—Tandy Dolin; Dafrey having a role—Thomas E. Shaffer; Unpun makes puns disappear—Seth Dorrity; Punny, creating puns—Bruce Morton; loss of the sense of humor—Brenda Roberts; cloudberries—Candace Suggs; Pook, Peek, Puck brought back, seeking the Mundane who can get to the Foop—Jaylin Allen; Cassaundra Centaur—Cathi Walker (When I checked for the email letter to see if there was any description or talent, I was unable to find it, so filled out the details myself, hoping that I didn't ruin it for Cathi); man-i-cure—

Kat Velayo; peacock—Jon Steenbeke; cyclepath—Tim Reddick; Lyn, who makes machines—Mari Rose; horror-scope—SupreMage; elderberries—Nicole Freeman; shrinking violet—Jennifer Richter; eye of the beholder—Nicole Scott; talking to the wind, Talent Agent—Daniel Forrest; Watt's Gnu—Ed Breest Jr.; fish swallowing half a person—Jackson Howa; scarf, warm but eats much—Christer Ward; Miss Erry, who loves company—Karalee J. Beierschmitt; Miss Steppe, who falls down; faux tangle tree—Russell Thompson; relatives of MareAnn—Krystal Houston; heart beet—Kathryn Voskuil; circle of friends—Julianne Burslem; dot matrix—Kathy; brain eyeball—Tim Kozloski; show and tell a vision—Kristina Gilbride; jumping to conclusions—Joshua Jarvise; castration—Ken Kuhlman; Siamese cats—(I lost the credit); decipher any code, intimidate anything, hide anything, have leprechauns in Xanth—Jamie Stoops; oxymoron strip—Jennifer Richter (I had to cut the figures of speech section short, so much of her suggestion was lost. It was that there be an oxymoron strip, run by a pretty ugly stupid genius named Mistress Mann, who makes oxymorons literal. The problem is, I have had an oxymoron character before, so this overlapped.); talent of seeing the result of a decision—Ashli Foust; the Internet as a net—Josh Millman, Daniel Forrest; the Web as a giant spiderweb—Daniel Forrest; Arachid, human/spider, crossbreed—Brittany Nelson; Demon Type-O—Dancer; Post Orifice where letters and articles go—Tham Shu Fen; move-E—Sean Thompson; flying goblin child with rainbow-colored wings, talent of enlarging or minimizing living things—Megan Ward; Stretch Ogre—James Johnston; Inebriated and Intoxicated—Ashley Treadway; nymph lode—Roger Fachini; talent of mixing metaphors—Jennifer Hoffmann; suit tree with flight suits—RWheel; tangle tree nymph with tangled hair—Jim Roberts; Xanthus the talking horse—Jenny Scott; goblin/harpy crossbreeds have talents—Katharine Capps (missed before); goblins have definition, harpies have strength in talents; talents occur once per species per generation—Richard Reeves; talent of bringing something forward or back in time—Joe Baity.

And stay tuned to this station for *Up in a Heaval* next year. The Demons are not through with their games.

mL   8-11